W9-BLR-003

Monument to Murder

This Large Print Book carries the
Seal of Approval of N.A.V.H.

A CAPITAL CRIMES NOVEL

MONUMENT TO MURDER

MARGARET TRUMAN

WHEELER PUBLISHING
A part of Gale, Cengage Learning

GALE
CENGAGE Learning™

Detroit • New York • San Francisco • New Haven, Conn • Waterville, Maine • London

Wheeler Publishing, a part of Gale, Cengage Learning.

Wheeler Publishing Large Print Hardcover.
The text of this Large Print edition is unabridged.
Other aspects of the book may vary from the original edition.
Set in 16 pt. Plantin.

LIBRARY OF CONGRESS CATALOGING-IN-PUBLICATION DATA

Truman, Margaret, 1924–2008.
Monument to murder : a capital crimes novel / by Margaret Truman.
p. cm.
ISBN-13: 978-1-4104-3827-0 (hardcover)
ISBN-10: 1-4104-3827-9 (hardcover)
1. Private investigators—Fiction. 2. Governmental investigations—Fiction. 3. Murder for hire—Fiction. 4. Savannah (Ga.)—Fiction. 5. Washington (D.C.)—Fiction. 6. Large type books. I. Title.
PS3570.R82M66 2011b
813'.54—dc22 2011016842

Published in 2011 by arrangement with Tom Doherty Associates, LLC.

Printed in the United States of America
1 2 3 4 5 6 7 15 14 13 12 11

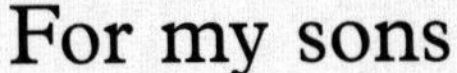

For my sons

Part One

CHAPTER 1

Mrs. Eunice Watkins was seated in the cramped reception area when Bob Brixton walked in on that steamy Savannah August morning. He was late for the appointment. He always seemed to run late during Savannah summers, reluctant to leave the AC of his apartment until the last possible moment.

After telling Mrs. Watkins that he'd be with her in a few minutes, he entered his office, followed by Cynthia, his secretary, assistant, and foil.

"Bad night?' she asked.

"Why do you always ask that?" he said. "I don't have bad nights or good nights. They're just nights. What's your read on her?"

"Seems like a nice lady," she replied in a drawl that seemed to thicken once summer arrived, like the humid air. "Very proper, didn't say much."

"No hint what she wants?"

Cynthia shook her head. "Where's your coffee?"

"I was running late and didn't stop. Send Mrs. Watkins in."

She escorted his potential client into the office, asked if she wanted coffee or tea — "No, thank you, ma'am" — and went downstairs to get Brixton an iced coffee from the deli that occupied the ground floor of the two-story building.

"Please, have a seat," Brixton said, indicating one of two green club chairs across the desk. He'd had only a fleeting glimpse of her as he passed through the anteroom. Now, he took a closer look. She was an attractive woman whose age he pegged at sixty, give or take a few years. She had probably been a beauty as a younger woman. Now, "handsome" was more apt. Her ebony face was relatively free of wrinkles, her gray hair carefully coiffed. She sat ramrod erect, hands folded on a purse that rested on her lap. Her carefully pressed dress had a tan-and-white floral pattern and she wore a lightweight white cardigan, hardly necessary considering Mother Nature's sauna outside. She locked eyes with him as though doing some sizing up of her own. No smile. Waiting for him to say something.

"So, Mrs. Watkins, you're obviously here because you feel I might be of help in some matter."

"Yes, sir, that's right."

"A personal matter?"

She looked down, then back up. "A very personal matter, sir. You were an officer with the Savannah Police Department as I'm told." She spoke slowly, deliberately. Brixton figured that she was a born-and-bred Georgian and her accent supported that.

"Uh-huh. A few years ago."

"I thought that might be helpful."

"How so?"

She gathered her thoughts before continuing. He had the feeling that she was girding against crying and gave her points for that. Weeping women always unsettled him.

"I was wondering if you might remember a case from a number of years ago. It involved my daughter, Louise Watkins."

Brixton leaned back in his chair and closed his eyes in a display of trying hard to recall. He opened them and said, "Can't say that I do."

"My daughter was murdered."

"I'm sorry to hear that. Tell me more."

"It happened sixteen years ago, in 1994."

And she expects me to remember that far back?

"My daughter had recently been released from prison when she was killed. Murdered in cold blood."

"How was she killed?" he asked.

"She was shot on the street. Someone in a car drove by and fired at her."

"They ever find the shooter?"

"No."

Brixton drew a deep breath and came forward in his squeaky swivel chair. "If you're here to ask me to try and solve your daughter's murder, Mrs. Watkins, I'm afraid I'm going to have to disappoint you. That's a police matter. I'm a private investigator."

She looked in the direction of the office's only window, in which the air conditioner did its blessed work, and returned to him. "There's more to Louise's death than the fact that she was murdered."

He squirmed against a back spasm. He wanted a cigarette. He didn't smoke in the office because Cynthia had put down her size-seven foot and threatened to quit if he did. It looked like he was in for a lengthy tale and he hoped that when it was over he'd at least have a paying client. Business had been slow, as slow as the way people walked in summery Savannah.

"Go on," he said to Mrs. Watkins as Cynthia carried in his iced coffee. "Stay around," he told Cynthia, "take some notes."

If having a third person in the room recording what she said unnerved Mrs. Watkins, she didn't show it. She said matter-of-factly, "My daughter was paid to go to prison."

Cynthia stopped writing and looked at Brixton.

"That's an unusual allegation, Mrs. Watkins," he said.

"But it's true."

"You're claiming that your daughter was paid to take the rap for someone else?"

"Yes, that is what I am saying."

"What was she in the can — in prison for?"

"Manslaughter. She was accused of having stabbed someone to death."

The case started to come back to him in fragments. Sure. Louise Watkins. Drug addict. Eighteen or nineteen years old. High as a kite on drugs and booze. He hadn't caught that case while with Savannah PD but was close to the detective who had. Brixton had been with the Savannah PD for eight years at the time it took place and had been promoted to detective just one year prior to that.

The stabbing had occurred in Augie's

parking lot, one of those clubs that come and go and lure the gotta-be-hip crowd, the young crowd, with a bouncer at the door making sure the teenyboppers he let in showed enough skin, and the macho young guys weren't wearing flip-flops on dirty feet. Class act all the way, until it was closed by the department's narcs for selling drugs over and under the bar. As Brixton recalled, she'd claimed the guy had tried to rape her and had stabbed him in self-defense, which the judge evidently bought when he sentenced her, a lenient sentence that had nettled Brixton's fellow cops.

"The case is coming back to me now. How much time did she do?"

"She was in prison for four years."

Four years for stabbing a guy to death. She got off easy.

"So, you're claiming that your daughter didn't do it."

"That's right, Mr. Brixton."

"So, who did?"

"I don't know, but I believe my daughter when she said she wasn't the one, that she'd been paid to confess to it."

"*Paid?* Somebody at the club paid her to say that she'd killed the guy?"

A nod, and stiffening at the disbelief in his tone.

"Who?" he repeated.

"I don't know. That's why I've come to you, Mr. Brixton. I was hoping that you could find out for me."

He took a swig of coffee, swiveled in his chair, and grimaced against a shooting pain in his right knee. Brixton's chiropractor called him his retirement fund, a walking orthopedic nightmare, arthritis in every joint, spinal X-rays that read like a train wreck, and one knee that bowed out five degrees, causing him to walk as though carrying a loaded suitcase on the opposite side. Taking a bullet in the bad knee hadn't helped. Not that he didn't get around pretty good. It was just that there was always pain, sometimes worse than other times, nothing to cause him to ask for a wheelchair at airports or get offered a seat on a bus. Annoying, that's what it was. Annoying. Every sign of getting older was annoying.

"Let me ask you something, Mrs. Watkins," he said. "Your daughter's murder happened sixteen years ago. How come you've just now decided to open it up?"

She chose her words carefully. "My son, Lucas — he was three years older than Louise when she was killed — is a man of God, Mr. Brixton. Lucas is pastor of the Southside United Freedom Church. He has been tormented ever since the day Louise was killed — not by her murder; that was bad enough — but by her having spent four years in prison for a murder that she did not commit. I should tell you, Mr. Brixton, that Louise was a problem child. She became addicted to drugs when she was thirteen and left home at seventeen, living on the streets, begging for money to support her habit, and I'm ashamed to say selling her body. She was eighteen when she went to prison, twenty-two years old when she was killed. In a way she acted honorably in taking money to keep someone else out of prison. It's better than the other ways she'd sunk to on the streets."

"Your son's the one who wants the case reopened?"

"Yes, and I now agree with him. When Louise died, I felt it was best to allow her to rest in the sort of peace she hadn't found when she was alive, to rest in God's kingdom, to forget all the pain she had suffered, and to let me cherish my memories of her before she got into trouble. But Lucas has always said that Louise deserves to have her name cleansed, not for the way she lived her life in those final years but from the sin of having taken another person's life. She didn't kill that man in the parking lot, Mr.

Brixton. She was paid to say that she did."

"Your daughter told you that she'd been paid to assume responsibility but didn't name the person who'd paid her?"

"She said she'd promised never to reveal it. I admired her for that."

"What did she do with the money?" Brixton asked.

"She gave it to me."

Her resolve not to cry crumbled and she wept silently, ladylike, never changing her erect posture, simply pulling a tissue from her purse and dabbing at her eyes. "Sorry," she said softly.

"That's all right," he said. "Want some water?"

"No, thank you."

"How much?" he asked.

"Pardon?"

"How much money was involved?"

"Ten thousand dollars."

Four years behind bars, twenty-five hundred a year. She'd sold out cheap, although based upon the lifestyle her mother claimed she'd had, a bed and three squares a day might have seemed like winning an all-expense-paid trip to Hawaii.

"She gave it to you just like that?" he asked.

"Actually, Mr. Brixton, Louise didn't

personally give me the money. It arrived shortly after she'd been convicted of the murder."

"Who gave it to you then?"

"I don't know. I returned home one day and there was an envelope wedged between my screen door and the other door. I opened it and found ten thousand dollars in cash. I was shocked, as you can imagine."

"But you said you knew it came from your daughter."

"Not at that moment. I mentioned it to her the next time I visited her in jail. That's when she told me how she'd agreed to confess to the crime in return for the money. I pleaded with her to tell the authorities but she was adamant. She said that jail was the best place for her to get straightened out, get off drugs, and find God. She also said that she wanted me to have it for all the pain she'd caused me. That's all she said. I pleaded with her again not to do it but Louise was always headstrong. I hid the money away."

"Until now."

"Yes, until now."

Brixton surreptitiously glanced at his watch. Cigarette time.

"Okay," he said, "I'll see what I can find out from friends still with the PD. My fee is four hundred a day plus expenses."

He expected her to express shock. Instead, she issued her first smile of the morning and said, "That will be fine. I still have the ten thousand and I'm willing to spend all of it to clear her name."

Brixton experienced dual silent emotions — pleasure at seeing a nice payday, and a desire to reach out and hug her for what she was determined to do. Her dead daughter had been a junkie, a drunk, and a hooker, no hesitation in admitting that. Yet, her main concern was to prove that she'd gone to prison an innocent person. Go figure. It didn't seem to matter a hell of a lot at this point, but who was he to challenge what was important to a client?

"I'll need some up-front," he said.

"Will a thousand be sufficient?"

He caught a small smile on Cynthia's face. "Yeah, a thousand will be fine. You can trust me. I'll give an honest accounting of my time and expenses."

"Yes, I'm sure you will."

"By the way, Mrs. Watkins, what brought you to me? There are bigger investigative agencies in Savannah."

She stood and ran her hands over the front of her dress. "I don't think I'd be comfortable with a larger agency," she said.

“I’m sure they have more-important cases to look into.”

He didn’t take it as a put-down.

“You aren’t from Savannah, are you?”

“No, ma’am, I’m not. I came here from Washington, D.C. I was born in Brooklyn.”

“I knew that from the way you talk.”

“I never got around to picking up a drawl.”

“When can you start on my case?”

“Well, I’ve got a couple of others I’m in the process of wrapping up but I’ll get to it as soon as I can.”

Cynthia’s raised eyebrows chastised him for stretching the truth.

“Cynthia will take down all your contact information in case I have to reach you,” he said. “And there’s a short retainer agreement for you to sign. Simple. You can bail out anytime — and so can I. I’ll be in touch.”

Chapter 2

Brixton did what he usually did after a new client left — he asked Cynthia for her take. Cynthia Higgins was savvy, with an antenna that picked up on subtleties Brixton sometimes missed. She'd been working for him since he started his private investigative agency four years ago, and not only had an uncanny talent for cutting through BS, she also put up with him. On top of that, he appreciated that she was a splendid-looking female, rounded where she was supposed to be, with an open face, a high-octane smile, and a mane of blond curls. She prettied up what was basically a drab office, which saved him the expense of buying decorative things. Her husband, Jim, worked for a company that conducted ghost tours of Savannah. Savannah is known as the most haunted city in America. Brixton wasn't sure whether he believed in ghosts but kept an open mind.

"A nice lady," Cynthia responded, "but I'm not sure what she wants you to do, find out who murdered her daughter or identify who the kid took the fall for."

"Seems to me she's more interested in finding who paid the daughter off than who killed her."

"Maybe one and the same. Sounds like an archaeological dig you're going on, sixteen years since she was murdered, twenty years since she went to prison. Lots a' luck."

Brixton endorsed the thousand-dollar check Mrs. Watkins had written and asked Cynthia to deposit it. "I'll be back in a few minutes," he said.

He paused in the hallway to look at the new sign he'd had installed on the door to his office "suite" — ROBERT R. BRIXTON, PRIVATE INVESTIGATOR. Many people called him Bobby, which annoyed him. "Bobby" was okay in high school, but it was no name for a grown man, any more than calling the lady he occasionally slept with his "girlfriend." He was too old to have a girlfriend, and he hated "significant other." He referred to her as "Flo" because that was her name.

He puffed away on the street and pondered the meeting he'd just come from. Mrs. Louise Watkins had handed him a formidable challenge. The Savannah PD hadn't been able to solve her daughter's murder and probably hadn't tried very hard. Ex-cons with a history of drug addiction and turning tricks never ranked high on the priority list. Brixton didn't see how he could do any better. As for the daughter having been paid off to go to prison on someone else's behalf, any chance of coming up with that other person was zilch at best, since the answer had been buried with the kid. But he'd give it his best shot with no guarantees. If the stone wall was too high to scale, he'd cut bait and not milk the mother for any more of her ten grand than was fair.

"Enjoy your cigarette?" Cynthia asked when he returned.

"No. It's too hot out to enjoy anything."

"Better than snow."

"And if you didn't buy all the secondhand-smoke nonsense, I'd be enjoying a cigarette in my air-conditioned office."

He slid behind his desk, called Savannah PD, and asked for Detective St. Pierre. Wayne came on the line.

"Bob Brixton," he said.

"Well, well, well," St. Pierre said, "a voice from my not-too-distant past. How in hell are you, Bobby?"

St. Pierre knew that Brixton didn't like

being called Bobby and did it to irritate him. Brixton didn't bother to correct him the way he used to. "I'm hot," he said, "patiently waiting for December."

"You never did get acclimated to our fine weather, did you, Bobby? If you were back up north you'd —"

"Yeah, I know, I'd be bitching about the snow. I need some time with you, Wayne. I've got a case that goes back a few years. You worked it. Louise Watkins. Did time for manslaughter, a stabbing at that dump Augie's, and then got herself killed shortly after she was released."

"Rings a bell, Bobby. What's it to you?"

"I'll tell you when I see you. I can pop over now."

"Oh, no, my man, not this morning. I've got a meeting to go to."

"Then I'll buy you lunch, or dinner."

"You must have picked yourself up a good-payin' client. I just happen to be free this evening and have been hankerin' for some of Huey's red beans and rice ever since I got back from the Big Easy. How's that sound?"

"Sounds all right as long as you don't expect me to eat grits. Huey's at seven."

The meeting with Eunice Watkins was the only one he had scheduled for the day, and the chances of having another potential client pop in unannounced were as likely as a sudden cold front dropping the temperature thirty degrees. He told Cynthia that he'd be at the *Savannah Morning News* going through back issues, got in his car, and drove to the paper's plush headquarters on the city's rapidly developing western suburb. An old friend, a reporter who covered the crime beat, was there and settled him in the paper's morgue, where back issues were preserved on microfilm.

He didn't find much of interest on Louise Watkins, nor had he expected to. There was a four-paragraph article on the unsolved stabbing in the parking lot of Augie's, and a follow-up piece a week later when Louise Watkins came forward to admit having wielded the knife. The reporter mentioned that Ms. Watkins was known to be a drug user and had been arrested twice for soliciting.

He fast-forwarded to four years later, when Louise was released from prison and gunned down on a Saturday afternoon on a street in a less-than-savory part of town. The police characterized it as a drive-by shooting; no suspects had been identified. There was no second story.

He returned to the office and spent the

rest of the day paying bills and catching up on paperwork. Cynthia left at four to take care of some personal business, and he closed up fifteen minutes later, going to his apartment, where he sacked out in front of the TV with a beer before heading back out for dinner.

St. Pierre was already there when Brixton arrived. The younger detective was a foppish sort of fellow, fond of brightly colored bow ties and pastel sport jackets. Because he was tall and angular, and reed-thin, clothes draped nicely on him. He wore his now-graying hair longer than most cops, swept back at the sides and curling over his shirt collar. That he became a cop was unlikely considering his background. He was the only son of a Savannah couple ensconced in the city's upper social strata, had gotten a degree in fine arts from SCAD, the Savannah College of Art and Design — today the nation's largest art school — and it was assumed that he'd continue his education in that field with an eye toward becoming a museum curator. But he had made an abrupt U-turn and announced that he intended to take the test to become a Savannah cop. According to him, the decision almost killed his mother: "She took to her bed for weeks the way southern women sometimes do," he had once told Brixton with a chuckle, "probably a case of the vapors." But his parents eventually got over it, at least on the surface. Never having married, Wayne St. Pierre was the quintessential gadfly; his idiosyncrasies were legion. He was an unlikely cop if only because of the wealth, money, and property left him by his parents. The richest cop in America? Could be. But he was a good homicide detective, especially when it involved members of Savannah's upper crust, the sort of people John Berendt made hay with in his *Midnight in the Garden of Good and Evil.*

"You're looking good," St. Pierre said as they shook hands and Brixton motioned for a waitress to take his drink order. St. Pierre's usual concoction was already on the table, a sidecar made with Tuaca, a brandy-based orange-vanilla liqueur. It looked refreshing.

"Beefeater martini," Brixton told the waitress, "cold and dry, shaken, with a twist."

"So," St. Pierre said, "tell me about this new client of yours."

Brixton recounted for him what had transpired at his meeting with Louise Watkins's mother. St. Pierre listened attentively, taking an occasional sip of his drink. When

Brixton was through, St. Pierre raised his eyebrows and said, "Seems to me you're chasin' another Savannah ghost story."

"Ghost, hell," Brixton said. "The daughter was only too real. So were the bullets that killed her."

St. Pierre shrugged.

"Metro termed it a drive-by shooting."

"That's right."

"But from what I've read, she was alone on that street."

"True. I refreshed my memory before comin' here. That little girl was all alone."

"Which says to me that she didn't accidentally get in the way of a shooting meant for someone else. She was the target."

"Nothing in the files to support that, Bobby."

"But it makes sense, doesn't it? And knock off the Bobby stuff."

His grin was wide and mischievous. "I forgot that you're sensitive to that name. My apologies."

"For the sake of argument, Wayne, let's say I'm right. Let's say that she was the target. She'd just gotten out of prison, where she spent four years doing time for someone else, someone who'd paid her off. Maybe that person wanted to make sure that she didn't change her story once she got out of the can and point a finger at him. Possible?"

"Everything's possible, Robert. That's what makes life so inherently fascinating."

Brixton finished his drink and motioned for a refill. St. Pierre did the same.

"You said you refreshed your memory, Wayne. Does that include going back into the files on when she confessed to the stabbing at Augie's and was sentenced?"

"What files?" he said. "There's not much. I called Joe Cleland before I came here."

"How is Joe?"

"As irascible as ever. He claims to be enjoying his retirement but I don't believe him. Joe was the one who took her statement. Remember?"

Brixton nodded.

"He said she just walked into headquarters and told someone at the desk that she wanted to confess to the stabbing. Joe was summoned and took her into a room where she told him her story, said she'd been drinking at Augie's and went outside with this guy, said he tried to rape her and so she stuck a knife in him like any upstanding young woman would do to preserve her virginity. Sweet little thing, wasn't she, walkin' around carrying a big ol' knife like that? She had turned tricks as I recall.

Maybe he got from her what he wanted but didn't want to pay for it."

"Maybe, but I don't think so. She told her mother — who, by the way, is a very nice lady — that she'd been paid to admit to the stabbing but wouldn't tell her who it was. That's honorable. Sort of. She wanted her mother to know that she wasn't a killer, but wasn't going to betray this other person. You know what I think, Wayne?"

"Mind if we order first?"

"Not at all."

Red beans and rice with andouille sausage for him; Brixton opted for a New York strip steak.

"So here's how I see it. I believe the mother. Louise Watkins was paid off to go to prison. Ten thousand bucks is pretty tempting for someone in her situation. She sees it as a way of paying back her family for all the heartache she's caused them. I also think that maybe this person who handed her ten big ones figured she'd get fifteen, maybe twenty years, but the judge takes pity on Louise, figures she's been punished enough in her young life, and slaps down four. She walks out a free woman and this other person makes sure that she never tells the real story. Boom-boom. Not to worry."

Their meals were served, which got Wayne off the hook from having to comment immediately to Brixton's what-if. They dug in, saying little except for small talk with Wayne doing most of it. When they'd finished, St. Pierre dabbed at his mouth with a napkin. "Excellent," he said. "Truly excellent. Now, my old friend and colleague, here's what I think of your thesis. I think you're creating a scenario to justify going forward with this client of yours. I think Savannah's ghosts have taken possession of you. It happens, you know."

Brixton laughed. Maybe St. Pierre was right, he thought. Maybe that special aura that surrounds Savannah, Georgia, had invaded his soul and caused him not to think clearly. He dropped the subject — for that evening — and they lingered over hot, black coffee.

"Know what surprises me?" St. Pierre asked.

"What?"

"That you elected to stay in Savannah when you retired from the force. I figured you'd be packed and gone, back to Washington or New York."

Brixton shook his head. "When I first got here I figured that's exactly what I'd do. Put in my time. Earn the pension check.

But this place grows on you, like the Spanish moss on those oak trees. Maybe it's the funny way you people talk, funny but charming. My ex-wife is a southern girl, from Virginia."

"So you've said."

"Go back to Washington? Why do you think I left there? They built the city on a swamp, and swamp creatures keep showing up. They're known as bureaucrats and elected officials."

Brixton had ended up in Washington, D.C., because the New York PD had put on a hiring freeze. But four years had been enough. He'd had it with politics playing a role in every aspect of his life, including policing. Savannah was expanding its force and he figured it was worth a try. His marriage had broken up; he was footloose and fancy-free. So he took the Savannah job and now here he was, years later, with a pension check and his own private investigative agency that sometimes generated enough income to pay its bills. Why hadn't he taken the money and run? Who knew? Inertia probably.

Brixton covered the check. As they left, they paused to look at a TV set over the bar. Video of the president of the United States and the first lady showed them hosting an event on the White House lawn for some of D.C.'s disadvantaged children.

"Warms your heart, doesn't it, to see one of our own in the White House," St. Pierre said.

"Maybe it warms *your* heart, Wayne," Brixton said. "I'm not from here. Remember?"

"That's right. You are a Yankee interloper who came to our fair city to find fame and fortune."

Brixton grinned.

"And did you? Find fame and fortune?"

"What I found is humidity and the stink from those paper plants that settles over everything in summer. She's good-looking."

"Mrs. Fletcher Jamison, first lady of the land? Yes, she is a fair thing, youngest first lady since Jackie O. Mrs. Kennedy was thirty-one on inauguration day. Jeanine was thirty-eight. Jack and Fletcher robbed the cradle."

They went to the street.

"Washington's almost as hot and humid in the summer as this place is," Brixton commented.

"Another fifty years or so and you'll get used to our weather, my friend. In the meantime, stay in touch. If you decide to go ahead with this case, I'll do what I can to help."

Go ahead with the case?

Brixton had already made that decision.

CHAPTER 3

Brixton left a sleeping Flo Combes in bed when he got up the next morning. She'd worked late at the touristy clothing shop she owned in the historic district and announced when she got home that she intended to sleep in. They'd sat up until midnight watching an old black-and-white movie, made a halfhearted attempt to kindle some passion, gave it up with mutual yawns, and went to bed — to sleep.

Brixton stood in her bathroom and took in his image in the mirror, turning left and right to present more-flattering perspectives. He was in decent shape for a fifty-year-old man. Despite his aches and pains, he exercised regularly at his apartment and at a local gym. A shade under six feet tall, he'd managed to keep excess weight off his midsection and to maintain muscle tone in his upper arms and chest. He knew one thing: no matter how he deteriorated as he grew older, he'd always have his wiry, gunmetal-silver hair, which he kept closely cropped.

When Brixton was a cop he had a reputation as a tough guy, not mean or bullying but someone you wanted at your back when the situation went downhill. He was also known as a tough kid while growing up in the Red Hook section of Brooklyn; plenty of scraps had sent him home with a bloody nose or black eye. That pleased his father. The old man worked nights as a bartender in some of the borough's rougher neighborhoods and wouldn't have stood for his only son backing away from a fight.

His decision to pursue a career in law enforcement was accepted by both his father and mother. Although Mrs. Brixton quietly hoped that her son would go to college and become an accountant or a lawyer, or at least land a white-collar job, that route had no appeal for Robert, although he did go to college, CCNY, and graduated with a degree in business administration. But the thought of spending his adult life behind a desk was anathema and he queried the NYPD. No jobs available. A friend said he'd heard that the Washington MPD was hiring, so Robert applied there and was hired. It took four years to decide that he and the nation's capital weren't made for each other.

That's when he headed for Savannah, one of the nation's first planned cities. James Oglethorpe had arrived there in 1732 with 114 colonists and had laid out the new city according to a plan he'd used in England. Brixton had to admit that Savannah was a pretty city, and the people were friendly for the most part. There was, of course, that entrenched genteel, aristocratic set that Wayne St. Pierre had grown up in and that Brixton found too precious for his liking. But in the main he'd enjoyed his twenty-four years there — except every summer.

He showered and dressed, kissed Flo on the forehead, and swung by his own place to change into fresh underwear and a clean shirt. He called a number on his cell phone that was answered by Joe Cleland, the retired detective who'd taken Louise Watkins's confession twenty years earlier. Brixton and Cleland had partnered for a while and he liked the beefy, African-American cop with the booming voice and ready smile.

"Joe, Bob Brixton."

"Hello, Robert. I figured you might be calling. Wayne said you were working the Louise Watkins case."

"Seems like it, Joe. Spare me an hour?"

"Anytime, my man."

Brixton got directions to Cleland's house and headed there in his 2004 Subaru Outback.

Cleland lived in a small one-story redbrick home set on a lovingly maintained piece of property. Brixton noted as he got out of his car that behind the house was a preserve of sorts that afforded plenty of privacy. Cleland heard his arrival and opened the front door before Brixton reached it. They shook hands, gave each other a quick hug, and went inside where Cleland had laid out coffee and a platter of Danish pastries. "Good coffee," he said. "I guarantee it. I'm particular about my coffee after all those years of drinking station-house motor oil."

"It was pretty bad, wasn't it?" Brixton agreed as he took a chair at the dining room table, poured himself a cup, and plucked a raspberry cheese Danish from the platter. "How's retirement treating you?" he asked.

"Just fine," Cleland replied, joining him. "I keep busy with the garden, grow the best damn lettuce and tomatoes in Chatham County. Of course, it gets a little lonely now and then with Beatrice gone." Cleland's wife had died of cancer less than a year after he'd retired.

"You look good, Joe."

Cleland patted his sizable belly and

laughed. “Hard as a rock,” he said. “So, you want to talk about Louise Watkins. Funny, lots of perps I dealt with are all fuzzy in my brain but I remember her. I remember when she came into the barracks and told the desk officer she wanted to confess to a killing.” His laugh was rueful this time. “They called me to the desk and I took her back into one of the interrogation rooms. Man, she was pitiful, looked like she could use a good meal.”

“She’d been running loose for too long,” Brixton said. “She just blurted out her confession to you?”

Cleland nodded his large head. “That’s about it, Robert. She rolled through her so-called confession like she’d been rehearsing it for weeks.”

“ ‘So-called confession’?”

“That’s the way it struck me. I mean, it didn’t set right the way she did it. I sat there wonderin’ why she was doing it. Hell, chances were that no one would ever link her to that stabbing, no earthly reason for her to give herself up. Of course, she did tell us where the knife was. We dragged that portion of the inlet and there it was, just like she said.”

“Prints?”

“Partials. The lab said they were sufficient

to make a match with her."

Brixton wondered why Louise's mother hadn't mentioned that. "Did you press her?"

"Sure, but she never backed off from what she'd said, just repeated it almost word-for-word. I had her write out her statement, watched her hands shake while she did. I left her alone for a while and talked to the chief about my suspicions that she might be lying."

"And he said?" Brixton waved away his response. "No," he said, "I can imagine what he said. He told you not to look a gift horse in the mouth. You had a live one, which meant the stabbing wouldn't end up in the cold-case file."

" 'Sometimes we get lucky,' was what he said."

"Not lucky for her," Brixton said. "You testified at her sentencing."

"Sure did. The public defender just went through the motions. Hell, she'd already been found guilty based on her confession, so he focused on the sentencing. Her mother, a good woman, testified on her behalf. So did an older brother. He was going to divinity school I believe."

"Seems like their testimony worked," Brixton said. "She only got four years."

"That's right. The DA wasn't happy about

it but I was. The way I figured it, she'd get straight behind bars, come out and maybe put some sort of a life together without drugs and booze. I'd kept up with her while she was incarcerated. A friend of mine at the prison worked with the kid and kept me in the loop. Louise Watkins made good use of her prison time, Bob, earned her GED, took advantage of the drug-rehab program, and came out clean." His laugh was more of a grunt. "My friend, she told me that Louise had a real talent for numbers, could do all sorts of math in her head. She — my friend — was going to help find Louise a job with an accounting firm or something else where she could use that talent. But then —"

"Then she was gunned down."

"That hurt, Robert. I had intended to contact her when she was released to see if I could help her find her way. I never had any kids and maybe was looking to play daddy to somebody. I never got the chance."

"What would you say if I suggested that she might have taken the rap for someone else?"

"You mean for a friend? That would have to have been one special friend."

"For money. Ten grand."

"Who?"

Brixton shrugged. "That's one of the things I'm being paid to find out, along with who shot her."

"You really think you can do that?"

Another shrug. "I'll try. Did she say anything, *anything* when you were with her that might help me?"

Cleland finished a cream puff and a swallow of coffee. "No," he said. "I wanted to question her further but the chief nixed that, told me to take the statement, cuff her, and turn her over to the DA's office. That's what I did."

"What about the guy who got stabbed? From what I've heard, she claimed he'd tried to rape her."

"I don't remember much about him. Fairly young, twenty-four, twenty-five. I reviewed the crime-scene photos in preparation for testifying at her sentencing. Good-lookin' fella, came from Atlanta. Autopsy showed plenty of drugs in his system, no surprise since he was hanging out at Augie's."

"Good-looking enough that he didn't need to rape anybody for sex?"

"I'd say so, but you never can tell what a junkie'll do."

Brixton stretched and grimaced, rubbed his right knee.

"When are you gonna get that knee replaced?" Cleland said.

"One of these days."

It had happened during Brixton's final year on the force. He and his partner had been dispatched to pick up a parole violator and were met with a hail of bullets, one of which hit Brixton in the knee. His partner killed the fugitive and called for backup. After undergoing surgery, Brixton had spent the next six months in rehab, and had been assigned to a desk job until his retirement papers came through.

There wasn't much else he could ask Cleland, at least at that juncture, and they settled into easy conversation about their days together on the streets of Savannah. Cleland took Brixton out a back door to show off his vegetable garden, which Brixton dutifully admired. Of all the things he enjoyed doing, gardening wasn't among them. An hour later Cleland walked him to the front door. Brixton looked up the quiet street at a small, red pickup truck parked at the curb. He'd noticed what he assumed was the same truck behind him on the highway on his way to Cleland's. Sun on the windshield obscured the driver's face. Brixton clapped his former partner on the back before he got into his car and drove off. The red truck remained parked.

His visit with Joe Cleland hadn't resulted in his learning anything tangible, but it did accomplish one thing.

He believed Eunice Watkins.

CHAPTER 4

Brixton dialed the number he'd been given for Eunice Watkins. He wanted to see whether Louise's mother was home and up for a visit. An answering machine picked up his cell phone call. He didn't bother to leave a message, deciding to stop by her house anyway if only to get a feel for the atmosphere in which the daughter had been brought up.

The address was in the Pinpoint section of Savannah, about eleven miles from downtown. Inhabited primarily by African-Americans, it had been established by freed slaves following the Civil War and was one of the last bastions of Gullah-speaking people, a Creole language patterned after several West African languages. As Brixton entered the town he saw a sign proudly proclaiming that it was the birthplace of Supreme Court Justice Clarence Thomas.

The Watkins place was one of a dozen

similar homes that sat side by side on a tree-lined street. He pulled up in front of the house number he had and surveyed his surroundings. The only activity was a few school-age kids playing and a delivery truck from which furniture was being carried into a house across the street. A recent vintage Ford sedan was parked in the Watkins driveway.

He got out and went to the front door, rang the bell. Based upon his unanswered call, he didn't expect to find her at home. But a curtain on a narrow vertical window next to the door was pulled aside, the sound of a sliding deadbolt was heard, and she opened the door.

"I hope you don't mind my just stopping by," Brixton said. "I tried calling but got your answering machine."

"I've been letting the machine take calls," she said.

To avoid bill collectors? he wondered.

"Please, come in," she said, stepping aside to allow him to enter.

An air conditioner in a living room window exhaled barely cool air into the tidy, pleasantly furnished room. A spinet piano occupied a short wall at the base of stairs leading to the second level. The hardwood floor glistened from a recent waxing, its center covered by a hooked rug of various colors. An older-model TV with its bulky back sat on a TV cart with wheels across from a couch covered in a green-and-white-striped fabric. Two chairs in a matching pattern flanked it.

"Please, sit down," she said. "Would you like some sweet tea? I made some fresh this morning." Sweet tea was a Savannah stalwart enjoyed year-round, well-steeped tea with plenty of sugar added.

"That would be nice," Brixton said. "Thank you."

While Mrs. Watkins fussed in the kitchen, Brixton walked around the small living room, stopping to peruse books on a tall bookcase interspersed with a variety of small, framed photographs. There were photos on the piano, too, and a cluster of them hung on a wall near the TV, each one perfectly straight. Brixton could never get his photos to hang straight and wondered whether the lady of the house spent a good part of her day keeping them in line. One picture on a bookcase shelf caught his eye. It was a color photo of a group of six teenage girls, three black, three white. They seemed happy in the shot, mugging for the camera the way teenagers do. He'd just picked it up to take a closer look when she returned with the tea and he put the photo back on the shelf.

"Is that your daughter in that picture?" he asked.

"Oh, my, yes, it is."

"Looks like a happy occasion."

"It was. Louise was sixteen when it was taken, a year before she left home. She was taking drugs by then only I didn't know it. I suppose I preferred not to know, turned a blind eye on what she was doing, wanted to believe only good things about her. What a glorious smile she had, light up a room. You can see it in that photograph." She left, returning seconds later with two other pictures of her daughter. Louise Watkins had, indeed, been a pretty girl, and the smile her mother had cited was evident in both shots. Brixton thought that showing him the pictures might cause her to tear up but she didn't. She placed them on a coffee table next to the pitcher of tea, and a plate of brownies, and urged him to sit and enjoy her offerings, which he did.

She asked why he'd stopped by.

"I just wanted to touch base with you again," he answered. "I spent time with two colleagues from the police department. One is still there, the other has retired. He was the one who took down Louise's confession."

"Detective Cleland," she said. "A nice man. He testified at her sentencing hearing."

"Right. He told me that he never quite believed her confession. It sounded rehearsed to him."

A flash of spark lit up her eyes. "Exactly," she said. "Louise was paid to say what she did."

Brixton nodded.

"I asked Detective Cleland, and other policemen, to question her further, to press her to tell the truth," she said, "but they didn't. It was like they didn't care enough to do it."

Brixton debated trying to explain why no one probed deeper at the department — that they were happy not to have another murder or manslaughter case to pursue. Confessions make everything so much easier for a cop, even when they might not reflect reality. A bird in hand, in this case a bird named Louise Watkins.

The phone rang. She allowed it to sound four times before the answering machine, which was next to the TV, picked up. After her outgoing message, the caller grunted and hung up.

"Another one," she said flatly.

"Another what?"

"Another call. I received two last night."

"From whom?"

"I don't know. A man. Both times he said something like, 'Don't be stupid.' "

"That's all he said?"

"Yes. And there have been two others like that one just now. He hangs up."

"Has this happened before?" Brixton asked.

"No. Never."

Brixton stood, arching against a pain. "Excuse me," he said, "bad back."

"Would you like an aspirin?" she asked.

"What? Oh, no, no thanks."

He walked to the bookcase and brought the photo of the six girls back to her. "Schoolmates?" he asked.

"No, Mr. Brixton. That was taken at a retreat at CVA."

"The Christian Vision Academy on Ogeechee Road?"

"Yes. The school held a retreat, inviting young girls of color to their campus for a weekend, sort of an outreach to bring the races closer together. It was a nice gesture. Louise didn't want to go but I insisted. From the looks of things in the picture she had herself a good time. She told me she did when she got home."

Brixton cleared his throat before saying, "I need to ask you a question, Mrs. Watkins. I don't mean to upset you but —"

"You go right ahead and ask any question you wish, Mr. Brixton. Most of my upset is behind me."

"Yeah. Well, when Louise was on the streets as a — as a prostitute — did she work for anybody?"

She looked puzzled.

"Did she have a boss, a pimp, a guy who managed her, if that's what you'd call it?"

"I don't think so."

"Did she ever mention any of the other women she worked with?"

"No. Louise never said anything about those times. She was embarrassed enough, I suppose, that I even knew."

"How did you know?"

"She called when she was arrested. I bailed her out."

"Well, thank you, ma'am, for the talk and the sweet tea. It was excellent."

He picked up the photo of the six girls again and looked closely at it before returning it to the bookcase.

"I was so pleased that Louise went to that retreat," Mrs. Watkins said. "Maybe if she'd spent more time with girls like that she wouldn't have strayed into trouble the way she did."

Brixton didn't know whether she was right or not and didn't comment.

"But I suppose that wasn't possible. Louise didn't have much opportunity to be with young women like those in the picture. They come from —"

"The other side of town?"

"Yes, I suppose you could put it like that, Mr. Brixton. Thank you for coming all this way to see me."

"Next time I hope to have more to report."

"Would you be needing another check?"

"No, ma'am, not yet. Thanks for the hospitality. I'll be in touch."

Chapter 5

Cynthia was in a foul mood when Brixton returned to the office. Her husband, Jim, had done too good a job of weaving scary ghost stories into his commentary during one of the tours he'd hosted the night before, causing a mother with two frightened, small children to complain loudly about his lack of sensitivity where children were concerned.

"What'd Jim say?" Brixton asked.

"He told her that if she didn't want her precious little darlings to be afraid, she shouldn't take them on a ghost tour."

"Sounds reasonable to me," Brixton said.

"She complained to the tour operator and demanded her money back."

"You husband was right," Brixton said.

"Not if he loses his job. You got a call from an attorney who's looking for an investigator. Here's his number."

"Thanks."

Brixton returned the attorney's call and made an appointment to meet with him later that afternoon. His next call was to Wayne St. Pierre at the police barracks on Habersham, at the corner of Oglethorpe.

"Nice dinner last night," St. Pierre said. "Did I thank you? I think I did but if I didn't, I do now."

"You thanked me. Wayne, I need to access arrest records going back fifteen, sixteen years. Louise Watkins had been arrested for soliciting at least a few times. I'd like the names of other hookers who were brought in with her on those nights."

St. Pierre laughed. "They're probably grandmothers by now, Bobby."

"I hope they are. Can do?"

"I'll check and get back to you."

He called less than an hour later. "Ready to write?" he said. "Your Ms. Watkins was dragged in with three other lovely ladies of the night, a couple of them veterans of the streets." He rattled off the names.

"Whoa," Brixton said. "Wanda Johnson? Isn't she the one who left the biz and established some sort of mission for hookers, get 'em off the street and into the straight life?"

"That's her. Moved to Atlanta, got plenty

of TV coverage when she opened her mission."

"The other names don't ring a bell but that's okay. I'll try Johnson first. It's a long shot that she'll remember Louise Watkins, but worth a stab. Thanks, Wayne."

A few calls to Atlanta gave Brixton a number for Wanda Johnson's Refuge Project. Brixton placed the call and, after being put on hold, Wanda came on the line. Brixton introduced himself, told her why he was calling, and said he'd like some time with her.

"Louise Watkins, you say?" Ms. Johnson said in a husky voice. "I do remember her, sort of a lost soul as I recall. Didn't belong out there on the streets, but then again none of my girls do. Sure, happy to see you, Mr. Brixton. When do you want to come?"

"Tomorrow?"

"Sounds fine with me long as it's in the daytime. I'm out doing God's work most nights."

They agreed on a time, noon the following day, and he received directions.

"I'll be in Atlanta tomorrow," Brixton told Cynthia when she came into his office with checks to sign. He told her why.

"You're really into this case, aren't you?" she said.

"Just doing what I promised, looking for information about what happened to Mrs. Watkins' daughter."

"You buy her theory that her daughter was paid to go to prison?"

"Maybe. If it's true, her murder might be linked to it." He raised his hand against her reservations. "I know, I know, it's all supposition at this point. But I owe it to my client to at least try and prove that she's right. Will I? Prove it?" A shrug. "I'll give it a week. If I haven't made any headway, I'll tell her I bombed and suggest she save the rest of the money her daughter gave her."

The attorney's office was too close to drive to but far enough that by the time Brixton walked there in the late-afternoon sun and humidity, his shirt stuck to his body and perspiration ran down his face. He'd put on a tie to look professional even though he knew it wasn't necessary. Old habits die hard. Besides, he wasn't pleased with society's casual approach to dress these days. He'd been on airplanes where his seat companion, if male, was dressed as though he were going to a mud-wrestling contest. Females too often viewed a commercial flight as a teenage sleepover with plenty of skin showing. He had nothing against female skin, liked it as much as the next guy. But it was a matter of time and place, like going to see a potential client wearing a tie.

He knew the lawyer by reputation, a matrimonial specialist with a not particularly savory image. *Probably needs a tail on a philandering husband or wife to see whether the guy really did go bowling with his buddies every Tuesday night, or whether she actually attended weekly Tupperware parties at a girlfriend's house.* He had done his share of those assignments since opening his agency and never felt clean when one was concluded and he'd turned over his notes, photographs, videos, or audio files. But that kind of work was bread-and-butter for most PIs, and he'd invested in some pretty esoteric electronic equipment to stay competitive with larger agencies. That he charged less than those bigger agencies gave him a certain advantage.

His expectation was correct: the attorney had a client, a husband, who was convinced that the missus was cheating on him and wanted proof before he filed for divorce. Brixton didn't care who slept with whom, no matter who they were, everyday Joes or hot-shot celebrities. The tabloid mentality that TV, newspapers, and magazines had adopted left him cold. But he didn't write the rules when it came to divorces. A buck was a buck, and he'd been successful in rationalizing those assignments, and compartmentalizing them from real life, his *own* real life.

He accepted the assignment, got an up-front on the fee, and left the office. He didn't like the guy the moment they shook hands, sized him up as smarmy, one of those attorneys who'll deliberately prolong a divorce case to keep the fee meter running. The guy had giggled rather than laughed, and spent part of the meeting telling Brixton about some of his juicy cases, which Brixton didn't want to hear. It turned out that the husband who wanted his wife followed owned a fairly popular restaurant down on River Street. Brixton knew the place from his days on the PD, and had eaten there a few times since retiring. He wouldn't go again.

He debated grabbing a taxi back to the office but decided instead to stop in a bar and grill a block from the lawyer's office building. It was a dark, quiet place, at the perfect time, too early for the happy-hour revelers and long after the lunch crowd had departed. The bar's AC was operating full-blast, which turned Brixton's damp shirt cold and clammy. He pulled off his tie and settled at the end of the long bar, behind which a sallow-faced man in his early thirties took care of business. Brixton ordered a gin and tonic and sighed. A wave of depression settled over him.

It was a familiar feeling. He tended to be depressed. At least they'd told him he did, "they" being his ex-wife and two pop-psychologist daughters, his boss at the Washington, D.C., MPD, his chiropractor, primary care physician, and a few others including a nosy, chatterbox neighbor, the bartender at his favorite hangout down the street from his apartment, and Flo Combes, his current lady friend. He never argued with them; what was the use? It wasn't as if bouts of the blues rendered him useless, curled up in the fetal position for days on end. If he was depressed it was because he had reason to be. Perpetually happy people got on his nerves. There was plenty to be depressed about. All you had to do was turn on TV at any hour, or spend your days as a cop dealing with the dregs of society.

"You want another?" the bartender called from where he was drying glasses.

"No. Hey, do I look depressed to you?" Brixton asked.

He meant it as a joke, but the bartender looked at him as though deciding whether his customer was crazy and about to cause a scene.

"Forget it," Brixton said as he tossed down some cash and left, aware that the bartender was watching his every step, poised to reach for the baseball bat he undoubtedly kept behind the bar.

Brixton walked slowly in the direction of his office. A police cruiser passed with two uniformed officers in it. It brought back memories and he smiled for the first time that afternoon.

Half a block from his building he noticed the red pickup truck parked across the street, the driver sitting stoically behind the wheel, windows open, puffing on a cigarette. Brixton realized he hadn't had a cigarette since leaving the attorney's office and wanted one. Instead, he crossed the street and went up to the passenger side of the truck, leaned on the door, and smiled. "Hello," he said.

The driver was big and bulky, a dyed blond with a scraggly reddish blond beard, wearing a faded blue-and-white short-sleeved shirt open to his navel, and jeans. His face and massive arms were sunburned, an outdoors kind of guy. He scowled at Brixton.

"Why do I get the feeling that you're

interested in me?" Brixton asked, widening his smile.

"Get lost," the driver said.

"For some reason I've seen you too often where I've been," Brixton said, taking note of the shotgun rack over the driver's seat.

"What the hell are you, some fag trolling for queers. Get lost!"

"Oh, you shouldn't talk like that," Brixton said, maintaining his pleasant disposition despite wanting to reach in and smack him.

The driver started the engine, snapped the gearshift into Drive, and burned rubber as he spun away from the curb, almost dragging Brixton with him. Checking the truck's license plate was second nature to Brixton and he wrote it down on a receipt he pulled from his shirt pocket. It was at times like this that he wished he were still on the force, whipping out his badge and weapon and taking the blond hulk down a peg.

The brief confrontation snapped him out of his dark mood. After a quick cigarette, he went to the office, poured himself a thimble-size shot of scotch from a bottle he kept in a desk drawer, put his feet up on the desk, and processed what had transpired over the past two days. A few things nagged at him.

The first was the series of phone calls Eunice Watkins had starting receiving.

The second was the moron in the red truck.

She hadn't received such calls until she'd visited him the day before.

And the pickup and its driver had started showing up at the same time.

Coincidence?

Possibly.

Then again . . .

The ringing phone interrupted his introspection. It was Wayne St. Pierre.

"I'm callin' to invite you to a soiree at the old homestead," St. Pierre said.

"What's the occasion?" Brixton asked.

"Do I need an 'occasion' to throw a party? Just havin' a few friends over for cocktails and thought you and your lovely lady, Miss Flo, might like to join us. Day after tomorrow. I know, I know, it's last minute but spur-of-the-moment invites are always the most fun. Seven o'clock? Elegant casual dress. No need to bring anything except your charming selves."

Brixton's first reaction was to question why he and Flo were on the invitation list. St. Pierre was known to throw parties at the mansion his parents had left him, and Brixton had been to a few when he was still a cop. But he hadn't been invited to one since his retirement.

"Not sure about Flo," Brixton said, "but I'll be there."

"Splendid. There'll be a gracious plenty of top-shelf whiskey, and I'm bringing in a chef for the occasion who'll take you back to that Savannah we knew before all you interlopers from the north invaded."

"I'll let you know about Flo," Brixton said.

"You're a fine gentleman, Robert Brixton. I think you'll enjoy the other guests I've rounded up. See you then."

"Wait, Wayne, I need a plate run." He read it off the paper in his shirt pocket.

"First thing tomorrow," St. Pierre said. "Got to run. Bye."

CHAPTER 6

Brixton stayed in his office until nine, closing time for Flo's shop. They went to dinner at Vic's on the River, one of his favorite Savannah restaurants, and lingered over after-dinner drinks in the bar. He'd told her little about the Watkins case the preceding night. Now, with shimmering snifters of brandy in their hands, he filled her in.

"And you believe the mother's story?" Flo said.

"Yeah, I do."

The skeptical expression on her face said volumes.

"You don't *buy* it," he said.

She wrinkled her nose, a sure sign that it hadn't passed her smell test.

"I know it goes back a long way," he said, "which makes it tough to nail down. But yeah, I do believe the mother. Where the hell would the girl get ten thousand to give her? Joe Cleland — a detective I used to work with — he took the daughter's confession and told me he didn't believe her."

"But they convicted her anyway?"

"Sure. Case solved. Solving cases always looks good when budget time rolls around."

"Didn't she have an attorney?"

"Court-appointed. George English, an old-timer, retired."

"And you're convinced that her killing is linked to her having taken the rap for someone else."

"For the ten grand. She gave it to her mother."

Another nose wrinkle.

"I don't know, Bob," she said. After a long pause and a slow, deliberate taste of her brandy, she said, "Have you ever thought of getting out of the business you're in?"

His laugh wasn't completely sincere. "I seem to remember you asking me that before."

She placed a nicely manicured set of long fingers on his bare wrist. "I worry," she said, "that's all. If this Louise Watkins was killed to keep her from pointing out the real killer, whoever did it won't be thrilled that her mother wants to reopen the case."

Not that the thought hadn't crossed his mind. But he hadn't dwelled on it. Louise Watkins's travails went back twenty years.

Whoever might have been involved was undoubtedly long gone and disinterested, maybe dead. The possibility that anyone would be keeping tabs on the mother for all these years was remote at best.

"Actually, it's her son, Lucas, who wants to reopen the case. He's a minister."

"Whoever."

He hadn't told her about the red pickup yet. Her comment about being worried convinced him that it was better left unsaid.

"Staying with me tonight?" she asked after Brixton had paid the bill.

"Can't. I'm going to Atlanta in the morning and need an early start."

"What's in Atlanta?"

"It's *who's* in Atlanta," he said. He told her about Wanda Johnson, aka Puddin' Johnson, and why he wanted to see her.

"Think she'll remember this Watkins girl after so many years? How many hookers has she dealt with?"

"She says she does remember her. It may not amount to much but I think it's worth the trip."

They drove to where she'd parked her car next to the shop. They embraced and he considered changing his plans for the night. But he girded against the urge, saw her safely into her car, and watched her drive away.

It was raining hard the next morning when he stumbled out of bed. The alarm clock said six and he didn't debate it. He'd stayed up late watching an Atlanta Braves game on TV, and mulling over his life, something he found himself doing with increasing regularity. And, as usual during these moments of introspection, much of the time was spent reflecting on his failed marriage and the two daughters it had created.

He'd met Marylee Greene shortly after joining the Washington, D.C., police department. Their mutual attraction was instantaneous. It was also culture shock for the Brooklyn-born Robert Brixton. Marylee was nothing like the girls he knew back home, nor were any of the other young women he'd met in the nation's capital. They tended to be bubbly and gushy, their southern accents only adding to that persona. There wasn't any gushing in his Brooklyn home while he was growing up, with his dour father and taciturn mother.

Marylee had been a cheerleader at the University of Maryland, and Brixton expected her to launch into a "Give me an M, give me an A" at any moment no matter the setting or occasion.

They'd crossed paths for the first time when Brixton, a rookie patrolman, was summoned to a restaurant where a customer had gotten out of hand over his bill. Marylee was on duty as a hostess — she'd majored in European literature and hadn't yet found a job in D.C. calling for that particular knowledge — and greeted Brixton as he and his partner came through the door. The fracas was quickly settled. The irate customer left, and Marylee gave Brixton the information he needed to complete his report. She was taken with his strong, youthful face and snappy uniform, he with her dazzling smile, shapely figure, and fashionably styled blond hair. He didn't know whether asking for a date while on duty was against MPD rules but did it anyway.

They were married six months later, to the chagrin of her mother, who considered police service a necessary albeit lower-class way to make a living.

Marylee became pregnant the first month of their marriage and Jill was born nine months later. The second pregnancy occurred as soon as Marylee's physician told her it was okay to have sex again. Janet arrived nine months after that.

Things went downhill from there. Brixton had become disenchanted with his job, which was a mild reaction compared to Marylee's revised view of being married to a cop. With her mother, arms crossed, supervising the move, Marylee, Jill, and Janet vacated the apartment in The District and headed to the family home in Maryland. Brixton didn't contest the divorce or the amount of child support and alimony. Marylee's mother had been left a lot of money when her husband died, and Brixton got off easy. Within months he'd resigned from Washington's MPD, been hired by the Savannah Police Department, and moved to that quintessential southern city where there were plenty of other Marylees that he assiduously avoided. Flo Combes was originally from Staten Island. Enough said.

Brixton's daughters considered him a bit of a flake, which was okay with him. He called weekly, sent the checks on time until they reached eighteen, and managed a visit every couple of months. He missed watching them grow up but didn't wallow in that disappointment. The older girl, Jill, went on to receive a degree in accounting from Maryland University and landed a good job with a firm in Bethesda, where she met her husband. Brixton had attended the wedding a year ago and proudly walked her down the aisle. Janet proved to be less conventional. She dropped out of college and became involved with the music industry in capacities that Brixton never fully understood. Most recently she claimed to be promoting rock concerts in the D.C. area featuring bands Brixton had never heard of, nor wanted to. He knew she was into the rock world's drug scene and had warned her on many occasions of the ramifications of that life. She always listened but he was certain that his words fell on deaf ears. That he was now a private investigator, a private eye, amused Jill and Janet, whose knowledge of what private eyes did came from TV. All in all, and with the exception of worrying about Janet's lifestyle, his life was pretty good, except for those times when he was sure it wasn't.

He left Savannah at seven. The 250-mile drive to Atlanta usually took him about four hours, but the rain and two accidents on I-75 slowed him down. On the long list of things he didn't enjoy, long drives were at or near the top. His orthopedic problems were made worse when behind the wheel for longer than a half hour, and the number of yahoos sharing the road seemed to increase each day, gobbling messy sandwiches while driving, blathering on cell phones, and more recently dunderheads composing text messages on the highway while doing seventy-five.

The only positive thing he found about driving long distances was the time it gave him to think. Shutting off his cell phone while behind the wheel was as second nature to him as silencing it in theaters. There was no call important enough that couldn't wait until he'd arrived at his destination and gotten out of the car.

He'd researched Wanda Johnson on the Internet the night before. Now in her early forties, she'd been turning tricks for years — Vegas, Boston, Chicago, Atlanta, and finally her hometown, Savannah. Her rap sheet took up enough pages to fill a novella; the Savannah PD's vice squad knew her well enough to call her by her nickname, "Puddin'."

She'd had her epiphany following her last arrest. A local clergyman, whose flock consisted of the city's criminal population, did for Puddin' whatever it is that clergymen do. Presto! Wanda gave up "the life" and started counseling other hookers to get off the streets — and their backs — dump their pimps, and start living straight.

She got plenty of local press for it but soon decided that there weren't enough clients in Savannah to sustain her efforts. She packed up and moved to the big city, Atlanta, where there were more in need of her services, and more civic-minded money to sustain her mission.

Wanda Johnson's Refuge Project was housed in a storefront in a seedy section of the city, flanked by a boarded-up former take-out-chicken shack and an active pawnshop. A fresh coat of white paint and a tastefully painted sign above the door caused it to stand out from its surroundings.

Brixton stepped through the door and was greeted by a young black woman seated behind a makeshift desk created by a hollow door on two file cabinets. A large bulletin board featured dozens of color snapshots of women who Brixton presumed had been rescued from the streets by the mission's founder. A series of six watercolors depicting city life were grouped on one wall along with a clock with an Atlanta Falcons face, some photographs, and a large blackboard.

Brixton introduced himself and said he had an appointment with Ms. Johnson. The receptionist disappeared through a door and reappeared moments later accompanied by

Wanda. Now a stout, middle-aged woman, she wore a flowing white linen robe with colorful embroidery at the hem, cuffs, and neckline, and a floppy red hat, a far cry from what she must have worn during her days as a prostitute. Her dark brown face was heavily made up: vivid red lipstick, greenish eye shadow, and pink rouge. She extended her hand and said, "I don't remember seeing you around Savannah. You ever work vice?"

"No, ma'am."

"The vice squad cops were pretty nice, not out to bust chops."

"I hope you told them that."

"Every time they hauled me in," she said with a hearty laugh. "Come back to my office, if that's what you can call it. Times are tough."

"So I've heard."

Her office wasn't much bigger than a good-size walk-in closet. She'd squeezed a yellow vinyl couch that had seen better days into the space along with a small, round table that functioned as a desk, the only thing on it a cordless telephone. Another bulletin board held photos similar to the ones outside, as well as a large calendar. There were photos of Wanda receiving awards of some sort from politicians, and candid shots of her with Atlanta athletes at what Brixton assumed were fund-raising events. A through-the-wall air conditioner chugged away noisily. There were no windows. She must have sensed Brixton's reaction to the space because she said, "Most of the money we raise goes to help the girls, the hospital and rehab fees, help 'em with their rent, psych counseling, stuff like that. I don't need no fancy office."

"Most nonprofits could take a lesson from you."

"Glad you see it that way."

She directed Brixton to the couch, then sat in a swivel office chair. "So," she said, "you want to know about Louise Watkins."

"That's right."

"What is it you want to know about her?"

Brixton grinned. "As much as you can remember."

"That might not be much."

"Anything will be helpful."

"Mind if I ask why you're interested in her?"

"Not at all. As I told you, I'm a PI now. Louise's mother came to see me. Louise went to prison for stabbing a guy outside Augie's. Remember that joint?"

"Sure I do. Down and dirty."

"Her mother claims that Louise confessed

to that stabbing in return for ten thousand bucks, claims her daughter didn't stab anybody."

"Just like a loving mother."

"I believe her."

"Cops aren't usually that gullible."

"I'm not gullible, Wanda. The detective who took the confession didn't believe it either."

"She got herself killed," Wanda said matter-of-factly.

"Not long after she got out of prison. She did four years."

"Gunned down as I remember."

"That's right, in broad daylight. She was alone on the street. The cops say it was a random drive-by shooting. I say she was a target."

They were interrupted by two young women, one black, one white, who walked in without knocking. They eyed Brixton suspiciously.

"What's up?" Wanda asked them.

"Betty's making trouble again," one said.

"Is she?" said Wanda. "You tell Miss Betty that she'd best shape up or she'll be answerin' to me. You got that?"

They laughed and left.

"A couple of your saves?" Brixton asked.

"Uh-huh. You can take them off the street

all right, but it's harder to take the street out of 'em."

"I imagine."

"You were saying about Louise getting gunned down. Let me tell you what I remember about Louise Watkins. Like I said on the phone, she was just a confused little puppy, didn't have what it took to turn tricks. It's a hard business, you know, takes a certain kind of woman to survive it. Probably best she was sent down. I don't think she would have lasted long as a hooker, probably have gotten herself cut up or worse by some pervert."

"Did you and she talk much?" he asked.

Wanda shook her head, which sent her red hat into motion. "Just once or twice. I remember once after she'd been busted. Might have been her first time only I can't be sure. Anyways, she told me that she loved her momma and didn't want to hurt her, only she already was hurtin' her. She was drugged up that time. Damn drugs. She was pretty heavy into it, selling, too."

"Louise Watkins was a drug dealer?"

"Minor league stuff, Mr. Brixton. She peddled pot, some coke, nothing big time. She used to hang around Augie's, sell to some of the teenyboppers who hung out there, too. Mostly white, girls and guys whose mommies and daddies never believed their precious kids were using. I told Louise to knock it off, told her that they'd take her down hard if she got busted dealing junk."

"Did she listen to you?"

"Probably not. I was just another whore handing out advice."

"She should have listened to you."

"Most don't, but enough do to make it worthwhile."

"Did Louise have friends?" he asked.

"I suppose. She wasn't out on the street long enough to get close to other hookers, but she hung around with some people at Augie's." She snorted. "Friends? They were only friends as long as she had junk to sell. There are no friends in that world, Mr. Brixton."

"Did you know her when she confessed to the stabbing and was sentenced? I mean, were you in Savannah at that time?"

"Sure I was."

"What'd you hear on the street about it?"

"Not much. Shame she got nailed. Too bad it happened. The smart thinking was that she was turning a trick in the parking lot, he got pissed about something, put some muscle on her, and she poked him. Didn't she claim that he tried to rape her?"

"That's right."

"That doesn't make any sense, no need to rape a hooker unless you're broke and want it for nothing."

"That's the way I see it, too."

The time passed quickly and they talked until one, when she excused herself to keep another appointment. She walked him out to the reception area, where she pointed to a large glass bowl with the sign DONATIONS. He smiled, extracted a twenty-dollar bill from his wallet, and dropped it into the bowl.

"Thanks," she said. "You let me know how things turn out."

"I will, and thanks for seeing me. Keep up the good work."

"Oh, no fear of me stopping what I'm doing," she said. "Long as there be men there be hookers to save."

As he got into his car he remembered that his cell phone had been off since he'd left Savannah. He turned it on and saw that Cynthia had tried to reach him a half-dozen times. "Call me," she'd recorded in his voice mail. "It's important."

He dialed his office.

"Jesus, where have you been?" she said.

"Atlanta. I told you I was coming here."

"Your phone was off."

"I know. What's so important?"

"Somebody broke in here last night and went through your office, left a mess."

"Damn! You call it in?"

"Of course I did. Detective St. Pierre was here with a crime-scene type. They left an hour ago."

"I'm heading back now," he said, "should be there by five. Hang around, huh?"

"It gives me the creeps to be here," she said.

He didn't say it, but it gave him the creeps, too.

Chapter 7

Brixton decided that whoever had ransacked his office was an amateur.

He'd broken into more than one office during his tenure as a Savannah detective and knew that a pro wouldn't have destroyed the doorjamb during entry, nor would he have left things strewn all over the desk and floor. A pro would have jimmied the door neatly and made an attempt to put things back to prolong the discovery of the break-in.

"What do you think they were after?" Cynthia asked as Brixton surveyed the damage.

"I can't imagine. Then again, maybe they weren't after anything."

Her expression was quizzical.

"From the looks of it, nothing's missing. Any thief would have taken my surveillance equipment. My laptop's sitting on the desk. Your computer's still there. Nothing."

"Then why?"

"Maybe somebody was sending me a message."

He sat behind his desk and poured them each a shot glass of scotch. "Just a possibility," he said, and went on to tell her of the big man in the red pickup.

"He's been following you?"

"It looked that way. At least that's how I read it."

But then he waved away the scenario he'd just painted. He didn't want to spook her and possibly prompt her to quit. Since coming to work at his agency four years ago, the most upsetting thing that had happened to Cynthia involved the idiot last year who'd been fired from his bartending job after Brixton proved that he was ripping off the house. The bartender had somehow discovered that it was Brixton who'd fingered him, and had shown up at the office waving a samurai sword. Cynthia had hidden under her desk while Brixton calmed the man down until he was able to lay him out with two short, well-placed punches. Then the police hauled him off. He was deemed mentally unfit to stand trial and was remanded to a mental institution for evaluation. The last Brixton had heard of him was six months ago, when someone said that he'd moved to California. Perfect place for him.

"What did St. Pierre say?" Brixton asked her.

"Not much. The crime-scene techie dusted for prints on the door and some of the file cabinets. Detective St. Pierre wants you to call him tomorrow to file an official report. Want help cleaning up? I told Jim I'd probably be late."

"No, go on home. I'll take care of it. It must have been traumatic walking in this morning and seeing this."

She shuddered and wrapped her arms about herself. "I was afraid he might still be here. I got out fast and called the police from the deli."

"Smart thinking."

She started to leave, stopped, and said, "I forgot to ask how things went in Atlanta."

"Okay. Wanda Johnson was helpful."

"Glad to hear it. Why don't you get out of here, go have a nice dinner with Flo and call it a night. We can put things back together in the morning."

"Yeah, I might do that. See you tomorrow."

Her suggestion was appealing, and he almost acted upon it. But in the turmoil he'd forgotten that he was scheduled to follow the restaurant owner's wife that night to see whether she actually did attend a weekly Tupperware party.

According to the attorney, the party was supposed to start at eight, and he'd given Brixton the couple's address as well as a photo of the wife and a description of the car she would be driving. The last thing Brixton wanted to do at that moment was to tail an adulterous woman. But he'd already received an advance. Besides, there were bills to pay. He was always amazed at how pragmatic he could be when necessary.

He examined the office door and decided it would take more carpentry skill than a locksmith could provide. He'd call in a handyman in the morning. Whoever had broken in wasn't likely to take an encore. He turned out the lights and walked out, carrying with him the attaché case holding the camera and recorder he would use that night.

He showered at his apartment, changed into jeans, a black T-shirt, and sneakers, and stopped in at Lazzara's, his neighborhood hangout, a small Italian restaurant and bar on the corner owned by a fellow transplant from New York. Ralph Lazzara had also married a southern girl and moved with her to Savannah. And, like Brixton, the marriage hadn't lasted long. But by the time it disintegrated Ralph had already opened the restaurant and decided to stick with it. Living in Savannah was a lot cheaper than in Brooklyn.

"Hey, look who's here," Lazzara said when Brixton walked in. "Sam Spade himself. How's business?"

"Could be better. Let me have a Swamp Fox and an order of calamari. I don't have much time."

Lazzara plopped the bottle of locally brewed beer in front of Brixton and called in the calamari order to the kitchen. He joined Brixton at the bar. They were the only two people in the six-table restaurant.

"There was somebody in here this afternoon looking for you," Lazarra said.

"Oh? Who?"

"I didn't get his name. Kind of a weasel type of guy, you know, narrow face like a ferret I used to own. Dressed nice."

"What did he say?"

"He asked if I knew where Bobby Brixton lived, said he was an old buddy from Brooklyn."

"He called me Bobby?"

"Uh-huh."

"He sound like he was from Brooklyn?"

Lazzara laughed. "He didn't have any accent as far as I could tell, you know, he didn't talk like they do here."

"What'd you tell him?"

"I told him you were from the neighborhood but I didn't know where you lived. I figured that's what you'd want me to say."

"Somebody broke into my office last night."

"No? What'd they take?"

"Nothing as far as I can see. The only stuff worth anything is some electronic paraphernalia I use now and then. Everything was still there. It wasn't a burglary."

"Kids?"

"I don't think so. Where's the calamari? I have an assignment."

Lazzara disappeared into the tiny kitchen and emerged carrying the platter.

"Did this guy who was asking for me say anything else?" Brixton asked between bites.

"No. He had a sweet tea, thanked me, and left."

"Has a big, sunburned guy with blond hair, almost orange, and driving a red pickup been around?"

"A bubba?"

Brixton nodded.

"Doesn't sound familiar but I'll keep an eye out. What's the assignment you're on?"

Brixton finished the calamari and beer

and promised Lazzara that he'd stop back on his way home and tell him about it.

He drove to the address given him by the attorney and parked a few houses down on the opposite side of the street. The wife's car as described sat in the driveway. He looked at his watch: 7:45. The minute he looked up, the wife came from the house, got into her car, backed from the driveway, and drove off. Brixton fell in behind at a discreet distance.

He assumed that if she was going to a girlfriend's house, it wouldn't be far. But as they continued to travel, the husband's suspicions became more plausible. The route took them out of the residential area and to a highway leading south. It was twenty minutes past eight when she exited and turned into a motel parking lot.

Here we go, Brixton said to himself as he took a parking spot two cars removed. He pulled an expensive digital camera with a monster telephoto lens from the case and rolled down his window. She got out of the car, fluffed her hair, straightened her mini-skirt, and crossed the lot in the direction of the rooms. Brixton had never been to a Tupperware party but doubted whether women at them would be dressed the way she was.

As trysts go, this one proved easy for

Brixton. The door she paused at had a bright light over it that afforded plenty of illumination for the camera. Too, the motel's name in red neon was low enough above the door to be in the frame. The wife turned before knocking, as though to make sure that no one was watching (*She should only know,* Brixton thought), and he squeezed off a rapid-fire series of shots catching her full-face. The man with whom she was rendezvousing stepped outside to greet her with an embrace, giving Brixton a clear shot of him, too.

They disappeared inside. Brixton checked to see that the photos had come out — they were excellent quality — and replaced the camera in the case. Two hours later, after dictating his observations and times in the digital recorder, he drove off with mixed emotions. He was pleased at how easy it had been. The husband would have proof of his wife's infidelity, the attorney would look good for having hired the right PI, and Brixton was spared a succession of future evenings hoping to catch her in the act. On the other hand, he'd intruded into someone's personal life, an intrusion that would result in pain for everyone involved. He felt anything but proud as he made his way back to the city but knew he'd feel better once he'd picked up the lawyer's second check.

Lazzara's Restaurant was busier than when Brixton had been there earlier. All the tables were taken, and four of the five stools at the bar were occupied. Brixton took the vacant one and ordered a scotch and water. Lazzara, who was bartending, asked, "How'd it go?"

"Fine. An easy one."

Lazzara leaned over the bar. "That guy who was in earlier looking for you came back. Not long after you left."

"Asking for me again?"

"No. He had a drink and some pasta and left."

Brixton thought of his trashed office and wondered if there was a connection between this stranger and the break-in.

"You want something to eat?" Lazzara asked.

"Yeah, that'd be great."

"I've got an eggplant special."

"I don't eat eggplant."

"That's right. I forgot. The usual?"

"That'll be fine."

The couple next to him tried to engage him in conversation but he wasn't in the mood for chitchat with strangers. He politely disengaged and focused on his veal parmigiana. The couple left, as did most of the diners at tables. Lazzara joined Brixton on his side of the bar.

"Put it on my bill, Ralph."

"Sure. Tell me more about what happened at your office."

Brixton filled him in, and told him of his surveillance that night of the wayward wife without mentioning names. "Did the guy asking for me look like the type who'd break in someplace?"

"Not the way he was dressed. Like I said, sharp dresser, expensive suit, fancy tie. You think there's maybe a connection?"

"Probably not." Brixton stood and clapped a hand on his friend's shoulder. "The veal was great, Ralph. It's been a long day."

"You look beat. Go crash. It'll do you good."

Brixton took his case of electronic gear and stepped out onto the sidewalk. The rain that had soaked the city earlier had cleared, leaving Savannah in a soupy, humid mist that made it hard to breathe. He headed in the direction of the building in which his one-bedroom apartment was located, eager to strip down, take a shower, and bask in the AC. The street was quiet, the few small stores that lined his route closed for the night, heavy metal gates secured over their windows and doors.

As he approached the corner, he thought he heard a noise coming from an alley that ran between his building and the adjoining one. A few more steps brought him even with the dark shaft. It happened fast. Two men who'd been lurking in the alley's shadows rushed him. The first caught him flush on the side of the face, knocking him to one knee. The second man grabbed him from behind in a stranglehold while the first rammed his fist into his gut, then smashed his nose. Brixton tried to bring up the attaché case as a shield but it was ripped from him. He tumbled face-forward, hands outstretched in search of the case, his momentum bringing his already battered face into contact with the hard sidewalk. He squeezed his eyes closed against the pain in his head; he heard their footsteps as they ran from the scene and disappeared around the corner.

Brixton remained motionless on the sidewalk until his senses had cleared. He opened his eyes and managed to pull himself up so that he was on all fours, and vigorously shook his head in an attempt to regain some semblance of clarity. He got to his feet, fell, and tried again. This time he was successful, although he was anything but steady. He gently put his fingers to his face. When he pulled them away, they were sticky, wet with his blood. He brought his hand back up to his mouth. No teeth missing. *Count your blessings.*

He leaned against the metal grates protecting the stores and used them as props to retrace his steps back to Lazzara's. He reached the window and looked inside to where Lazzara was busy cleaning up behind the bar. Brixton felt as though he might vomit. Lazzara saw him and rushed through the door. "What the hell?" he said.

"I need to sit down," Brixton said.

"Sure, sure," Lazzara said, grabbing Brixton's arm and helping him stay erect as he guided him into the restaurant.

Brixton slumped on a bar stool.

"You got mugged?" Lazzara asked.

"I got jumped. Two guys." It was at that moment that he realized that his attaché case was gone. "They took my case, dammit! I had pictures from tonight's assignment. Damn!"

"Okay, take it easy," Lazzara said. "You need to see a doc."

"No, I'm all right."

"The hell you are."

Lazzara brought a cloth soaked in cold water from behind the bar and applied it to Brixton's face. "You're a mess. Your nose is busted."

Brixton pressed his fingers against it and groaned at the pain.

"Come on, man, you need the ER."

Brixton didn't argue. After telling the chef to lock up, Lazzara walked Brixton to his car and drove him to Memorial Health University Medical Center, in midtown, where Brixton was seen by a young physician. Lazzara had been right: Brixton's nose was broken. Aside from that, there didn't appear to be any other serious injuries.

"How did this happen?" the doctor asked after patching Brixton up.

"I was jumped by two guys," Brixton answered.

"Have you notified the police?"

"I, ah — I will once I leave here. I was a cop."

"Were there weapons involved in the assault?"

"Not that I know of."

Brixton had mentioned to Lazzara during the drive to the hospital that he wasn't carrying his licensed handgun. "Not that it would have done me any good," he said. "They were all over me before I could even move my hands."

"You didn't see 'em?" Lazzara asked after they'd left Memorial and were on their way back to the restaurant.

"Enough to ID them? It was dark and they were quick."

"Maybe you shouldn't go back to your place," Lazzara suggested.

"No, it's okay. I got mugged, that's all."

Which didn't accurately reflect what he was thinking. Sure, he might have been the victim of a simple street assault, a couple of guys who spotted the attaché case and figured it might contain a million in cash. But that didn't wash for Brixton. There was more to it than that. How many coincidences could there be in the space of two days?

He'd been followed by the good ol' boy in the red truck. A stranger had shown up at Lazzara's asking for him. Someone had broken into his office, gone through his files, and left without the laptop tucked under his arm. And now this.

These incidents were enough to make him believe that his taking on the Louise Watkins case was, one way or another, connected. He couldn't conjure why that would be, but it was too compelling to be dismissed. It was all too much to process during the ride back. His broken nose throbbed and his head ached. On top of his injuries, there was the theft of his attaché case. The camera and digital recorder were insured, covered under the policy he carried on his office. But there was no insurance on the photos of the restaurant owner's cheating wife and her lover-boy.

He thought back to what he'd captured with the camera. The photos were of no use to anyone except the husband and his attorney. They'd have to be content with Brixton's written report of what he had witnessed the wife doing. But chances were that they wouldn't accept it as proof and that he'd have to follow her again, using a new camera. Maybe they'd feel sorry for him because he'd sustained injuries in the line of duty. On second thought, the attorney wasn't the sort of guy who'd feel sorry for anyone.

Lazzara unlocked the restaurant door and put on the overheads. Brixton sat at the bar. "Mind if I smoke?" he asked. Smoking was prohibited in all restaurants in which food was the primary draw.

"No, go ahead," Lazzara said, sliding an ashtray that hadn't been used in years across the bar. "Drink?"

"Yeah, that'd be great. Scotch, neat."

Lazzara joined him. "How you feeling?"

"All right."

"You want me to call Flo?"

"No. No sense worrying her. I'll talk to her in the morning."

"You gonna call the cops and report it?"

"Tomorrow. I have to file a report on the break-in anyway. Might as well do both at once."

They lingered at the bar for another half hour, when Brixton announced that he was going home. Lazzara locked up again and walked him to the entrance of his building.

"Sure you're okay?" he asked as they stood inside the cramped lobby that served the building's six apartments.

"I'm fine. Thanks, Ralph. I owe you."

Lazzara laughed. "I'll put it on your bill."

"Yeah, you do that. Thanks again."

As Lazzara walked back to where he'd parked his car, he passed the scene of the attack on his friend. He looked down at the red stain left by Brixton's blood on the sidewalk and hoped that it wasn't a down payment on worse things to come.

CHAPTER 8

Brixton woke at six the following morning on his couch, where he'd collapsed the night before. He hadn't bothered to undress, just kicked off his shoes and curled up; sleep had come in seconds.

He went to the bathroom and examined his bruised face in the mirror. One side was swollen and had turned purple and green. His nose, which he always thought was one of his better features, was puffed and discolored. Other than that, he was his usual handsome self.

He showered, dressed in chinos and a pale yellow button-down shirt that he thought went nicely with his wounds, and added a light blue linen blazer. He checked himself in the mirror again and knew that people would want to know what had happened to him: "Walk into a tree?" they'd ask.

He wouldn't reply, "You should see the other guy."

He called Cynthia at home to tell her that he'd be in late, asked her to call the handyman they'd used before to repair the door, and headed out, stopping for a bacon-and-egg sandwich and coffee, which he carried to a small park across the street from the Metro barracks at Habersham and Oglethorpe. When he finished eating, he paused in front of a statue of a man in uniform; the sign read ABOVE AND BEYOND, LEST WE FORGET. A list of Savannah police officers who'd given their lives in the performance of their duties appeared below, starting in 1901 with an officer named Harry L. Fender and continuing through more recent years. Brixton had stood before that statue on the first day he'd reported for duty as a Savannah cop and silently hoped that his name wouldn't be added to the roster.

The entrance to what the cops called "Metro" was covered with a portico supported by columns. A large blue sign with gold lettering announced that this was the SAVANNAH-CHATHAM METROPOLITAN POLICE DEPARTMENT, the result of a merger in 2003 of the Chatham County Police and Savannah City Police. Brixton entered the reception area, where the desk was manned by a pair of formidable female uniformed officers, one of whom Brixton recognized.

"Hey, Detective Brixton, how are you?" she asked.

"Not bad — and don't ask what happened to my face."

"Won't say a word," she said, laughing.

"Is Detective St. Pierre in?" Brixton asked, aware that the second officer was eyeing his bruises.

"I think so. He expecting you?"

"Expecting to hear from me. Thought I'd drop in instead of calling."

"I'll see."

St. Pierre appeared minutes later. He took one look at Brixton, cocked his head, and said, "I suppose the other fellow looks worse."

"I wish that were the case, and let's skip the clichés. Got a minute?"

"For you, Bobby? All the time in the world. Come on back."

St. Pierre shared an office with another detective, who was out investigating an armed robbery. Brixton took a chair and said, "Two reasons for my being here, Wayne. The first has to do with my face. I was jumped on my block last night by two goons. They stole the attaché case I was carrying, which contained an expensive digital camera and tape recorder. I had photos in the camera from a surveillance job I did last night."

"Following some misguided wife or husband?"

"As a matter of fact that's exactly what I was doing."

"You waited until this morning to report it?"

"I was in no mood last night to hassle with it. I'm reporting it now."

"That's good of you, Bobby. I'm sure that the second reason for your visit is what happened at your office night before last."

"You were there," Brixton said.

"Ah certainly was. Made a mess of your door, didn't they?"

"That they did."

"Your lady-Friday said she didn't think anything was missing."

"She was right. You pick up on anything while you were there?"

"Can't say that I did. We dusted for prints."

St. Pierre sat back and made a show of scrutinizing Brixton.

"I know," Brixton said, "I don't look so good."

"Ah wasn't admiring the handiwork those two fellas did on your ugly face, Bobby. What I *am* wonderin' is why a nice fella like you wants to waste his time like a character in a Raymond Chandler novel. Hell, you could get yourself hooked up with some respectable company here in Savannah, head up their security department and spend your sweet days watching shoplifters on a monitor."

It hurt when Brixton smiled. "I can't imagine a worse way to spend a day," he said. "I might ask you the same question. With all your money you could be spending your days mixing juleps and charming southern women with your wit and good looks instead of sitting here." He indicated the cramped, cluttered office with a wave of his hand.

St. Pierre laughed. "You miss the point," he said. "Being an officer of the law gives me a certain cachet that other handsome, wealthy Savannah gentlemen lack. I'll get you a report form for last night. No, better make it two. Seems like your troubles come in pairs."

When St. Pierre returned, Brixton asked whether he'd had a chance to run the plate on the red pickup.

"As a matter of fact I did. Seems it's an old discarded plate taken off a vehicle that was junked."

"But the pickup wasn't junked."

"I'd say that the fella driving that red truck didn't want anybody to know who he was or where to find him, probably put those old plates on to make sure that didn't happen. What's your interest in the truck?"

"I think the guy was following me."

"Oh. Well, whoever he is he probably has his legit plates back on the truck now. Following you, you say? What is goin' on with you, Bobby? A break-in to your office, a mugging, and bein' followed."

"That's what I'm trying to figure out." Brixton stood and stretched. "Thanks, Wayne. I'll fill out these reports outside. This office gives me claustrophobia."

"Before you go," St. Pierre said, "what about my soiree? You and Flo will be there?"

"I haven't mentioned it to her yet. I will later today and let you know. Actually, I don't look like a happy partygoer."

St. Pierre put an arm around Brixton's shoulders and walked him from the office. "What I suggest, my friend, is that you concoct some intriguing story. You know, like you were hurt trying to protect a young lady's virtue, or thwarted a terrorist attack right here in downtown Savannah."

The handyman was busy trying to repair the broken office door when Brixton arrived and didn't look up. But when he entered the reception area, Cynthia took one look and said, "Oh, my God, what happened to you?"

"I thwarted a terrorist attack last night on Bay Street."

"You *what?*"

"I lied. I got jumped by two guys when I was going home after the assignment. They ripped off my camera with last night's photos in it. Ralph Lazzara took me to the ER. I look bad but I'm fine."

Cynthia had done a good job of straightening up the mess.

"Anything seem to be missing?" he asked.

"No, but it's hard to tell with so many papers."

"Nothing of value in them," he said. "I'd better call Flo."

He reached her at the dress shop and told her what had happened.

"And you didn't call me?" she said.

"I didn't want to worry you. Hey, I'm all right, got patched up nicely at Memorial. Look, Wayne St. Pierre has invited us to a party at his house tonight."

"Tonight? Thanks for the advance warning."

"I was busy thinking of other things. I'd like to go, rub elbows with Savannah's upper crust."

"I thought you didn't like Savannah's upper crust."

"I don't. Can you close up early?"

She sighed audibly. "I suppose I can have Carla cover for me. Do I have to dress up?"

"Sure. Basic black with pearls and plenty of rocks on your fingers."

"Bob!"

"Elegant casual. Isn't that what they say at restaurants? I'll pick you up at six."

He asked Cynthia to get him the phone number of the Southside United Freedom Church and dialed it. The call was answered by a man with a deep, cultured voice.

"I'm looking for the Reverend Lucas Watkins," Brixton said.

"You are speaking with him."

"My name's Robert Brixton. I'm a private investigator working for your mother."

"Yes, my mother mentioned you."

"I was wondering if I could stop by and talk with you about the case."

"About my sister, Louise, you mean. Hearing her referred to as a 'case' is a bit unsettling for me."

"Yeah, well, I — Could we get together to talk about Louise?"

"Are you thinking of today?"

"If it's okay with you. I can be there within the hour."

"All right. You have the address?"

"I do."

"The rectory is directly behind the church. It's a white, one-story frame house. I'll await you there."

Brixton's next call was to the Christian Vision Academy, where the photo of Louise and friends had been taken during a weekend retreat. He was shuttled around until he connected with the school's headmistress, Mrs. Farnsworth.

"I have absolutely no recollection of a young woman named Louise Watkins," she said after Brixton explained the reason for his call.

"I don't expect that you would," Brixton said. "Her mother has a photograph of Louise with some of your students at the retreat. I thought that if I showed you the photo, you could help identify who's in it with her. I know it's a long time ago, the late eighties, but I really would appreciate your help."

"Well," she said after a pause and a meaningful sigh, "I suppose I would be willing to do that. But I must say that our students come from prominent families here in Savannah, from all over the state as a matter of fact. Their privacy is of paramount importance to us."

"Sure, I understand," he said. "I just need

some help in sorting things out. I'll arrange to get the photo from her mother and call you when I have it. Will you be in all day?"

"Yes."

"Hopefully I'll get back to you by early afternoon. Thanks very much for your assistance. Have a nice day."

A call to Eunice Watkins confirmed that she would be at home and that he was welcome to come by and pick up the picture, provided he returned it. It was one of her favorite photographs of her daughter because it showed Louise in happier days. He said he understood and pledged that the photo would be back in her hands safe and sound.

The Southside United Freedom Church was on a leafy street in a virtually all-black area, surrounded by modest houses on small plots of land. A group of boys dressed in Little League uniforms — he gauged their ages as somewhere between ten and twelve — milled around in front of the church, waiting for someone to pick them up and deliver them to a ball field. Brixton parked on the street and approached them on his way to the rectory.

"Got a big game today?" he asked.

His question was met with shouts followed by high fives. The other team didn't have a chance, if their bravado was any indication.

Brixton looked past them and saw a man he assumed was the minister standing on the small front porch in front of the rectory. He was imposing in height and weight. He wore a black suit and white shirt with a clerical collar. His salt-and-pepper hair and beard were neatly trimmed. He raised his hand. Brixton returned the wave.

"Looks like a bunch of all-stars out front," Brixton told him.

The Reverend Lucas Watkins laughed. "Their enthusiasm makes up for any shortfalls on the playing field. Come in, Mr. Brixton."

The inside of the rectory was neat and orderly, the air smelling of fresh paint. "Coffee, tea?" the minister asked.

Brixton opted for coffee. Watkins had a glass of water. They sat in what Watkins termed his study, a compact, nicely furnished room with floor-to-ceiling bookcases on one wall and a large open window looking out over a small backyard. A set of lacy orange-and-yellow curtains fluttered in a welcome breeze. Brixton noted that among an array of photographs hanging behind the desk was a large color photo of Eunice Watkins with her daughter. He commented on it.

"Breaks my heart every time I look at it," Watkins said, slowly shaking his head. "Louise was a victim and paid the price."

"A victim? Of what?"

"The society we live in, Mr. Brixton. She fell under the influence of evil people who inhabit it."

Brixton was tempted to challenge the statement. As far as he was concerned, today's society was no different than it ever had been and most people didn't fall victim to anything. For Brixton, life amounted to nothing more than a series of decisions. You make good ones, and barring some freakish act of nature or accident, a tornado or being hit on the head by an air conditioner falling from a high window, things go pretty smoothly. Make bad decisions and things don't go so well. But he wasn't there to argue philosophy.

"I understand that it was you who urged your mother to come see me about Louise," he said.

"That's correct, Mr. Brixton." Watkins's voice filled the room and Brixton visualized him delivering a fire-and-brimstone sermon. "However, I didn't suggest you specifically. I simply told her that she might engage the services of a private investigator."

"Had your sister told you about being

paid to go to prison? I know she told your mother."

"No, she did not. Louise and I suffered the sort of sibling rivalry that occurs in most families. Being older and male, I had different interests and friends. I felt my calling to God at a very early age, Mr. Brixton, and Louise was aware of it. I, of course, was aware of *her* lifestyle and the wrong path she was going down. It wasn't a situation conducive to her sharing intimate thoughts with me, although I tried to reach her. I regret I was unable to provide a counterbalancing influence."

"You're referring to her drug use."

"Yes."

"But I'm under the impression that your mother — and now I assume you — are more interested in clearing her name regarding the stabbing than in finding out who shot her when she got out of prison."

"Being shot is not a sin, Mr. Brixton. She happened to be at the wrong place at the wrong time. But to have spent four years behind bars for a crime she did not commit is a legacy I believe should be corrected."

"When did you learn of Louise's claim that she'd been paid to take the rap?"

"A few months ago. My mother, bless her,

carried the burden of knowing for all these years."

"What caused her to finally confide in you?"

"My mother isn't well, Mr. Brixton. I believe that she wished to unburden herself of this before answering her final call."

Brixton nodded. It was as good a reason as any. He noticed for the first time since entering that the house, and particularly this room, was relatively cool even without an air conditioner running. Maybe it was a perk of being close to God. If so, he might consider stopping in at a church from time to time, at least until fall arrived.

Brixton wondered just how ill Eunice Watkins was but didn't ask. *Stick to the reason you're here,* he silently reminded himself.

Sounds of a happy commotion from outside interrupted their conversation. "Excuse me," Watkins said, standing. "The boys are about to leave for their game and I have to see them off. The church sponsors the team."

Brixton followed him to the front porch and stayed there as Watkins went to where the team stood alongside a school bus. The youngsters had now been joined by a handful of adults, presumably their parents.

When they saw Watkins approaching, conversation died. The moment he reached them, the boys and their parents lowered their heads in prayer, with Watkins leading. When their heads came up, Watkins shouted, "Play hard but fair! You carry God's name with you." The whooping and hollering resumed as the team scrambled onto the bus and the adults retreated to their cars parked in driveways up and down the street.

"I'm impressed," Brixton said when Watkins rejoined him on the porch.

"With what, Mr. Brixton?"

"With the respect they obviously have for you."

"To be more accurate, sir, it's the respect I have for *them*. Are we finished?"

"Yes, unless you can remember something that will help in my investigation."

"Might I ask *you* a question?" he said.

"Sure."

"I know nothing about you, Mr. Brixton, except what my mother has told me. She says you seem like an honest, honorable man. My mother is prepared to pay a large sum of money to you in the hope that truth will prevail."

"The ten thousand your sister gave her."

"She told you that?"

"Not to worry, Reverend. I'm not out to spend your mother's money beyond what it'll take to find out the truth."

"I wasn't suggesting that you were."

"But the implication was there. Look, anytime you or your mother wants to call this thing off, let me know and that'll be that. In the meantime, I'm working as best I can, considering how long ago this all went down."

Watkins extended a large hand. "I see why my mother has put her faith in you, sir," he said. "Please call on me at any time."

Watkins went inside the house, leaving Brixton on the porch. He walked to the street and gave a thumbs-up to the kids as the school bus pulled away. Their parents' cars left their driveways and fell in line behind the bus. But Brixton's attention went to one car in particular. It had been parked at the curb a few houses removed from the church and was driven by a white man who cast a fast glance at Brixton as he joined the parade. He didn't look familiar to Brixton, a nondescript sort of man with a pinched, elongated, ferretlike face.

The way Lazzara had described the man who'd been looking for him the preceding day.

Chapter 9

Brixton got in his car, made a U-turn, and headed in the direction the bus and entourage had taken. But by the time he caught up with them a few blocks away, the last car in line, the one driven by Ferret Face, had veered off and was gone.

As he drove to Eunice Watkins's house he reflected on the conversation he'd just had with her son. He had to give the padre credit for not commenting on his battered face. He'd never even winced. Aside from that, Brixton had been uncomfortable meeting with the minister.

That feeling was nothing new. He'd been ill at ease around ministers and priests going back to when he was an altar boy in his family's local Brooklyn parish. He'd been baptized like all good Catholic babies, and confirmed in the faith, attending Sunday Mass on a regular basis with his mother while his father slept in after getting home from his Saturday-night shift behind the bar.

When Brixton left home to join the Washington MPD, he put worshipping behind him — until he met and married Marylee Greene and had two kids with her. The Greene family was devoutly Catholic, and Brixton went along, although he knew that he was only going through the motions. Their daughters were dutifully baptized in the Catholic faith and he attended Mass with them whenever his shift allowed. If his faith had been weak before becoming a D.C. cop, nights spent on the city's mean streets did nothing to strengthen it. And the breakup of the marriage brought a sense of finality to any belief in a higher power. He hadn't set foot in a church since.

He and the Jewish Flo Combes were a perfect match in that regard. At thirteen her parents had celebrated her coming of age with an elaborate bat mitzvah at a local catering hall. She'd dated plenty of young men, many of them not Jewish, which was all right with her parents. Neither her mother nor her father was especially observant, and their attendance at the local synagogue was restricted to the high holy days.

When Flo graduated from the Parsons School of Design in Manhattan and launched what she hoped would be a successful career as a clothing designer, she fell hard for a handsome young Jewish fellow who was in his third year of residency at a New York City hospital. Their marriage had lasted even fewer years than Brixton's had — two years, two months, six days, to be precise. Her husband turned out to have an increasingly serious prescription-drug problem that set his emotions on a roller coaster, placid one moment, volatile to the point of physical abuse at the next. Fortunately, no children were involved and they parted amicably, as amicably as possible in such circumstances.

Flo soon tired of the Manhattan rat race and looked to relocate to a more serene environment. A high school friend had moved to Savannah and encouraged Flo to join her there. She packed up, found an apartment in this quintessential southern city, got bank backing for her dress shop, and happily settled in to her new life. There were beaus there, too, of course, but along came Robert Brixton, fresh from twenty years as a homicide detective with Metro, and their distinctly secular, off-and-on relationship took off. Although they disagreed about many issues, they were in concert on one important one: neither wanted to be married again.

Eunice Watkins greeted Brixton and, unlike her son, gasped when she saw his face.

"It's a long story," he said. "I'm fine. Not to worry."

She invited him in for sweet tea. He declined, explaining that he had appointments to keep. She'd put the photograph in a plastic bag and taped it closed.

"You take good care of that now," she said.

"You have my word," he said. "Oh, I've been meaning to ask whether you've received any more strange phone calls."

"No, thank the Lord."

"That's good," he said. "You let me know if you do. I'll try and have the picture back to you later today, but it may be tomorrow."

"That will be fine," she said.

"I spent time with your son this morning."

"Lucas called and said you'd paid him a visit."

"I'm sure you're very proud of him."

"I thank God every day for him," she said. "Every day. I'll be prayin' for you, Mr. Brixton," she added, indicating his face.

"I appreciate that," he said.

His next stop was the Christian Vision Academy. He'd been on those grounds before as a cop, two calls, as he recalled, having to do with suspicious-looking people hanging around. The private girls' high school was the butt of occasional jokes, mostly about its reputation as being snobbish and priggish, the students' families coming almost exclusively from Georgia's A-list stratum. But it had a sterling reputation for turning out fine young southern women who, for the most part, went on to marry fine young southern men after leaving CVA and majoring in finding suitable husbands at college. A few had strayed over the years from the religious teachings that supplemented the school's academic curriculum, and Brixton had once arrested one of those rogue fine southern young women in a drug bust. He'd arrested people from all walks of life as a cop, both in Savannah and in D.C., including a House member in the nation's capital, and some wealthy types in Savannah. Money never buys morality was how he saw it.

CVA's campus was set on a dozen acres of gently rolling land with an abundance of live oaks, crepe myrtles with purple and white flowers resembling crepe paper, and sweet bay magnolias. The administrative building stood on the tallest rise, an imposing antebellum mansion that Brixton figured probably looked like Tara in *Gone With the*

Wind, although it had been so long since he'd seen the movie that he couldn't remember what Scarlett's plantation home looked like. Smaller buildings, architecturally designed not to clash with the main building, housed classrooms and other functional rooms.

He pulled into a visitors' parking area in front of the main building, turned off the engine, unwrapped the photograph, and spent a few moments examining it. He looked up as a group of six young women wearing the school's green-and-black uniforms exited the building and passed the car, their voices shrill, their laughs giddy. The white girls in the photograph weren't wearing uniforms, probably, he assumed, so as to not make the three African-Americans feel out of place. He focused on Louise Watkins's wide smile and felt a twinge of sadness. What had led her into a life of drug use and hooking, and why would she give up four years of her young life for ten thousand dollars? Who knew? Decisions! You make good ones and you do okay, bad ones and you end up like her. His creed.

Mrs. Farnsworth was a tall, staunch lady in her sixties. In some ways she was the clichéd image of a head mistress of a prestigious girl's school. But her pink suit and frilly white blouse, coupled with a pleasant smile, softened her beyond stereotype.

She invited him to take a seat in her large, handsomely furnished and decorated office and asked if he wanted a soft drink or coffee. He declined. He was aware that she was eyeing his beat-up face and headed off any questions. "I was mugged last night near my apartment," he said. "But I'm feeling fine."

"So much crime," she commented.

He nodded and got right to the point by handing her the photograph. She put on half-glasses and spent more time than he thought necessary to look at it.

"Taken at one of our weekend retreats," she said flatly and handed back the picture.

"That's what I was told by Louise Watkins' mother," he said. "Louise is the third black girl from the left." He handed the photo back to her.

Farnsworth perused it again and shook her head. "This was so long ago," she said, and the picture ended up back in Brixton's hands.

"What I'm hoping is that you can identify the other young women in the photo, Mrs. Farnsworth." He gave her the photo again.

"Hmmm." She adjusted her glasses. "I don't know the names of the black girls in the picture, or of two of our students."

"Two?" he said. "But you know the name of one?"

She placed the photo on her desk and smiled. "Oh, yes," she said. "I can't miss that vibrant face and lovely smile."

Brixton waited for her to elaborate.

"The girl on the far right is Mitzi Cardell." She placed the accent on the *dell*.

"Sounds like you knew her pretty well."

"And still do, Mr. Brixton. Her name isn't familiar to you?"

"Afraid not."

"Mitzi was an outstanding student, top grades, a class leader, an exemplary young woman. That she's gone on to great success surprised no one here at CVA."

"What does she do?" Brixton asked, wishing he already knew.

"Why, Mitzi Cardell is one of Washington's leading hostesses, Mr. Brixton, and a confidante to many of our government's leaders." She laughed. "Some say that many members of Congress, and the White House for that matter, don't make important decisions without conferring first with Mitzi."

"Really? I don't follow the Washington social scene too closely. I lived there for a while but that was years ago."

"It's fitting that she'd ended up in Washington. Her best friend here at school was Jeanine Jamison. That's her name now that she's our first lady. Jeanine Montgomery was her maiden name. I'm sure she's grateful to have Mitzi close-by to help ease the incredible pressure she must be under as first lady. They were inseparable here, just as they are in Washington. Mitzi is one of our major fund-raisers, and the first lady has lent considerable support to our efforts in that regard as well."

"This Ms. Cardell," Brixton said. "Her family from Savannah?"

"Yes. Wonderful people, pillars of the community."

It took a few moments for the name Cardell to register with Brixton, big shots in Savannah, plenty of money, their names in the society columns every now and then. The old man led the annual St. Patrick's Day parade on a few occasions; Savannah's St. Patrick's parade was the second largest in the United States, second only to New York City. Go figure. Brixton recalled being introduced to him at a fund-raiser for a charity dedicated to providing funds to the families of cops wounded or injured in the line of duty. Typical titan of industry was Brixton's reaction to shaking his hand. Cardell had made his money in real estate, and there had been rumors that he'd pulled a few shady deals including payoffs to elected officials to secure prime downtown property. Business as usual.

"That's the best I can do," Mrs. Farnsworth said.

"You've been generous with your time," said Brixton. "I appreciate it."

She walked him from the building, looked up into a pristine blue sky, and said, "I've been blessed with helping nurture so many outstanding young ladies during my years here."

"Must be nice seeing your students go on to bigger and better things."

"Very satisfying, Mr. Brixton, very rewarding."

Brixton got into his car and turned on his cell phone, which had been off all day. There were messages from Cynthia. He called the office.

"You know," she said upon answering, "you should get in the habit of leaving your cell phone on, Bob. It's so damn frustrating trying to reach you."

"Yeah, I know. Sorry. What's happening?"

"A restaurant owner called to say he needed you to do some undercover work at his place. And that attorney called to get a report on the wife you followed last night."

"What'd you tell him?"

"I told him I'd have you call."

"I will."

He'd been avoiding making that call all day.

"Are you coming back to the office?"

"Later. The handyman get the door fixed?"

"Uh-huh. He left his bill."

"Okay. I should be back within the hour."

While Brixton dialed the attorney's number, Mrs. Farnsworth placed a call of her own from the office. "Mr. Cardell, it's Waldine Farnsworth at CVA."

"Hello there," he said in a loud voice colored by his Savannah roots. "To what do I owe this pleasure?"

She told him of Brixton's visit and of his interest in the girls in the photo. "I pointed out Mitzi to him. I hope that was an appropriate thing to do."

"You say he's a private detective?"

"Yes. He gave me his card."

"Ah'm sure there's nothing to it, Waldine, but I appreciate the call."

"I just thought you'd want to know."

"Much obliged, Waldine. I'll have to get over there one of these days to talk some about raising some more money for that fine school of yours."

"I look forward to that," she said, and the conversation ended.

Brixton reached the attorney from his car.

"What've you got from last night?" the attorney asked.

"The husband's right," Brixton replied. "She met up with a guy at a motel south of here." He gave the attorney the name of the motel and its location.

"Damn good work, Brixton. You've got pictures, tapes?"

"Well, let's just say I *had* pictures."

"What's that supposed to mean?"

"I got a good set of pictures of the two of them hugging in front of their motel-room door, but I got mugged. The bastards took my attaché case that had my camera and recorder in it."

"Oh, that's wonderful. That's really wonderful, Brixton."

"Couldn't be helped."

"It sure as hell won't help my client. What do you think I should do, tell him that you *say* you saw his wife with this guy at a motel? That'll do a lot of good, Brixton. He needs proof to bring to the judge, hard proof."

"I understand that, but you see, I got beat up and —"

"I don't need excuses, dammit, I need

evidence, hard evidence. What you *say* doesn't mean squat. What'd I hire, an amateur?"

"No, you hired a good PI who got his face busted up trying to keep a couple of bozos from stealing my expensive camera and your client's pictures. I should have the check from my insurance agent within a week and I'll follow her again once I buy a new camera."

"I should have gone to a *real* agency," the attorney growled, "somebody who knows what he's doing."

"You know what?" Brixton said. "I think that's exactly what you should do, get somebody else."

"What about the advance I paid you?"

"Sue me for it, pal. I consider it a down payment on my pain and suffering."

He clicked off the phone.

It took Brixton a few minutes to calm down. His thoughts ran rampant. He considered going to the attorney's office and punching him out, but he'd end up in jail if he did that. He thought of contacting the husband's wife and telling her to cool it with her lover. That wouldn't accomplish anything, he decided, and contented himself with having blown off the attorney and keeping the advance payment.

Eunice Watkins was home when Brixton dropped off the photograph. He didn't stay.

Cynthia was packing up to leave by the time he walked into the office.

"Half a day?" he said.

"Very funny. I have errands to do," she said. "It's quiet around here. I mean, unless you want me to stay."

"No, go on. I have to leave, too. Flo and I are going to St. Pierre's place for a party tonight."

"The way you look?"

"Thanks for the vote of confidence. First thing in the morning go online and find out everything you can about a Mitzi Car-*dell.* She's supposed to be some big-shot D.C. hostess who was friendly with the president's wife."

"Why?"

"Cynthia, I'm not in the mood for twenty questions. Just do it, okay?"

"Testy, aren't we? I'll take care of it. Enjoy the party. And lock up tight when you leave. I'd hate to have to go through this again."

Chapter 10

Flo Combes owned the building in which she lived, a two-story row house constructed in the mid-1800s of large porous bricks known as "Savannah grays"; its second-floor balcony covered with scrolled ironwork typical of vintage Savannah houses. She occupied the top floor and rented the lower one to the owner of an art gallery that featured local artists, many of them products of the Savannah College of Art and Design, Wayne St. Pierre's alma mater.

"You look terrific," Brixton said when Flo opened the door dressed in a knee-length white silk sheath.

She winced at the sight of his face. "Oooh," she said. "You really did a number on yourself."

"I had nothing to do with it," he said.

She gently touched the side of his face. "Hurt?" she asked.

"Only when I laugh. You look — different."

"Like it?" she asked. "I had my hair done this afternoon and I told her to do something different with it. She came up with this shorter cut."

"Looks great," he said, and he meant it, although he preferred the longer version. Discretion prevailed and he didn't say it. She'd been blessed with a mane of luxuriously full and healthy hair, so richly black that it gave off almost a purple sheen. It was the first thing he'd noticed about her the night they met.

"So," she said, "why are we invited to this shindig? You and Wayne haven't been close since you left Metro."

"It's this case I'm working on. He's been helpful inside the department. Besides, I get a kick out of him, always have. He's funny."

"That's not necessarily flattering."

"No, I mean I like him. It's just that I've never known another cop like him. It must be his money."

"You used to wonder whether he was gay."

"I don't think he is. Not that it matters. He's had plenty of girlfriends."

"That doesn't always mean anything," she offered.

"Ready to go?"

"Do I look sufficiently *southern?*" she asked, striking a pose.

"You look sufficiently *Staten Island,*" he said. "Perfect!"

Wayne St. Pierre's home was located on Monterey Square on Bull Street between Taylor and Gordon Streets, amid equally impressive homes, all of them old, large, immaculately maintained, and owned by wealthy Savannahians. That old money was behind each front door was as evident as if they had neon signs on them that flashed RICH!

Piano music and the voices of party revelers came from the house as Brixton turned over his car to a young man St. Pierre had hired for the evening as a parking valet. "I want a cigarette before we go in," Brixton said, pulling one from his jacket pocket and lighting it. He'd taken only an initial puff when the door opened and St. Pierre appeared, dressed in a purple silk smoking jacket, black pants, white tux shirt open at the neck, and red-and-yellow carpet slippers with toes that turned up.

"What are you doing out here?" he asked. "Sneaking a smoke like some homeless character? Come on in and bring your cigarette. The antismoking crowd doesn't have jurisdiction over the old homestead."

He turned to Flo. "You look absolutely ravishing, my dear," he said, taking her hand and kissing it. "Come in, come in. Plenty of good whiskey for all, food catered by Susan Mason herself, and nothing but Johnny Mercer music."

They followed him inside, where two dozen men and women stood in conversational bunches, drinks in hand, their laughter filling the room along with music from a Yamaha Disklavier player piano. Two uniformed waitresses passed trays of canapés and other finger food. A few smoking guests had gathered around a sizable ashtray.

"Bar's over there," St. Pierre said, indicating a far corner of the large living room. He left them to welcome another arriving guest.

Brixton said into Flo's ear, "We don't have to stay long."

She laughed and led him to the bar.

St. Pierre rejoined them as they waited for one of two bartenders to make their drinks. He was accompanied by a tall, deeply tanned man with rugged features. His pearl-gray suit had Savile Row written all over it. "Bobby and Flo, say hello to Warren Montgomery."

They shook hands.

"We've met before," Brixton said, "when I was with Metro."

"One of Savannah's finest?" Montgomery said. "Not still on the force?"

"No. I retired four years ago," Brixton replied as the bartender handed them their drinks.

"Warren's our president's father-in-law," St. Pierre said.

"I know that," Flo said. "We've never had the pleasure of meeting. It must be exciting being that close to the seat of power."

Montgomery gave forth with a self-effacing laugh. "I don't think I'd choose the term *exciting,* Ms. Combes. *Annoying* might be more like it. They wanted to assign a couple of Secret Service boys to keep me safe." Now it was a guffaw. "I told 'em that I had my own security people and that they could save the taxpayers money by lettin' me take care of myself. If more citizens felt that way we might be able to balance the damn budget there in D.C."

"You get to see your daughter much now that she's in the White House?" Brixton asked.

"I get there occasionally," he replied. "Even got to sleep in the Lincoln Bedroom on one occasion. They say it's haunted but I never saw any ghosts parading around. Got enough ghosts here in Savannah without havin' to go to Washington to see them."

Then, as though noticing Brixton's black-and-blue face for the first time, he said, "Judging from your face, I'd say being retired from the police is a dangerous undertaking."

"An accident," Brixton said.

"Can't be too careful these days," Montgomery said. "Good meeting you folks." He strode away.

"I'm going out for a cigarette," Brixton announced.

"You can smoke right in here, Bobby," St. Pierre said.

"I don't like blowing smoke in people's faces."

"Robert's a very considerate smoker," Flo explained.

St. Pierre slapped him on the shoulder. "Looks like some of our famous southern manners rubbed off on you. Go on out back." He pointed to french doors that led to a brick patio.

"You go ahead," Flo said. "I'm not leaving the air-conditioning. Besides, I'm enjoying the music."

The disk inserted in the piano contained only Johnny Mercer songs recorded by a local professional pianist, the ivory keys moving magically without anyone seated on the piano bench. It segued from one Mercer tune to another — "Fools Rush In," "Autumn Leaves," "Satin Doll" (with music by Duke Ellington), and "Laura," Flo's favorite song, written with the composer David Raksin. Mercer had been a lifelong Savannah resident; his family's ancestral home, across the square from St. Pierre's, had become a tourist destination, hosting thousands of visitors each year. He'd written the lyrics to more than a thousand songs and composed the music for others, many of which became classics. He ranked right up there as a Savannah favorite son.

It was a typical summer night, hot and steamy, although a breeze had developed, which helped a little. Brixton lit up and sat on a stone bench in front of a piece of statuary, a six-foot-tall naked woman holding a bunch of grapes. Savannah was full of statues, many celebrating the city's heritage, which went back to 3500 BCE, when the Biblo lived there. Oglethorpe's arrival in 1732 marked the birth of modern Savannah. Brixton respected the city's history but didn't have any particular interest in it. For him it was an alien land in which he'd ended up through circumstances. No, he decided as he sat on the bench and thought about it, he'd ended up in Savannah because he'd decided to come there, and he was still there because he'd decided not to leave. He didn't believe in fate. You made your own fate.

As this train of thought occupied him, he realized that he was becoming depressed. The shrill female voices inside, coupled with loud males', oiled by the free-flowing booze, grated on him. He lit a second cigarette. He knew he should go back inside and join Flo but dreaded it, actually dreaded it. They never should have come. He should have declined St. Pierre's invitation, made an excuse — his face was excuse enough — and spent the evening with Flo at some quiet restaurant, or in one of their apartments.

He was sinking deeper into this morose state when the doors opened and St. Pierre came through.

"Bad form, Bobby, leaving that lovely lady alone in there with a bunch of men on the hunt."

"I was just about to come in," Brixton said, snuffing out the cigarette on the bricks at his feet and adding it to the first butt, which he held in his hand. "You need an ashtray out here."

"The ground is fine, my friend."

"You travel in impressive circles, Wayne," Brixton said as he stood and maneuvered against a pain in his back.

"Ah was surprised when Warren said he'd stop by tonight," St. Pierre said. "You can imagine how busy he is with his real estate interests and having a daughter in the White House."

"Yeah. I'm sure he's a busy guy."

"Come on in, Bobby, and meet some of my other friends. Most of 'em are pretty nice once you get to know them."

Brixton forced some life into his voice. "Okay," he said, "but no more 'Bobby.' "

St. Pierre delivered a fake punch to Brixton's abdomen. "You've got my word, Robert, and a southern gentleman's word is his bond."

Brixton and Flo stayed another hour. St. Pierre introduced them to a handful of others at the party, a few from Savannah's artsy crowd whom Brixton considered too precious for his taste, and some of the host's wealthy neighbors who reacted to Brixton's battered face by cutting short their conversations. When it was time to leave, St. Pierre walked them to where they waited for the car parker to fetch Brixton's Subaru.

"Thanks for inviting us, Wayne," Flo said.

"It was my pleasure." He looked at Brixton and frowned. "Looks to me, Robert, that you could use a vacation, considerin' everything that's been happening to you lately. You know, go lie on a beach someplace, drink some fancy rum drinks, and relax."

"I might do that, Wayne."

"Wonderful seeing both of you. Stay out of trouble, Robert. There's no case worth gettin' beat up over."

Part Two

CHAPTER 11

On most summer days, Washington, D.C., is as miserably hot and humid as Savannah. But on this day it was as though a large dome had been placed over the city built on a swamp and someone had switched on a gigantic air-conditioning unit. The temperature had dropped twenty degrees and the humidity was low. The sky was cobalt blue — like a fall sky — and the brisk breeze from the northwest was invigorating.

A perfect day for sightseeing.

The tour guide of a double-decker, open-top sightseeing bus parked in front of Union Station stood by the door and greeted passengers who'd paid for a tour of the city, including a man in his late thirties with a pencil mustache, who used a thin walking stick with a gnarled head. Aside from his cane, Emile Silva looked like any other tourist — chino pants, white sneakers, and a white shirt worn loose.

"Good morning," the guide said pleasantly.

"Good morning to you, sir," Silva replied, equally as pleasantly, "a perfect day for a tour." The guide accepted his prepaid ticket and watched him slowly, presumably painfully, climb the stairs one at a time to the open upper level, where he took a seat behind a couple who spoke to each other in a combination of Kurdish and English.

Silva looked down to where a dozen high school students led by their teacher came from Union Station and milled about until their tickets were collected and they were allowed to board.

"All right, everyone," the tour guide said as the driver started the engine, "off we go. We'll be stopping at the sites listed in your brochures and you'll have time to get off and take all the pictures you want before we proceed to the next stop. Please stay in your seats while we're moving for your safety and comfort."

The bus pulled away and the tour guide started his spiel about Washington and the many landmarks they'd be passing. Silva heard the comments but wasn't particularly interested in them. He'd recently taken this tour twice with different drivers and guides, so he knew in advance what would be said.

That left him free to focus his attention on others on the bus, particularly the couple in front of him, who demonstrated enthusiasm at what they were seeing.

The couple and most of the other tourists got off the bus at the U.S. Capitol to take photographs of the imposing structure, particularly the almost twenty-foot-tall statue of a woman, *Freedom,* that sits atop the building's nine-million-pound cast-iron dome. Some of the young people on the tour were too busy horsing around to pay attention to what the guide said about the Capitol, and Silva viewed them with disgust.

With everyone back onboard, the trip continued — Washington's compact Chinatown, Ford's Theatre, where Lincoln had been assassinated by John Wilkes Booth, the monuments to the Korean, Vietnam, and Second World wars, and the Holocaust Museum. Some of his fellow tourists lingered at those locations, knowing they could board another passing bus at any time. Silva remained in his seat.

But when they reached Washington Harbour, a riverside complex of restaurants, shops, an office building, a condominium, and an inviting promenade that offered panoramic views of the river, Silva got up, stretched and yawned, and hobbled down the stairs, leaning on his cane. The Kurdish couple headed straight for the promenade and stood looking out over the river and its boat traffic. Silva came up next to the man, a burly fellow wearing a black suit, white shirt, and black tie. His wife wore a colorful, long-sleeved velveteen outfit that ran straight from her neck to her ankles; a "lira belt" fashioned of coins strung together provided a waistline.

"It's a beautiful city, isn't it?" Silva commented.

"Oh, yes," the wife said.

"Your first visit?" Silva asked.

The husband nodded.

"How long will you be staying?" Silva asked, following the line of usual questions asked of tourists.

"One more week," the husband replied.

"You're from . . . ?"

"We are Kurds, the northern part of Iraq," the husband said.

Silva had inched closer until his hip touched the husband's.

"It's the best way to see a city on a first visit," Silva said, "taking a bus tour. Once you've gotten an overall view, you can choose what to follow up on."

As he said it, a woman in a pale blue jogging suit seemed to have lost her balance when she was abreast of them and fell against Silva, pushing him harder into the husband.

Silva grunted.

The husband said "aah" and reached down to touch his ankle, the one closest to Silva.

"I'm sorry," the jogger said. "I really am sorry."

"It's all right," Silva said.

The woman jogged away. Silva turned to the husband, who was now crouched down. He'd rolled down his black sock and was examining and rubbing his ankle.

"Are you all right?" Silva asked.

"A bite maybe," the husband said. He straightened up and smiled at Silva. "Clumsy woman," he said.

"But pretty," Silva said, which made the wife laugh.

"Yes, pretty," the husband agreed. "But clumsy."

Silva looked back to where the sightseeing bus was parked. "I think the driver is about to leave," he told the couple.

"Yes, we had better go," said the wife.

They started to walk away but stopped. "Are you coming?" the husband asked.

"No," Silva said, a broad smile crossing his face. "I think I'll stay here and have lunch at one of the restaurants, get on a later bus. Go, enjoy yourselves. It's a beautiful day for it."

He waited until everyone had boarded and the bus had disappeared from view before getting into a taxi, which took him to the garage near Union Station in which he'd parked his car, a black Lexus sedan. He drove to his home across the Potomac River in suburban Maryland, a remodeled Victorian shielded from view of passersby by a seven-foot high hedgerow and numerous trees. He used a remote device to open the three-car garage, parked the Lexus alongside two other vehicles including a new black Porsche — all three vehicles had recently been reregistered to his mother's address in suburban Virginia — and took the walking stick to an area of the garage devoted to woodworking. He removed the head of the cane and extracted its triggering mechanism, using a hammer to smash it. Within seconds the table saw had cut the stick and its thin metal shaft into a dozen small pieces, which he secured in a green plastic garbage bag and added it to another bag containing household trash.

He entered the house and went to a sizable room that contained an elaborate home theater system, a floor-to-ceiling wall of books, and a workout area that included a weightlifting bench and an elaborate treadmill. He sat behind his glass-topped desk and dialed a number. A woman answered.

"Good job," he said.

"Thanks."

"He said you're clumsy."

She laughed.

"I'll be in touch," he said.

He ended the call and stripped down to his shorts and sneakers. With a large plasma TV tuned to a local TV news channel, he stepped up onto the fast-moving treadmill and smiled as his tension melted away.

CHAPTER 12

Some pundits compared Mitzi Cardell to that famed D.C. hostess of yesteryear, Perle Mesta, who reigned over Washington society as the "hostess with the mostest," particularly during the Truman and Eisenhower presidencies (Truman would eventually name her ambassador to Luxembourg).

Married to Pittsburgh's steel baron George Mesta, she was the only heir to his $78 million fortune when he died in 1925. Feeling unaccepted by Pittsburgh's social elite, "Pearl" Mesta changed the spelling of her name to "Perle" and moved to the nation's capital, where she brought together presidents and their first ladies, senators, congressmen, cabinet members, and other political movers and shakers at lavish bipartisan soirees. Her fame eventually reached far beyond the District of Columbia: the composer Irving Berlin based his smash Broadway musical *Call Me Madam,* starring

Ethel Merman, on her.

Mitzi eagerly accepted having the Mesta torch passed to her. She'd married John Muszinski, founder and CEO of Muszinski Financial Group, a man twenty years her senior, and it was his wealth that supported their glittering Washington lifestyle. Mitzi decided early on to use her maiden name, Cardell, which she felt would be more readily accepted than Muszinski by Washington's social set.

An invitation to Mitzi's parties at her Georgetown mansion was one of the most coveted in town.

But there were differences between dinner parties hosted by Mitzi Cardell and those staged by Perle Mesta. Perle had been a Democrat who liked Republicans and was an early supporter of the Equal Rights Amendment. Mitzi Cardell and her wealthy husband were staunch supporters of the right-wing Fletcher Jamison administration and had little tolerance for alternate viewpoints. Too, Perle Mesta's parties were almost purely social; whatever political advantages resulted from having attended were incidental. Not so with the gatherings choreographed by Mitzi. They often had a motive behind the gaiety, gourmet food, and top-shelf liquor, and she built the guest lists around a political issue, bringing together Washington political power brokers with similar interests in the subject du jour.

The major difference between being a D.C. social hostess back in Mesta's day and the society in which Mitzi Cardell functioned was the city itself. Washington's bitter political partisanship had torn apart social niceties between Republicans and Democrats. No longer did rivals on the floor of the Senate or House of Representatives put aside their policy differences at the end of the day and get together at dinner parties, or sit down for a friendly game of poker. Mitzi's guest lists had to be carefully vetted to ensure that like-minded people sat next to and across from one another. Elected officials raced to their home districts as often as possible, leaving behind bureaucrats, agency heads, and staffers to fill spots at her dinner table. It was a new, often dismal era in which Mitzi Cardell was forced to entertain, and she was well aware of it.

This unseasonably cool evening was no exception. The unstated topic was the law, and the guests represented various members of D.C.'s legal community. Among the dozen guests were Mackensie Smith and his wife, Annabel Lee Smith.

Smith had been one of the city's most respected defense lawyers, his client list ranging from drug dealers to politicians whose greed had reached the criminal level. When his first wife and their only son were slaughtered one rainy night on the Beltway, victims of a drunk driver — and when the drunk driver received a minimum sentence — Mac's zeal for the courtroom waned. He closed his practice and accepted a teaching position at George Washington University's law school, where he imparted his legal wisdom and keenly honed cynicism to a new generation of attorneys. Although he no longer practiced law, he was much sought after as a consultant and had advised Mitzi Cardell on a few legal matters, his primary role having been to refer her to attorneys for whom he had respect and who he knew would do right by her.

Annabel, too, had been an attorney, a busy and successful matrimonial practitioner. She had not married, although the lineup of potential suitors was long. After eventually tiring of mediating between warring spouses, she decided it was time to abandon the law and pursue her private passion, pre-Columbian art. She, too, shuttered her law practice and opened a gallery in Georgetown.

Mac and Annabel knew each other professionally and had ended up at some social events together. He was well aware and appreciative of Annabel's natural beauty, and his good looks and quiet, thoughtful demeanor hadn't escaped her. She was tall and striking, with ivory skin and copper hair, her laugh infectious, slightly wicked. Mac was a man whose self-confidence never strayed over the line into egotism, as was the case with too many attorneys Annabel knew. They started dating, although Mac quipped that *dating* was too youthful a word for people their age — both were in their early fifties. Their courtship progressed to Mac's marriage proposal, which Annabel eagerly accepted. They were married in the National Cathedral and set up blissful housekeeping in an apartment in the Watergate complex, its name infamous, its amenities many.

Of the twelve guests at the dinner table, the attorney general of the United States was the most prominent, at least in terms of government rank. "Delighted you agreed to join the commission, Mac," he said, referring to a task force established by Justice to study proposed new legislation affecting sentencing guidelines. Smith knew that his inclusion in the group was a tip of the hat

to creating a nonpartisan look to the commission; he'd not made a secret of his dissatisfaction with the Jamison administration.

"The ramifications of the legislation are substantial," Smith said. "It could dramatically change the legal system."

"And as far as you're concerned, not for the better I take it," the AG commented lightly.

"I haven't made up my mind yet," Smith said. "We still have testimony to get through."

A law professor from Georgetown University, an acknowledged Jamison supporter, weighed in with his views on the proposed legislation, his stance at odds with the way Smith saw things. Smith turned to Annabel and said, "Wonderful dinner."

"Superb," she said, understanding his need to shift conversational gears. She lightly placed her hand on his.

Mitzi Cardell occupied the seat at the head of the table. It was no surprise to anyone that her husband, the "man of the house," hadn't been assigned that seat. Although Mitzi's wealth was the result of her husband's financial success, she ran the show when it came to dinner parties. That she was the first lady's closest friend only added to her clout.

Along with being well connected in Washington, Mitzi Cardell was an extremely attractive woman who turned heads wherever she went, with soft blond hair always perfectly coiffed, a slender figure that wore designer clothes well (she was on *Washingtonian Magazine*'s best-dressed list every season), and a politician's penchant for saying the right thing and smiling at the right time. There were those who resented her wealth and position, who viewed her marriage to the older John Muszinski as representing gold digging at its finest. But those comments were always whispered, by those who vied to be elevated to inclusion on her guest lists.

"How is Mrs. Jamison?" Annabel asked.

"She's terrific!" Mitzi replied. "She'll go down in history as the most effective first lady ever."

Mac Smith silently considered that a gross overstatement, but others at the table heartily agreed with their hostess's assessment.

Following dinner, Mitzi announced that cordials would be served in the library. As everyone left the table, a housekeeper came to her and said that she had a call. "Be a dear and take it," she said to her husband, who nodded and disappeared into another room.

"So, Mac, how's the tennis game?" a congressman asked after their drinks had been served.

"Slow," Mac said. "My knee keeps acting up."

"But he never uses it as an excuse when I beat him," Annabel said. "He's still tough on the court, although I let him win now and then."

"A wise wife," the congressman agreed. "Can you believe this weather? In all my years in Washington I've never seen it so cool at this time of year."

"I'm sure the president will take credit for it," Smith said.

"As well he should," the congressman said, laughing.

Smith just smiled.

Mitzi asked Annabel, "Looking forward to Jeanine's tea?"

"Very much," Annabel said. "I'm eager to see the redecorating she's done at the White House."

"You'll love it," Mitzi said. "She has such wonderful taste — in everything."

"So I've heard."

Smith sneaked a look at his watch and said quietly to his wife, "Time to be going."

Mitzi had already decided the same thing and smoothly indicated that the party was over. She and her husband stood at the door and said good night to their guests. When the last one had gone, and after checking on the cleanup being performed by the household staff, they retired to their bedroom, where she sat at a dressing table removing her makeup while John changed into pajamas and a robe.

"Your father called," John said.

"Is he all right?"

"He's fine. He said some private investigator visited Waldine Farnsworth at CVA."

"A private investigator? Did he say why?"

"Something to do with a photograph of a black girl and you that was taken at a retreat at the school."

"*What* black girl?"

He shrugged. "Louise something. He wants you to call him first thing tomorrow. It sounded important."

Mitzi said nothing as she turned and stared into the mirror.

"Something wrong?" he asked.

"What? No, nothing's wrong. I can't imagine what it's all about." Her laugh was forced. "A picture with a black girl taken when I was a student there? God, that's aeons ago."

Her husband climbed into bed and returned to a book he'd started nights earlier. Had he looked over at his wife, he would have seen the changed face that peered back at her from the mirror. It hadn't changed because she was now without makeup, or because of fatigue she felt after the party and the long day leading up to it.

The change came from within.

Chapter 13

Emile Silva cupped a mug of steaming black coffee in his hands as he stepped out onto his secluded rear patio. It was two days since he'd played tourist and visited Washington Harbour. The cooler weather had held, although that morning's forecast called for a return of heat and humidity later in the day.

He wore a red silk kimono over his nakedness, and flip-flops. The coffee was to his liking. Silva was a coffee snob who took pains to buy and to mix what he considered the perfect brew. A pair of cardinals that called his property home flew between trees, causing him to smile and to imitate their call. Life was good. He'd slept well and felt rested, ready for the day, which would involve an hour of strenuous exercise followed by an alternating hot and cold shower. His meeting wasn't until eleven that morning, plenty of time for him to continue cataloging his extensive CD collection before he needed to leave.

He chose to drive the Porsche that morning. The feel of its powerful engine and the control he exerted through its manual transmission was orgasmic. He took Western Avenue, crossed the Potomac on the Chain Bridge, and proceeded southeast on the Washington Memorial Parkway until reaching his destination, a relatively new two-story modern office building a few miles south of the Pentagon. While it had all the trappings of any other small office building in the area, it differed because of its lack of large windows. The stucco structure had only a pair of narrow vertical windows flanking the entranceway, and horizontal ones of the same size across the second level.

He swiped his card in a reading device at the door, entered, and walked down a hallway to a rear office in which two men sat leaning over papers on a low, oval coffee table. They looked up at Silva's arrival. One closed the folder they had been reading.

"Good morning, Emile," he said.

"Good morning to you."

"Coffee?"

Silva's grimace delivered his answer.

"It went well?"

"Of course," Silva said as he took a hard

candy from a bowl on the table.

"He was hospitalized," said the other man.

"Two, three days," Silva said. "He'll be gone. You told me to be here this morning. You have another assignment for me?"

"Yes. Dexter has the details."

Silva followed them down a set of stairs to a basement room. The use of a card as well as a key was necessary to gain access to it. It was a windowless space with thick concrete walls and soundproof baffling on all surfaces. Heavy locked metal cabinets lined one wall; a workbench ran the length of the opposite one. A folding metal table surrounded by four folding metal chairs sat in the middle of the room. A short, slender bald man with thick glasses and wearing a tan suit sat in one of them.

"You have your bags packed?" he asked in a pinched voice that matched his appearance.

"They're always packed," Silva replied.

"Good. You're needed overseas. Here is what it involves."

At George Washington University Hospital, Afran Mutki was fading fast. His wife had brought him there from the hotel in which they were staying when he complained of difficulty breathing. His chest had felt heavy and constricted, and he ran a fever. By midnight he'd begun to turn blue and his lungs had started to fill. His blood pressure dipped precariously low.

"We have a diagnosis on him yet?" a nurse asked the senior physician who'd been assigned the case.

"No, dammit. I've ordered more tests, but the way he's going, I doubt if the results will matter."

By the next day, Mutki had begun to hallucinate and suffered a series of seizures. There was blood in his urine.

"His body's shutting down," the physician told colleagues as they pulled out everything from their medical bag of tricks in an attempt to save his life.

That afternoon, Mutki's kidneys, spleen, and liver failed. He was pronounced dead at 8:51 that night.

Afran Mutki was fifty-three years old, married, had three children, and worked as a journalist. His home was Erbil, the largest Kurd city in northern Iraq. As far as the hospital staff knew, he and his wife were in the United States on a tourist visa, seeing the sights, buying souvenirs and gifts to take back to their children. His wife, shaken by the sudden loss of her husband, was now faced with arranging for his remains to be transported back to Iraq. But those plans would be put on hold after two calls from the hospital.

The first was made to Dexter, the slender man with the pinched voice, by a member of the hospital's administrative staff. "There's been a death in the family," was all he said before hanging up.

The second call was to the Washington MPD. It was placed by Dr. George Bennett, the physician who'd tried valiantly to save Afran Mutki's life. Bennett had been practicing medicine for forty years and was close to retirement. He'd seen it all and was considered a superb diagnostician. Before making the call, he'd huddled with the younger physicians who'd assisted him.

"He went fast," one said.

"A hell of an infection," said another.

"Ricin," Bennett said flatly.

They looked at him quizzically.

"It has all the trappings of ricin poisoning," Bennett said. "You're too young to remember the Markov case. About thirty years ago in London. He was a Bulgarian, a journalist who defected to London, where he kept up his criticism of the Bulgarian government. They — or someone working on their behalf, probably the Russians — got rid of him, poisoned him with ricin.

That red pimple on Mr. Mutki's lower leg. He complained about it, said he thought that he'd been stung by some insect. Markov, as I recall, had a similar complaint. His assassin — and he *was* assassinated — had used a specially rigged umbrella to inject him with a tiny pellet containing ricin."

"Real cloak-and-dagger stuff," said one of the younger physicians, chortling.

"Real life-and-death," Bennett corrected. "I have no idea whether it was ricin or not but it's a suspicious death in any case. The police have to be informed, an autopsy performed."

Bennett reported Mutki's death to the authorities and ordered an autopsy with instructions to pay particular attention to the tiny raised red mark on the deceased's lower leg.

Interest in the sudden, unexplained death of the Kurdish journalist, Afran Mutki, wasn't limited to the physicians who'd treated him, the MPD, and the man known as Dexter.

Mutki's handler at the State Department knew of his illness only hours after he'd been admitted to the hospital. His death spurred an emergency meeting of the handler and others at State who gathered in the Iraq Section in the agency's Foggy Bottom facility. Also present were two CIA agents who worked the Iraq Desk at Central Intelligence.

"Go over Mutki's importance again," one of the agents said.

The handler obliged. "Mutki, as you know, has been a leading voice in the Kurds' dissatisfaction with the approach taken by Baghdad. He's been writing and broadcasting his belief that the Kurds are victims of the Iraqi central government and of our government. President Jamison has been particularly interested in Mutki and his activities and isn't happy with what he's learned. This is a delicate time in Iraq. We don't need someone like Mutki stirring up trouble in the north."

"We've been tracking him since he arrived in the States," the CIA representative said. "What was the purpose of his trip?"

"He was here at State's invitation," the handler explained. "We were hoping to help nurture a different perspective on his part."

"He was loose in the city," the CIA agent said.

"His choice," replied his handler. "He said that he and his wife wanted to spend time exploring the city. We worked with the Kurdistan embassy to schedule their trip, got them sightseeing and theater tickets. It's not like he was in any danger. Nobody knew who he was, just another foreigner exploring D.C."

The second CIA agent raised his eyebrows. "It looks like *somebody* knew who he was," he said curtly. "The hospital and MPD are treating it as a suspicious death. We hear that the doctor in charge of the case even mentioned the possibility of ricin poisoning."

That bit of news brought a momentary halt to the conversation.

"Does the embassy know that?"

Mutki's handler at State answered, "We're meeting with them at noon. Hopefully we can keep this under wraps until an autopsy determines how he died."

"Lots of luck," the CIA agent said.

"We've had a few media queries," the representative from State said. "We're working on a response now."

"Ricin? Jesus! If it's true, the Iraqi government is going to have the spotlight trained on it big-time."

"The White House?" a CIA agent asked. "Have they been informed?"

State nodded. "Of course. The president

is calling the Kurdish prime minister later today."

"To say what?"

"To say how sorry he is that one of their leading journalists has died."

"How sorry *is* he?"

"Let's not be cynical. The president didn't like what Matki was writing and broadcasting, but —"

"Forget I said that."

"Ricin! Don't tell me it's another umbrella attack," said the older of the CIA agents.

"It's all speculation at this juncture," said State.

That's the way it was left — for the moment. The two CIA agents departed the meeting and headed back to CIA headquarters at Langley.

"We need someone present at the autopsy," the older agent said. "Get one of our cleared docs to sit in on it."

"Shouldn't be a problem."

"Everything's a problem," was his older colleague's terse reply.

At noon that day, Dexter met with a man at a local McDonald's.

"Has Emile left yet?" Dexter was asked.

"He's flying out tonight."

"Cancel the trip."

Dexter looked up from the cheeseburger he'd just picked up.

"We need a low profile for a while. Keep Emile here. I'll let you know when it's time to activate him again."

"All right," Dexter said and took a bite of his burger.

Chapter 14

Dexter called Silva's cell phone to inform him that his overseas mission had been scrapped. Silva took the call at his mother's house in suburban Virginia, where he'd arrived earlier that afternoon. He regularly visited her, sometimes as often as four or five times a week. She wasn't well. She suffered from congestive heart failure, emphysema, and diabetes; a portable oxygen tank was kept close to her side. Emile was her only child. She'd given birth to him at the age of forty-three, a year before her husband died in a hunting accident.

"Who was that?" she asked from her favorite living room chair after he'd ended his call.

"The office."

"Where is your office?" she asked.

He smiled, sat on a hassock at her feet, and patted her gnarled hand. "You always ask me that, Ma-ma, and I always tell you that I have many offices. I'm a consultant. I go from office to office. I was supposed to fly somewhere tonight but that trip has been postponed." He gave her his widest smile. "That's good news because it means I can spend more time with you."

"That will be nice," she said in a weak voice. "You never come and stay long."

"Now don't say that, Ma-ma. Sometimes my business takes me away from home but I always rush back to see you. I brought you your favorite soup."

"What kind?"

"Oh, Ma-ma, you know what your favorite soup is, crab chowder. I'll heat it up for you now."

He emptied the container of soup into a saucepan and heated it on the stove, taking tastes as he did so. The smile that seemed pasted on his square, dusky face when he was with her had disappeared the moment he entered the kitchen. It took resolve to feign pleasure at being there. The house smelled as though an old person lived in it, sour and oppressive, dusty and depressing, the drapes always closed, a TV on twenty-four hours a day. And there was the smell of the cigarettes she smoked despite her frail health. A large ashtray next to her chair was always filled with foul-smelling butts. She was visited each day by a nurse, and twice a week by a cleaning woman, but that was inadequate for the task. The nurse had recently told him that it might be time for his mother to be admitted to a nursing facility, but he wouldn't hear of it, nor would he consider moving in with her. He'd rather see her die than allow either of those things to happen.

When the soup was ready he ladled it into a large bowl, carried it to the living room, and he placed it on a special wooden table that brought it close to his mother.

"Where's the crackers?" she whined. "I like crackers with it."

He returned to the kitchen and brought back two packages of saltines. "There you go," he said. "Enjoy."

"Aren't you eating, Emile?"

"I had lunch before I came," he said as he tucked a napkin beneath her chin. "You go ahead."

"Will you play music for me later?" she asked.

"If you wish."

He left her to enjoy her soup and went upstairs to what had been his boyhood bedroom. It was exactly as it had been when he left home to join the marines, all the toy bears and dogs lined up where they belonged, the bed made with his favorite sheets, which featured tanks and combat airplanes, the wallpaper, now faded from sunlight, picturing the planets. The mural on the ceiling depicted the heavens. Lined up on top of a dresser were framed photographs of him — his high school graduation, wearing his marine uniform on the day of his completion of basic training, shots with his mother when he returned home on leave, and of him with his dog, a small, mixed breed he'd named Lucky who turned out to not be as lucky as his name. Emile never allowed the dog to be loose outside the house. But one day his mother left the door open and Lucky ran outside and was hit by a passing car. Emile was devastated by the loss of his best friend, a pain that had stayed with him to this day. He couldn't watch a TV show or motion picture showing animals in distress; his only charitable donations each year went to various shelters and animal-rights groups.

"Emile," he heard his mother call.

He went to the head of the stairs and said, "I'm here, Ma-ma."

"I finished my soup."

"I'll be down in a second."

"Remember we're going to have music."

"I remember, Ma-ma."

He returned to his bedroom, opened the closet door, picked up a case from the floor that contained a clarinet, and carried it downstairs. She'd lit up again, despite another freshly lit cigarette in the ashtray. The blue smoke stung his eyes.

"Was the soup good?" he asked as he took the empty bowl and napkin from her.

"It wasn't hot enough."

"I'm sorry. I'll heat it better next time."

He washed the bowl in the kitchen sink and put it in the dish drainer.

"Emile!" she commanded.

He went to her. "Yes, Ma-ma?"

"You said you would play music for me."

He sat on the hassock and removed the clarinet parts from their case. He'd owned the instrument since high school, when he played in the school's marching and swing bands. There had been a time when he dreamed of becoming a jazz musician, like Benny Goodman or Artie Shaw, and he had practiced a lot during that period. But his interest in a musical career soon faded and he turned to his other interest — stories of military conflicts and the weapons used in them.

With the clarinet's parts securely joined, he removed a reed from the case and attached it to the mouthpiece, wetting it first with his saliva. He blew a few test notes before asking, "What would you like me to play?"

"You know what I like," she said sternly.

He nodded. His mother's first name was Rose, and one of her favorite songs was "Honeysuckle Rose." He started the tune, establishing a tempo with which he was comfortable and tapping his foot loudly on the wooden floor to keep a steady rhythm. His playing was sloppy, he knew, and unintended squeaks erupted from time to time. But a glance at his mother told him that she was enjoying it, and so he continued until he'd finished the piece.

"Did you like that, Ma-ma?"

"It was very good, Emile, very good. Play something else for me."

He knew what she wanted and started playing "Rose Room," his foot now coming down on the floor even harder and louder.

"Stop!" she said. "You'll hurt your foot. I don't want you to hurt your foot." She extracted a throw pillow from behind her and handed it to him. "Use this," she instructed.

He placed the pillow beneath his foot and began the song again. His mother had closed her eyes and sang some of the lyrics in a voice so low that they were barely discernible. Emile finished the song. It appeared that she'd fallen asleep, but when he got up she stirred, opened her eyes, and said, "Play more for me, Emile."

"I can't, Ma-ma," he said. "I have to go now."

"You never stay."

He didn't argue with her this time. He bounded up the stairs, took apart the clarinet, put the pieces in the case, returned it to the closet, and looked at himself in the mirror. The anger on his face was almost palpable. After a series of deep breaths, he went downstairs. His mother had gotten up and had made it to the front door. As he kissed her on the cheek, the odor of talcum powder and stale cigarettes was almost overwhelming.

She ran her fingers through his hair and cooed, "My darling little Emile, my precious little boy."

He kissed her again and made his escape, waiting until he was outside to allow the trembling to begin.

Chapter 15

Those in government who thought that the death of Afran Mutki and the suspicion surrounding it could be kept under wraps also believed that politicians made decisions based upon what was good for the country rather than what would help them perpetuate their positions of power.

A forensics team at GW Hospital launched a full-fledged autopsy on Afran Mutki, beginning with the removal of a tiny pellet from his ankle. It measured 1.52 mm in diameter, the size of a pin head, and was made of 90 percent platinum and 10 percent iridium. Two 0.35 mm holes had been drilled in the pellet, which created the cavity in which the ricin, a poison found naturally in castor beans, had been inserted. The small holes in the pellet had then been covered with a substance that had a melting point of 37 degrees Celsius, or 98.6 Fahrenheit — the temperature of the human body.

Once inside Mutki, the coating had melted, opening the holes and allowing the ricin to be absorbed into his bloodstream. A written report was rushed to CIA headquarters, in Langley, Virginia, and to FBI headquarters, on Pennsylvania Avenue NW, and the pellet itself was delivered to a CIA lab at Langley. A strict media blackout was imposed on all involved.

Which didn't keep the story from seeping out and quickly becoming front-page news and the lead-in to TV newscasts. It really took off when one of the young physicians who'd worked with Dr. Bennett told a reporter (off the record, of course, and without attribution) that ricin poisoning was being considered as the cause of the Kurdish journalist's demise.

This young physician went on to educate the reporter about the Markov case thirty years ago as though he'd personally been there, and the Markov murder took on new life in the nation's capital along with this latest *assassination.*

A spokesman for the Iraq embassy in Washington provided a statement to the inquisitive press denouncing rumors that its government had had any involvement in Mutki's death, and offering condolences to his family. The spokesman took to task the media for speculating that the Iraqi government might have silenced Mutki because of his criticism of the Baghdad regime. "This is a deliberate smear of our democratic society," he said, "and it is deeply resented."

The State Department picked up on the Iraqi protest and asked in a written statement that the rumors circulating about the possible cause of Mutki's death be discounted until a more definitive cause of his demise had been determined. "The Iraqi government has come a long way in establishing a democracy in which journalists are free to express their views," said the statement. "We ask that the media wait until more facts have been established."

A Kurdistan Regional Government representative demanded that the United States government launch an official investigation of Afran Mutki's "murder" and bring those responsible to justice. "This esteemed journalist has been assassinated on U.S. soil" — yes, they used the word *assassinated* — "and it is incumbent upon the government of the United States to bring those behind it to swift justice."

While Mutki's death and the controversy surrounding it had joined other hot political topics being discussed across Washington — in day-care centers and on tennis courts, in the halls of Congress and in launderettes — it was of little interest to Mitzi Cardell. She found most topics debated at her dinner parties boring, even irrelevant. What mattered was her social calendar, who would be seated next to whom in her salon, and whether the purveyor of food for those occasions understood that the shrimp had to be firm, not flabby.

After showering and dressing on the morning following the dinner for the attorney general, she called Jeanine Jamison's private number at the White House.

"This is Mitzi Cardell. May I speak with the first lady?"

"She's unavailable at the moment, Ms. Cardell," the man said.

"When would be a better time to call?"

"She has a very busy schedule today."

Mitzi bottled her anger. She knew the man functioning as Jeanine Jamison's buffer, Lance Millius. He'd been one of Fletcher Jamison's closest confidants during the recent presidential campaign, a loyal and politically smart insider who was destined for a top White House job should Jamison win, as his chief of staff perhaps, or an equally powerful position. There was considerable buzz around Washington when Jamison named Millius the first lady's chief of staff, lots of speculation that the new president didn't trust his wife and wanted a strong hand making sure she didn't stray from the party line or commit a verbal gaffe. That the post hadn't gone to a woman also raised a few practiced eyebrows around D.C., including Mitzi's.

But his gender wasn't what really riled her. She considered him an arrogant, overly ambitious young man whose only true loyalty was to Lance Millius, someone Ayn Rand obviously had in mind when she championed a sense of self. Mitzi sometimes wondered whether the first lady was having an affair with Millius. Wouldn't she love to be privy to *that* bit of juicy insider gossip.

She'd shared her dislike of him with her childhood friend, but Jeanine had dismissed her complaints: "Lance is an incredibly loyal and effective chief of staff, Mitzi. I think he'd lay down his life for me. Besides, the president has faith in him."

Mitzi hadn't pursued it, although she'd wanted to. If she had, she would have had to admit to her friend that what really irked her was having someone — anyone — stand between them. Had achieving the White House gone to her friend's head? she sometimes wondered. Jamison's win, albeit by an extremely narrow vote, represented a victory for Mitzi, too. Having her best friend in the White House was a dream come true because it solidified her position as the city's most important and influential hostess. Access to power has always been paramount in Washington, and Mitzi had carefully cultivated relationships with the city's leading figures. Jeanine was the prize in her black book of private phone numbers and e-mails. Having a snotty young twerp like Lance Millius loom between them was anathema.

"It's important, Lance, that I speak with her today," Mitzi said.

"I'll make her aware that you called, Ms. Cardell."

Ms. Cardell. Refusing to call her Mitzi was his way of establishing himself as a gatekeeper to be reckoned with. *Screw you,* Mitzi thought. "Thank you, Lance," she said.

The click in her ear hurt.

Across town, Mackensie Smith sat with other members of the commission charged with gathering input from experts on the proposed new legislation on sentencing guidelines. He listened attentively as two witnesses, both retired federal judges, limned their views of what the legislation would mean in courtrooms across America. When they'd completed their testimony and had answered the panel's questions, Smith and his colleagues retired to a private dining room where they were served lunch.

"So, Mac, what do you make of this Mutki flap?" Smith was asked by a lawyer with whom he'd butted heads in his previous life as a trial attorney.

"I only know what I've read," Smith responded, "and we all know that that's not a basis for coming to a conclusion."

"You don't distrust the media, do you?" his friend said sarcastically.

"On occasion. However, despite the media's deteriorating reputation, it's still the only true check-and-balance we have. But as far as this Mutki thing goes, I just don't know. I remember when the Markov case broke. I avoided people with umbrellas for weeks."

"If it did involve the use of some high-tech device and exotic poison like ricin, it was ordered from on high, that's for certain. He was a thorn in the side of the Baghdad government." When Smith didn't respond, he continued. "I was talking to a source at MPD. He tells me that they've tracked down the driver and the tour guide of the bus that Mutki was on and have questioned them. From what I understand, it was during that trip that Mutki complained of something stinging him on the ankle."

"Were the driver or guide any help?"

"I don't know. The Bureau's involved, too, and undoubtedly the CIA. It puts the president in a spot, doesn't it?"

"One of many spots he's in."

"I hear that you were a guest last night at Mitzi Cardell's home."

"Yes. Lovely evening."

"I always knew you were an A-list kind of guy."

Smith chuckled. "A moment of fleeting fame." He looked at his watch and sighed. "One more panel of witnesses and we can call it a day. I'm not sure we're learning anything worthwhile."

"Just business as usual, Mac. You know how the game is played. Going through the motions is de rigueur. Let's set up dinner with our wives sometime soon."

Emile Silva had taken his luggage with him, intending to go straight to the airport from his mother's house. He drove home and deposited the large suitcase in a closet. The bag was seldom emptied; he never knew when he would be dispatched on a moment's notice to some far-flung destination and didn't want to be hampered by having to pack each time.

The visit with his mother had unsettled him more than it usually did. She smelled of death, a smell that caused him to come close to gagging at times. Silva was especially sensitive to odors and had been since he was a child, suffering headaches and nausea when confronted with an odor that no one else in the vicinity detected. As he grew older he found himself avoiding crowded, confined spaces. How many times had he changed seats on a bus to escape a woman wearing an offensive perfume? He hated cigarette smoke, yet he decided that the smoking ban in restaurants had only cleared the air for other equally obnoxious smells to permeate. And he was convinced that he could smell trouble. People who were about to cause trouble gave off an odor that only he could detect.

He drove to a post office in The District where he maintained one of several post office boxes. He withdrew an envelope from it and carried it to his car. Back home, he counted the cash in the envelope, $125,000 and a $30,000 check drawn upon an account titled MTE Enterprises and payable to Silva Consulting. Silva didn't always agree with his "employer" but the payment was consistently on time and in full.

He placed the cash in a wall safe in which an additional $400,000 was secured, and drove to his local bank, where he deposited the check into his Silva Consulting checking account. In a few months he would charter a private jet in Miami to fly to an offshore island where the safe's contents would be added to an account already holding almost $2 million, no questions asked.

He spent the afternoon swimming in the pool he'd had installed shortly after purchasing the house and lolled poolside reading *Sun Tzu and the Art of Modern Warfare* by Mark McNeilly. A pile of books on military tactics and practices was beside his bed, and his collection of war films on DVD was extensive.

He napped late in the afternoon. After spending a few hours going through his CD collection, he got into the Porsche and drove to the 701 Restaurant on Pennsylvania Avenue, where he enjoyed his favorite dishes there, its renowned clam chowder and steak tartare.

He was home by nine. At ten his driveway alarm signaled that a car had arrived. Dressed in his red kimono and flip-flops, he went to the door and greeted his visitor, a tall, statuesque blonde with slightly oversized facial features and wearing a miniskirt, knee-length black boots, and a scoop-neck yellow T-shirt. She followed him to the bedroom, where he put a CD of operatic arias on the sound system, and sat in an overstuffed chair. Without any instruction she removed her clothing and stood naked.

"Go on," he said, "walk around."

She paraded about the large room until he told her to stop directly in front of him.

"I told you not to wear perfume," he said.

"I'm not, sugar. I never do when I'm with you."

"I smell it."

"Maybe it's the soap I used," she said, sensing a rising anger in his voice. "I bought a new soap and used it just before I came. I thought —"

"I don't pay you to think," he said. "I don't like that soap."

"Sorry, sugar," she said. "I won't use it again."

"Go on, walk," he said as he opened his kimono.

Fifteen minutes later, after she'd sashayed around the room and struck a series of provocative poses, he relieved himself.

"Feel better?" she asked.

"I always do when you're here," he said. "Go on, get dressed, I have things to do."

She went downstairs and found the usual envelope containing five hundred dollars on a table near the door.

Chapter 16

The man known as Dexter pulled into the parking lot of his favorite McDonald's and went inside. He ordered what he always ordered, a cheeseburger, fries, and a soft drink. He'd just settled at a table and removed the wrapping from his burger when the man he was to meet walked in and joined him. This particular McDonald's had been the chosen scene of their infrequent clandestine meetings for the past six months. Was it time for a change? Probably.

"Aren't you eating?" Dexter asked.

"I'm not in the mood. I just came from a meeting at the White House."

"The president?"

"No. Some of his intelligence people. They say the old man is furious at how things went down with Mutki."

Dexter had just raised the burger to his lips. He paused, lowered it, and said, "Why would he feel that way? It went smoothly."

"It isn't a matter of *how* it went, Dexter. It's a matter of *where* it happened."

Dexter took a bite, chewed, and said, "We chose the ideal place for it to happen. We researched it thoroughly before he came."

"It shouldn't have happened here in the States, not in Washington, D.C."

"You should get something to eat," Dexter said. "It looks strange for you to be sitting here without eating."

His luncheon companion drummed his fingertips on the table.

"You were well aware," Dexter said, "that the method, timing, and location were our choice, just as it's always been. It can be no other way."

"It may be necessary to reevaluate that, Dexter."

Dexter shrugged, finished his burger, and dipped a fry into ketchup. "That, of course, is up to you and your people," he said in a casual tone that mirrored his lack of concern. "But I remind you that the process put in place by the highest echelons of your agency has served you well." His smile was thin. "Get something to eat. I'm uncomfortable sitting with you."

His companion leaned across the table and said in almost a whisper, "I don't appreciate being on the receiving end of the president's wrath. Surely you can understand that."

"Of course I do, but it really can't be a concern of mine or my people. We do what we do, and we do it well. Political ramifications or administrations don't interest us."

His visitor stood and Dexter assumed he was going to the counter to order. Instead, he left and disappeared into the parking lot.

Fletcher Jamison, president of the United States, was in a foul mood. Foul moods were not the exception for this president. His temper was, as those close to him had experienced, volcanic. Jamison was a tall, angular man with a heavy five-o'clock shadow that seemed to match his frame of mind, a black, grainy beard line that accentuated his jowls, which were prominent, and his scowls, which were numerous. There were those who thought he looked something like former President Nixon, although he was considerably taller than the thirty-seventh president of the United States. Others said he was "Lincolnesque" because of his height and prominent nose. Physical comparisons failed to define Jamison, the nation's forty-fifth president. It was his style, his demeanor that characterized him for those with whom he interacted in the

White House and in Congress. “He has a mean streak,” some whispered after an especially brutal session with him. “He has a nasty gene,” others said.

Voters seldom saw that side of him, although his tough talk on a variety of issues, domestic and international, promised them a man who wouldn’t kowtow to anyone, friend or foe, just the sort of president the country needed in hard times. His hair-trigger smile and large hand that landed on the shoulders of thousands of voters endeared him to them, a stern father figure who would undo all the mistakes of the past administration, who would reestablish America as the best and most powerful nation in the world, calling the shots around the globe and putting home-grown laggards on notice that they’d better get their act together. Although it was never played — the separation of church and state was still sacrosanct — you could almost hear “Onward Christian Soldiers” played each time he left the White House and mingled with the masses.

He’d conducted a meeting earlier that day with a member of his National Security staff whose primary responsibility was as liaison with the Central Intelligence Agency. The topic was the death of the Kurdish journalist Afran Mutki. Jamison had recently expressed his unhappiness with Mutki's postings from Iraq in which he scorched the Iraqi central government for its treatment of the Kurds, and Jamison had made his feelings known to his staff.

News of Mutki's death had reached Jamison after he and his wife had retired for the evening to their private quarters on the second floor. The president took the call, smiled, hung up, and shot his fist into the air.

"What was that about?" the first lady asked from where she sat browsing through *Washingtonian Magazine.*

"That Kurdish journalist, Mutki, is dead," Jamison answered.

"That makes you happy?" she asked absently.

"He was stirring up trouble for the Iraqi government, and that meant trouble for me. These writers who think they know so damn much give me a royal pain in the ass. They get it wrong most of the time. What the hell do they contribute except confusion?"

She continued skimming the magazine.

"How was *your* day?" he asked.

"Busy, as usual. I got a call from Mitzi. She sounded upset."

Jamison snorted. "Your friend always

seems upset. What's the matter this time, her napkin supplier on strike?"

She lowered the magazine to her lap and said, "That's cruel."

"No, it's accurate. She's a hysteric, Jeanine."

"She is not. Anyway, we're having lunch here tomorrow."

"What's she upset about?"

"I don't know. She said she'd tell me at lunch."

"She's so damn dramatic. Don't forget we're having the Israeli PM here tomorrow."

"That's at four. Mitzi and I are meeting at noon."

"Are arrangements set for dinner with the PM?"

"As far as I know. I'll confirm everything in the morning with the staff."

Jamison sat in his favorite chair and looked out the window. "You happy?" he asked.

His question surprised her. Of course she was happy. She was living in the White House with all the accompanying perks, the first lady of the land, the pinnacle of power for a woman. Happy? Was politics corrupt?

"You didn't answer me," Jamison said.

"I'm happy. I wish there was a little more time to escape, just escape, but yes, I am happy. Are you?"

"I'm not sure I'd call it happy, Jeanine. Winning the election made me happy. Why shouldn't it? This country needs a new direction and I'm the one to lead it there. I just never realized how many people there are who'd like to take me down."

"You knew that when you decided to run."

"I know, I know, but they're warped, Jeanine, warped, vicious people. They look for every little thing to criticize. If it weren't for the Secret Service I'd have taken a bullet like the Kennedys by now."

"Don't talk that way, Fletch."

"It's true, babe.

She dropped the magazine to the floor, went to him, sat on his lap, and caressed his cheek. "We need some time away from here," she said.

"That'd be nice."

"I'm going to Savannah for that fund-raising event for CVA. Maybe we could —"

"When's that?"

"Next week. Maybe we could spend a few days down on Tybee Island with the Warrens."

He shook his head. "Not a chance."

"Then I suppose we'll just have to find an hour of escape right here."

She kissed him softly on the lips, then

increased the pressure. They left the couch, slipped out of their bedclothes, and climbed into the king-size bed.

“If that red phone rings I’ll scream,” she said with a playful giggle.

“Don’t worry about that, babe,” he said. “If the world is about to blow up I’ll just suggest it be put off for an hour. Hell, I am the president of the United States.”

She laughed again as she straddled him. “An hour?” she said. “Sure you can make it last that long?”

CHAPTER 17

Annabel Lee Smith arrived at her Georgetown gallery early the next morning. A shipment of four rare, painted baked clay Mayan plates had arrived the afternoon before and she wanted to create an appropriate display for them. She'd purchased them in Mexico the preceding month from a collector with whom she'd dealt before, and based upon her growing expertise in things pre-Columbian she was confident that she'd made a wise purchase, and one that conformed to U.S. regulations regarding the importation of antiquities.

Walking into the gallery always filled Annabel with a sense of calm and pride. She'd developed her interest in pre-Columbian art while in undergraduate school and had devoured every book she could find on the subject. She continued her study of it during law school and after she'd gone into practice, always thinking of opening a gallery but unable to make the dramatic decision to abandon law to pursue her dream.

Meeting and falling in love with Mac Smith had been the turning point. He'd encouraged her to take down her Esq. shingle, find the right location, and indulge her passion. The space in trendy Georgetown was charming and she loved being part of the neighborhood's commercial community. Owning the gallery brought her into contact with pre-Columbian collectors around the world and she'd made numerous trips to seek out rare finds.

She'd never looked back.

By ten o'clock, she'd arranged the plates on a large, glass-covered pedestal in the center of the gallery, having taken a few minutes to circle it slowly and admire the presentation. She had then retreated to her office at the gallery's rear to compile a list of area collectors who might be interested in the new arrivals, and was busy with that task when the chime sounded, indicating that someone had entered. She got up from her desk and went to greet her first potential customer of the day.

"Good morning," she said.

"Good morning," Emile Silva said. "Mind if I just browse?"

"Please do. Do you have an interest in pre-Columbian?"

"I've just begun to develop one," he said.

"That's wonderful. If you have any questions, please ask."

Like any shop or gallery owner, Annabel took a moment to size up her visitor. He was of average height, and she estimated his age as mid-to-late thirties. Black hair cut short and fringed with a hint of gray at the temples framed a square, solid, dusky face. He wore blue jeans that looked to Annabel to be more expensive than run-of-the-mill ones, a pale blue button-down shirt, and alligator loafers sans socks; he was a good-looking man whose compact muscular build testified to regular workouts.

"It's a very nice gallery," he said as he perused items along one wall.

"Thank you," she said.

She busied herself behind the counter while he browsed without comment. After ten minutes he said, "Thank you. The pieces are very nice."

"Would you like to be on my e-mail and mailing list?" she asked.

"No, I don't think so."

The door opened and Annabel's husband came through it.

"This is my husband, Mackensie," Annabel told the visitor. "I'm sorry. I didn't get your name."

Silva smiled, fixed Mac in a hard stare, shook his head, and left the gallery.

"A buyer?" Mac asked.

"Just browsing. See? I arranged the new plates."

He admired the display along with his wife. "Looks great," he said.

"I hope they sell."

"You didn't know him?" Mac asked.

"Who?"

"The man who just left."

"No."

"He wasn't anxious to give his name."

Annabel laughed. "He probably didn't want to be inundated with e-mail and mailings from me. I don't blame him."

"Free for lunch?" Mac asked.

"Sure."

"Founding Farmers by the World Bank, say twelve thirty?"

"See you there."

They kissed, then Mac stepped out onto the sidewalk where Silva stood looking into an adjacent shop window in which expensive women's shoes were displayed.

"Beauty of a different sort," Mac commented as he came up beside him.

"What?"

"Women's shoes and pre-Columbian art. Beautiful but different."

"Yes, I suppose that's right," Silva said.

The men looked at each other without saying anything else before Silva walked away.

Mac watched him navigate shoppers and disappear into another shop. There was something about the man that bothered Mac. He'd become an astute judge of people, honed by dealing with every possible variety of criminal when practicing law. This man with whom he'd had only the briefest of contact triggered something visceral in the former attorney, nothing he could put his finger on but there nonetheless. It was in the eyes, he decided. There was a coldness there that Smith had seen too many times before, a lack of affect that he'd learned was characteristic of a certain type of man. He made a mental note to suggest to Annabel at lunch that, should the man come into the gallery again, she be on her toes.

Silva, too, had had a negative reaction to this man who was the gallery owner's husband. This was someone to stay away from and Silva was sorry that he'd visited the gallery. He didn't know why he felt that way but the presentiment itself was sufficient. Maybe it was the aftershave lotion this man named Mackensie wore, or an odor emanating from his pores. No matter. This was a man who could spell trouble for Silva — for anyone — someone to be avoided. Not that his reaction to Smith mattered. He would never visit the gallery again or have occasion to bump into Annabel's husband anywhere else.

He was scheduled to meet with Dexter at noon and had decided to spend the latter part of the morning perusing Georgetown's shops, which he enjoyed doing. Annabel's gallery was just one of his stops. He had no interest in pre-Columbian art, or any art for that matter, but it had looked like an attractive space in which to kill time.

Emile had assumed that his meeting with Dexter would be at the office building near the Pentagon, but he was mistaken. Dexter had said something about the need to avoid going to that place and had suggested a Burger King on K Street, which amused Silva. Meetings not held at the office were always conducted in fast-food restaurants because Dexter, and those for whom he worked, had decided that such places were safe, based on the assumption that men involved in high-level nefarious activities wouldn't stoop to that gastronomic level. It didn't matter to Silva, although he detested fast food and would have preferred to meet in higher-class establishments like 701 or Citronelle, The Palm, or Tosca. But his job wasn't to make decisions. His job was to kill, something at which he was very good.

As he drove to his rendezvous with Dexter, Mac Smith's face kept injecting itself into his thoughts, and Annabel's, too. She was a beautiful woman — too beautiful for her husband. He played out a fantasy of slowly slashing the husband's throat while a naked Annabel looked on. That brought a smile to his face as he pulled into the lot and parked.

Dexter was already at a table wedged into a corner away from others. "Order something," he said when Silva came to the table. Silva returned with a tray holding a chicken sandwich and a Diet Coke.

"You pick the nicest places to meet," Silva said through a smile.

"It serves its purpose," Dexter responded.

"Why was my trip abroad canceled?" Silva asked.

"It became inconvenient to send you."

"Pity. I was looking forward to getting away. So, why am I here today?"

"We may have another assignment for you."

"Where?"

"That hasn't been decided yet. But in the meantime I want you to leave the city for a few weeks until the Mutki affair cools down."

Silva laughed and tasted the sandwich. "I never realized how much of a storm that would create."

"It was handled poorly."

Silva frowned. "Not by me," he said.

"By everyone. Our sponsors have made their displeasure known to me."

Dexter's mention of his "sponsors" triggered a series of thoughts for Silva. He'd never been sure who gave the orders for someone to be eliminated using the group headed by Dexter that was headquartered in the Virginia office building. That facility was relatively new. When Silva first started working for the enterprise there had been no central location. All orders came from hotel suites. But it was decided — by whom, Silva didn't know — that it would be best to establish a business front with space to house the various instruments, technology, and weapons used to carry out the group's missions.

Emile Silva had intended to make a career out of the marines. But a series of incidents in which his rage overflowed, resulting in physical attacks on fellow servicemen, led to a decision by his superiors that he was mentally unstable, unable to function in the corps' structured environment. He'd fought that finding but had been unsuccessful, and left the service with a general discharge — and a need to seek revenge on those former comrades-in-arms whose testimony had been the basis for his dismissal. One in particular topped his retribution list.

Silva and Buddy Carcini had become friends while in uniform, as much of a friendship as Silva, constitutionally a loner, was able to develop with anyone. Carcini was a fast-talking Italian from New York who appreciated Silva's cockiness and jaundiced view of the world, and of authority. They were competitive in many aspects of their service, on the shooting range, in hand-to-hand combat drills, and in a special sharp-shooting unit both had applied for and been accepted into.

It was off the base where the problems between them emerged and festered. It seemed to Silva that Carcini spent every hour off-duty chasing girls from the local town. Silva went along with him on some of his hunts but was never comfortable with his buddy's sweet talk to each young woman they met. It wasn't that Silva was shy. He could talk as good a story as Carcini, and a number of the girls made it obvious that they were taken with him. But when it came time to follow through, to entice a girl into a local motel or into the backseat of a borrowed car, Silva backed off, much to Carcini's amusement. But after a few episodes like this, Carcini's amusement turned to sarcasm, and then to questions about whether Silva was a closet homosexual.

Silva had finally had enough. One night as Carcini slept in their barracks, Silva pulled a switchblade knife from where he'd secreted it in his bunk, silently went to Carcini's bunk, clasped a hand over his mouth, and pressed the blade against the New Yorker's throat. "If you ever call me a fag again," Silva hissed, "I'll cut your throat from ear to ear."

The next morning, Carcini saw blood on his pillow. When he looked into the mirror, he saw that the knife had traced a four-inch-thin red line just beneath his Adam's apple. He considered not reporting the attack but the cut was too blatant to go unnoticed. Besides, he'd had it with Silva. And there was patriotism to be considered. The marine corps didn't need a flaming fag in its ranks. He told his superior what had occurred, and the captain passed the story up the chain of command. This wasn't the first experience the brass had had with Silva and his penchant for settling every argument with physical force. It was time to get rid of him, and Carcini's testimony was the basis for his removal from the corps.

Silva maintained his proud bearing as he walked out of the hearing. He paused where Carcini was seated, smiled at him, and left the base and his career in the United States Marines behind.

It took several years for the right circumstance to present itself for Silva to be in contact with Buddy Carcini again. Carcini had left the corps and was working and living in Chicago according to posts on his Facebook and Twitter accounts. Silva, who'd supported himself in Washington as a bouncer at topless clubs and by applying muscle for local bookies and mobsters, went to Chicago, staked out where Carcini worked and lived, and spent three days shadowing him. On the third night, when Carcini left a girlfriend's apartment at three in the morning, Silva followed him to where he'd parked his car.

"Hey, Buddy, remember me?" Silva asked as Carcini, who'd had too much to drink, fumbled to insert his key in the lock.

Carcini turned and squinted in the dimness of the streetlight.

"Emile, Buddy. Emile Silva," he said with a throaty laugh.

"Oh, Jesus, I'll be damned," Carcini said. He extended his hand. Silva grabbed it, pulled him close, and rammed a knife into Carcini's throat, severing the jugular vein. His former friend slid to the pavement and was dead in less than a minute. Silva wiped the knife on Carcini's shirt and walked away, a satisfied smile on his face. He took the next available flight back to Washington and assumed that the murder of his former friend and fellow marine would become another in Chicago's unsolved-cases file. He knew one thing for certain: he'd never felt more alive than that night.

He continued to work odd jobs in the D.C. area until one night when he met a well-dressed man in a bar. They fell into an easy conversation and the topic of what Silva did for a living came up. He mentioned his work as a bouncer.

"You can handle yourself, huh?" the man said.

"I do pretty well."

"Ever been in the military?"

Silva said that he'd been a marine, and after some gentle probing by the man he told him why he had left the corps. "I don't like to be pushed around," Silva added as an explanation for having threatened his fellow serviceman, leaving out the reference to his sexuality.

"I'd have done the same thing," the man said.

"There are people in this world who don't deserve to live," Silva said.

"I couldn't agree more."

Their conversation flowed easily, with Silva's drinking companion smoothly segueing from topic to topic until it settled on politics.

"As far as I'm concerned," Silva said, "all this pantywaist diplomacy with these bastards around the world who hate us is a waste of time. We should just take 'em out, get rid of them."

The man agreed with this, too. He'd agreed with every philosophy Silva had espoused.

"Same with some of the lefties in this country. What good are they? We're too soft, that's our problem. I think Jamison might finally put us on the right track. What do you think?"

"I like the new president. He's tough, doesn't take guff from anyone including our so-called allies."

"If I were calling the shots I'd turn Iran

and North Korea into parking lots, bomb 'em to oblivion."

The man laughed gently. "I'm not sure I agree with that approach but I see your point. You say you work as a bouncer."

"On and off."

"I know someone who might be looking for a person with your skills and outlook," the man said.

"Really? What kind of job is it?"

"It would be best if he described it to you. He has a small, privately held company that does contract work for the government. Very low-key, not on anyone's radar screen."

"What, like Blackwater, private security?"

"Similar. If you're interested, I'll pass along your name and contact information. No guarantees, of course, but it might be worth exploring. Nothing to lose, as they say."

"Makes sense to me."

Silva gave him his name and phone number before leaving the bar. Two days later he received a call. "My name is Dexter. A colleague of mine says you might be the sort of person we're looking for."

"Yeah, he said you might be calling."

"I would like to meet with you."

"Sure. Just tell me where and when."

Silva met Dexter in a suite in the Hyatt

Regency on Capitol Hill. He disliked the little man from their initial handshake, disliked his thick glasses and nasal voice and creviced bald head. He also disliked the little man's careful choice of words, never anything concrete, just beating around the bush and talking in vagaries. After forty-five minutes, Silva asked him to get to the point about the job and whether he was being seriously considered for it.

"Have you ever killed a man?" was Dexter's answer.

This sudden directness caught Silva off guard. He fumbled for an answer, which seemed to amuse Dexter. "It shouldn't be hard to answer," he said through his smile. "Either you did or you didn't."

"All right, I did." Silva decided that he could make that admission without being specific, not incriminating himself with any particular crime.

"What were the circumstances?" Dexter asked.

"That's my business," Silva said.

"I appreciate discretion."

"Yeah, well, it happened because I needed to right a wrong."

"A noble motivation. Did you use a weapon?"

"Knife," Silva said, realizing he was now

revealing too much.

"And how did you feel after you'd righted this wrong?"

"I felt — I felt good. It was the right thing to do."

"I'm sure it was. How would you feel about killing someone you don't know?"

Silva held up his hands and said, "Whoa. What is this, some set-up?"

Dexter allowed the comment to pass. He said, "I'm talking about killing someone to right wrongs."

"What, a hit? Hey, forget I was even here. I'm not into anything illegal."

"Why do you assume it would be — illegal?"

"Because —"

"What if it were sanctioned by your own government?"

"Huh?"

"When the government decides to do something in the interest of national security, or because our way of life is being threatened, it's hardly illegal. In fact, it's for a common good, for the good of the citizens of this wonderful country."

"Then that would make it all right I guess."

"You would have killed the enemy when you were a marine, wouldn't you?"

"Of course."

"Killed on behalf of your government."

"Right."

"Not all soldiers in the fight against tyranny and the destruction of our precious way of life wear uniforms, Mr. Silva. Some of our most patriotic citizens have been people exactly like you, men who treasure our democracy and who don't hesitate to do what needs to be done to preserve it."

"Sure, I agree with that," said Silva. "But I thought I came up here to be interviewed for a job."

"Oh, that is exactly what I'm doing, Mr. Silva. I happen to have a job opening for which you might be perfectly suited. I should add that it pays handsomely for very little work."

Silva smiled for the first time that afternoon. "You've got my attention," he said.

"Good."

"What's the name of your company?" Silva asked. "What's your name? All I know is 'Dexter.' "

"Best that it be left that way for the moment. I would like to meet with you again."

"Sure. Anytime."

"I'll be in touch."

He was, two days later. Silva met again with Dexter and the man who'd befriended him in the bar. That man's name was never mentioned, nor was Dexter's last name. But their intentions were clear to Silva.

He was now a paid assassin for the United States government.

CHAPTER 18

Mitzi Cardell woke with a headache and sour stomach. She'd had a series of nightmares that had caused her to toss and turn, and she'd awoken a few times with a gasp, her chest pounding. It was good that she and her husband slept in separate beds.

He'd gotten up early to catch a plane to attend a business meeting in London. She had pretended to be asleep when he kissed her on the forehead and said, "I'll be back soon. I love you."

With him gone, she got out of bed, went into her private bath, and viewed herself in a large theatrical mirror surrounded by bulbs. She didn't like what she saw. "Calm down," she told herself, using ineffective words.

She went downstairs dressed in a robe and slippers and went to the kitchen, where a member of the staff was cleaning up after John's breakfast.

"Mr. Muszinski got off all right?" Mitzi asked.

"Oh, yes, ma'am. Would you like breakfast now?"

"What? No, no, thank you. Not yet."

She went to her office and dialed her father's number in Savannah.

"I hope I didn't wake you," she said.

"I've been up for hours, sweetheart. John told you I called last night?"

"Yes. What is this all about?"

"Are you alone?"

"Yes."

She heard him shut a door and return to the phone. "Ah've done some checking on this private investigator who visited Waldine Farnsworth. He's a former Savannah police officer, now retired."

"You told John that he was asking Waldine about Louise. Louise *Watkins?*"

"Evidently. I've already had some of my people take a look at this detective and his interest in Ms. Watkins. Seems he's working for the girl's mother."

"Working for her? What does that mean?"

"From what Ah gather — and Ah really don't know that much yet — the mother hired this detective to find out who shot her daughter when she got out of prison."

Mitzi had been wound as tight as a spring

since getting out of bed and during the conversation with her father. Now, she drew a deep breath and leaned back in the chair.

"Mitzi, honey, you there?"

"Yes, Daddy, I'm here. That was so long ago. How could anyone think they can find out who shot her after all these years? It was some drug addict, a drug gang sort of thing. Happens all the time to them. We have plenty of that here in D.C."

"You're absolutely right about that," he said. "Even Sherlock Holmes couldn't solve that shooting."

Tension gripped her again and she leaned forward. "Do you think he's also prying into her stabbing that fellow outside the club?"

"That's what I understand, but I need to check on it further. Like I said, I've already had some of my people look into it."

She leaned back again and fell silent.

"Mitzi?"

"Yes, Daddy, I'm here. Please find out what this is all about."

"That's exactly what I intend to do. I've already taken steps to cut this private eye fellow off at the knees, so to speak. My suggestion is for you to put it out of your mind. Believe me, honeybunch, nothing will come to it. It'll all blow over if it hasn't already."

"I'm sure you're right," she said, not at all

convinced that he was. “What’s this detective’s name?”

“Brixton. Robert Brixton. He’s got himself an office in town, been a private investigator for a couple of years. The way I figure it, he’s just tryin’ to generate some business for himself. You know how these private eyes are, low-life, real low-life.”

“Of course. Is there anything else?”

“Not at the moment, sweetheart. Now you do what I suggested and put the whole silly thing out of your pretty little head, heah?”

“Yes, Daddy, I hear. Thank you.”

“My pleasure, and I’ll get back to you if I find out anything else.”

“Good, Daddy. Thanks again.”

She hung up and turned to face the window. At least the sun was shining, she thought. Wearily, she went upstairs, took a long, hot shower, dressed in the outfit she would wear to lunch with Jeanine Jamison, then went back downstairs to the dining room. One of the housekeepers made her an omelet; she picked at it and left most of it uneaten.

Had she been free to do what she wanted that morning, she would have climbed back into bed and pulled the covers up over her head. But people would be arriving in a half hour to discuss a fund-raising project and it was too late to call it off. And, she had her lunch date with Jeanine Jamison at the White House.

The meeting lasted until eleven. Mitzi thanked them for coming and called for her driver. After going through White House security, which had been tightened even more because of recent breaches of it, she was allowed to enter and was led by a member of the first lady's staff to Jeanine's office in the East Wing.

"Hi, Lance," Mitzi said to Lance Millius, Jeanine's chief of staff.

"Hello, Ms. Cardell," he replied, looking up only momentarily from something he was reading.

Mitzi forced a smile and took a seat along the wall. It was ten minutes before the first lady bounced in, looking fresh and alive. "Mitzi," she said, "sorry to be late. I'll just be a minute more." To Millius: "Are things straightened out with the rabbi about tonight?"

"Everything's worked out," he said. "No problem."

Mitzi and Jeanine were about to leave when the first lady's assistant in charge of flower arrangements came into the office in a state of near hysteria. "I need to talk with you, Mrs. Jamison."

Jeanine shrugged and made a gesture to Mitzi that said it was beyond her control. They disappeared into Jeanine's private office. Fifteen minutes later Jeanine returned, grabbed Mitzi by the arm, and waltzed her out the door to a small, private dining room one floor above, where two members of the waitstaff stood at the ready. "Hope what I ordered for us is all right with you," Jeanine said as they sat at the nicely set and adorned table.

"I'm sure it will be fine," Mitzi said.

"It's great to find some time together," Jeanine said. "My schedule is insane these days."

"So I read," Mitzi said. "You're going back to CVA next week?"

"Yes. I didn't know how I'd ever squeeze it in but it's hard to say no to Waldine when it comes to raising money."

"She's lucky to have someone in your position willing to do it."

"All for the old alma mater, huh?" Jeanine said with a laugh. "So, how are things at the Cardell residence? John okay?"

"John is fine. He's off to London, some business meeting. Jeanine, there's something we have to talk about."

They'd just been served cups of vichyssoise. Jeanine sat back and adopted a concerned expression. "Oh?" she said. "Sounds as though it's serious. Are you and John — ?"

"No, no, nothing like that." Mitzi surveyed the room. "Is this room secure?"

" 'Secure?' Of course it's secure."

"I mean there's no tape recorder running, anything like that?"

"Mitzi, don't be silly."

"I know there's always a tape running in the Oval Office. Nixon and the tapes. Lyndon Johnson."

"Mitzi —"

"I know I'm being foolish. It's just that —"

A waiter delivered their salads and conversation ceased. When he was gone and the door was closed behind him, Mitzi said in a low voice, "My father called last night. I didn't take the call because I was in the middle of a dinner party. I called him this morning. He told me that a private detective named —" She consulted a scrap of paper she'd brought with her. "His name is Robert Brixton."

"A private detective?"

"Yes."

"What about him?"

"Daddy says he visited Waldine Farnsworth and asked her about a photo he had with him."

"So?"

Mitzi drew a breath before continuing. "The picture was taken during one of those weekend retreats we used to have at the school. Remember?"

"Sure. But what does a photo have to do with anything?"

"I'm in the picture, Jeanine. So is Louise Watkins."

The first lady's dismissive tone changed now. Mitzi watched as her childhood friend processed what she'd just heard, lips pressed tightly together, eyes narrowed. Finally, she said, "Oh."

"Daddy says this detective is working for Louise's mother and trying to find out who shot her when she got out of prison."

Jeanine guffawed. "Fat chance of that ever happening."

Mitzi's pained expression told Jeanine that her friend had more on her mind, so Jeanine asked.

"Daddy says he thinks this detective is also looking into why Louise went to prison. The stabbing of that guy."

"I see."

"I'm sure there's nothing to it," Mitzi said. "Daddy says not to worry. But — but I am worried, Jeanine."

"Your father is right," Jeanine said. "Go on, eat your soup before —" She laughed. "I was going to say before it gets cold, but it already is."

For the rest of the meal the first lady kept the conversation away from the topic of Brixton and his visit to the headmistress of the Christian Vision Academy. Mitzi had visibly relaxed and they laughed at gossip each had to spread about Washington bigwigs, which included tales of sexual indiscretions. By the time Mitzi left the White House she was in considerably better spirits than when she'd arrived.

Jeanine attended a last-minute meeting in preparation for the dinner that night with the Israeli prime minister. Before heading to the family's private quarters to change for the evening, she took Lance Millius aside. "Do me a favor, Lance, and have someone check out a private detective in Savannah named Robert Brixton. Just a favor for an old friend."

She walked away, leaving him looking after her quizzically.

Chapter 19

Mitzi's emotional wires were crossed when she returned from lunch.

The conversation with Jeanine had been soothing but only to an extent, and Mitzi's contribution to their light banter toward the end of lunch had been forced. Her father, too, had been comforting. She knew him to be a man of action. He'd do whatever he could to blow away this unwelcome intrusion into her structured, satisfying life.

But alone in her study — and without their dismissals of her fears to hang on to — the feeling of dread that had consumed her earlier in the day returned, and memories of twenty years ago dominated.

She was seventeen years old on that hot, humid summer night in Savannah. She'd told her parents that she was going to spend Saturday night at Jeanine Montgomery's house but failed to mention that Jeanine's parents would be away overnight and wouldn't be back until Sunday.

She and Jeanine had been close friends since grade school. Mitzi's mother often joked that the girls were joined at the hip, like Siamese twins. Their parents were also friends. Ward Cardell had made a fortune in Savannah real estate. Warren Montgomery was a successful banker, although most of his wealth had come through an investment firm he headed. The Cardell and Montgomery families were scions of Savannah society, movers and shakers, powerful forces behind elected officials. Numerous civic organizations listed Montgomery and/or Cardell on their letterheads, and their yearly financial contributions to area charities were unfailingly generous.

Their parents approved of the relationship between the girls, each of whom was an only child. Mitzi tended to be somewhat flighty, a nervous young girl with a sweet disposition who tended to talk fast. Jeanine was a cooler head, more sophisticated than her bosom buddy yet appropriately immature at eighteen. Their parents considered them exemplary examples of young southern womanhood, well mannered and bright, their outlook on society properly shaped by their parents' staunchly conservative politics. Most of all, the girls were considered levelheaded, at least when compared to other female teenagers who the Montgomery and Cardell families considered prime examples of wasted youth, those who hung out with the wrong people at places like Augie's, an infamous teen hangout. Ward Cardell had tried to have the club shut down and almost succeeded. But some slick legal maneuvering by the club's attorney staved off the closure and it continued to draw large crowds each night.

Mitzi had dinner with the Montgomerys at their home on that Saturday. After dinner she and Jeanine went to Jeanine's bedroom to listen to a Black Sabbath album that Jeanine had bought that day at a local record store. They played the music at a low volume, knowing how much Mr. and Mrs. Montgomery disliked that sort of "decadent" music. But once Jeanine's parents had left the house, the volume was raised and the girls played air guitars and sang along with the musicians before getting down to more serious matters, like whether Miss Farnsworth, who'd never married, had ever had sex. The cutest boys were dissected, the most nerdy girls verbally devastated. It was all great fun, but the night was young and they were brimming with restless energy.

While Jeanine had supplied the music, Mitzi had provided the evening's other stimulant — four marijuana cigarettes she'd bought that afternoon on a Savannah street corner. Mitzi wanted to light up in Jeanine's room but Jeanine didn't want to leave behind the telltale odor. They went to a gazebo in the expansive rear yard and puffed awkwardly on two of the joints, claiming to be higher than they were. Savannah's infamous sand gnats, "no-see-ums," were out in force that night; the smoke from the joints provided something of a barrier against them.

"Want the other?" Mitzi asked.

Jeanine shook her head as she crushed the butts in a piece of foil she'd brought from the kitchen. "Want to go to Augie's?" she asked.

Mitzi giggled. "Yeah," she said, "I know. You want to see if that cool guy is there again."

On a previous trip to Augie's, Jeanine had struck up a conversation with a good-looking man in his mid-to-late twenties. He told her that his name was Allan and that he was a talent scout for a major theatrical agency in Atlanta, who was spending time in Savannah in search of new talent. Jeanine didn't necessarily buy his story but it didn't matter. She was smitten with his curly black hair that hung down over sleepy bedroom eyes, a three-day growth of beard, his nonchalant persona, and most important, his overt interest in her.

"Think my dad would like him?" she asked playfully.

"Your daddy would shoot him," was Mitzi's reply.

"You know, I believe he would," Jeanine said.

Augie's was officially off-limits to the girls. But the club represented an adventure, a forbidden place where those "other" kids hung out, many of them African-Americans who symbolized danger, another world to explore in "officially" integrated Savannah.

Jeanine drove her father's Cadillac convertible; he was a car buff and owned six automobiles of various makes. When they pulled into Augie's parking lot they were surprised at how many cars were already there. Rock music, mixed with raucous laughter, spilled through the club's open door and into the lot, where a dozen teens smoked cigarettes or pot and sucked on cans of beer.

The girls found a space, got out, and approached the club. They expected to have trouble getting in because of their age but a hefty young man charged with checking IDs was busy chatting with friends, and the girls slipped by.

Inside, the recorded music was loud, the conversation even louder. They found space at the bar and ordered beers. The bartender eyed them suspiciously but didn't question their ages, just plopped the bottles in front of them and told them how much they owed.

"I feel like I'm dressed funny," Mitzi said.

Jeanine agreed. Their designer casual clothes were out of place in the club where ragged jeans and T-shirts were the norm.

Their attention went to a small area in front of where a DJ played music. Two black couples danced. As they watched, a young black girl wearing a green miniskirt, a low-cut yellow sleeveless blouse, and sandals came up to them.

"Hi'ya doin'?" she slurred.

"We're doing fine," Mitzi said. She squinted against the room's smoke and garish lighting and looked more closely into the girl's reddened eyes. "I know you," she said.

"Yeah?"

"You were at a retreat at CVA once. I remember."

"Yeah?"

"Your name is —"

The girl laughed. "Can't sometimes even remember my name," she said dreamily. "Louise. You got any money, buy me a drink?"

Jeanine and Mitzi looked at each other.

"Sure," Mitzi said. "Order what you want."

She ordered a brandy and soda from the bartender, whose expression said he knew this girl named Louise only too well and didn't think much of her.

Jeanine turned away from them and focused on the bottle of beer in front of her. The tap on her shoulder startled her. She looked up into Allan's face. "Hey, glad you came back," he said.

"Oh, hi."

"You're with your friend again."

"Mitzi. Her name's Mitzi." She realized that her voice was shaky. He was leaning against her; she could smell aftershave or cologne, and beer on his breath.

"Buy you a beer?" he asked.

"I already have one. Thank you."

Jeanine split her attention between him and the conversation Mitzi was having with Louise. "I get by," she heard Louise say, "doin' a little of this, a little of that. I don't see you in here much."

"We don't come much," Mitzi said. "Our parents —" She didn't want to appear to be an overprotected white girl.

"Feel like a walk?" Allan asked Jeanine.

"Oh, I don't know. I —"

"You lookin' for some good weed?" she heard Louise ask Mitzi.

"I don't think so. We have some."

"Good weed, the best, better than what you get on the street. I got some snow, too."

"Snow?"

"Coke. The Big C. Snort it up. Take you up to heaven."

"Oh, I don't think so. But thanks."

"Come on," Allan said to Jeanine. "Let's get some air."

Jeanine indicated Mitzi. "I'm with my friend and —"

"What, she can't be alone for a few minutes?"

She liked his deep voice.

"So?" he said. The feel of his hand on her bare arm was blissful.

She said to Mitzi, "I'm going out for some air. It's stuffy in here."

Mitzi gave her a knowing smile, which prompted Jeanine to punch her arm before getting up and following Allan outside. They walked through rows of cars until reaching a secluded corner of the lot where a metallic-blue Mustang convertible was parked. "It's mine," Allan said.

"It's beautiful. My father is into cars. He has six of them."

"He must have some loot, huh?"

"He's — he's a businessman."

"Yeah? So am I."

"It must be exciting discovering new talent. Is there anyone I know who you — ?"

His answer was to pull her to him and kiss her hard on the mouth. She struggled against him as he ground his pelvis against hers.

"Hey, cut it out," he said as she pulled back. "Come on, you want it. You know you do. Get in the car."

"No, I won't. I'm going back inside."

One hand went to her throat. He pushed her back against the car, her head pressing into the soft convertible top. With his other hand he reached into his pocket. He withdrew a switchblade knife and clicked it open, held it up in front of her eyes. "Don't make me use this, baby. Just get in the car and —"

Jeanine brought her knee up into his groin. He grunted and doubled over but continued his grip on her neck. The knife came up again, this time the point of its blade was at her throat. "No!" she shouted as she grasped his wrist and twisted with all her strength. Now the knife was pointed at his midsection. She pushed against it and felt it cut through his skin and penetrate his chest cavity.

"Jeanine!" a female voice shouted.

Jeanine heard Mitzi but was too shocked to respond. She felt as though all life had been drained from her. She leaned back against the car as he slid down, his hands on her in search of something to grab, down to his knees, and then keeled over to one side.

"Jeanine!" Mitzi said again as she arrived at her friend's side. "What — ?"

Jeanine collapsed against Mitzi, who kept her from falling.

"Oh, shit!" Louise Watkins said.

Jeanine looked down at her pale blue blouse, which was stained with his blood. Her hands shook uncontrollably and her breath came in spasms.

"We have to call the police," Mitzi said.

"No," Jeanine said. "I can't —"

Louise bent over the body. She grabbed the knife and pulled it from him. "Got to get rid of this," she said, more to herself than to them.

"Please, let's go," Jeanine said. "It was an accident. He tried to rape me."

She leaned on Mitzi as they headed for their car. Louise followed, muttering about not wanting trouble. When they reached the car, Mitzi opened the passenger door and pushed Jeanine onto the seat. She turned to see Louise climbing in the back. "What are you doing?" she asked.

"Just get me out of here," Louise responded.

Mitzi got behind the wheel. "The keys," she said to Jeanine. "Give me the keys."

Jeanine fumbled in the little purse she carried, found the keys, and handed them to her friend. "My father will kill me," she said.

"He doesn't have to know," Mitzi said.

"But the police," Jeanine said.

"Forget any police," Louise said from the backseat. "Come on, get movin'."

As they left the parking lot they passed a couple walking in the direction of where Allan's body lay.

"Oh my God," Jeanine said, sinking down in the seat and wrapping her arms tightly about herself.

"Got to get rid of this knife," Louise said.

"Your blouse," Mitzi said.

Jeanine loosened her arms, looked down, and emitted a tight whine.

"Take a right there," Louise said as they approached an intersection. A minute later they came to a narrow bridge over a tributary from the sea. "Stop!" Louise said. Mitzi hit the brakes. Louise opened her door and tossed the knife over the low concrete railing. A second later a splash was heard.

"Take off your blouse," Mitzi said as she hit the accelerator. Jeanine absently did as instructed. "Give it to Louise," Mitzi said. Jeanine obeyed. "Where can we get rid of it?" Mitzi asked Louise.

Louise gave Mitzi directions. They arrived at a Dumpster behind a department store. Louise got out and dropped the blouse into the Dumpster, leaning into it to scatter garbage over the bloody garment.

"Where are you going?" Mitzi asked Louise.

She gave her the address of a run-down two-story apartment building on the edge of downtown.

"You live here?" Mitzi asked.

"Sometimes," Louise said. "You got any money?"

"Yes, I —" Mitzi handed Louise all the cash she had. "Jeanine, money," she said. Jeanine fished cash from her purse and handed it into the back.

"You just forget everything," Louise said. "Just forget it, you heah?"

"Yes," Mitzi and Jeanine affirmed.

They watched Louise get out of the Caddy and go into the building.

Jeanine started to cry. "I'm freezing," she said, her teeth chattering.

Mitzi ignored her and drove to the Montgomery house, where she parked the car where it had been earlier in the evening. Jeanine, wearing her bra, sat shivering. "Come on," Mitzi said. "Get out before anyone sees you."

They went inside. Jeanine got out of her clothes and took a shower. Mitzi followed. Wearing bathrobes, they put what washable clothing there was in the washing machine and sprayed other items with air freshener in an attempt to rid them of the odor of cigarette and marijuana smoke.

"What are we going to do?" Jeanine asked as they sat in her bedroom.

"I don't know," Mitzi said. "Nothing, I guess. Nobody knows what happened. I mean, nobody knows it was you and him."

"Somebody knows," said Jeanine. "That girl, whatever her name is —"

"Louise Watkins."

"She knows. You think she's going to say anything?"

"Don't be silly. She's a drug pusher, probably a prostitute. She doesn't want anything to do with the police."

"But other people in the bar. The bartender. People sitting near us."

"Look," Mitzi said, grabbing Jeanine's wrist and looking her in the eye, "nothing will happen if we just stay calm. Try to forget about it. You said he tried to rape you. He's was a bum, trash. Good riddance."

They stayed up talking for most of the night. Mitzi left at noon on Sunday; Jeanine's parents returned at six that evening.

"Had a good time with Mitzi?" Mrs. Montgomery asked.

"Oh, sure," Jeanine said. "We just hung out."

Her father had settled in his favorite reading chair in the living room and started to go through the Sunday paper. "Look at this," he said, referring to a short article on the slaying at Augie's the night before. "It was bound to happen. That place should have been shut down months ago."

Mrs. Montgomery took the paper from him and read. The reporter had little to report — a man, Allan Resta, twenty-five years old, a resident of Atlanta, had been found stabbed to death next to his car in the parking lot of Augie's. The weapon was missing and no suspects had been identified. Witnesses said a young woman had accompanied the victim from the club just prior to his murder, and officials were seeking this individual. The victim's mother in Atlanta had been informed of her son's death by phone.

The next morning, Mrs. Montgomery asked Jeanine if anything was wrong.

"No. Why do you say that?"

"I don't know, dear, you look worried about something."

Jeanine manufactured a dismissive laugh. "No, Mother, everything's great."

Everything *was* great in the Montgomery household until five o'clock that afternoon when two Savannah detectives arrived at the door. Mrs. Montgomery answered.

"Ma'am, we'd like a word with your daughter, Jeanine Montgomery," one detective said.

"My daughter? Why?"

"Just a routine inquiry, ma'am. Is she at home?"

Jeanine was summoned from upstairs. The detectives got right to the point: "Were you at Augie's Saturday night?"

"Augie's?" She made a face. "I never go there."

"One of the people we interviewed said that she thought she'd seen you there."

"I hesitate to intrude, Detective," Mrs.

Montgomery said, "but I assure you that my daughter doesn't frequent places like that."

The two men looked at Jeanine, waiting for an additional comment from her.

"No," she said, "I wasn't there. My mother is right. I wouldn't be caught dead in a place like that."

"Sorry to have bothered you," said one of the officers. "The witness said she wasn't sure that she'd seen you but we had to follow up. I'm sure you understand."

"Of course we understand," Mrs. Montgomery said. "You're doing your job, and you do it very well, all of the Savannah police. Would you like coffee or a soft drink?"

They declined the offer and left.

Jeanine's father was, of course, told of the police visit when he returned home that evening. "Glad you straightened them out," he said after his wife had recounted the reason for the visit and its outcome. "Ridiculous thinking someone like Jeanine would be involved in anything as tawdry as that."

The following day, Jeanine was home alone when a call came.

"Hey, this is Louise," Louise Watkins said.

"Who?"

"Ah, come on, don't play dumb with me. Louise, from Saturday night. Remember?"

"Yes, I remember. How are you?"

"Not so good. I need to talk to you."

"I don't think that would be such a good idea," said Jeanine.

"Better you talk to me than to the cops."

Jeanine felt as though she'd been hit in the stomach. The message was clear. This girl named Louise was going to blackmail her. Where would she get the money? From her parents? She'd rather die than tell them what had happened. *Please, dear God, make this go away.*

Louise told her of a street corner where she wanted to meet later that afternoon.

"Please don't do this," Jeanine said, aware as she did so that she sounded pathetic. She summoned her control, steadied her voice, and said, "I'll meet you there."

Louise hung up.

Jeanine called Mitzi and told her about the call.

"You aren't going to meet her, are you?" Mitzi said.

"What am I supposed to do?" Jeanine countered. "She knows everything that happened and can tell the police."

Mitzi paused in thought. Finally she said, "Jeanine, it was an accident. The guy tried to rape you. Maybe it would be best to just tell what happened."

"Tell *who?* My parents? They'd kill me. I'd never be able to go out for the rest of my life. Maybe this Louise isn't looking for money to keep quiet. We can meet and find out what she wants. No harm in that."

"*We* meet her?"

"Yes! You were there with me. I need you, Mitzi."

Another pause before Mitzi said, "All right. This stinks."

"I know. I'll meet you there at four."

The street corner was in a shabby part of the city. Louise was waiting when they arrived. She was dressed like a streetwalker and had obviously been using drugs. The flesh around her left eye was discolored, black-and-blue.

She led Jeanine and Mitzi into a small, weed-choked park with two broken benches. Jeanine noticed three young black men loitering near a fence separating the park from a junkyard. It was stiflingly hot but she was chilled by the circumstance of the meeting and its location.

"What do you want?" Jeanine asked Louise.

"I need money. I need money bad."

"I'm sorry that you do," Jeanine said, "but

I don't have any money to give you; maybe a few hundred dollars but —"

Louise snickered. "That not what I mean. Things are bad for me, got to get away from here."

"Again, I'm sorry but —"

"Your family got money, big bucks, right?"

"Leave my family out of it!" Jeanine was surprised at the strength in her voice.

"I took care of you," Louise said, "got rid a' the knife and all. You owe me. You don't pay me, I got to go to the police."

"No, don't do that," Jeanine said. "Please."

The three men approached. One said to Louise, "Hey, bitch, come on. What you hangin' 'round with these white chicks for?"

It was as though Louise didn't have any choice except to go with them. She said to Jeanine, "You be back here tomorrow, same time, and bring a thousand dollars with you. You hear me?"

Jeanine and Mitzi watched Louise leave with the men.

"What can I do?" Jeanine asked, tears beginning to roll down her cheeks.

"I don't know," Mitzi said, "but maybe I can talk to my father and see what he suggests."

"Tell your father?"

"You have a better idea?"

"My parents will know then."

"It looks to me like they're going to know anyway, at some time. My dad's a pretty cool guy. We'll talk to him together and ask him not to tell your folks. There's no other choice, Jeanine."

The thought of sharing with Mitzi's father what had happened on Saturday night was terrifying to Jeanine. But Mitzi was right, and she didn't see any alternative. Maybe Mr. Cardell would put up the money to satisfy Louise. Jeanine hung on to that thought as they drove to the Cardell home, where Mitzi's father practiced putting on the back lawn.

"Daddy, we have to talk to you," Mitzi said. "Jeanine's in trouble."

Jeanine bristled for a moment at being painted as the only one in trouble. After all, Mitzi had broken the rules, too, by going to Augie's, and she had been involved in the cover-up. But she was in no position to quibble about relative guilt.

They sat in the Cardell kitchen, where Mitzi's father poured glasses of sweet iced tea. "Now, Jeanine," he said, joining them at the table, "what's this trouble you're in?"

It took Jeanine time to compose herself and to form her thoughts. When she was ready, she said, "Mitzi and I went to Augie's

Saturday night. My parents were away overnight and we — well, we decided to go."

Cardell fixed his daughter with a harsh stare, which she avoided by casting her eyes down.

Jeanine continued recounting the events. She hadn't gotten very far when Cardell stopped her. "You were there when that fellow was murdered?" he asked.

Jeanine nodded.

"Don't tell me that —"

"It was an accident. He tried to rape me. It was his knife and he threatened to kill me. It just happened. He held the knife and we fought and it went into him."

"Jesus!" Cardell muttered, shifting in his chair and looking out the french doors. He turned to his daughter. "You were there when it happened?"

"No, Daddy. I was with the black girl who —"

"What black girl?"

Jeanine answered his question, ending with, "She wants a thousand dollars or she'll go to the police."

"My God," he said, again diverting his gaze to the outdoors.

"I don't want my parents to know," Jeanine said.

"Oh really?" Cardell said. "A little late for

that, isn't it?"

Jeanine started to cry.

Cardell ignored her tears and asked, "Who is this black girl you were with?"

"Her name's Louise Watkins," Mitzi replied. "She's a drug dealer and a prostitute."

"And you hung out with someone like that?"

"I didn't 'hang out' with her, Daddy. I met her at the bar and —"

"And she wants a thousand bucks to keep quiet."

The girls nodded.

"What makes you think she'll stop at a thousand?" he asked. "You give in to blackmailers and they keep coming back for more."

Another set of nods.

Jeanine said, "She said she has to get away. She looked like somebody had beaten her up. I think she's in trouble and will take the money and leave Savannah."

"You can't count on that. When are you supposed to meet her again?"

"Tomorrow afternoon."

"Where?"

"Downtown."

A last look at his private putting green outside the french doors preceded his next and final response to their situation. "I want to meet this girl named Louise but I don't want to do it downtown. Can you convince her to go with you to a place I name?"

Mitzi and Jeanine looked at each other.

"I suppose so," Mitzi said.

Chapter 20

The following afternoon, Jeanine and Mitzi drove to where they were to meet Louise Watkins. She looked even worse than she had the day before. A cheek sported a new bruise and she walked at an angle, as though to straighten up would be painful.

Jeanine, who was behind the wheel, pulled to the curb by the run-down park and motioned for Louise to come to the car. She balked at first and indicated that they were to come to her. Neither Mitzi nor Jeanine made a move. Mitzi repeated Jeanine's hand motion. Louise looked around and slowly, tentatively approached. She stood beside Mitzi, who sat in the passenger seat.

"What's going on?" Louise asked through the rolled-down window, her words affected by drugs.

"Get in," Mitzi said.

Louise frowned as she tried to gather her thoughts. "You got the money?" she asked.

"No, but we're going to someone who does," Jeanine answered.

Louise was visibly conflicted. She hadn't expected this change in the scenario she'd written for herself and the meeting.

"If you want some money, Louise, you'll have to come with us," Mitzi said.

The girls in the car waited while Louise processed this.

"Who?" Louise asked.

"You'll find out," Jeanine said. "We can't sit here all day."

Louise looked up and down the street and saw two of the young black men who'd been there yesterday heading her way. Jeanine wondered whether Louise was afraid that they were about to take her to some secluded spot and kill her. They would be going to a secluded spot but murder wasn't part of the script. *Maybe it should be,* Jeanine thought.

Louise opened the rear door and tripped as she got in. She slammed the door shut and sat wedged against it as though seeking refuge.

Jeanine drove south, reaching Victory Drive and continuing until she took a right onto Waters Avenue. Louise said little except to ask a few times where they were going. "You'll see soon enough," Mitzi responded.

They crossed the Diamond Causeway from the Isle of Hope and entered the Skidaway Island State Park, a 533-acre preserve bordering a stretch of the Intracoastal Waterway called the Skidaway Narrows. Jeanine and Mitzi had been there many times on family outings. Jeanine followed a narrow roadway leading to an area where large earthwork fortifications built as Confederate defenses during the Civil War shared the land with abandoned moonshine stills. It was an overcast day with rain looming in the forecast, which had kept down the number of visitors. Jeanine parked and she and Mitzi got out. Louise remained in the backseat, taking in her surroundings, fear etched on her face.

"Come on," Mitzi said, opening the door for her.

The three young women walked along a path bordered by Savannah holly and magnolia trees and azalea and firethorn shrubs.

"Where the hell we going?" Louise demanded.

"We're here," Jeanine said as she saw a man standing alone near an entrance to one of the Civil War entrenchments.

Louise stopped. "Who's he?"

"Somebody who can help you," Mitzi said.

"This is Louise," Jeanine said when they reached the handsome, well-built young blond man in a tan suit, yellow shirt, and green tie. His name was Jack Felker; he was Ward Cardell's personal assistant and PR man.

"Hello," he said, and smiled.

Louise said nothing.

"You have nothing to be afraid of," Felker said, "but maybe I can help you."

" 'Help me'?" Louise said.

"Yes. I understand you're looking for money in exchange for forgetting something that happened last Saturday night at Augie's."

Louise cocked her head defiantly. "So? You got the money?"

"Yes," Felker said, "but first I need to talk to you. I'm told that you're looking for a thousand dollars to remain quiet about what happened at the club."

"That's right. Seems to me what I know is worth it."

Felker noticed that the battered black girl was starting to shake, probably because the drugs she'd taken earlier were wearing off.

"I'm told that you want the money to get away from the life you've been leading in Savannah," he said.

Louise kept her eyes on the ground as she

said, "I'm all messed up, that's all. I got to get me straightened out."

"And I'd like to help. Of course, you know that a thousand dollars won't go very far. It'll be gone before you know it and you'll end up back the way you were." When Louise didn't react, he continued. "What someone like you needs is a nice, long vacation where you can get yourself straightened out."

Louise nodded and shuffled her feet.

"I'm sure your mother and brother would be very proud of you."

The mention of her mother and brother caused her to look up at him with eyes now moist. Felker had done his homework before the meeting and knew about Eunice Watkins and Louise's preacher-brother, Lucas.

"You need to go to a place where they'll take care of you," he said, "make you healthy again, put you in classes that will teach you skills you can use later on in life. I know that your brother, Lucas, is a minister. You need God in your life, young lady, and there are places where God will be brought to you and made a part of your life."

"I — I just need the money."

"How would you like ten thousand dollars?" Felker asked.

Louise was stunned by the question; her fingers fluttered to her mouth.

"Did you hear me?" Felker asked.

"Yes, sir, I heard you."

"Well?"

"Ten thousand. You got to be joking with me."

"No, I'm not joking. But you have to do something in return."

"What I have to do?"

"Go to the police and tell them it was *you* who stabbed the man in Augie's parking lot."

"I didn't do that. It was her." She pointed at Jeanine.

"It doesn't matter who actually did it," Felker explained. "It was obviously an accident. The man tried to rape you. He used a knife. You grabbed the knife and in the struggle it killed him. By confessing to the crime you'll be given leniency. I assure you that the right judge will see it that way and will go very easy on you, give you just a few years in prison, where you can find yourself and find God, get off the streets, and become the sort of good young person your mother and brother want you to be. Believe me," he concluded, "what I'm offering you is a gift from God. We don't often get second chances in this life. I'm giving you a second chance, and so is God."

"I don't know. I —"

"The police will believe you. You threw the knife in the water and you know where that is. Your fingerprints will be on the knife unless the water has dissolved them, which I don't think will be the case in such a short period of time."

Felker sensed that she was softening.

"The women's prisons aren't there to punish. The facilities at Metro State Prison in Atlanta or the Lee Arrendale State Prison in Alto are there to help you forge a new life. Just think about it — free of drugs, maybe your GED diploma, and a bright future ahead for you."

When there was still no response, Felker said, "This is your one and only chance. You've obviously made some bad decisions in your young life. Don't make another one. And if you think you can go to the police with your story about someone else having done it, they'll laugh you out of court. You're a druggie and a hooker. How do you think that will play with the police and a judge?"

Finally Louise spoke. "You give me the money now?"

Felker chuckled. "I don't think so," he

said. "Here's what I suggest. Tomorrow you go to the police and tell them that you were the one who stabbed the man in the parking lot. I'll spend time with you tonight to help you come up with your story. Once you've been arrested, I'll arrange for ten thousand dollars to be delivered anywhere you say."

Louise turned her back on him and looked up into the gray sky. The initial raindrops of a storm that would soon become full-blown landed on her face. The wind suddenly picked up and blew Felker's blond hair into a swirl above his head. That, coupled with a dramatic flash of lightning behind, gave him an almost messianic quality. Jeanine and Mitzi waited. Louise slowly turned and said to Felker, "You promise about the money?"

"Yes, I promise," he said above a sharp clap of thunder.

"You give the money to my mother?"

"If that's what you want. Ten thousand dollars will be given to her anonymously. But you have to promise that you won't tell a soul about this. If you break that promise, you'll wish you were back on the Savannah streets." His tone had turned rock-hard.

Louise Watkins agreed. She would, of course, eventually tell her mother how she ended up in prison, but she would never reveal the source of the payoff. Nor would she ever know that the young woman for whom she'd sold out would one day become the first lady of the United States of America.

Chapter 21

Israel's prime minister and his wife were entertained that night in the State Dining Room by the president, the first lady, and a select group of one hundred invitees. Jeanine Jamison had approached the evening without enthusiasm. She found most state dinners unbearably dull: all the pomp and circumstance with which to contend; the briefing by State on the visiting head of state and his wife to ensure that certain topics would be raised, and avoided; the forced gaiety — the pomposity of it all. She'd taken an instant dislike to the prime minister's wife, a ravishingly beautiful brunette with an exquisite figure and lively, wide brown eyes. Jeanine never did like it when a female guest was more attractive, especially another first lady. She preferred dumpy ones or those with out-of-proportion facial features and bad teeth.

But feeling competitive with the prime

minister's wife wasn't the primary reason that her thoughts wandered away from the here and now — to the stabbing in the parking lot at Augie's twenty years ago, and its resolution as worked out by Mitzi Cardell's father and his PR man, Jack Felker, in Skidaway Island State Park.

She'd forgotten about it, had managed to store that nasty recollection away in one of the many compartments that she was capable of creating, especially for unpleasant memories. But Mitzi's lunchtime visit had been unsettling. The whole mess was now back, front and center, thanks to her childhood friend.

She wondered what her husband's reaction would be if she confided in him after all these years of secrecy. She looked at him as he laughed at something the PM had said and decided that sharing that sordid episode from her life wasn't worth risking his wrath. He was a man who detested anything that stood in the way of his goals; having a first lady who'd killed a man and avoided prison by a friend's father paying off a drug-ravaged black hooker wouldn't be taken kindly. There was a side of him, however, that might applaud how the parking lot situation had been handled. Fletcher Jamison believed that there were few problems that couldn't be solved with sufficient money and power. There had been plenty of rumors during his ride to political power about payoffs to bury unflattering episodes from his past both as an attorney and then as governor of Georgia, and Jeanine had personal knowledge of two of them, including one that involved her.

They had occurred during his one and only term as governor.

The romance between the governor and Jeanine had its origins while he was still married to his first wife, Claire. Jeanine had landed a job as his liaison with the state legislature, a position that brought them into close and daily contact. She'd been in that office only a month when he made it plain that he found her attractive and was interested in seeing her socially. His marriage, it was said, was rocky, held together only for the sake of political propriety, which he confirmed to Jeanine the first time they slept together, a week after the start of their flirtation.

Their trysts were catch-as-catch-can, a stolen hour in a hotel room, sex on the floor of his office after all other staff had gone home for the night, and once at her apartment, the riskiest of all their assignations.

Jamison had been linked to several extramarital affairs, none of which had ever been proved to the extent that local media dared to base stories on the allegations. Jeanine knew one of the women, a blonde nightclub hostess with multiple tattoos. The blonde had gotten pregnant and didn't want his baby, or *any* baby. Jamison arranged for her to visit a doctor in Atlanta who had a thriving business on the side doing abortions for the mistresses of well-connected men. Jamison paid the doctor and gave the blonde a generous going-away present in cash. Jeanine had heard about the cash settlement and asked Jamison about it during one of their hurried sexual romps. He denied it, of course. But a few weeks later, a departing disgruntled employee took Jeanine out for drinks, consumed too much, and confessed that he was the one who'd delivered the cash to the blonde, and to the doctor. That knowledge didn't elevate Jamison's character quotient in Jeanine's estimation, but by that time she'd set her eyes on replacing the current Mrs. Jamison and becoming first lady of Georgia. The governor's past indiscretions were stored in another of her mental compartments.

Following the sexual encounter at her apartment, she was approached by a local political reporter who'd been staking out that apartment since rumors of her affair with the governor had made it to the newsroom. The reporter told Jeanine of the story he was developing about Jamison's extramarital sex life, with Jeanine Montgomery as exhibit A.

She vehemently denied the allegation to the smug reporter, wondering as she did so what he'd do with the knowledge that only that afternoon she'd learned that she was pregnant with Jamison's child.

Knowing she was pregnant did not unduly upset her. She decided that it could be the catalyst to force Jamison to make a decision about their relationship, something she'd been looking for since their affair had commenced. He'd promised to end his marriage to marry her, but as far as she could see, he hadn't taken any steps in that direction.

That night, in tangled, sweaty sheets after lovemaking in a hotel, she decided it was time to draw a line in the sand. She told him that she was carrying his child, told him of the reporter's visit, and revealed that she knew about the blonde hostess and how he had arranged and paid for her pregnancy to be aborted. She ended by saying, "I want to be your wife, Fletch."

She expected an angry reaction. Instead,

he said, "And I want to be your husband, Jeanine. Claire and I have agreed that a divorce would be best for everyone involved — for her, for me, and for the kids. We've stayed together because I wasn't sure how being divorced would affect a run for the presidency. There's only been one divorced president, Ronald Reagan, and it sure as hell didn't hurt his chances for the White House. Claire and I will be announcing our decision at a press conference at the end of the week, irreconcilable differences, an amiable parting of the ways after a long and honorable marriage. We'll stand side by side along with our oldest son, Michael, a good family with the sort of values that have been lacking in American culture for far too long now."

He paused, and she concealed her incredulous smile.

"After a decent amount of time has passed, we'll announce our engagement."

She hugged him tightly, which aroused him.

"What about the baby I'm carrying?" she asked.

"I don't want another child, Jeanine," he said. "I've researched it. George and Martha Washington didn't have children, although she had two before being widowed.

Jackson and his wife never had kids. Harding and his wife — what was her name?; oh, right, Florence — Florence Harding had a son from her previous marriage that ended in divorce. Polk was sterile and Buchanan was a confirmed bachelor. My two kids from my marriage to Claire will do just fine. But another child? No. That won't work."

"Meaning?"

"You'll have an abortion — and we'll be a hell of a lot more careful from now on. Roll over."

It had worked exactly the way he'd choreographed it. Claire and their son stood proudly at his side as he announced to the public that he and his wife were parting, "But not as enemies, as is too often the case with divorcing couples these days," he intoned. "We've loved and honored each other for many years but now it's time for us to go our separate ways. Claire, as you know, has been extremely active in a variety of causes, each contributing to a better America. She will continue to serve the public good in these capacities — with my unbridled support, I might add. And I will continue to lead the great state of Georgia in new directions that will ensure a better life for all its citizens. I pledge to you that I will do everything in my power to bring back to Georgia the level of civility and morality that its people deserve."

Claire Jamison beamed. Their son pumped a fist into the air.

"Only Fletcher Jamison would dare to speak of getting a divorce and morality in the same speech," a veteran political reporter commented to a colleague.

"And nobody cares," was his colleague's reply. "I need a drink."

Jeanine and Fletcher Jamison bid good night to their distinguished visitors from Israel and retired to their private quarters.

"She's charming," he commented as he undressed.

"She's all show," was Jeanine's response.

"Oh?"

"A quarter inch deep. You were taken with her flashy beauty."

"She is a beautiful woman."

"According to some definitions," Jeanine said as she changed from her evening dress to a designer lavender jumpsuit and slippers.

"Where are you going?" her husband asked.

"Down to my office. I have some personal e-mails to catch up on."

"Do it in the morning," he said during a yawn.

"I want to do it now."

She kissed him on the cheek and padded downstairs, where her chief of staff, Lance Millius, sat hunched over a computer. He looked up at her entrance.

"What are you doing here?" she asked. "It's late."

"I suppose I could ask the same of you," he said lightly, not wanting to appear confrontational.

"I couldn't sleep."

"How'd the dinner go?"

"All right. Crushingly boring, but all right. Did you find out anything about the man I mentioned to you, Robert Brixton?"

He rolled his chair back and turned to face her. "Yes, I did."

"I'm listening," she said as she perched on the edge of a replica eighteenth-century desk. She'd replaced all the desks in her suite of offices with replicas of antiques shortly after moving in.

"I had a search run on Mr. Robert Brixton — work history, e-mails, phone records, credit cards, banking info, tax records — the works." He consulted a sheet of paper. "Let's see," he said. "Robert Brixton. Age fifty. Born in Brooklyn, attended City College of New York, graduated with a degree in business administration. Tried to join the NYPD but wasn't hired. Came to Washington, D.C., and became a cop here. Lasted four years. Married a Marylee Greene from Maryland, had two kids. Divorced. Quit the force here and went to Savannah, where he joined that city's police department. Retired in 2006, went into the private detective business. Runs his own one-man agency. Owes some back taxes but nothing major. Occasional traffic ticket. Had a reputation with the Savannah PD as a bit of a loose cannon. Tends to be a loner, has been identified as seeing a woman named Florence Combes, Jewish, also from New York. Here's a couple of photos of him."

"I'm impressed," Jeanine said.

"With what?"

"How much you've come up with in such a short amount of time."

"Just took a phone call." He handed her the paper.

"Did whoever you called want to know why you were looking for information on him?"

Millius shook his head. "Never came up." Now he cocked his head. "Why your interest in this guy anyway?"

"No special reason."

She glanced at the wall clock. Eleven fifteen. Not too late to call Mitzi, who was a known night owl.

"Thanks, Lance, for getting me the info. Leaving soon?"

"No. I'm still working out details of your Savannah trip next week."

"I could do without that trip," she said. "Go on home and get some sleep."

"Later," he said.

He obviously intended to stay. "I'll be in my office," she said.

"Okay."

She closed the door behind her and sat at her replica nineteenth-century desk, which contained only a telephone and a blank white legal pad with a pen carefully aligned with the pad's blue lines. She hesitated to make the call with Millius in the next office but decided she could do it quietly.

"Mitzi? It's Jeanine," she said in a low voice. "Catch you at a bad time?"

"No. My guests just left. A painfully dull evening. The new head of the TSA is a pompous ass if I've ever met one."

"Sorry. Mitzi, I think we should get together again soon about this — this Savannah project. You know I'm going there next week."

"Yes."

"I've come up with some information about the — about the man we discussed at lunch."

"Oh. Something bad?"

"No, no, but we should talk. Can you come here to the White House tomorrow at four?"

"Four? That's a problem. I have a meeting with the caterers for the Washington Opera party I'm hosting."

"Postpone it, Mitzi!" Jeanine said sharply.

"I — of course I will. Can you tell me about this information you've come up with?"

"Not on the phone. I'll see you tomorrow."

The first lady went to the outer office, where Millius continued to work on the computer.

"I think I'll get some sleep," she said.

"Good idea," he said without looking up.

He waited a few minutes after she'd left before checking her phone to see what number she'd called. Mitzi Cardell! Of all the people Lance Millius disliked — and the numbers were sizable — Mitzi Cardell was at the top of the list.

He packed up to leave. Before he did so, he consulted a directory of political operatives in Georgia, especially in the Savannah area. Because the president and first lady were from Georgia and the president had once been governor of that state, the network of political friends there was extensive. After jotting down a few names from the directory, he added that note to other materials he was carrying home.

"Robert Brixton," he muttered as he turned out the lights.

Part Three

CHAPTER 22

Cynthia Higgins was crying when Brixton walked into the office carrying a Styrofoam cup of coffee.

"Hey, what's the matter?" he asked.

"Jim . . . got . . . fired . . . last . . . night," she said, each word punctuated by a sob.

"Sorry to hear it," he said. "What happened?"

She blew her nose with gusto and drew some deep breaths. "He got into a fight with a customer on the ghost tour, some big, fat older guy with a snootful of booze and with a girl young enough to be his daughter."

"Always nice to see fathers treat their daughters to a night out."

"Daughter? Hell! Anyway, this drunk starts giving Jim a hard time, telling him the tour stinks and that Jim doesn't know squat about Savannah ghosts."

Brixton saw it coming and grimaced.

"So Jim tells him off in no uncertain

terms, and the drunk calls the tour agency and they ream Jim out. Turns out this slob has political and business connections in Georgia and threatened to put the agency out of business. That's it! Jim gets canned."

"Well," Brixton said, "Jim is — was — in the people business."

Cynthia flared. "Which doesn't mean he has to take guff from anybody."

Brixton held up his hands. "No, of course not," he agreed. "I'm sure he'll find another job soon. There's got to be a dozen ghost-tour operators in the city."

"His boss told him he needs anger management classes."

"Yeah, well, maybe he should look for another line of work."

"Maybe I should look for another husband. Sorry. I know it's not your problem, Bob. These calls came in earlier this morning."

Brixton took the slips of paper she handed him into his office and sat behind his desk, feet up on it. Two of the messages promised new clients, including another restaurant owner who wanted to establish surveillance on two employees he suspected of skimming. The third was from Detective Wayne St. Pierre.

"Hello there," St. Pierre said when Brixton

returned the call. "And how are you, sir?"

"Not bad. You called."

"As a matter of fact I did. I have good news for you."

"I'm always up for good news."

"We've found your missing camera and recorder."

Brixton swung his feet off the desk and straightened up in his chair. "Where?"

"A pawnshop in the Lamara Heights district."

"You canvassed them?"

"Not exactly. We did put out a bulletin to pawnshops describing the missing items. That doesn't usually amount to anything, but this particular law-abiding owner called and said he had them. Obviously looking for the citizen-of-the-year award."

"When did this happen?" Brixton asked.

"This morning. I thought you'd want to come with me to talk with the owner."

"Yeah, I'd like that very much."

St. Pierre gave him the address and they agreed to meet there in a half hour.

The pawnshop was in a row of seedy one-story buildings that had gone through a succession of owners and small businesses; gentrification wasn't spoken there yet. St. Pierre and Brixton arrived at the same time and entered the shop, where a wizened old man stood behind a small counter protected by Plexiglas panels. St. Pierre announced who they were and why they were there and they were buzzed into the owner's cramped domain. Brixton's eyes immediately went to his briefcase and its contents, which were displayed on what passed for a desk.

"That's it?" St. Pierre asked.

"Sure is," Brixton replied, picking up the camera. "They never even took this off," he said, referring to his name label that was still affixed to it.

"Who brought this stuff in?" St. Pierre asked the owner.

"Vinnie."

"Vinnie *who?*"

"I don't know his last name. He's a homeless guy who hangs around the neighborhood, has his hand out all the time, checks out Dumpsters and the like."

"Know where we can find him?" asked St. Pierre.

"Probably out on the street someplace."

While Brixton examined the contents of his briefcase, St. Pierre continued asking questions. "Did this fellow Vinnie say where he'd gotten it?"

"Said he found it in a Dumpster. Like I said, he checks them out and —"

"And you didn't question him?"

"Sure I did. I asked where he got such a good camera and recorder. He just said he found them in a Dumpster. I gave him a few bucks — a lot less than the equipment is worth — and figured I'd gotten a good deal. That's what I'm in business for, to find good deals. Anyway, I took them in and was going to display them when I got the message from the cops." He looked at St. Pierre over his half-glasses. "From law enforcement," he corrected. "As soon as I got that message I called in. I'm a good citizen, always have been."

St. Pierre filled out a form indicating that he'd taken possession of the items and handed it to the owner. "I'm sure we'll have more questions for you," he said. "In the meantime, how about we take a swing around the neighborhood and find this Vinnie character."

"I can't leave the shop."

St. Pierre looked left and right. "Doesn't look to me like they're breaking down your doors. Come on now. We find Vinnie and you can come back."

Brixton placed the camera, recorder, and other items into the briefcase and followed them outside. The owner locked the door and got into the back of St. Pierre's unmarked car. Brixton took the front passenger seat.

It took them less than five minutes to locate Vinnie. They spotted him sitting on the sidewalk in front of a vacant storefront a few blocks away. St. Pierre parked and got out of the car. Brixton joined him, leaving the pawnshop owner in the vehicle.

"Hello there, Vinnie," St. Pierre said with a smile. "Hot day, isn't it?"

Vinnie, who was probably younger than he looked — living on the street and foraging for food aged a guy fast — peered up at St. Pierre and Brixton through bloodshot eyes. His face was grimy beneath his stubble, his chino pants urine stained, his torn red T-shirt filthy. He wore heavy winter boots despite the oppressive heat.

St. Pierre motioned to Brixton, who held the open briefcase in front of Vinnie, displaying the camera. St. Pierre squatted and asked Vinnie where he had found it. It took the homeless man a minute to realize that he was being questioned by a police officer. When he did, he struggled to his feet and stumbled, trying to get away. St. Pierre grabbed his arm and gently pushed him against the storefront. "You're not in any trouble, Vinnie," he said. "We just want to know where you found these things."

"I didn't do nothing wrong," Vinnie said,

fear etched on his face.

St. Pierre assured him that he hadn't and repeated his question. Vinnie mentioned a Dumpster. St. Pierre told him to lead them to it. Vinnie did as instructed. The Dumpster was at the corner next to a building that was being demolished. "In there," he said. "I found it in there."

St. Pierre and Brixton peered over the edge of the Dumpster, which was filled with construction debris.

"Feel like getting dirty?" St. Pierre asked Brixton.

"No."

"Nothing to be found here," St. Pierre agreed.

They thanked Vinnie for his time and drove back to the pawnshop. As the owner was getting out, he asked, "What about the money I gave him? I'm out that money and don't have the camera."

"How much?" Brixton asked.

"Twenty."

"You ripped him off," Brixton said as he pulled out his wallet and handed the owner a twenty and a ten. "Thanks for calling it in."

"Like I said, I'm a good citizen."

Brixton accompanied St. Pierre to Metro, where the briefcase, camera, and recorder were dusted for prints. There weren't any.

"Thanks," Brixton said when he was handed back the briefcase and its contents.

"Mah pleasure, Robert," St. Pierre said as they walked outside together. "Things progressing on the Watkins case?"

"Nothing new to report but I'm still working it."

"No further sidewalk confrontations with the city's lower species?"

"If you mean have I been mugged again, the answer is no. How are things at Metro?"

"The bureaucracy lives on, Robert. How is your lovely lady friend, Miss Flo?"

"She's fine."

"Well, glad you got back your tools of the trade. Hot enough for you?"

"More than hot enough, Wayne. This weather stinks. Thanks again."

"Take care, Robert. Ciao."

Brixton poured two shots of scotch upon returning to his office and shared the good news with Cynthia.

"That's great," she said. "Now you can give the pictures to that attorney."

"Maybe, maybe not. Depends on how nice he is to me and how much money he comes up with. He's not on my list of favorite people." Brixton was good at understatement.

That day's edition of the *Savannah Morning News* was on the desk where Cynthia had dropped it earlier. Brixton picked it up and took a look at the front page. Dominant was a large photograph of a man surrounded by men and women holding campaign signs. The caption indicated that the man, Shepard Justin, had just announced his candidacy in the upcoming Savannah mayoral race. His smiling wife and two kids, whom Brixton judged to be no older than eight or nine, stood next to him in the photo.

Brixton read the accompanying article. Justin, an alderman and member of the city council, had held a news conference to make his announcement. He was quoted as saying, "It's time that this wonderful city had a mayor who understands the needs and aspirations of its citizens. I pledge to you that as your mayor I will restore dignity to city government, work in a nonpartisan way to bridge the gaps that have paralyzed important legislation, and establish a new and refreshing commitment to family values that have been neglected for far too long."

Brixton leaned closer to the page and squinted to see the man's face better. Although he wouldn't swear to it under oath in court, he was almost positive that Shepard Justin was the man he'd photographed the night he'd followed the restaurant owner's wife to the motel. "I'll be damned," he muttered.

"You'll be damned about what?" Cynthia asked.

"The guy in the picture, Justin, the alderman who's running for mayor."

"What about him?"

He told her of his conviction that it was Justin who'd been having an affair with his restaurant owner–client's wife and it was Justin whom the man he'd taken pictures of.

"Whew!" was Cynthia's response.

"Yeah, how about that."

Cynthia returned to the reception area. Brixton swiveled in his chair, opened the briefcase, and pulled out the camera. He turned it on and the digital screen lit up. He pushed the button that retrieved photos from the camera's disk. The message NO PHOTOS appeared in red.

"What the hell?" Brixton said.

He opened the camera to pull out the disk. The compartment was empty.

He got up and left the office.

"Where are you going?" Cynthia asked from behind her desk.

"A cigarette."

"You really ought to think about quitting, Bob."

He ignored her and went downstairs, where he dragged on a cigarette and tried to inject order into his jumbled thoughts.

What had happened to the photos he'd taken? Someone obviously had removed the disk. But why? *They wouldn't have bothered unless they knew what was on it.* They'd unceremoniously dumped the briefcase and everything in it into a Dumpster, hadn't even tried to sell the items, which meant that money wasn't the motive behind the attack on him, nor was admiring the art of digital photography on their collective shrunken minds.

He almost never had two cigarettes in a row but automatically lit the second one.

Had his muggers linked up the photos on the disk with the newspaper picture — with Shepard Justin? He had to assume that they had. The next question was whether they had attacked him because they already *knew* what was in the camera or had discovered it by chance after the fact.

If those photos were now in the hands of Justin's political enemies, they could be used to derail his mayoral ambitions. Not that Brixton cared whether Justin lost his bid to lead city hall. *Serve him right,* he thought, *bedding another man's wife. Another family values hypocrite.*

Now Brixton's thoughts shifted to whether the pictures that had been in the camera could be traced back to him. His name was on the camera, compliments of his Brother P-Touch label maker, and his name was displayed in other places inside the brief-case.

Who knew that he'd taken the photo-graphs and that he had them in the brief-case?

The only people he could come up with were the husband who was being cuckolded and the husband's attorney. Of course, Cyn-thia knew about the assignment, and he'd replayed the evening for his friend Ralph Lazzara after returning from the motel. But the assault had happened so soon after he'd taken the photos that he couldn't conceive of anyone having been informed about it and told what he'd be carrying.

He eventually decided that whoever had taken the disk from the camera wasn't interested in who'd taken the pictures. Chances were also better than good that they had looked at the photos, seen nothing of value in them, and tossed them in the trash. He lit a third cigarette as he came to these conclusions, looked at it, snuffed it out in an urn in front of the building, and went back upstairs, where Cynthia was packing up to leave.

"Hate to run out on you, Bob, but Jim called and said he needed to talk with me."

"Sure. Go ahead."

"Thanks. You're a sweetheart."

He was on his way out of the office when the phone rang.

"Dad. It's Janet."

"Hi, honey. How are you?"

"I'm okay but I've gotten myself into a little bit of a financial jam and need some money."

"What kind of a jam?"

"Oh, I got — it really doesn't matter, does it? I'll pay it back. I promise. I have some great new concerts coming up and —"

"How much do you need, Janet?"

"Five hundred? I could use more but —"

"Are you in some sort of trouble?"

"No, Daddy, I'm not in any trouble." Her tone hardened. "Look, if you don't want to help me out I'll —"

"I'll see what I can do and send you a check. It'll be a few days, though."

She turned soft again. "Thanks, Dad. I really appreciate it *and* I'll pay it back."

"Sure, honey."

"I have to run. You're a doll."

The line went dead and he sighed. It wasn't the first time she'd called looking for money, nor was it unusual for her to say that she'd pay him back. She never did. Once, he'd balked at sending money and called Marylee to discuss it. She berated him for not having been there for his girls throughout their entire lives and further accused him of putting money before his responsibilities as a father. He claimed that his ex-wife had cornered the market in self-righteousness, like her mother. That conversation had ended in a hang up and he'd never contacted her again concerning their youngest daughter's calls for cash.

He shook off the frustration Janet's call had created, picked up the phone, called the *Savannah Morning News,* and asked for Willis Sayers, a veteran reporter with whom Brixton had become friendly while a cop.

"Hello, my man," Sayers said. "Long time no talk, or is that a cliché?"

"It's a cliché. I need to pick your brain, Will."

"About?"

"About a family here in Savannah. The Cardell family, more precisely a daughter named Mitzi."

Sayers, a bear of a man, laughed like one. "Washington's leading social light. What about her?"

"Buy you a drink?"

"Now?"

"Yeah."

"Pinkie Master's on Drayton? In an hour?"

"Don't be late."

Chapter 23

It hadn't been necessary for Will Sayers to tell Brixton that Pinkie Master's Lounge was on Drayton Street. Brixton had been to the dive bar across from the Hilton Hotel, in Savannah's historic district, many times over the years. It had been around as long as Savannah had been, or so it seemed.

Brixton took a seat at the small, circular bar, which was sticky to the touch, and ordered what everyone else seemed to be ordering, a "tall boy PBR," a sixteen-ounce glass of Pabst Blue Ribbon beer. He was tempted to have a martini served in a plastic cup (Savannah is one of the few cities in which it's legal to carry drinks outside and consume them there) but decided to hold off. No telling how long an evening it would be. Willis Sayers had the reputation of being able to outdrink most men of normal size, which included Brixton.

He glanced down and realized that he was

seated where a brass marker was inlaid into the bar commemorating the spot where in 1974 Jimmy Carter allegedly had announced his intention to run for president. Al Gore had made a similar proclamation there in 1999.

Pinkie Master's was a rock-solid Democratic hangout frequented by a variety of types, students from SCAD, bikers, businessmen in suits, lots of media folks, and on this evening a private detective named Brixton, who looked up at the large Confederate flag, and a sign that read TIPPING IS NOT A CITY IN CHINA, proudly displayed behind the bar. He smiled.

Sayers arrived a few minutes later. He wore what he usually wore, baggy chino pants, a striped button-down shirt obviously purchased from a big man's catalog, wide red suspenders, and a red-and-white railroad handkerchief protruding from his rear pocket. He wedged his sizable girth past other customers, slapped Brixton on the back, and took the empty stool next to him. "Bourbon and a tall boy," he barked at the female bartender.

"A martini," Brixton told her. He'd almost finished his beer.

"How are you, Will?" she asked.

"Pretty damn good, hon. You?"

"Holdin' up."

Sayers turned to Brixton. "So, good buddy, you're looking to become a D.C. society type?"

Brixton laughed. "Hardly," he said.

"What's your interest in Miss Mitzi Cardell?"

Sayers's voice was as loud as his size and Brixton second-guessed meeting him at Pinkie's. "Maybe we can leave here and find someplace quieter," he suggested as the jukebox, which seemed never to be still, spewed out another obscure hit from the eighties and a group of customers started singing along.

"Sensitive?"

"Yeah, it is, Will, sort of sensitive."

"Have dinner plans?"

"No." He did, but he knew that Flo would understand if he canceled.

"Another round," Sayers told the barmaid. To Brixton: "We'll get some steam up here and head out. You buying?"

"Dinner? Sure."

They downed the fresh drinks and Sayers put it on the tab he ran at Pinkie's. Brixton called Flo on his cell and told her he was tied up on business. She wasn't as understanding as he'd hoped.

"Where to?" Sayers asked when they were

on the sidewalk beneath the Pabst Blue Ribbon sign that hadn't been illuminated in years.

"How about Bella's?" Brixton suggested. He was in the mood for Italian food and Bella's made the best manicotti in Savannah, no surprise since the owner — who was not named Bella — was originally from Brooklyn. He was also conscious of his dwindling bank account and the call from Janet looking for money. Bella's wouldn't break the bank. Time for another advance from Eunice Watkins.

Settled at a table in a far corner away from other diners — there weren't many — Brixton got to the point. He told him about the visit from Louise Watkins's mother and her allegation that her daughter had taken the rap for someone else in the stabbing incident in Augie's parking lot. Sayers listened attentively, but before Brixton could continue with the story, the big reporter interjected, "I remember that case, Bob. There always was a suspicion that she hadn't done the deed. At least I heard that from some cop friends."

"They were right," Brixton said. "She got ten grand, which she gave to her mother. From what I hear she did well in prison, got her GED, found out she was good with numbers and wanted a job. She comes out of prison and —"

"And wham! She's gunned down on the street."

"Exactly. You remember that."

Sayers nodded and refilled their glasses from their second bottle of Chianti.

"Okay," Brixton said and continued recounting for Sayers other aspects of the Watkins story. He eventually mentioned the photo shown him by Louise's mother of her daughter and two other black girls with three white girls on the CVA campus during a weekend retreat. "Mitzi Cardell was one of the white girls," he added.

Sayers shrugged. "Okay," he said. "What's the connection?"

"I don't know," Brixton replied, "but I need to find out. To be honest, Cardell is the only possible link I can come up with. What I was wondering is whether you know anything that might help me get to her."

Sayers ingested his final strands of spaghetti and patted his mouth with his red-and-white railroad handkerchief, which he'd tucked into his shirt collar. "No," he said, shaking his large head for emphasis. "But maybe I can point you in a direction."

The evening's alcohol intake had caused fuzziness in Brixton's brain, but the possibility raised by Sayers snapped him to attention. "Go on," he said. "I'm listening."

"Another bottle?" Sayers asked.

"No. I gotta work tomorrow."

To Brixton's chagrin, Sayers motioned for another bottle of Chianti. He leaned his elbows on the table and said, "First, my friend, I have some news for you. I'm leaving Savannah."

"That *is* news," Brixton said. "Retiring?"

"Hell no. The paper is sending me back to D.C. to open the bureau again."

Willis Sayers had been assigned to Washington a few years back but had been recalled when the failing economy took its hit on newspapers. Closing bureaus had become routine. But, as Sayers explained, with a former Georgia governor in the White House and a Georgia peach as first lady, reopening the D.C. bureau was a no-brainer.

"Happy about it?" Brixton asked.

"Yes and no. Lots happening in D.C., a lot more than the drivel I end up covering here. But I never did like our nation's capital or the people who make it run. Like Harry Truman said, if you want a friend in Washington, get a dog."

Brixton laughed appropriately.

"Anyway," Sayers continued, "I got to

know a few good people when I was there, including a guy named Mackensie Smith. He was a top criminal lawyer until some drunken yahoo ran into the car his wife was driving and killed her and their kid. He packed up the practice and took a gig at GW Law School. A really solid guy, straight shooter. He's comfortable with D.C.'s society crowd but marches to his own drummer. Married a knockout of a woman, Annabel, a ten. She was also a lawyer, mostly matrimonial, but threw in the towel, too, after marrying Smith. She owns an art gallery in Georgetown. I can give Mac a call and tell him you'd like to pick his brain about Mitzi Cardell."

"I'd appreciate that, Will." Buying dinner was beginning to pay off.

"Here's another guy you might look up. Ever hear of Jack Felker?"

"No. Who's he?"

"Felker used to be the PR guy for Mitzi Cardell's old man, Ward Cardell. A slick guy, smooth as a milk shake. Anyway, there's always been a rumor floating around about Cardell."

"What sort of rumor?"

"Hard to pin down. Cardell and the first lady's father, Warren Montgomery, are close. Word has it that Cardell owns Montgomery."

"*Owns* him?"

"Yeah. Seems Cardell did Montgomery a big favor years ago and —"

"What sort of favor?"

Sayers shrugged his large shoulders. "I don't know," he said and sipped wine. "It's all very hush-hush, underground stuff."

"You mentioned Cardell's PR guy, this Felker."

"Right, right. I'm told that Felker was mostly responsible for keeping his boss's name *out* of the papers. Cardell cut some pretty nasty deals along the way is how I hear it."

"Is Felker still working for him?"

"No. I heard just a few weeks ago that Mr. Felker is dying of cancer."

"Oh."

"I also hear that he's been telling friends about some of Cardell's deals that he had to keep sub rosa. Knowing you're dying tends to make some people want to fess up to past sins. You might want to look him up."

"I will," said Brixton.

As they parted in front of the restaurant, Sayers promised to call Mac Smith in Washington to alert him that he'd be receiving a call from Brixton.

"Can't thank you enough," Brixton said.

"Dinner was thanks enough, my friend. If you come up with a bombshell about Mitzi Cardell and the first lady, I get it first."

"Count on it," Brixton promised.

And then he went home, dreading the hangover that was sure to follow.

Chapter 24

Rain splattering against the window woke Brixton the following morning. He sat up and immediately fell back onto the pillow. His head pulsated and his knee ached from having been in the wrong position while he slept. He reached for a bottle of Tums he kept at his bedside and downed two.

A cup of black coffee and a bowl of fruit that was on the cusp of turning into an alcoholic punch settled his stomach down, and a shower helped with the headache, supplemented by two Tylenol.

He called Flo, whose voice testified that she was not happy.

"Sorry about last night," he said.

"You should be," she said. "I spent my birthday with Marla."

"Your birthday? No!"

"Yes! How was your dinner with the reporter?"

"Look, I'm really sorry about last night. I

mean, my dinner with Sayers from the *Morning News* paid off big, I think. He gave me some leads to follow up on and —"

"I'm glad to hear it."

She lightened up. "I was expecting a ten-carat diamond broach as a present from you last night."

Relieved, he said through a chuckle, "I have it right here with me. Dinner tonight? The Pink House?"

"Sounds good. Don't forget the broach."

He called Eunice Watkins and told her that he'd need another thousand up-front. "I've developed some promising leads, Mrs. Watkins."

"That's good to hear," she said. "Shall I bring a check to your office later today?"

"That'd be fine, Mrs. Watkins. If I'm not there just give it to my assistant, Cynthia." She sounded perfectly content, didn't have that change in tone people often adopt when asked for money. "Better make it two thousand if you don't mind. I may have to spend some time out of town and —"

"Of course."

Headache, sour stomach, aching knee, and a downpour were the only negatives to what otherwise was shaping up to be a good day — money in the bank and a not-too-angry Flo Combes. *Buy a card and a present before tonight,* he reminded himself as he left the apartment and headed for his offices.

He told Cynthia about having blown Flo's birthday. After rummaging through a desk drawer he found the slip of paper on which he'd written the names of Flo's favorite bath items — Fantasia Violet Soap and Cleopatra Body Wash. She was a fancy-soap addict, so she always smelled good. "Do me a favor," he said to Cynthia, handing her the note. "Run over to the Paris Market and pick up some of each."

He spent the next hour writing checks against the promised infusion of two thousand dollars into his account, including one to his daughter Janet. Eunice Watkins arrived at ten thirty with the check.

"Thank you," he said.

She nodded. "I spoke with Lucas this morning and told him that you had some leads. He wants to know what they are."

"Well," Brixton said, suddenly faced with the question of how much to reveal, "it involves some people who might know something that can help us. I'd rather not mention their names at this point."

"You said you might have to leave town," she said.

"Right. Washington, D.C."

"Someone there might be helpful?" she

asked, the first hint of incredulity he'd heard from her.

"That's right."

Silence filled the room.

"You'll have to trust me," he said. "Believe me, I'm doing all I can."

"I do trust you, Mr. Brixton, but Lucas — well, he is more of a businessman than I am."

A clergyman in a three-piece suit, Brixton thought.

She stood, straightened her dress, and said she looked forward to hearing from him. He assured her that she would.

He ran to the bank, deposited Eunice Watkin's check, mailed his checks, and returned as Cynthia walked in holding her purchases from the Paris Market.

"Thanks," he said. "You're a doll."

"Bob," she said, "I have something to tell you."

"Oh?"

"Jim and I are leaving Savannah."

"Wow. Where are you going?"

"Iowa. Jim is from there. His uncle, Sydney, owns a community bank and has offered Jim a job as a teller."

Brixton's laugh wasn't completely genuine. "Sounds good," he said against the sinking feeling he was experiencing. "I just hope he keeps his anger in check when a customer gives him a hard time." He knew the second he'd said it that it was wrong, and tried to cover with an even bigger, more manufactured laugh.

Cynthia let it go. "We're leaving a week from now," she said. "Sorry for the short notice but —"

"Hey," he said, "nothing's forever. I'll miss you."

"I'll miss you, too," she said and walked out as the tears came.

Brixton closed the door to his office before calling Wayne St. Pierre at Metro.

"Hi-ho, Robert," St. Pierre said.

"What do you know about a guy named Jack Felker?" Brixton asked. "He used to be Ward Cardell's PR man."

When St. Pierre didn't respond, Brixton said, "You there?"

"Yes, I'm here, Robert. Why do you ask?"

"I'd like to ask him some questions. Know how I can reach him?"

"Ah — of course. Give me a minute."

He returned with Felker's phone number. "I should alert you, Robert, that Mr. Felker is quite ill."

This time the silence was on Brixton's end. It initially sounded as though St. Pierre didn't know Felker. But here he was warning Brixton that the man was dying. Before he could ask how well St. Pierre knew Felker, the detective asked, "Does this have to do with the Watkins thing you're working on?"

"Yeah, it does, Wayne."

"Well, good luck. I must run now. Ciao!"

Brixton went over in his mind what he would say when he reached Felker. Once he had, he dialed the number. A man answered.

"Mr. Felker, my name is Robert Brixton. I'm a former Savannah detective who's now a private investigator."

"Yes?"

"I was wondering if you might be good enough to give me a few minutes of your time."

"For what?" Felker replied in a weak voice.

Brixton pictured the man with whom he was speaking, riddled with cancer, emaciated, eyes sunken, hairless thanks to the chemo, fading fast.

"Well, sir," he continued, "it might be best if we wait until we meet in person. Can we do that?"

"I don't know. I'm not well."

"Yes, sir, I've been told that, and I'm sorry for your troubles. Look, this has to do with a case I'm working on. It involves a young black woman who years ago was wrongly convicted of having stabbed someone to death. Her name was Louise Watkins."

Felker's voice gained strength as he said, "I have nothing to say about that."

Bingo! Translation: *I know about it but don't wish to discuss it.*

He hadn't said, "That name means nothing to me," or, "I have no idea who you're talking about." He'd said, "I have nothing to say about that." . . . "About *that!*"

He knows!

Brixton collected his thoughts before pressing on. He decided to toughen his stance. "Look," he said, "I know that you were Ward Cardell's PR spokesman for years, and that his daughter, Mitzi Cardell, knew Ms. Watkins at the time of the incident. All I want to do is ask a few questions — of you and hopefully of her."

"I'm not sure there's anything I can tell you."

Making progress, Brixton thought. He shifted gears. "Look, Mr. Felker, I *know* what went down twenty years ago with Louise Watkins. All I need is to fill in some holes. Whatever we talk about is off the record."

Would the bluff work?

He heard a deep sigh at the other end. Finally, Felker said, "All right, but there's little I can tell you."

"Whatever you can will be appreciated, sir."

They agreed that Brixton could come to the house that night at eight. "But please come alone," Felker said before hanging up. "I don't want anyone to know."

Brixton realized the moment he'd clicked off the phone that he'd already made dinner plans with Flo. If he hadn't forgotten her birthday he wouldn't have felt so conflicted about canceling another date. An early dinner was out of the question. She seldom closed her shop until eight, often nine. Besides, she'd want to make a night of it, dinner at the Pink House, after-dinner drinks at some bar with music, and home together for a celebratory roll in the sack.

He put off calling her and later was glad that he had. She called at one that afternoon to say that she'd forgotten that she'd promised to attend a fund-raising dinner with her friend Marla, and would he, Brixton, be terribly hurt if they made it tomorrow night?

"I was really looking forward to tonight," he said, not terribly proud of his lie but enjoying being able to milk it. "I just hope no one steals the broach before I get to give it to you."

"You can always buy another," she said

airily. "Thanks for understanding, Bob."

"That's me," he said, "Understanding Bob."

CHAPTER 25

Before leaving the office that afternoon Brixton called the restaurant owner who was looking to have a couple of his employees scrutinized and made an appointment to meet with him the following day. He was tempted to pass on the assignment, wanting to devote his full time to the Watkins case. But he knew that would be folly. He now had three thousand of the ten thousand dollars that Louise had given her mother and pledged to himself that he wouldn't take more unless absolutely necessary. Louise Watkins had sold her soul for the ten grand, and possibly lost her life because of it. If he didn't come up with the sort of information the mother sought, he'd bow out before taking more of what he considered blood money.

He had dinner at Lazzara's before heading for his meeting with Jack Felker, and told the owner of having retrieved his camera and recorder.

"That's great," Lazzara said.

"Yeah, except that somebody took the disk from the camera that had photos on it from my last assignment."

"Of the cheating wife?"

"Right. Put this on my tab, Ralph."

He was about to tell his friend that the man in the photos at the motel was running for mayor but decided that it was better kept to himself. He was sorry that he'd told Cynthia. What he didn't need at that moment was to become involved in some sordid political dustup. The fewer people who knew, the better.

As he drove to Felker's house he formulated the questions he'd ask, hoping they would result in useful answers. The problem was that he didn't know at that juncture what he was looking for. Coming up with evidence that definitively cleared Louise Watkins of the stabbing, and nailing down that she'd been paid to take legal responsibility, would be a home run. But he was pursuing Felker on the remote chance that his boss's daughter, Mitzi Cardell, had in some way been involved, and that Felker would both know about it and elect to admit it.

And what if he *did* admit that Mitzi

Cardell was somehow involved, laid it out all nice and neat as a deathbed mea culpa? What would he, Brixton, do with that information? Mitzi Cardell was a powerful figure in Washington, D.C., a close friend and confidante to the nation's first lady. *Get real,* he told himself as he approached the address given him. Maybe it was time to admit failure and get back to what paid the bills, following wayward spouses and restaurant employees who cheated the house. He debated turning around and going home but something kept him from doing that, stubbornness or pigheadedness. Take your choice.

The question of Louise's murder upon coming out of prison had been shunted to the back burner. Her family was less interested in solving it, which was good. Chances were slim to none that the twenty-year-old slaying would ever be resolved.

Felker's house was in midtown Savannah, the Ardsley Park community of expensive mansions and craftsman-style bungalows. Felker's residence was a house that fell in size between the mansions and the bungalows. Brixton parked at the curb and took in his surroundings. It was a well-lighted quiet street lined by Savannah's famous live oak trees, from which heavy strands of

Spanish moss hung low. Tourists were fond of taking home the moss, which gained its nutrients from the air, as a souvenir, often using it to stuff pillows. Bad decision. The moss contained mitelike creatures called red bugs, which cause intense rashes and itching.

He got out and slowly approached the front door, which was illuminated by a copper lantern above it. He took note of a red Corvette parked in the short driveway and a copy of that morning's *Savannah Morning News* on the front step. As he was poised to ring the bell, he was again struck with the sinking feeling that the trip would be for naught. Felker had finally agreed to the meeting because Brixton had pressed the issue, and although Felker's comment — "I have nothing to say about *that*" — said to Brixton that Felker did, indeed, know something about what had occurred twenty years ago, to think that he'd spill his knowledge of it to a stranger, a private investigator to boot, was more than unlikely.

He rang the bell and waited. When there was no response, he rang the bell again and pressed his ear to the door to make sure the bell was working. A faint chime came from somewhere inside. This time he both rang and knocked. Still nothing.

He came down off the step and moved to the side where he could see through a picture window whose purple drapes were open. The living room was well lighted by floor lamps and a small chandelier over a dining table. There was no sign of life. But as his eyes shifted from the larger room to a hallway leading from it to the rear of the house he saw the mound on the floor, a lump the size of a person, shrouded in the hallway's shadows.

He went back to the door and tried it. That it opened and easily swung away was a surprise that startled him. He stepped over the threshold and went to the hallway where he confirmed that the mound he'd seen was a body, presumably that of Jack Felker.

Brixton knelt on one knee and touched his fingertips to the neck in search of a pulse. There was none. He peered closely at the man's face, one side of which was exposed. There was no sign of blood or bruising. He wondered why Felker — and he had no doubt that's who it was — was dressed in a bathrobe over red silk pajamas and was barefoot. Either he'd intended to greet Brixton in his nightclothes or he had died earlier in the day before changing into street clothes.

Brixton had seen plenty of dead bodies

during his stints with the Washington, D.C., and Savannah police departments, and had witnessed many examinations by medical examiners. He used what knowledge he'd gained from those experiences to further examine the body. The corneas had begun to turn slightly milky, which told Brixton that he'd been dead for more than a few hours. He reached through the folds of the robe and pajama top and laid his palm against Felker's chest. The body had begun to lose warmth, although it hadn't become cold and clammy yet, leading Brixton to estimate that he'd died as many as six hours earlier. He placed his thumb on one of the deceased's eyelids and pulled it back, revealing petechial hemorrhages, minute blood clots lining the surface of the eyelid, presumptive evidence that he'd been suffocated.

He stood and returned to the living room. Why were all the lights on? If Felker had died during daylight hours, the lights in all probability would have been off.

He went to the window and drew the drapes closed. He knew that he should immediately call the police and not disturb the scene, but he wanted a few minutes alone in the house.

Felker's study was in a long, narrow room

at the back of the house. Its lights, too, were on. Brixton had noticed that the living room was extremely neat and tidy and had made the same observation while glancing into the kitchen. Yet, the study was a mess, with file and desk drawers open and papers tossed onto the floor and desk. Someone else obviously had the same intentions as Brixton did, to see what he could find among Felker's possessions. And that meant that Felker's death had probably not resulted from natural causes. It also meant that whatever Brixton might hope to find had already been taken.

Still . . .

He went to the desk and flipped through the papers on it. Nothing of interest caught his eye and he turned to one of the open four-drawer file cabinets, pulling out folders at random. A battered, dog-eared, empty folder caught his attention. Written on the tab was "Watkins." Judging from the file's condition, it was old, possibly as old as twenty years. He folded it so that it would fit into the pocket of his sport jacket and was about to look at other items when the sound of a patrol car's siren was heard from front of the house. Then, a second one sounded.

Brixton left the study and had just reached

the living room when the front door was flung open and four uniformed Savannah officers burst into the room, followed by two plainclothes detectives, including Wayne St. Pierre. One of the officers drew his weapon.

"Hey, put that damn thing down," Brixton said.

"*You're* here?" St. Pierre said.

"Looks like it," Brixton said.

St. Pierre's colleague went to the body in the hallway. "He's dead," he called out.

"Did you call it in?" St. Pierre asked Brixton.

"No. When was it called in?"

"Fifteen minutes ago," St. Pierre replied. "Anonymous call, suspicious death at this address."

"It's Felker, right?" Brixton said.

St. Pierre looked at Brixton quizzically. "How did you get in?" he asked.

Brixton recounted having rung a few times, looking through the window, and trying the door, which was unlocked.

St. Pierre looked at the drapes pulled tight over the window. "How did you see in with the drapes closed?"

Brixton sighed and sat on the couch. "I closed them," he said.

"Why?"

Brixton shrugged.

"What else did you touch, Bobby?"

"Nothing." Brixton got up and headed for the door.

"Whoa," St. Pierre said.

"I want a cigarette," Brixton said, opening the door and stepping out onto the small landing. St. Pierre followed. Brixton lit up.

"You have to admit, Bobby, that these are strange circumstances."

"How so?" Brixton asked, taking a long, satisfying drag. "Aside from the body in there, there's nothing strange about it. You gave me Felker's contact info. I called him and made a date to meet here at his house. I arrived and found him dead on the floor." Brixton waved off St. Pierre's next comment. "No, wait, there *is* something strange," he said. "You say somebody called in a suspicious death at this address fifteen minutes ago. It wasn't me. So, who was it, somebody who'd followed me here, or somebody who knew I'd be at the house at a certain time?"

"Were you followed?" St. Pierre asked.

"Not that I noticed, although I really wasn't paying attention. Getting sloppy in my old age."

"Who knew when you'd be here?"

Brixton ground out the butt with his shoe.

"Nobody, Wayne. You were the only one I told that I wanted to speak with him, and that's it."

A van from the medical examiner's office pulled up, followed immediately by a Metro forensics vehicle. St. Pierre directed them inside. When he and Brixton were alone again, St. Pierre asked, "Who told you about Jack Felker, Bobby?"

"Knock off the 'Bobby' stuff, Wayne. If you're trying to get under my skin, you're succeeding. As for who told me about Felker, it doesn't matter."

"Your call, Robert. But you're going to have to come down to Metro and give a statement."

"Why? It happened just like I told you."

"Why did you want to meet with Felker?" St. Pierre asked. "You said it had to do with the Watkins case you're working on. What possible connection could Felker have with that?"

"He worked for Ward Cardell."

"And?"

"I wanted to see if there was any connection between Cardell's daughter, Mitzi, and what happened to Louise Watkins."

"Really, Robert, what possible connection could there be?"

"Maybe there isn't, but I want to follow

up on every possible lead. I owe it to Louise's mother."

"I still don't understand how —"

Brixton was about to tell St. Pierre about the photograph of Mitzi with Louise at the retreat at the Christian Vision Academy, and the folded file folder in his pocket, but decided against it. "Forget about it, Wayne. You want a statement from me? Fine. I'm available anytime."

"We'll leave from here," St. Pierre said.

"By the way," Brixton said as St. Pierre was about to return inside, "take a look at Felker's study. It's a mess. Whoever killed him was looking for something."

" 'Killed him?' What leads you to that conclusion?"

"The mess in his study. Pretty obvious to me."

"The ME will determine cause of death, Robert."

Chapter 26

"You know, Robert, you could be charged with criminal trespass and breaking and entering," St. Pierre said after Brixton had provided a written statement. They sat in St. Pierre's office at Metro.

"Don't be ridiculous," Brixton said. "Do I look like the breaking-and-entering type?"

St. Pierre laughed. "I think the ridiculous one is you, Robert. Frankly, I'm concerned about you."

"Why?"

"Ah get the feeling that you've gone off the deep end with this Watkins matter."

"If you mean I'm working it as hard as I can, you're right."

"Working it *too* hard is the way I see it. It's a solid brick wall you're going up against."

"Really?"

"All this about the Watkins girl havin' been paid off to take the rap for a stabbing just doesn't make sense, at least not to this humble southern boy."

"Southern maybe, but I'd hardly call you humble."

"Be that as it may. What you said earlier this evening about the Cardell family has me worried. You do realize that they are very powerful people here in Savannah *and* in Washington, D.C."

"So?"

"How cavalier we can be," said St. Pierre. "You obviously believe that what happened twenty years ago to a doomed black hooker and drug addict is more important than how good, decent people are treated." Brixton started to respond but St. Pierre cut him off. "You're flailing about, Robert, chasing ghosts from twenty years ago, and not the sort of ghosts we all love and admire here in Ghost Town USA — and I might add who provide a nice bit of change to our economy."

"Know what, Wayne?" Brixton said as he stood to ease the pain in his back, "that doomed black hooker and addict named Louise Watkins was a human being, just like Mr. Ward Cardell and his family. The kid spent four years in the pen for something she didn't do, and got herself gunned down on the street when she was released. She came out of prison with her GED and a shot at putting together a decent, productive life. She's got a mother who loves her and a brother who does, too. They want her name cleared and that's what I'm trying to do."

"A noble undertaking to be sure, Robert, but a fool's errand. Want mah advice? Of course you don't, but I intend to give it anyway. You're not getting any younger, my friend. Time's afleeting. Go back home to Brooklyn or wherever it is that you're from up there in New York. Take that lovely lady of yours with you. She's from up north, too, isn't she? Get yourself a cushy job in security with a bank or with the TSA at one a' your airports up there. You're out of your element here, my friend. Don't get me wrong. Ah love you like a brother. Hell, we were brothers on the force for a lot a' years. I'd miss you sure as the sun will rise tomorrow but what's more important to me is that you do what's right for you."

"I'm touched, Wayne."

"And ahm flattered that you are. Not easy touching the cement head you've become. Let's both head on home now. Care to drop by for some libation?"

"No, thanks. Before I go, Wayne, you told me when I first contacted you that you'd taken a look at the Louise Watkins records from twenty years ago."

"That's right."

"Nothing in them of interest, you said."

"Right again."

"I'd like to browse through them. You said there wasn't much there."

"To be honest, Robert, I didn't do more than browse them myself. But sure, happy to oblige. When?"

"How about now?"

St. Pierre shook his head. "You are one stubborn man, Robert Brixton. You know where the records room is. I'll call and tell them you're on your way."

"Thanks, Wayne. I appreciate it."

St. Pierre made his call and escorted Brixton to the main lobby, where they shook hands.

"One last thing, Wayne," Brixton said.

"You've changed your mind and will accompany me home for a drink?"

"No. This guy Felker was murdered. I checked his eyes. Tiny red spots, just like the forensics books describe them. Presumptive evidence of suffocation."

"And the forensics books also point out that they can be caused by a number of other factors, none involving murder. Felker had terminal cancer, Robert. He died of his cancer. But the ME will confirm that. I'll pass along his findings soon as I receive them. Adios, my friend. And at least consider what I said this evenin'."

The officer in charge of the records room that shift had been there for years. He greeted Brixton warmly but said, "This ain't exactly kosher, Detective."

"Nice hearing me called Detective again," Brixton said, slapping the officer on the shoulder. "I won't be long." He gave him the information necessary for the Watkins file to be located. Five minutes later he was handed a slim folder. "That's all there is," the officer said.

"Looks like I'll be quicker than I thought," said Brixton.

He sat in a far corner of the room at a small, scarred desk illuminated by a single gooseneck lamp. He adjusted the lamp and opened the folder. Had Louise Watkins pleaded not guilty and gone to trial, the folder would have been considerably thicker. He read the typed reports filed by various officers assigned to the stabbing and its follow-up and saw nothing of potential interest. Fifteen minutes later, he'd gone through every piece of paper in the folder and was about to call it quits. But he absently turned over one of the reports. On its reverse side were notes handwritten in pencil that were faded to the point of being almost illegible. One of the notes contained the names of a few people who'd been interviewed following the stabbing but who didn't appear in the final typed report. One name screamed off the page at him: *Jeanine Montgomery.* Next to her name was written the date and time of an interview of her. Next to that was "Subject cleared."

Chapter 27

On his way home Brixton had stopped at Lazzara's for a drink and an order of mussels to go. Now in his apartment, he sat at a table by the window; the folded-up file folder and a piece of paper on which he'd copied the notation about Jeanine Montgomery lay next to the platter of empty mussel shells, leftover garlic bread, and a half-empty bottle of pinot grigio. He'd jotted down the name of the detective listed on the front of the report, someone with whom Brixton had worked while with Metro. That detective would be of no help, having died shortly after taking retirement.

The night had been a blur once he'd discovered Jack Felker's body and the police had arrived. Now, with solitary time to think, he tried to put things in perspective and to fathom what up to now had been unfathomable.

He cleared the dishes, brought his laptop

to the table, and started typing, hoping that the act of putting his thoughts into words would help. He started with a question: why had Jeanine Montgomery been interviewed by a detective following the stabbing in Augie's parking lot? Had someone seen her there that night and told the police? That seemed to be the only logical explanation. The detective who'd "cleared" Jeanine hadn't indicated why he'd come to that conclusion. Did she have an alibi for that evening? Had her family's clout influenced the officer to take her word that she hadn't been there? He'd seen that happen before — a cop, especially a young one, unduly impressed with someone's money and power.

Okay, he thought, *let's assume that Jeanine Montgomery* was *at Augie's that night. If so, could Mitzy Cardell have been with her?* There was nothing to indicate that she had been, but they were known to have been close friends since their early years. Bosom buddies. Their families were undoubtedly close. Augie's was a notorious dump, hardly the sort of place to which someone like Jeanine Montgomery would have ventured alone. Chances were that if she had, indeed, been at Augie's that night, she'd had a friend with her, a friend like Mitzi Cardell.

Both the Cardell and Montgomery families had plenty of money; paying ten thousand to protect one or both of the girls wouldn't pose a hardship.

He poured wine into his glass and rapped his knuckles on the table out of frustration. This was all a game of supposition and speculation, a what-if exercise. But that didn't mean it wasn't useful. He'd played what-if myriad times while with the Savannah PD and it had paid off big on occasion.

He continued with his imagined scenarios and two-finger typing.

He thought back to what his roly-poly journalist friend, Willis Sayers, had said about Ward Cardell "owning" Warren Montgomery. What had that been about? What were the possibilities? Had Cardell arranged to pay off Louise Watkins not to protect his *own* daughter but to protect her best friend, Jeanine Montgomery, who now happened to be America's first lady? Wow! That represented the biggest *if* of all.

He picked up the battered file folder. Why would Cardell's PR guy, Jack Felker, have a file labeled "Watkins"? Had Felker been involved in some way in choreographing the payoff to Louise?

Speaking of Felker, Brixton was convinced that the former PR man had been murdered, the mess in his study and the telltale tiny red dots on his inner eyelid testifying to it. Why? Who? Had Felker told someone that he'd agreed to speak with a private investigator who was delving into the Louise Watkins case more than twenty years later, and had that person made sure that Felker couldn't go through with the meeting?

Then there was Wayne St. Pierre's urging that he, Brixton, drop the matter and leave Savannah. He took it at face value, that St. Pierre had his best interests at heart. But was there more to it? St. Pierre ran with the city's elite when he wasn't getting down and dirty as a cop. Warren Montgomery had been a guest at St. Pierre's party that Brixton and Flo had attended, surrounded by Savannah's A-list, for which Brixton had disdain — or for any so-called A-list, for that matter.

Connect the dots, he told himself, *only do it better than the government is capable of doing to thwart terrorism.*

His office had been broken into, but nothing had been taken. A warning?

Eunice Watkins, Louise's mother, had received calls from an anonymous person who'd said, "Don't be stupid," before hanging up. Stupid about what, reopening the question of her daughter's imprisonment and murder twenty years ago?

Brixton had been mugged, his briefcase containing his camera and recording equipment stolen. Just a random street crime? Probably. Or did it have to do with the Watkins case, or what the photos on the camera's disk showed? If the latter was true, it had nothing to do with Watkins.

Had the driver of the red pickup been nothing more than a moronic bubba who showed up once too often, or had he been following Brixton?

And what about the nicely dressed, ferret-faced guy who'd been looking for him at Lazzara's Restaurant, and who was possibly the same man who'd followed him to Lucas Watkins's rectory?

He had no facts, no tangible evidence to link any of those events with his having become involved with the Watkins family. He was perfectly willing to chalk them up to coincidence. Coincidences happen, more regularly than we like to admit. What bothered him was that in his four years as a private detective he'd never had such things happen to him. It was the timing. They all coincided with his taking on the Watkins case.

He turned back to the question of Jeanine

Montgomery. She now lived in the White House, at 1600 Pennsylvania Avenue, surrounded by security guards and shielded from anything unpleasant by layers of screeners. Fat chance of ever getting to ask her about the stabbing.

There was her father, Warren Montgomery, who lived right there in Savannah. Calling him and asking about it would probably result in Montgomery's using his political clout to get his PI license revoked. The same with Ward Cardell. Titans of industry. Successful businessmen. Good at screwing people and getting their way.

Jack Felker's death now loomed larger and more meaningful than ever. Here was a guy who might possibly have told what he knew about Cardell's involvement in what had happened at Augie's that summer night. It was a long shot but Felker, supposedly close to dying, conceivably could have provided some answers. Brixton had almost forgotten about Felker's death as he grappled with the other questions that boomeranged around in his brain.

He was sure that Felker had been murdered. Was it because he knew too much and had agreed to meet with Brixton? That was a good possibility. No, it was even better than that. Why else kill the guy? It wasn't a robbery gone wrong. Whoever rifled through his files wasn't looking to steal something of value, something that could be peddled through Savannah's underground of stolen goods. He was after information — just as Brixton had been. And he'd probably gotten what he was after. The empty file folder with WATKINS on the tab had obviously contained information. Sloppy to have left the empty folder behind. It might not have contained anything relevant but it did confirm to Brixton that Felker, who had been associated with Ward Cardell at the time, knew something about what had gone down with Louise Watkins. And it was reasonable to assume that Cardell did, too.

He saved what he'd written, closed the laptop, and emptied the wine bottle. He was brimming with energy, and anger, and felt as though he might burst at any second.

The phone rang. It was Flo.

"How was your fund-raiser?" he asked.

"Boring. How was your evening?"

"Not boring. Feel like a nightcap someplace?

"You okay?"

"I'm not sure. The lobby lounge at the Marriott Riverfront in a half hour? It's usually quiet there. I need to vent."

She said she'd meet him there.

As he prepared to leave the apartment he glanced at the slip of paper on which Will Sayers had written Mackensie Smith's Washington phone number. He'd make that call first thing in the morning. He'd decided that there was only one person with whom he had a chance of finding out what had happened in Augie's parking lot twenty years ago, and that was Mitzi Cardell.

Jesus!

Chapter 28

Brixton stayed at Flo's house that night. When he awoke the following morning he felt strangely relieved and enjoyed a new-found sense of control.

The Watkins case had overwhelmed him. He'd decided on his way to meet Flo that he was in over his head, out of his element, and not up to the challenge of finding the answers sought by Eunice Watkins and her preacher-son, Lucas. But Flo lent an open ear, as she usually did when he was down in the dumps and feeling impotent. She also wasn't the sort of woman who equated love and caring with agreeing with everything that he said. She questioned him, gently chided him for falling into an uncharacteristic funk, and challenged his conclusion that he'd never be able to follow through on Mrs. Watkins's behalf.

"You owe it to her to keep trying," she'd said over their second glass of wine.

"I know," he said, "but I've run out of ideas. It's not like there are plenty of sources to give me the answers, locals, people who were there and know the truth. I thought that Felker might be one of those people but somebody made sure that he wasn't. That leaves me with Cardell and his daughter, Mitzi. She's now a big mucky-muck in D.C. Fat chance of getting to her."

"Wait a minute, Robert," Flo said. "You have this contact in Washington that Will Sayers gave you, Mackensie something or other."

"Mackensie Smith. I intend to call him tomorrow. But what am I supposed to say, that I want him to use his influence to get Mitzi Cardell to sit down with me and admit what really happened twenty years ago? What if she was the one who stabbed the guy at Augie's. Will she happily fess up? I don't think so. And what if — I've been playing the what-if game all night — what if it was her buddy, Jeanine Montgomery, who poked the guy? She's the first lady of the land, for Christ's sake. I'm out of my league on this one, babe."

"Maybe you are," she said, "but that doesn't mean throwing up your hands and slinking away. You have nothing to lose by contacting this Mackensie Smith, going to

Washington, and seeing what can be accomplished there. If you fall on your face, so what? You can hold your head high for not having quit on Mrs. Watkins."

They made love after returning to her house; at least his growing sense of impotency didn't include *that* brand of it. As he fell asleep he pondered the conversation they'd had at the Marriott bar. He wanted to buy what she'd said, wanted to wave away all his doubts and forge ahead. It didn't work, and he finally dozed off still filled with visions of failure.

But he felt different in the morning, full of resolve. Flo was amused that he hummed a tune while making breakfast, and he seemed lighter on his feet.

"Thanks," he told her as he was about to leave.

"Go get 'em, tiger," she said.

Cynthia had left a message on the answering machine. She wouldn't be coming in until later in the day, something to do with meeting with their landlord to attempt to get out of their lease. That was all right with Brixton. He enjoyed being alone in the office with a cup of hot coffee from the downstairs food shop.

There had been other messages on the

machine, including one from a man who said it was important that he speak with him that day. No name, but he left a phone number. Brixton returned that call before trying to reach Mac Smith in Washington.

"Thank you for getting back to me," the man said. "Would it be convenient to meet with you later this morning?"

He sounded old, as though age had sapped his voice of energy.

"That depends. What's it about?"

"It's not something I wish to discuss on the phone."

Brixton had heard that plenty of times before.

"I suppose I can squeeze you in today," Brixton said. "Who am I speaking with?"

"What time will you be free?"

"Whoa, hold on. Who are you and why do you want to meet with me?"

"Let me just say, sir, that it has to do with a series of photographs."

"What photographs?"

Brixton knew even before the words came out to what the man was referring — the shots he'd taken at the motel.

"Just name the time, sir," the man said.

"An hour from now."

"I'll be there," the man said and hung up.

The conversation sent Brixton's mind racing in a direction other than Louise Watkins. The missing camera disk had always been in his thoughts but had never stayed front and center for very long. Now it was back and he cursed the distraction it created.

The number Sayers had given him for Mac Smith was Smith's apartment in the Watergate. He answered on the first ring.

"Mr. Smith, my name is Robert Brixton. I'm a friend of Willis Sayers."

"I've been expecting your call," said Smith. "Will mentioned that I'd be hearing from you."

"I'm not quite sure what it is I'm looking for in contacting you," Brixton said, "but it has to do with a case I'm working on. I'm a private investigator."

"So Will said. I don't know what help I might be but I'm certainly happy to meet with you. Are you planning on being in the Washington area anytime soon?"

Brixton hadn't made definite plans to go there but Smith's question forced the issue. "Yes, I will be coming, but I want to be sure that my trip will coincide with you being available."

"My schedule's pretty flexible," Smith said, "and I don't have plans to be away in the near future. Just give me a date when you'll be here and I'll make sure I'm open."

"How about if I get back to you once I've firmed up my plans?"

"Makes sense to me. Look forward to meeting you."

Brixton was buoyed by the call. Smith sounded like a nice guy. Flo was right: he should go to Washington to see what he could accomplish regarding Louise Watkins. If he came up a cropper, the trip wouldn't be a total waste. He could arrange to visit his daughters in Maryland, something he hadn't done in much too long a time.

The feeling of relative exuberance faded fast when his visitor arrived at ten thirty.

Brixton knew who he was, Scott Wilson, a lawyer who'd been practicing in Savannah far earlier than Brixton's arrival. He'd seen him around the courthouse and had read profiles of him in the paper. Wilson was a white-collar attorney, never dirtying his hands with common criminals. His clients were business types and politicians, and he was known as a consummate, smooth-talking dealmaker. Few of his cases ever reached court. He also had a reputation as a foppish sort of dresser, and this morning testified to it: white suit, pale blue silk shirt, wildly patterned blue-and-green tie, and highly polished shoes with pointy toes that screamed French or Italian. He had a mane of flowing white hair, pink cheeks, and lively blue eyes. The first-cast southern attorney out of central casting.

They shook hands. "Scott Wilson," the man said.

"I know who you are, Mr. Wilson. Have a seat."

Brixton directed him to a chair across the desk. "What can I do for you?" he asked. "You mentioned photographs."

"That's correct."

"Okay, so tell me about these photographs."

Wilson's smile was meant to be friendly but there was adversarial steel behind it. "Maybe it would be better if *you* told me about them, Mr. Brixton."

Brixton recrossed his legs and returned the smile. "Hard for me to do," he said, "without knowing what photos we're talking about."

"Oh, I think you know what I'm speakin' of," Wilson said. "I'm referrin' to a series of pictures you took at a certain motel outside of town."

Brixton's laugh was as phony as Wilson's had been. "Oh, *those* photos."

"Yes, sir, *those* photos. I represent a client who has a specific interest in them."

I bet you do, Brixton thought. "Who might

that be?" he asked.

"My professional obligations prohibit me from divulging his identity," Wilson said. "I have the feeling that you are a man who prefers direct talk, no beating around the bush." He said it with one eyebrow cocked and Brixton wondered how he could get one to go up and not the other.

"My client has authorized me to pay a handsome sum for the photographs, Mr. Brixton."

Brixton was confused and was sure that his expression mirrored it. Why would they think that *he* had the photos? *They* obviously had them. But even if they didn't — even if someone else had possession of them and was attempting to blackmail Wilson's client before turning them over — there was no reason to confront the one who had taken the pictures.

"I know the photos you're referring to," Brixton said, "but I don't have them."

Wilson's face reflected skepticism.

"Somebody mugged me the night I took them and stole the camera. I eventually got the camera back but the disk was missing. No disk, no photos."

"That may be, Mr. Brixton, but it doesn't assure me that you don't have a duplicate set."

"Of course I don't," said Brixton, edginess creeping into his voice. "How could I have a set of dupes? The camera was stolen hours after I took them. I never had a chance to do anything with them."

Wilson examined a crease in his trousers and then diverted attention to his polished fingernails. Brixton disliked polished fingernails on men. "The problem, you see, is that whether you have a duplicate set or not, you are aware of their existence. Your name was on the camera they were taken from. I'm sure that you at least took a peek at your handiwork to be sure that the camera functioned properly."

Brixton didn't confirm or deny.

"And I further assume that you have been able to identify the people in the photos."

"You assume a lot of things," Brixton said.

"I'm paid to do that, Mr. Brixton. Let me cut to the chase, which I *also* assume you would appreciate. As I said earlier, my client is prepared to pay you a handsome sum for —"

"For photos I don't have."

"For forgetting that you ever took them."

"Oh, I get it," Brixton said. "Your client might be embarrassed if the public got to see those pictures, might cost him a few votes."

Brixton's comment obviously resonated with Wilson, and Brixton had a moment of doubt about having indicated that he knew who the attorney's client was, the same man in the photo kissing the restaurateur's straying wife — Shepard Justin, candidate for mayor of Savannah. But he immediately resolved that it didn't matter. He was tired of the cat-and-mouse game Wilson was playing, had had enough of *assuming.*

"I've been told that you tend to be a man who enjoys straight talk. That was your reputation when you were a police officer."

Brixton nodded.

"And since you evidently know my client's identity and his reason for having retained me to represent his interests, you are probably sitting there confident that you have the upper hand."

"No, you're wrong. The only thing I'm confident of is that you wasted a trip here." He realized that his voice had begun to reflect the anger he felt and worked to modify it. He leaned forward on his desk and spoke in the sort of hushed tone that he might use with a friend to whom he was giving advice. "Let me put it this way, Mr. Wilson. I don't give a damn about those pictures or your client. But I'll ask you a question. Who came to you with the disk?

Whoever that was is the guy who beat me up and stole my camera."

"An anonymous source, Mr. Brixton."

"And you paid for it. Right?"

Wilson stood and dusted off lint that wasn't there. "I have come here today to make you a very generous offer."

"A very generous bribe, you mean."

"Call it what you will. I am prepared to offer you twenty thousand dollars for your assurance that you will forget that you ever took those photos."

"I've already forgotten about them," Brixton said.

"Or perhaps you have a duplicate set and don't feel that twenty thousand is enough for them. I also find your dismissal to be foolhardy, Mr. Brixton. We aren't dealing here with a run-of-the-mill situation. We are talking about a man's political future as well as the future of this city. I sincerely hope that you don't regret your brash, unwise decision. It could have unfortunate consequences."

"Is that a threat?"

"Good day, sir."

"Good day to you, *sir.* Take your money and tell your slimy client that screwing another man's wife doesn't strike me as the sort of trait I look for in my elected officials.

Not that I expect anything better from them. Thanks for stopping by, Mr. Wilson. Should be an interesting election."

Wilson gave another insidious smile, did a little bow, and left. After he had, Brixton went downstairs, lit a cigarette, and reviewed the conversation. If Cynthia had been privy to it, she would have told him that he'd been stupid not to take the money and run. In retrospect, she might have been right. He didn't have a duplicate set of the photos, nor did he have any intention of telling anyone that the man at the motel was the same one running for mayor. He could have taken the money for doing what he'd intended to do all along — nothing.

But he also knew where Wilson and his client, Shepard Justin, were coming from. Whoever had mugged him and stolen the camera realized after looking at the disk that the guy smooching in front of the motel room was Shepard Justin, future mayoral candidate, and approached Justin's campaign people with an offer to sell them the shots.

Who were the two mugs who'd attacked him? He'd probably never know. Two things were certain. The first was that they'd let Justin's people know that the camera had been wielded by Robert Brixton, private eye, and Justin wanted to tie up that loose end with a bribe. The second obvious truth was that the two goons who'd mugged him either were smart enough to examine the photos and link them to Justin — which he doubted — or knew someone else who could.

When Cynthia walked in later that morning, Brixton asked her if she'd told anyone about his having identified the man in the newspaper photo as the Don Juan at the motel.

"Just Jim and —"

"And?"

"I don't know, I might have mentioned it to some friends at dinner last night. Is something wrong?"

"No, nothing's wrong, Cynthia. But don't spread it around any further, okay?"

"Sure. Okay."

He was glad she'd be leaving town.

He met later that day with the restaurant owner, collected an advance, and said he'd start the assignment when he returned from Washington.

"How long will that be?" he was asked.

"Just a couple of days," he answered, without having a clue as to how long he'd be away.

He called Mac Smith at five and told him

he'd be in Washington in two days. Smith invited him to dinner, which Brixton accepted. He booked a room online at the Hotel Rouge, on Sixteenth Street NW, where he'd stayed the last time he'd been in D.C. Flo had also stayed there on his recommendation and liked it. It wasn't the cheapest hotel in the nation's capital but it wasn't one of those venerable Washington hotels where you paid through the nose for their vaunted reputation. He also called Jill and Janet to say he'd be in the Washington area and wanted to visit with them. Jill sounded pleased and suggested they meet at her mother's house. That wasn't what Brixton had in mind but he agreed. Janet was vague; "I'm real busy," she said. "Let me know the day you'll be here and I'll try to find time."

Find time. For her father. Maybe I had it coming, he decided as he got ready to leave to meet Flo at Lazzara's for dinner. He was almost out the door when Wayne St. Pierre called.

"Just leaving," Brixton said.

"And Ah wouldn't think of stopping you, Robert. I was just callin' to see if you and Ms. Flo might like to join me and a few other guests for dinner tomorrow night, nothing fancy, just good booze, good food, and stimulating conversation."

"Sounds nice, Wayne, but I'll be out of town for a few days."

"Oh? Going home to visit your Yankee friends up north?"

"No, Washington."

"As in D.C.?"

"Right."

"Goin' there to give our esteemed president a piece of your mind, I'm sure."

"Yeah, I might stop in and give him a few pointers. Wish we could make it, Wayne. Thanks for asking. Maybe when I get back."

"You can count on it, Robert. Travel safe."

"I will. Thanks again."

He and Flo enjoyed dinner at a Lazzara's and spent the rest of the night at his apartment. Contemplation of making the trip was bittersweet for him. On one hand, he was glad to be taking action instead of simply mulling things over. What did the shrinks say? Any action is better than no action. At the same time, he didn't look forward to returning to the scene of his initial foray into his law enforcement career, and where his overactive male hormones had led him into a disastrous marriage. He would visit his daughters while there but hoped that it wouldn't entail spending much time with Marylee and her mother. It wasn't that he didn't like them. It was more a matter of their not liking him and making it obvious.

The following morning he placed a small suitcase in the trunk of his car, kissed Flo goodbye, and headed for Washington, D.C. The reality of the situation into which he'd plopped himself hit him hard soon after he'd left Savannah's city limits and was cruising on the highway.

He had a Savannah mayoral candidate angry at him and possibly after his head.

He was hoping to involve Washington, D.C.'s most influential hostess in a twenty-year-old murder.

And if he was successful, he might end up exposing the first lady of the United States as, if nothing else, an accomplice to murder.

Dale Carnegie, author of *How to Make Friends and Influence People,* could have taken a lesson from Robert Brixton.

Part Four

CHAPTER 29

Emile Silva sat impatiently at a Wendy's in suburban Washington. Dexter had said to be there at one and it was now twenty minutes past.

Silva had returned the day before from a visit to his offshore bank, where he'd deposited another large sum of cash. He'd intended to stay there for two weeks but had soon become bored. And there was the episode with the black prostitute that had angered him almost to the point of physical violence. She'd taken offense that he wanted only to watch her nude gyrations and refused to touch her. She'd considered it a personal affront. Was it because he didn't like her body, or because she was dark-skinned? She'd cursed him, called him a faggot and a pervert. He'd dismissed her harshly, holding up a knife and threatening to kill her. The encounter had left him shaken and he'd decided to return to Washington despite Dexter's order to stay away longer.

He was about to leave the Wendy's when Dexter walked in. He went directly to the counter and ordered a sandwich and soft drink, which he took to the table.

"You're late," Silva said.

"Get something to eat," Dexter said. "It looks strange for you to be sitting here without eating."

"I'm not hungry."

Dexter's expression was disdainful. Silva saw his reflection in the other man's thick glasses and thought how much he would enjoy killing the arrogant little bastard.

"I was surprised when you called," Dexter said. "You were supposed to be away for much longer."

"I wasn't happy. Is there another assignment for me?"

"Not at the moment but one is currently being discussed. The decision is being made at the highest level."

Silva snickered. "I hope it comes through soon," he said. "I don't like to lose my edge."

"I will let you know the minute I hear something. You do realize, Emile, that your service has a built-in expiration date."

"What does that mean?"

"There comes a point when someone with your particular skills has outlived his usefulness. It has nothing to do with your performance, which has been outstanding. But there is a strategic need for new faces from time to time. The old faces can become a liability. You were informed of that when you joined us."

What Dexter said was true, although Silva had dismissed it at the time. Was he now being told that he was being cut loose? *You'd better think twice about that,* he thought. He'd once asked Dexter about those who had preceded him as assassins but hadn't received an answer. Were they "eliminated" once their service was terminated to ensure that they weren't able to tell tales out of school? He knew that was a good possibility and pledged to himself that he wouldn't allow it to happen. He'd kill them first. He would survive.

"I suggest that you maintain a low profile now that you're back," Dexter said as he finished his sandwich and swallowed what was left of his drink. "There is to be no contact until I need you. Understood?"

Silva's noncommittal shrug annoyed Dexter but he said nothing. He got up and left without another word.

Silva exited the restaurant shortly after

Dexter had departed, got into his Porsche, and drove home. He'd seldom thought about being dismissed, but the fact that Dexter had pointedly raised the issue was of concern. Were plans in the works to replace him? He couldn't allow that to happen. He *wouldn't* allow it to happen.

He changed into workout clothes and was about to mount the treadmill when the phone rang.

"Mr. Silva?"

"Yes."

"This is Dr. Rahmi. I'm calling concerning your mother." She spoke with an East Indian lilt.

"Mother? Is something wrong?"

"I'm afraid so, sir. Your mother was taken to the hospital earlier today. Your name is listed as her family contact."

"Is she — ?"

"We're conducting tests to determine why she collapsed."

"Is it terminal?"

"Oh no, sir, although she is in serious condition. The next twenty-four hours will determine the cause of her collapse and the prognosis for recovery."

"Where is she?"

The doctor gave him the information.

"I'll be there right away."

"Yes, I would suggest that, Mr. Silva."

He clicked off his cordless phone and sat at his desk. "Poor Ma-ma," he said. But his words didn't reflect what he was feeling. A pervasive feeling of glee consumed him and he started to laugh. It began with a series of giggles that grew into helpless hysterical laughter as though he'd just heard the funniest comedian tell the funniest joke. It racked his body until his ribs hurt and he began to cough. He rubbed his eyes and sniffled, sliding down in the chair until he'd fallen off and was now sitting on the floor, arms wrapped tightly about him, his eyes pressed closed.

Two hours later, he stood at her bedside. Tubes protruded from every area of her frail body.

"Ma-ma?" he said. Her eyelids fluttered. She smiled and softly said his name.

"Goodbye, Ma-ma," he said as a nurse entered the room and asked him to leave while she initiated a procedure.

"She won't be in pain, will she?" he asked.

"No, she isn't feeling any pain. She's heavily sedated. I'll tell you when you can come back in. I know you want to be with her every possible second."

"She's my mother," he said, impressed with how bereft he could sound.

"And a wonderful one, I'm sure," said the nurse. "Please. I won't be long."

After leaving the hospital, Silva stopped in to see his attorney and told him of his mother's condition.

"Doesn't sound good," the attorney said.

"No, it doesn't. You have her will."

"That's right. She leaves everything to you."

"I'll want to sell her house, of course." Had he followed his true instincts, he would have had the place bulldozed.

"I can handle that," the attorney said. "I work with good real estate agents."

"I want to put my house up for sale, too," said Silva.

"Oh? Thinking of moving out of the area?"

"Yes, to someplace warm and quiet."

The attorney laughed. "I wouldn't mind doing that myself."

"You'll handle it?"

"Sure. You want me to start the process now?"

"Yes, start it now," Silva said, the conversation with Dexter about possibly outliving his usefulness fresh in his mind.

Mackensie Smith and his wife, Annabel Lee Smith, worked together in the kitchen of their apartment in Washington's infamous

Watergate complex. The apartment was large and airy, with a sizable balcony that afforded them unobstructed views of the Potomac River and Georgetown beyond. They'd bought the apartment shortly after marrying in a small, private service at the National Cathedral, officiated by Mac's friend, a young Episcopal priest. To say that they were happy was to state the overtly obvious.

"What do you know about this fellow?" Annabel asked while washing lettuce. Mac was busy whipping up a mustard sauce to go with the swordfish that they would grill on the balcony.

"Not a lot, Annie, aside from what Will Sayers told me. He's a private detective in Savannah who's working on a case that has a Washington connection. He used to be a D.C. cop. Will says he's a stand-up guy, a straight talker."

"How will someone like that ever deal with people in this town?" she said with a meaningful laugh.

"It isn't *that* bad," he said.

"Seems to me it's getting worse, nothing but double-talk and spin coming out of Congress and the White House." Of the two, Annabel tended to be more direct in her evaluation of politicians and the nation's political climate. Her views had hardened since Fletcher Jamison took office. To be blunt, as she was capable of being, she considered him an unintelligent man void of convictions and easily manipulated by those around him.

Mac didn't pursue the discussion, not because he disagreed but because he didn't want to get the evening off on the heavy, depressing subject of politics. "Will says that this case Brixton is working on goes back twenty years. Not easy digging up information about a case that old."

"What does he want from you?" she asked after putting the salad ingredients into a spin colander and giving it a whirl.

"I really don't know, but we'll find out soon enough."

As the Smiths prepared dinner, Brixton was just getting out of the shower at the Hotel Rouge. He was glad he'd chosen to stay there. The room was spacious and nicely furnished, everything in various shades of red to reflect the hotel's name. He also liked the location, on Washington Circle and close to DuPont Circle. He'd taken a walk shortly after checking in and was surprised at how much he enjoyed being back in Washington. It was a beautiful day, cooler than it had been in Savannah when he left. He'd never debated that the city was nice on the eyes. It was its people that he'd never been comfortable with, not the average citizen but those involved in government. And Washington, D.C., was a one-industry town — government and the politics that went with it.

Showered and dressed, he got into a taxi parked in front of the hotel and headed for the Watergate.

"It's nice of you to invite me to dinner," he said after drinks had been served on the balcony. The sun was beginning to go down, the red ball setting the waters of the Potomac on fire. "What a view!"

"That's what sold us on the apartment," Annabel said. "It changes hour by hour."

"You were a police officer here in D.C.," Mac said.

"A long time ago. I lasted four years. Got married, had two kids, got divorced, and headed for Savannah, where I've been for the past twenty-four years."

"Why Savannah?" Annabel asked. "You said you were from New York."

"Somebody told me they were looking for cops there. I heard it was a pretty nice city so I figured I'd give it a try. Twenty years on the Metro force. Took the retirement check and opened my agency."

"How's business?" Mac asked.

"Up and down. I catch enough cases to pay the rent. Right now I'm up to my neck in the case that brings me to D.C."

He started to explain but Annabel said, "How about waiting until we're through with dinner? I'm sure you're hungry, Robert. I know I am."

They fell into easy conversation during dinner — sports, politics-lite, television and movies — and Brixton felt very much at home, as though with old friends. It wasn't until they'd returned to the balcony that he was asked to tell them about the case. He almost wished they could skip it. It had been a lovely evening and he didn't want to ruin it by introducing what they might view as a wild-goose chase by an inept, naïve investigator.

He started from the beginning, recounting the visit from Eunice Watkins and her claim that her daughter, Louise, had been paid to plead guilty to a stabbing that she hadn't committed. Mac and Annabel listened intently, hanging on his every word, nodding or asking for occasional clarification. He avoided mentioning Mitzi Cardell or Jeanine Jamison, referring to them only as two young white women who might possibly have been involved.

"Fascinating," Smith said when Brixton had taken a pause for a coffee refill and to consider what to say next.

"You're convinced that one of these girls was the one who stabbed the victim, and whose family paid off Louise to take the rap?"

"Yeah, I am," Brixton said. "I was naturally skeptical at first, but things have happened that lead me to believe it."

"What about these two other girls?" Smith asked. "Do you know their whereabouts?"

Brixton hesitated and sipped his coffee. Mac and Annabel waited for his response. Finally, Brixton said, "Yeah, I know where they are. They're right here in Washington."

"Oh?" Smith said. "Have you contacted them?"

"No. I was hoping you could help me do that."

"Who are they?"

"One is Mitzi Cardell. The other is Jeanine Jamison."

Chapter 30

What was intended to be an early-evening dinner turned into a lengthy discussion that lasted well into the night.

Up until the time Brixton mentioned Mitzi Cardell and Jeanine Jamison, Mac and Annabel had exhibited normal interest in Brixton's tale and had asked few questions. But now, over snifters of Rémy Martin, the atmosphere had changed. The couple's legal backgrounds kicked into gear and the questions were more frequent, and probing.

They pressed Brixton for evidence to back up his belief that either Mitzi or Jeanine had stabbed the victim in the parking lot. He had few hard facts to offer and admitted that his allegation was based solely upon connecting a series of fuzzy dots. He summed up everything he knew — the photo in which Mitzi and Louise appeared; the detective's pencil note on the back of his report indicating that he'd questioned

Jeanine Montgomery; Detective Cleland's doubts as to Louise's truthfulness when she confessed; the folder in Jack Felker's file drawer labeled "Watkins"; Ward Cardell's reputation as a wheeler-dealer; and Willis Sayers's comment that Cardell "owned" Jeanine Jamison's father, Warren Montgomery. There were also the phone calls to the mother in which she was warned not to be stupid; the break-in to Brixton's office shortly after having taken the case; the belief that he was being followed; and, of course, the question of why she had been shot to death on a Savannah street shortly after coming out of prison.

But most important, he told his hosts for the evening, he fervently believed Eunice Watkins.

"Everything you say makes sense," Mac Smith said, "but it's mostly supposition. I'd hate to go into court to try a case based on what you've got."

"I know, I know," Brixton agreed. "But I promised Louise Watkins' mother that I'd do my damnedest to get the answers she's looking for. Look, I'm not out to hurt Ms. Cardell or Mrs. Jamison. Hell, I *know* who they are. All I want is to be able to report back to Mrs. Watkins with conviction that her daughter didn't stab the guy. That's her main concern, not her daughter's murder. The same goes for Louise's brother, the reverend. It's possible, isn't it, that she was killed to keep her from telling someone that she hadn't been the one with the knife that night?"

"Everything is possible," said Smith. "But again, it's flimsy."

"I shouldn't have wasted your time like this," Brixton said, standing and leaning on the balcony railing. "I just thought that if I could spend a few minutes with Mtizi Cardell, ask her some questions, I'd have at least closed the circle, done everything I could."

Smith joined him at the railing while Annabel removed their cups and dishes to the kitchen. "You want me to try and arrange a meeting with Mitzi," he said.

"That's what I was hoping," Brixton responded. "I figured that since you knew her, were a close friend, she might listen to you."

"I'd hardly call our friendship close, Robert. Mitzi Cardell knows hundreds, maybe thousands of people in this city. She's made a career out of knowing people and entertaining them at her home. Annabel and I were her guests not long ago, just part of the pack. I have given her some off-the-record legal advice on a few matters but I'm not a practicing attorney. Let me ask you a question. Do you intend to accuse her of the crime?"

"No. I don't know whether she did it or not. The same with Mrs. Jamison. All I want to ask is whether they were at Augie's that night, see if she was with Louise Watkins and might remember the incident. Louise was convicted of manslaughter, got four years for it. I have to figure that the statute of limitations has run out in Georgia so it wouldn't matter if Cardell or anyone else *did* admit to it."

"Maybe not as a matter of law, Robert, but it sure would matter with her social standing. And there's the question of the first lady's possible involvement. You're probably right about the statute of limitations. I can easily check on that in the morning."

Annabel rejoined them. "Another cognac?" she asked.

"No, thanks," Brixton said. "I'm already over my limit." He turned to Mac. "Will you ask if she'll see me?"

"I want to think about it some more, Robert. I'll let you know tomorrow. If I do, I'll have to tell her why you want to talk to her. I don't want her blindsided."

"Fair enough," Brixton said.

"And I'd be surprised if she agreed to it. A final question, Robert. If what you say is validated, and you report back to the girl's mother, what do you think *she'll* do with the information?"

"I don't know," Brixton said, accompanied by a shrug. "Maybe it will be sufficient just knowing the truth. I suppose she could go to the press and publicly vindicate her daughter's memory. That's really not up to me." He laughed. "Will Sayers would love the story if it pans out."

"Yes, I suppose he would."

"I really appreciate this, Mac."

"As I said, I'll let you know tomorrow. You'll be in Washington for a while?"

"Until I get to see her, or know she's refused. I'm going to visit one of my daughters tomorrow in Maryland. Here's my cell phone number. Thanks for a great evening."

"It was our pleasure," Annabel said.

After Brixton left, Mac and Annabel sat in Mac's office.

"Do you really think you should ask Mitzi to see him?" she asked.

"Mixed emotions about it, Annie. On the one hand I'm not anxious to be the one to raise this with her — assuming what he says is true. On the other hand, if he *is* right, a serious miscarriage of justice has occurred. All things considered, I think I should follow through. I'm not acting as Mitzi's attorney, just a friend and conduit of the message. I'm sure she'll say no and that'll be the end of it. I told Robert that I would tell her what it's about — without suggesting that she might have been involved — and let her make her own decision."

"No matter how it comes out," Annabel counseled, "Mitzi won't be happy knowing that there's someone in town who thinks she might have been involved in a twenty-year-old homicide."

"And if our first lady might also have been involved —"

"I'd rather not think about *that.* I don't need a nightmare to keep me awake."

Chapter 31

Smith called Brixton at the hotel the next morning to say that he would contact Mitzi Cardell and inform Brixton of the result. But as Brixton drove out of the city on his way to visit Jill, he had second thoughts about using Smith as an intermediary. While he appreciated the distinguished attorney's willingness to make the call, he wondered whether it might be more effective to call Cardell cold and catch her off guard. He reflected back on times during his tenure with the Savannah Metro force when he'd made such calls and how taking the person by surprise had paid dividends. In some cases, the people on the receiving end blurted out things that had proved to be incriminating, or at least had led him to another level of the investigation.

Too late now, he decided as he navigated D.C.'s traffic snarls until reaching less-crowded roads outside the city. As he got closer to the house, his thoughts shifted from Louise Watkins to the reception he might receive, not by his daughter but by Marylee and her haughty mother. His nerves were on edge and he drew deep breaths to lower his pulse rate. *Just stay cool,* he told himself. *Don't let them get to you. Focus on Jill and let whatever comments Marylee and her mother make roll off your back like water off a duck.*

The problem was that he wasn't a duck.

Marylee's faux colonial house looked like all the others in the neighborhood, lots of white cedar shakes and contrasting shutters, blacktop driveways and manicured lawns, probably all built at the same time by the same architect and contractor. He wondered as he pulled in front of the three-car garage why Marylee had never married again. Had her experience with him so soured her on the thought of tying the knot for a second time? She was a good-looking woman who kept herself in shape on the tennis court and in the large pool behind the house. Had her overbearing mother scared away potential suitors? That had to be it, he decided, although that was pure supposition albeit a satisfying one.

Marylee came out of the house and greeted him at the car. She wore a white tennis outfit that showed off her cute bottom and shapely bronzed legs.

"I'm a little late," he said. "Traffic."

"It's okay. I want you to know that Mom isn't well."

"Oh? What's the problem?"

"She has cancer. Lymphoma. She's been going through chemo and radiation."

"I'm sorry to hear it. Is it — ?"

"Terminal? We're all terminal, aren't we?"

"Unfortunately."

"I mention it because she's resting and might not be up to joining us."

Was it too callous to be pleased that she wouldn't be part of the gathering? Probably. He said nothing.

"Is Jill here yet?"

"No. She's on her way."

"I'm sorry Janet couldn't make it."

Marylee's raised eyebrows said it all. "Come on in," she said. "There's someone I'd like you to meet."

He followed her through a door to the kitchen.

"Coffee?" she asked.

"Sure. Black, no sugar."

"You used to take sugar and milk."

"I've changed," he said through a smile. "You haven't."

Their conversation stopped when a man

dressed in tennis whites and sporting an impossibly deep tan entered.

"Robert, this is Miles. Miles Lashka."

The men shook hands. "Good meeting you, Robert," Lashka said. "I've heard nothing but good things about you."

I bet.

"Miles and I play tennis a few times a week," Marylee said. "I'm getting better, thanks to him."

"Don't listen to her," Lashka said. "I hear that you're a private eye. Must be an exciting life."

"Anything but," Brixton said as Marylee handed him his coffee. "What do you do for a living?"

"I'm someone Shakespeare wanted to kill. I'm an attorney, estates."

"Oh," Brixton managed and refrained from saying that he agreed with the Bard.

Their inane back-and-forth was interrupted by Jill's arrival. She gave her mother a hug and kiss and did the same with Lashka, which nettled Brixton. She then kissed her father on the cheek and said to all, "Well, this is the perfect occasion to make an announcement."

Everyone's eyes went to her.

She struck a pose, hand on hip, the other in the air. "Ta da! I — am — pregnant!"

There was silence until Marylee blurted, "That is wonderful news, Jill. When are you due?"

"Eight months." She turned to Brixton. "You're going to be a grandfather."

"Yeah, looks like I am," he said. He hugged her. "Congratulations."

"Mother will be thrilled," Marylee said. "A great-grandchild."

"How is she?" Jill asked.

"All right. Tired. The treatments."

Brixton took in Lashka, who leaned against the counter while the family reacted to the news, and wondered whether there would be a second announcement, that Lashka and Marylee were engaged or planning some other antiquated ritual. He didn't have long to ponder it because his cell phone rang. "Excuse me," he said and went outside.

"It's Mac Smith."

"Hi. Any luck?"

"Afraid not. I spoke with her. She refuses to talk to you."

The news deflated Brixton but he said, "No surprise, huh? I really appreciate what you tried to do."

"Nothing ventured, as they say. I'm off to a meeting but I'll be back at the apartment in a few hours if you want to stop by. I'd like to discuss this further with you."

"Okay. I'll do that. Thanks again."

He clicked off the phone and took a moment to digest the news.

Mitzi Cardell's reaction certainly wasn't unexpected. Smith wanting to talk about it again later in the day was. Had Smith learned something from his conversation with her that might be of interest? Brixton couldn't imagine what that might be and decided it was useless to speculate. He returned inside and joined the group, which now included his former mother-in-law, who wore a pale blue satin bathrobe and slippers. She looked like hell.

Smith ended his call to Brixton and prepared to leave the apartment. Annabel had left hours earlier to tend to business at the gallery. Smith glanced down at notes he'd taken during his call to Mitzi, which included one handwritten line in quotes and underlined.

"Mitzi, it's Mac Smith."

"Good morning, darling. How nice to hear your voice."

"Have I caught you at a bad time?"

"It's always a bad time, Mackensie. I don't know what's happened to this city over the past two years. I simply cannot find trustworthy help these days. I've changed caterers twice and still haven't found one who meets my standards."

Smith laughed, not because he thought it was funny but because it was typical Mitzi Cardell, all aflutter about things that few others cared about. He said, "I'm calling for an unusual reason, Mitzi, and with an equally unusual request."

"Sounds intriguing. Does the CIA want to recruit me for some clandestine mission?"

"As a matter of fact they do, but that's grist for a later call. Mitzi, I've been put in contact with a gentleman through a mutual friend. His name is Robert Brixton. He's a private detective in Savannah, Georgia, and —"

Her frothy tone was gone as she said, "A private detective? Why would you be calling me about *that?*"

"He's working on a case in Savannah that goes back more than twenty years. It has to do with a stabbing that took place in the parking lot of a nightclub there and —"

"Mac, I can't possibly understand why you would be bothering me with something like this."

"The reason I am, Mitzi, is that this Mr.

Brixton would like a few minutes of your time to ask some questions. I said that since I knew you I would call and run it by you."

There was a cold silence on the other end.

"Of course," Smith said, "if you'd rather not take the time I —"

"That is precisely the point, Mac. I do not wish to take the time to speak with this private detective about some sordid stabbing that occurred aeons ago. It sounds as though this man is just looking to stir up trouble and I'm amazed that you would allow yourself to become involved."

"I'm not *involved,* Mitzi, and I certainly understand you not wanting to take time from your busy schedule to meet with him."

"I'm glad you understand, Mac. I'm sorry if I sounded critical of you, but to think that some ages-old common street crime involving black drug dealers — Savannah's crime rate continues to rise, especially in the black community — would find its way here to Washington through this — what did you say his name was?"

"Brixton. Robert Brixton. His interest is in a young woman who might have been unfairly convicted of the crime."

"I've never heard of him or this stabbing or of any young black woman. I really must run, dear. Please tell him that I am not available."

"Of course," said Smith. "Forget I ever mentioned it. But if you want to speak with him, he's here in Washington, staying at the Hotel Rouge on Sixteenth."

"I certainly intend to forget it, Mac. You and your lovely wife must join us again for dinner before much time passes. I'm putting together a party a few weeks from now that you and Annabel would fit into splendidly."

"And we'd be pleased to attend. Thanks for your time, Mitzi."

Smith had been making notes during their conversation, a habit honed during his years as a practicing criminal attorney. He focused on one line he'd written and put quote marks around it and underlined it: ". . . any young black woman."

Mitzi, too, did something after ending her conversation. She called the White House.

"It's Mitzi Cardell," she told Lance Millius. "Please put me through to the first lady." She'd taken a few minutes before placing the call to try to calm down, to bring her breathing under control.

"She's not available, Ms. Cardell."

"This is urgent. I need to speak with her now!"

"I'll pass along your message, Ms. Cardell."

"No, that's not good enough. Find her!"

"I'm sorry, Ms. Cardell, but that is quite impossible. I'll tell her of your call and mention that it's important."

"Yes, you do that."

She slammed down the phone and was sorry that she had. Getting tough with Millius wouldn't accomplish anything.

She waited anxiously for Jeanine to return the call, pacing rooms, curtly fending off questions by the household staff, and ignoring demands on her by outsiders. It was an hour later when the first lady returned her call.

"Jeanine, thank God it's you."

"What's going on, Mitzi? You sound panicked."

"Because I am, and you will be, too."

"Do you think you can pull yourself together and tell me what this is all about?"

"Brixton, that private detective from Savannah."

"Him again? What is it this time?"

"Yes, it's him again, and it's about the same thing."

"This is ridiculous, Mitzi. What can he possibly know?"

"It's obvious that he knows plenty, Jeanine. He had a friend call — Mackensie Smith — to try and set up a meeting with me."

"Who's that?"

"A lawyer. He teaches at GW."

"He's gotten a lawyer involved?"

"Yes. Jeanine, we have to do something and do it now! If this were ever to boil over and become public it would mean — well, you *know* what it will mean."

"Mitzi, you've got to calm down. We can think this through. Where is he now?"

"Brixton? He's here in D.C. at the Hotel Rouge on Sixteenth Street."

"Have you talked to your father?"

"No."

"Call him and see if he knows anything more about this aside from what he told you previously. Get back to me after you do."

"All right, but tell that bastard Millius to put me through the minute I call."

"Just do what I suggested," Jeanine said and hung up.

Ward Cardell had just come in from a swim when his daughter called.

"Hello, honeybunch, how are ya?"

"Terrible."

Her father laughed. "What's the matter, had a foul-up at one of your dinner parties, some drunk congressman fell asleep at the table with his face in the vichyssoise?"

"I'd welcome that, Daddy, after what I've just gone through."

"Hold on now, honey, while I get me into a robe. Ah've been swimmin'. Hot as Hades here."

He listened to her recount the call from Mac Smith. When she was finished, his voice assumed gravitas. "Let me make a few calls about this Brixton character," he said. "Sounds like he's a hard man to get a message through to. Don't you worry. I'll take care of it."

If his words had been intended to comfort and assuage her concerns, they hadn't. She'd no sooner ended that call when she dialed Jeanine Jamison's private number again. Millius answered. "It's Mitzi again. Is she there?"

"Hold on, Ms. Cardell."

Jeanine came on the line. "You talked to your father?"

"Yes. He says not to worry, but I *am* worried. Can you talk where you are?"

"I'm in my office."

"Why does Millius answer your private line?"

"Because I've asked him to. Look, Mitzi, maybe we should get together."

"Soon."

"Tonight. Fletch is off on a trip, back late tonight. Come for dinner."

"I have a dinner party tonight, the Brazilian ambassador and his wife."

"Your choice."

"I can't cancel. Can I come after dinner? I don't care what time it is."

Jeanine's sigh indicated what she thought of that suggestion, but she said, "All right. But make it as early as possible. Develop a headache before dessert. Goodbye."

Brixton stayed for lunch at Marylee's house but made his excuses as soon as it seemed acceptable. "I have to get back to D.C.," he said.

"Business?" Miles Lashka asked.

The attorney, who sat next to Marylee at the table and made a habit of touching her hand and whispering in her ear, struck Brixton as a phony but probably a successful one. He'd spent a good deal of time discussing the trouble he was having with his backhand, and if Brixton heard "Miles says" or "Miles thinks" or "Miles knows a lot about that" from Marylee one more time he would've been tempted to tip the table over on them. Was Marylee about to marry this guy with a deficient backhand? If he cared, he would have taken her aside and advised her to dump him. But the truth was that he didn't care, at least not about what she decided to do with her love life.

His daughter was more ebullient than he'd ever remembered, the pregnancy undoubtedly contributing to her bubbly conversation. As for his mother-in-law, she begged off lunch and went to take a nap.

"Hope you're feeling better," Brixton said as she left the room.

"Goodbye, Robert," she said, her words trailing behind her.

Brixton bid goodbye to everyone, giving Jill an especially warm hug and kiss. "I think it's great that you're going to have a kid," he said.

"If it's a boy I'm going to name him Robert," she said.

It touched him.

"Hope your backhand gets better," he said to Lashka.

"Just a matter of practice," said the attorney with a wide grin — he had perfect teeth — and a manly slap on Brixton's arm.

He drove back toward The District but pulled off at a rest stop to make calls on his cell phone. The first was to Flo at her shop.

"How's it going?" she asked.

"Not so good. Mac Smith called Mitzi

Cardell and got the brush-off. I just left Marylee's house. Jill's pregnant."

"Congratulations, Grandpa."

"I'll forget you said that. What's happening in sunny Savannah?"

"Hot. Wayne St. Pierre called. He said that he'd invited you to a party but since you're out of town he wondered if I'd like to come stag."

"Men go stag."

"Whatever. I told him where you were staying in case he wanted to reach you."

"Marylee has a boyfriend."

"Good for her."

"He's a quarter-inch deep. A lawyer."

"Your favorite people.

"I'm heading for Mac Smith's place now. He said he wanted to talk more about the case."

"Good. I'm not going to Wayne's party."

"Your call. I'll stay in touch."

His next call was to Cynthia at his office. She reported that nothing was new, no calls from potential clients or bill collectors. "Oh," she said, "Will Sayers called from the newspaper. He wanted you to know that he's heading for Washington a few days sooner than he expected. Here's his phone number there."

Brixton found a scrap of paper in the car

and jotted down the number. After ending the call with Cynthia he got back on the road and continued toward the center of Washington. As he drove he had an idea. What if he could persuade Sayers, a member of the almighty press, to call Mitzi Cardell and ask for a statement from her about the Louise Watkins investigation? He wasn't sure Sayers would do it based upon the little Brixton had as evidence, but it was worth a try.

A half hour later he parked in the Watergate's garage and was on his way up in the elevator to the Smiths' apartment.

Chapter 32

A meeting took place that afternoon in the windowless basement room of the two-story modern office building south of the Pentagon. Dexter sat in one of four folding metal chairs at the folding metal table.

Across from him was a man of medium height. His hair was the color of beach sand after a rainstorm. His cheeks were slightly pockmarked, his ears larger than his face called for. He wore a light green T-shirt, jeans, and white sneakers. Although he was slender, the muscles of his arms were nicely defined and his chest strained against the shirt's fabric.

"You realize, James, that your work will be spasmodic," Dexter said in his pinched voice. "You'll be on call at all times and are to take orders only from me. We will meet at various locations chosen by me. You are also aware that while your assignments will be generously compensated, the duration of your employment can end at any time. Is this all understood?"

"Sure, I understand," James Brockman said.

He'd been recruited over the course of months, carefully vetted including a psychological evaluation, and meticulously informed of his responsibilities should he be called upon to undertake an assignment for his employer.

"You've impressed us, James. Your sense of duty and patriotism is exemplary. So few of us have the privilege and honor of serving this great nation in such a direct way in its time of need."

"I'm happy to serve."

"I know that you are. I suggest that you fall into your normal lifestyle, doing nothing to attract attention. I believe that the advance you've been given is sufficient for you to enjoy a financially sound lifestyle until you're needed."

"No problem."

"Fine. You'll hear from me soon."

Dexter ignored Brockman's extended hand and his newest hire left.

Bob Brixton sat with Mac Smith in Smith's home office.

"And she mentioned a young black girl

without you having said it?" Brixton said after Smith had filled him in on his call to Mitzi Cardell.

"Yes, which says to me that she's obviously aware of what occurred in that parking lot twenty years ago."

"I had an idea while driving," Brixton said. "Willis Sayers is here reopening the *Savannah Morning News* bureau. I was wondering whether he'd be willing to call her and ask some questions. If she thinks the media is on to it she might decide to open up a little."

"It's worth a try, I suppose," Smith replied, "although it could backfire, cause her to stonewall even further."

"You're right, but I'd still like to give it a try."

Smith pointed to his phone. "Be my guest," he said.

Brixton dialed the number given him by Cynthia. Sayers picked up immediately.

"It's Bob Brixton."

"Hey, pal, how goes it?"

"Okay. I'm sitting here with Mac Smith."

"Say hello."

"Shall do." He filled Sayers in on what had transpired and suggested that he call Mitzi.

"Yeah, I think it's a good idea. If what you

told me back in Savannah is true, I might get this bureau off to a hell of a good start. Where are you staying?"

"The Hotel Rouge on Sixteenth Street. Here's the number."

"You'll hear from me."

Sayers didn't waste any time in calling Mitzi Cardell. Before Brixton even left Smith's apartment in the Watergate, the rotund reporter was on the phone. Mitzi's social secretary answered.

"This is Willis Sayers, Washington bureau chief for the *Savannah Morning News.* I'd like to speak with Ms. Cardell."

"What is it in reference to?"

"A story I'm working on about a crime that occurred in Savannah twenty years ago."

"Please hold."

She went to where Mitzi was reviewing the menu for that night's dinner party for the Brazilian ambassador and his wife. "There's a reporter from the Savannah paper on the line. He wants to speak with you."

"About what?"

"Something to do with a twenty-year-old crime in Savannah."

Mitzi sat heavily in her chair.

"You okay?" her secretary asked.

"Yes, I'm fine. Tell him I'm not available."

The secretary told Sayers what she'd been instructed to say.

"Here's my number. Please have her call me as soon as she's free."

It was a busy day at Annabel Lee Smith's gallery. There seemed to be more tourists than usual. Hordes of men and women deftly avoided bumping into one another on Georgetown's congested Wisconsin Avenue and M Streets, the centers of this trendy albeit commercial section of the nation's capital. Shops of every description lined the streets, a browser's paradise. The attractive window display that Annabel had created stopped its share of admirers, many of whom decided to explore further inside — and to enjoy a refreshing dose of air-conditioning.

She was engaged in conversation with a visiting couple from Germany whose knowledge of pre-Columbian art was impressive, and Annabel thought she might have a potential paying customer. But they said they'd return another day, and Annabel walked them to the door. As she bid them farewell, she looked outside and saw Emile Silva staring at the gallery. It took a few seconds for her to recognize him. When she did, she realized that he was the man who'd been in the gallery a few mornings earlier, the man for whom Mac had developed an instant suspicion. She avoided his eyes and closed the door. A moment later the bell over the door sounded and he entered.

"Hello," he said.

"Hello."

"I've been here before," he said.

"Have you?"

"Yes. You don't recognize me?"

"I'm sorry but I don't. I'm getting ready to close." They were alone.

Silva ignored her and slowly, deliberately went to each piece of art and stood before it before moving on to the next piece.

"Is there something specific I can help you with?" Annabel asked, moving close to the telephone on her desk.

"No, nothing specific."

"Well, I'm sorry but I really have to close up now. Thank you for stopping by."

He turned and stared at her. What was he thinking? she wondered. Was he angry? She now realized what it was that had set Mac on edge about him. His eyes were dull, dead, as though disconnected from his brain, separated from his emotional cortex.

What should I do? she wondered. *Demand*

that he leave? Try to coax him out the door?

Before she could decide on a course of action, he smiled, turned, and was gone, carrying with him the visual image he'd created of her naked. He'd mentally stripped her of her clothing.

Annabel shuddered as though she were, indeed, naked, chilled. She went to the door, locked it, turned the sign so that it read CLOSED, and slumped against the wall.

Chapter 33

". . . And so we've managed to pull ourselves out of our six-month recession far faster than more developed economies and are well on our way to solid financial footing. We predict a five-and-a-half-percent growth in our gross national product this year with little risk of inflation."

Mitzi fought to continue feigning interest in what the Brazilian ambassador was saying. He was a charming man personally, but he enjoyed pontificating about his country's more enlightened economic policies. Others at the table seemed interested in his prognostications, but all Mitzi could think about was leaving for the White House. She considered doing what Jeanine had suggested, pretend to fall ill and excuse herself. But that would have cast a pall over the party, something she was loath to do.

As they left the dinner table, her husband, John, asked if she was feeling well.

"Yes, I'm fine," she said. "Just tired."

"Maybe you ought to cut back on the parties," he whispered, "take a breather. We can get away and —"

"Have you ever been to Brazil?" the ambassador interrupted.

"No, I've never had the pleasure," Mitzi responded.

"I have business connections there," her husband said, "and have spent many pleasurable weeks in Brasília." He and the ambassador crossed the room to join others who were being served after-dinner drinks in the library.

Mitzi excused herself, went to a quiet room, and called Jeanine's private number.

Lance Millius answered.

"It's Mitzi Cardell."

"She's not available at the moment, Ms. Cardell. Can I leave a message?"

"No, no, I'll call again later."

It was another hour before the gathering broke up and guests scattered to wherever it was they were going. John Muszinski kissed his wife's cheek and announced that he was going to bed. "Coming?" he asked.

"No, I'm wide awake. I told Jeanine that I might get together with her once the party broke up."

"At *this* hour? Whatever for?"

"She, ah — she wanted to run a few ideas by me. She's heading to Savannah for the school's fund-raiser and wanted my input."

"Can't it wait until tomorrow?"

"Oh, God, no, John. My schedule is overflowing tomorrow. You run along and get a good night's sleep. I won't be long."

His face reflected his confusion but he knew not to press once she'd made up her mind. "As you wish," he said and planted another kiss. "Don't be too late."

Mitzi spent a few minutes checking on the cleanup. Satisfied that it was going smoothly, she went to her study and called Jeanine. Again, it was Millius who picked up the phone. Mitzi announced herself. "Just a minute, Ms. Cardell."

"Successful party?" Jeanine asked.

"I suppose so. I'm heading there now."

"I've arranged with security."

"Good."

A half hour later, Mitzi sat with the first lady in her office.

"Does he have to be there?" Mitzi asked, referring to Millius, who worked at a computer in the anteroom.

"Forget him, Mitzi. Okay, so this Brixton character is in Washington and tried to reach you. That doesn't mean he knows anything."

"It's worse, Jeanine. I got a call from a reporter for the Savannah paper, some guy named Sayers."

"I've heard the name."

"He told my secretary that he wanted to talk to me about a twenty-year-old crime that happened in Savannah. The stabbing! Jesus, the press is involved now."

Jeanine sat back and rubbed her eyes. "That *is* cause for concern. How did he get onto it?"

"I don't know. Probably this Brixton. This is all about to come tumbling down on you, Jeanine."

Jeanine lowered her hands and leaned forward. " 'Tumbling down on *me*'?"

"Well, yes, of course. It was you who stabbed him and —"

"And it was your father who paid the Watkins girl to go to prison."

They stared at each other, their eyes transmitting their conflicting thoughts.

"Look," Jeanine finally said, "there's nothing to be gained by deciding who's more to blame. The important thing is to come up with a plan to head it off. Do you have any suggestions?"

"No." Mitzi twisted her fingers; she was on the verge of tears.

After a thoughtful pause, Jeanine said,

"There's a lot more at stake here than having paid off Watkins. Do you realize what this will do to Fletch and his presidency?"

"I wasn't thinking about that," Mitzi said.

"Well, I think you'd better start thinking *about that,* Mitzi."

"This is terrible," Mitzi said.

"How did you leave it with the reporter?"

"I said I wasn't available. He left his number."

"You didn't call him back."

"Of course not."

"We have to assume that whatever this reporter knows he got from Brixton, and what can Brixton have? Damn little. It's not like it happened yesterday, for Christ's sake. It happened over twenty years ago. What about this attorney friend of yours?"

"Mackensie Smith? I don't know what Brixton has told him."

The tears came.

"Stop it!" Jeanine said. "Crying isn't going to solve a goddamn thing."

"My reputation will be ruined," Mitzi said as she fished a Kleenex from her purse.

"*Your* reputation!" Jeanine snapped.

"We can't let this happen," Mitzi said and blew her nose.

"No, we can't."

"Did you ever tell Fletcher about it?"

Mitzi asked.

"Of course not."

"Maybe —"

"Maybe I should have? You're right. I can't allow him to be surprised by this, wake up and read about it in the papers. Can this Brixton be bought off?"

"How would I know?"

"I'm sure the reporter can't be. Your lawyer friend?"

Mitzi shook her head. "No. He's —"

Jeanine got up and paced the room, her hand to her forehead. When she resumed her seat she said, "I'll have to tell Fletch about this. He's due back any minute now."

"What do you think he'll say?"

"He'll blow his stack. Maybe you should tell John."

Mitzi shuddered.

"I know this," Jeanine said. "I'm not going to see my life or Fletch's presidency ruined because of some dime-store, white-trash private detective looking to make a buck."

Jeanine's hard tone was palpable, and Mitzi recoiled from it.

"I'll talk to Fletch tonight. You go on home. I'll call you tomorrow. In the meantime don't mention this to anyone. Got that? Not anyone!"

CHAPTER 34

Fletcher Jamison, president of the United States, blustered into the White House, followed by a gaggle of attentive aides. He'd just returned from giving a speech in support of his agenda to rescind regulations on financial institutions that had been imposed by the preceding administration. It had gone over well with the handpicked crowd, and the warm reception they gave him was a welcome tonic after what had otherwise been a bad day. Congress had balked at his most recent budgetary proposals, and the latest polls showed his popularity heading for the tank. A small group of vocal, sign-carrying opponents had made their feelings known outside the auditorium.

"Jerks!" Jamison had muttered once back in the limo and headed for the airport where Air Force One awaited him.

"They're meaningless," an aide said. "All mouth, no substance."

"You'd think they'd get a life," the president said.

"They like to protest," the aide said. "They latch on to any reason to carry their stupid signs and chant slogans."

"What the hell do they want from me?" Jamison snarled as the limo and security vehicles neared the airport. "The media takes these polls and twists them to suit their agenda."

"Exactly," another aide enthusiastically agreed.

Jamison had grabbed a fast nap on the flight back to D.C., although it hadn't done anything to improve his disposition. His aides knew to stay clear when he was in one of his moods, and they did so until he was back in the White House, had received a quick briefing on the day's headlines from his political adviser, and headed for the first family's private quarters, where his personal assistant stood at attention, ready to accept Jamison's discarded clothing and to fetch him anything he might want. As usual, it was a glass of his favorite Tennessee mash whiskey with a splash of water, and popcorn.

Jeanine waited for him in her bedroom. She'd rehearsed what she would say and how she would say it, choosing her words carefully, dismissing the incident in the parking lot as a frivolous teenage evening gone awry, making light of it while at the same time letting him know of her concern for what it might mean should the story end up in the media. She chose a deep pink cashmere sweater to wear, a favorite of her husband's, and form-fitting black slacks. Her musings took many directions, including the possibility that offering sex might mitigate his reaction to bad news. It had worked before.

I should have told him about it when we first started going together, she thought. He had plenty of skeletons in his closet, too. But she hadn't mentioned it for fear of losing him, of crushing her chance to become the first lady of Georgia. That she'd end up in the White House was beyond any dreams she had conjured, and when he announced that he was running for the presidency it seemed too late to spring a complication like murder on him.

She tried to imagine all the negative fallout that might occur if the story broke, and none of it was pretty. His political opponents would jump on it and turn it into a media circus, night after night of coverage on what had become a 24/7 news cycle, talking heads analyzing its meaning to death, pundits making cruel remarks, the late-night comedy shows, Jon Stewart, and *Saturday Night Live* having a field day.

"Maybe the president should dispatch his wife to kill off his opponents," the comics would quip.

"The president means it when he says he wants to *slash* the budget."

"If the president pulls a John Edwards on his wife he'd better watch his back — in bed!"

"Jeanine Jamison, our own Lizzie Borden."

Those visions made her cringe in the chair as she awaited his arrival.

He'd changed into his nightclothes in his private dressing quarters before entering the bedroom. She sprang to her feet, crossed the room, and kissed him. He noticed what she was wearing and asked why.

"Oh, I just thought I'd try and look pretty for you."

"Well, you do."

His assistant arrived with the whiskey and popcorn. "Would you like something, ma'am?" he asked.

"Yes, I would, a glass of Chablis please." The assistant left and she asked the president how his day had gone.

"The speech went fine. The rest of the day makes me wish I'd stayed governor of Georgia."

"That bad, huh?"

"The goddamn polls. They mean nothing, but the media lives and dies by them."

Her wine was delivered and they sat across a small table from each other in front of the draped window. She raised her glass. "To good days ahead," she said with a wide smile.

"I'll drink to that," he said, touching the rim of his glass to hers.

"Fletch, there's something we have to talk about."

"Oh? Sounds heavy."

"I suppose it is. No, it really isn't. You see —"

"You having an affair?"

She guffawed and spit out some of her wine. "Don't be ridiculous."

He shrugged and drank.

"Fletch, something happened many years ago in Savannah that I've kept to myself all these years."

Nothing from him.

"You see, when I was a teenager — a silly teenager, I admit — I went to a local hangout with Mitzi when my folks were away for the weekend. It was a dive called Augie's. Lots of kids from the other side of the tracks hung out there and I suppose it represented danger to us, an adventure, you know, tasting something forbidden."

He seemed disinterested, simply grunted and tasted his drink again and took a handful of popcorn from the sterling silver bowl.

"Something happened there, Fletch, that — well, it was something bad."

"I know, you tried marijuana. Shame on you."

"It was more than that," she said. "There was also a young black girl there. Her name was Louise Watkins."

"So?"

"So, we got into a conversation with her, at least Mitzi did. I was talking to a young guy who invited me outside. I'd seen him before and —"

"So it wasn't your first time there."

"No, it wasn't. Anyway, I went outside with him and —"

"Spare me the details, Jeanine."

"He tried to rape me, Fletch."

That got his full attention. He put down his glass and leaned toward her. "He *tried* to rape you? Did he? Rape you?"

"No. I — I — he had a knife and threatened to use it unless I got in the car with him."

"Bastard!"

"Yes, he was a bastard, Fletch. I —"

"What happened?"

"He tried to use the knife and I fought him and the knife got turned around and it went into *him.*"

"He — ?"

"He died."

"He was killed?"

"Yes."

"Then what happened?"

"Here's where it gets complicated, Fletch. I mentioned the black girl, Louise Watkins. She'd come out of the club with Mitzi, saw what happened, and helped us get away."

"Get away?"

A tear formed in Jeanine's right eye. "We ran. This girl threw the knife in a river or stream and we went home like nothing ever happened."

"You were never connected with it?"

"That's right."

He stood, parted the drapes, and looked out over the lighted lawn and shrubs. "I'm shocked, of course," he said without looking at her, "but it turned out all right." He leaned over her. "There's nothing else, Jeanine? That was the end of it? What did the police do, chalk it up as another unsolved homicide?"

She avoided his eyes and said, "Not exactly."

"I hate 'not exactly.' Be specific. What

then? They accused someone else of the crime?"

"Yes."

"That person did time for it?"

"Yes."

"Tough on that unfortunate person but —"

"The black girl was convicted of it."

"How — ?"

"She was a screwed-up girl, Fletch, a drug dealer and prostitute. She didn't go to prison for long, just four years."

"That's good to hear."

"She tried to blackmail us."

"What?"

"She tried to blackmail me and Mitzi. She wanted a thousand dollars to keep her mouth shut."

"You paid her?"

"No. Mitzi's father did, ten thousand dollars."

"Ward Cardell paid her ten thousand bucks? You said she wanted a thousand."

"Just to keep quiet. Mr. Cardell paid her more money to confess that she did it and to accept the prison term."

His laugh reflected amazement rather than joy. "And she bought it?"

"Yes."

"Did you have any contact with her after

she came out of prison?"

"No. She was murdered days after she got out. Someone shot her on the street. They said it was one of those drive-by shootings, probably drug dealers."

Jamison pressed a button that summoned his personal aide. "Another drink," he said.

"Ma'am?" the aide asked Jeanine.

"What? Yes. Another wine."

Jamison took his seat across from her again. He stared her down, causing Jeanine to avert his gaze. "Okay," he said, "let's pick up where we left off. From what you're saying, this whole sordid affair happened long ago, past history, so why bring it up to me now?"

"Because it's surfaced again, Fletch."

"How?"

She told him about Brixton, and about the newspaper reporter who'd called Mitzi. "And there's a D.C. lawyer involved, too, somebody named Mackensie Smith."

"I've met him. You say this Brixton is involved in the case? How so?"

She explained that he was representing Louise Watkins's family, which was all that she knew. She awaited his reaction, ready to brace against an angry tirade. With his second drink in his hand, he said in measured tones, "This obviously has the potential to turn into a major flap, Jeanine, the sort of bombshell this town thrives on. Do you have any idea of what the ramifications are?"

"I've been running them through my mind all night, Fletch. I know I should have told you this years ago but —"

"Let's not play the should-have, would-have game, Jeanine. It's too late for that. This private detective has to be stopped. I assume he's the one feeding information to the reporter."

"It looks that way."

"How much has Mitzi confided in her father?"

"I know she's spoken with him a few times. I encouraged her to."

"Ward Cardell has been a friend throughout my career, a loyal supporter. I can call him."

"Maybe you shouldn't."

"I'll think about it. You've made quite a mess of things."

"I certainly didn't mean to, Fletch. It was all so long ago and I was young and —"

"This guy Brixton is the problem. He has to be shut down before he goes any further."

"What do you want me to do?"

"Nothing. Just keep your mouth shut. I'll take care of it."

She tried to entice him into bed but he balked. "I have some thinking to do," he said and left the room.

Chapter 35

Jeanine Jamison had waited up almost two hours for her husband to return and finally dozed off well past midnight. When she awoke that morning after a restless, nightmare-laden sleep, he was gone.

She'd stumbled to her dressing table and observed herself in the Hollywood-style mirror. She didn't like what she saw. Bags under her eyes were exaggerated and dark; her eyes lacked the sort of gleam associated with being alive.

She showered, and dressed for the day with the help of a female aide, trying all the while to sound her usual self, upbeat and positive. It wasn't easy, with what she'd gone through the night before. The president's reaction had been surprisingly benign, although she was certain that he seethed inside. He didn't need this complication to add to what he faced each day from a cantankerous Congress and a constituency on the verge of abandoning him and his agenda. She wanted desperately to do something to resolve the mess she'd led him into but had no idea what that might be.

Mitzi's involvement hadn't struck Jeanine as a problem while leveling with the president. But in the gray light of early morning it loomed large. Her friend was known to be flighty and easily sent off-balance; her husband often joked that his wife tripped over bobby pins and paper clips. Was she likely to lose control and blurt something out to the wrong person? Could she be depended upon to keep their confidence and not do something rash? Jeanine couldn't be sure, and she dwelled on this while breakfasting in the private dining room.

What would Fletch do now that he knew? When he'd left the bedroom he said he had some thinking to do. What did that mean? What *could* he do? Would he confide in close aides and garner their opinions? She hoped he wouldn't. It was embarrassing enough to have gotten into such a mess without the people with whom she interacted on a daily basis knowing that she'd stabbed someone to death, and had gone along with the scheme to cast the blame on another.

Louise Watkins!

That scene twenty years ago at Augie's was as clear in Jeanine's mind as the evening it happened. Shortly after the incident she would think of Louise sitting in a prison cell and suffer oppressive guilt. But those moments eventually passed, as unpleasant ones often do, and it was rare that she found herself immersed in such introspection. Of course, when Louise emerged from prison and was gunned down, the guilt had resurfaced. But that, too, had passed with time. . . .

Until now!

Damn this private detective named Brixton. How dare he threaten to drag something from the past into the present and hurt others in the process? Her mind was like a fast-moving slide show of emotions — anger, then a return to feelings of guilt, oppressive remorse, back to anger, and on to wishing it had never happened. But it *had* happened. And it was happening all over again.

It was now possible, more likely probable, that the world would know what had gone down that steamy summer night in Savannah.

Who currently knew?

The detective, Brixton.

The reporter, Sayers.

The lawyer, Mackensie Smith.

Her friend, Mitzi Cardell.

Mitzi's father, Ward Cardell.

The president of the United States.

Were there others?

She had to assume that there were.

Of course there were.

She was deep into these upsetting thoughts as she went downstairs to her office, where her staff awaited. Missing was Lance Millius. She asked about him.

"He called in, Mrs. Jamison. He has some personal business and will be here after lunch."

Millius's absence wasn't upsetting. She was aware that he worked impossibly long hours and was entitled to as much time off as he needed.

Other members of her staff conferred with her about projects for which they were responsible, and she forced herself to concentrate on what they said, banishing those other nasty thoughts to their own compartment. But they rushed back to the forefront the minute there was a lull in the conversation and she wondered how she would get through the day.

Millius had been up and out of his Bethesda apartment early that morning. He'd received a call at six from President Jamison's chief of staff, Chet Lounsbury, who said that the president wanted to meet with him privately; he was to tell no one, including the first lady.

"What's it about?" Millius asked.

"I haven't the slightest idea," Lounsbury replied, sounding annoyed.

The relationship between Millius and Lounsbury was tenuous at best. It wasn't lost on Lounsbury that despite being chief of staff to the president of the United States, his counterpart in the first lady's office maintained a closer, strangely special relationship with the president. It went back to Jamison's tenure as governor of Georgia, when Millius was his right-hand man in more ways than one. Rumors abounded about the role the young man played in the governor's inner sanctum. Some said that Millius was the cleanup man for Jamison's indiscretions. There were even those who claimed that there were dead bodies in Jamison's past and that Millius had had a hand in arranging for certain individuals to be "neutralized." It was all juicy political gossipmongering, of course, and no one had ever developed evidence to support the rumors.

When Millius was named the first lady's

chief of staff, it had set off another round of rumors and speculation. Some considered it a demotion for Millius, and he was asked that question a few times by reporters. His boilerplate response served to cut off further inquiries, although skepticism remained: "The president feels that the first lady will play a vitally important role in his administration and wants me to help her achieve her goals. I consider working directly with her to be a welcome challenge as well as an opportunity to help shape the president's ambitious agenda for the American people."

Millius's boilerplate statement was dutifully reported, while the reporters covering him laughed among themselves. No one pressed Lance Millius for a more cogent comment. From the day Fletcher Jamison took office it was understood by the press corps that Lance Millius had the president's ear. Offend him and you offended the president of the United States. Goodbye press pass. Goodbye access. Goodbye career.

"Where?" Millius asked Lounsbury.

"The Treaty Room, nine thirty sharp."

The line went dead.

Millius looked down at the silent receiver in his hand and smiled. He had little use for

Lounsbury and enjoyed those moments when his West Wing counterpart was unhappy.

After showering and dressing, he retrieved his new silver Lexus from his apartment building's garage and drove to the White House, where he parked in his reserved spot. He passed through security and chose a route to the second floor of the West Wing that circumvented the first lady's suite of offices in the East Wing.

One of Jamison's personal aides who'd been awaiting Millius's arrival went to summon the president. While waiting, Millius went to a large overmantel mirror on the west wall and checked his appearance in it. Satisfied, he sat in a chair on the visitor's side of the Treaty Table on which President McKinley had signed the peace treaty with Spain in 1898, which ended the Spanish-American War. The room had been the private office of a succession of first ladies until Rosalynn Carter moved in and preferred that her office be on the first floor in the East Wing, closer to the center of government and political activity, closer to her husband.

He was studying the ornate Victorian chandelier above him when Jamison entered, closing the door behind him. Millius stood but Jamison waved him back down and took his chair on the opposite side of the table.

"There's a messy situation looming that I want cleaned up before it happens," Jamison said.

Millius nodded.

"It involves the first lady, but I don't want your participation in it known to her."

"All right, Mr. President."

"It's a long, convoluted story, Lance. I'll try to be as brief as possible. You don't need to know all the details. It involves a man named Robert Brixton. He's a —"

"Sorry to interrupt, sir, but there's something you should know."

"What's that?"

"I'm aware of this man, Brixton. The first lady asked me to run a background check on him."

Jamison's expression mirrored his surprise. "When did she do that?"

"A number of days ago. I had the check run and provided it to her."

"Did she tell you why she wanted it done?"

"No, sir, and I didn't ask. I mention this only to let you know that I already know something about him."

"I suppose she forgot to mention it to me.

It doesn't matter. It gives you a head start. You have the results?"

Millius hesitated. He'd made a photocopy of the dossier on Brixton and taken it with him. He said, "I have access to it, sir. What do you want me to do?"

Jamison didn't hesitate. "I want this Brixton shut up."

"Could you be more specific, sir?"

"Do I have to be?"

Millius's silence confirmed to the president that further specific instructions weren't necessary.

"I'll only say this, Lance. If Brixton is allowed to continue delving into the first lady's life — into my life by extension — it could have a terrible impact on my administration."

"I'll have to be away from the office for a while, Mr. President. Will you speak with Mrs. Jamison and — ?"

"There's no need for that. I don't see this dragging out for very long. She's off to Savannah. She'll be there for a few days. Get this thing done before she comes back."

Jamison stood and looked as though he had something else to say. Millius waited. The president came around the Treaty Table, slapped Millius on his shoulder, and was gone.

■ ■ ■ ■

The first lady's chief of staff followed the route he'd used when he'd arrived to avoid Jeanine's offices, got in his car, and drove away from the White House grounds. He crossed the Potomac over the Key Bridge, pulled off the road, opened the trunk, and removed the Brixton file he'd claimed to have taken home with him. He got back into the Lexus, pulled a cell phone from the glove compartment, chose a stored number, and pushed the speed-dial button.

"Hello."

"It's Lance."

"How are you?"

"I'm fine. I have a message for you."

"Good."

"Can we meet?"

"I think so. When?"

"Now."

"Where are you?"

"In Virginia, right off the Key Bridge."

"The Island in a half hour. The parking lot."

Millius ended the call.

Millius next called the Hotel Rouge.

"Mr. Brixton please. He's a registered guest."

The desk clerk rang the room. "I'm sorry but Mr. Brixton doesn't seem to be in at the moment."

Good, he thought. *He's still registered there.*

He waited a few minutes before driving away and heading for the Theodore Roosevelt Island and Memorial, a ninety-one-acre marshland and wildlife sanctuary in the Potomac between the Key and Theodore Roosevelt Bridges, a fitting tribute to the ecologically minded twenty-sixth president of the United States. He entered the island from the northbound lanes of the George Washington Parkway, pulled into the parking lot, and walked to the eighteen-foot tall bronze statue of Roosevelt, where the man he was meeting stood. They shook hands and strolled casually to an area void of tourists.

"What do you have?" asked the man, who was dressed in a gray suit, white shirt, and tie.

Millius handed him the envelope containing the Brixton report. The man tucked it under his arm and they continued their walk, stopping again in a grove of trees.

"This is from the top?" the man asked.

"Yes. It has to be done quickly."

The man smiled. "I believe they call it 'stat' in emergency rooms."

"I suppose."

"The reason?"

"I'm not at liberty to say."

"Where?"

"Here in Washington. He's staying at the Hotel Rouge, on Sixteenth. There are photos of him in the envelope."

"I'm not sure how fast they can act."

"Whatever it takes. The funds are there."

"Sounds important."

"It is. Anything else you need from me?"

"Not at the moment. If there is I'll contact you."

"Good. You leave first. I'll follow later."

Millius watched him saunter away and breathed a sigh of relief. He hadn't been sure that he could put it into motion that quickly. In past cases it had involved a lot of strategic planning that meant days, sometimes weeks of delays. *Business must be slow,* he thought as he returned to the Roosevelt statue and read from the four granite tablets surrounding it, each containing Roosevelt's thoughts on nature and the state. *Roosevelt would be proud,* he thought as he walked away. *He was a man who appreciated action.*

The man with whom Millius had met returned to his office at CIA headquarters, in

Langley, Virginia, and went to his office, a small space behind a sign: STATISTICAL RECONCILIATION. He sat behind his desk and perused what Millius had given him. There wasn't a doubt in his mind that the request had been initiated by the president. Millius was Jamison's point man when it came to arranging unusual assignments at the CIA. His word was as good as the president's, and had been since Fletcher Jamison was governor of Georgia.

Chapter 36

The office of Statistical Reconciliation, STAT-RECON, was tucked away in a secluded corner of CIA headquarters. Its existence went back more than sixty years under other names. Its stated mission was to analyze statistical information gathered by various agency intelligence sources. Its budget as included in the agency's annual report to Congress was modest; its official listing on the CIA's organizational chart showed it reporting to the chief of Statistical Intelligence. It was manned, according to staffing reports, by four people. Its current leader was the man who'd just met with Lance Millius on Roosevelt Island.

STAT-RECON was the outgrowth of a small, secret wing of the agency that came into existence in the late 1950s under the blanket term *Executive Action.* While the CIA was created to garner intelligence from America's Cold War enemies, it was decided that it would also be necessary, at times, to take a more proactive stance — in other words, to "eliminate" selected enemies who posed a distinct threat to the nation's security. The National Security Council (NSC) and its internal "Special Group," also known as the 40 Committee, whose mandate was to "counter, reduce and discredit International Communism," was established to oversee the Executive Action group within the CIA. These assassination attempts, either through direct action initiated by the CIA or by supportive groups within the target's own country, necessitated establishing a clandestine operation to undertake "wet jobs," the killing of foreign leaders — and others — when called upon to do so by the president and his top intelligence officials.

Because of its secretive nature, its operations and budgets were shielded not only from congressional oversight but from other top government officials. It functioned as a separate entity within the intelligence community, answerable to no one except the highest echelons of the CIA and NSC. There had been concern when the group was formed that because of its clandestine structure there was the possibility of perversion of its reason for existing. But that was considered a small price to pay when compared to the potential gains it could achieve.

Attempts were made on the lives of such foreign leaders as Patrice Lumumba of the Congo; Fidel Castro of Cuba; Rafael Trujillo of the Dominican Republic; Ngo Dinh Diem of Vietnam; and General René Schneider of Chile. Some succeeded, some didn't. But always these undertakings were conducted with "plausible denial" uppermost in mind.

The fear that such a secret organization within the government might be used for nefarious purposes was well founded.

In the 1950s, a small group of wealthy men, primarily oil barons from the Southwest, got together to discuss what they considered the downward path the nation was taking. At that time, the president, John F. Kennedy, had captured the American public. The White House had become Camelot; the youthful president could do no wrong in the eyes of most Americans. But the small group of wealthy men saw things differently. Kennedy's agenda concerned them. He talked of pulling back support for the South Vietnamese government, which they viewed not only as creating an opening for a Communist takeover of Asia — the "domino effect" — but as negatively impacting the financial health of the military-industrial complex. Too, Kennedy's failure to support the Cuban exiles and their 1961 attempt to topple Fidel Castro, or to destroy Castro during the Cuban missile crisis of 1962, said to them that it was time to alter the course of the nation they professed to love, no matter how dramatic the required actions might be.

Their initial financial support of projects aimed at carrying out their vision was soon enhanced by donations from other wealthy men across the country. In effect, they created a government of their own with its own purpose — to rid the country of leaders whose visions for the nation clashed with theirs. They found willing accomplices within a small, rogue group of CIA operatives, and a complex web of financial fronts was established to further fund operations.

As always, plausible denial was a sacrosanct concept, both for the rogue element within the CIA and for this group of men. From the beginning, the actual dirty work was farmed out to individuals and organizations far removed from those who gave the orders. Members of organized crime were called upon from time to time to carry out hits on the group's selected targets. In some cases, warped individuals with the wherewithal to eliminate a selected target, and who believed in the group's brand of perverted patriotism, were utilized.

The wealthy cabal's success in ridding the country of those they felt were taking the nation in the wrong direction began in spectacular fashion on November 22, 1963, in Dallas's Dealey Plaza, when President John Kennedy was shot dead. Five years later, on June 5, 1968, the slain president's brother, Robert Kennedy, a candidate for the presidency, was gunned down in the kitchen of a hotel in Los Angeles where he'd just given his victory speech after winning the California Democratic primary. In both cases, plausible denial was effectively implemented. Official reports on both assassinations concluded that the killers of the two Kennedys were lone gunmen acting alone. No conspiracy was determined. The group and its backers were free to continue their "crusade."

As the years passed, it was decided that a more well-ordered assembly of on-tap killers was needed. That's when three men in Washington, D.C., each a former CIA operative, established a clearinghouse, an employment agency of sorts to provide selected individuals to accomplish further assassinations as deemed necessary. Included among the three was a small, bald, bespectacled man known to his colleagues, and to those he recruited as paid assassins, only as Dexter.

Carrying the folder containing information on Robert Brixton, the man left Langley and drove to a parking lot in Maryland, where he used a special cell phone to make a call.

"Dexter?"

"Yes."

"Morris," he said, using the predetermined code name.

"Yes?"

"Can we meet in an hour? I have something for you."

"Of course. Number Seven."

Number Seven was on a list of meeting places shared by Dexter and his caller, the parking lot of a Roy Rogers fast food outlet on Belle View Boulevard in Alexandria, Virginia.

Dexter placed the cordless phone back in its cradle in his office in the building south of the Pentagon. Visitors to the building saw a small sign on the front, Z-STAT ASSOCIATES, which was registered as a legitimate corporation whose official source of business was providing consulting and administrative services to the CIA's Office of Statistical Reconciliation.

He left the building and went to where the meeting would take place.

The man handed him the envelope. "There's an urgency to this," he told Dexter.

"He's here in Washington?"

"The Hotel Rouge, on Sixteenth."

"It will be taken care of," said Dexter. "The usual fee."

"That will be fine. Let me know when it's completed."

"Of course."

The fee would be six hundred thousand dollars paid through the multimillion-dollar hidden fund at the CIA, provided by nameless, faceless rich men scattered across the country.

Chapter 37

Bob Brixton met for breakfast with Will Sayers. The rotund Savannah reporter, now Washington bureau chief, consumed a hearty platter of eggs, pancakes, bacon, and sausage as he listened to Brixton recount the events of the past few days. The private detective's frustration was evident as he told Sayers of Mac Smith's failure to arrange a meeting with Mitzi Cardell. That Sayers had also come a cropper in trying to speak with the D.C. hostess only added to Brixton's glum mood.

"Maybe I ought to just pack up and forget about getting people to talk," he said as he picked at a bowl of fresh fruit and the remains of a Danish pastry.

"That's one possibility," Sayers said, "but it doesn't sound like you."

"What *does* sound like me?" Brixton said, more to the fruit bowl than to his breakfast companion. "Tilting at windmills? Chasing my tail in circles? I couldn't sleep last night because I kept thinking that even if I could nail down that Mitzi Cardell and her father had something to do with the murder, and paying off Louise Watkins to go to prison, what's the end result? Nobody's going to indict them back in Savannah. The statute of limitations ran itself out long ago. What's to be gained? It makes for a juicy story, puts a dent in Mitzi Cardell's reputation, but so what? I'm not out to hurt her or her father."

"I thought you wanted to find out what really happened for your client, the kid's mother."

"Yeah, that would be nice, give her a sense of closure. That's what's been keeping me going, to do right by her. But is it worth it?"

"Only you know that, Robert. Why don't you pick up the phone and call Mitzi directly?"

"Oh, I thought of doing that when Mac Smith offered to give it a try. Fat chance she'd talk to me after she blew off you and Smith."

"Well," Sayers said, wiping his mouth on the red-and-white railroad handkerchief he always carried, "I'd at least give it a try before you throw in the towel." He motioned to the waiter for a coffee refill as

Brixton's cell phone rang.

"Bob, it's Cynthia. You actually have your phone on."

"I never turned it off from last night. What's up?"

"Detective Cleland called twice. He says it's important that he speak with you."

"You give him my cell number?"

"I didn't want to do that until I talked with you."

"It's okay. Give it to him. You getting ready to leave town?"

"We put it off a week."

"What else is happening?"

"Not much. How are things going with you?"

"They're not. Going anywhere, I mean. I'll stay in touch."

Brixton and Sayers were about to leave the restaurant when Brixton's phone sounded again.

"Robert, it's Joe Cleland."

"Hey, Joe. Cynthia said you'd called. What's up?"

"Something I thought you ought to know. Sitting down?"

"Yeah, I'm sitting down."

"Seems like the obit section of the *Morning News* gets read by lots of people, including the prison population over at Coastal

State, in Garden City. Catch this, my friend. There an inmate there, name's —" He read from a piece of paper. "Name's Ginell Johnson, doing thirty to life for a homicide. Looks like he's coming to the end of his sentence, the life portion. The Big C, terminal. Anyway, I hear from an old buddy who works there that this Johnson found God a few years back, turned into a born-again something or other. Looks like he wants to copper his bet when he gets to the Pearly Gates by confessing to other murders he committed but was never accused of."

Sayers started to say something but Brixton waved him off as he listened to what Cleland had to say next. "Johnson claims that he was hired to kill a young gal whose name happens to be Louise Watkins."

Brixton sat back and exhaled a stream of air. Sayers's raised eyebrows asked what was going on. Brixton raised an index finger. "What else?" he asked Cleland.

"Johnson says he was given the contract for the hit on Ms. Watkins by none other than Mr. Jack Felker."

"Whew!"

"I thought that would grab your attention."

"It sure as hell does, Joe. Felker worked for Ward Cardell."

"I'm well aware of that, Robert, only I wouldn't necessarily go overboard in linking Cardell to this."

"Is this guy Johnson credible?"

"According to my buddy. He's got nothing to gain by claiming it, no plea deal in the works unless it's to put in a good word upstairs — *way* upstairs."

They ended the call and Brixton clicked off his phone.

"You look like you just won the lottery," Sayers said.

Brixton recounted the conversation for the reporter.

"That's intriguing," Sayers said after Brixton had finished.

"Yeah, it sure is."

"Felker, who just happens to be one of Ward Cardell's close associates, puts out a contract for a hit on the girl who he paid off to falsely confess to a crime that Cardell's daughter actually did."

"That may be going too far at this point," Brixton said.

"Maybe, but it's delicious to contemplate."

"Know what I think, Will?"

"What?"

"I think I *will* take a shot at reaching Mitzi Cardell."

Chapter 38

Emile Silva received two calls in quick succession.

The first was from Dr. Rahmi, the physician in charge of his mother's care at the hospital. "We'll be sending your mother home today. She's made a remarkable recovery."

"I know. It's — it's wonderful." The words stuck in his throat. He knew that she'd rallied to the point of being released. "That's good news," he said.

"She's a feisty lady, Mr. Silva. Frankly, I didn't think that she'd make it when she was brought in."

"Yes."

"I'm going to put you on with one of our social workers. Some decisions about her care will have to be made."

"All right."

The social worker came on the line. "Your mother will need continuing care," she said.

"It's my recommendation — and the doctors agree — that she be placed in a nursing facility."

"That sounds fine," he said.

"But she refuses to go," said the social worker. "She insists upon being in her own home. That will mean arranging for consistent nursing care, perhaps not round-the-clock but close to it."

"She wants to go home?"

The social worker laughed. "She certainly does, Mr. Silva. Your mother has a mind of her own. She says that you're a wonderful son and will do everything you can to make her transition from the hospital to home as smooth as possible."

"Of course, whatever is necessary." He began to shake and fought to keep it from his voice.

"I need to meet with you as soon as possible to discuss permanent care at home for her. Can you come in this afternoon, say, at three?"

"Yes. No, I have business meetings. I'll call you when it's convenient for me."

Her silence told him that she wasn't pleased with his reply. "I'll make it soon," he added, and the conversation ended.

He sat at his desk, stunned by the news. Anger overwhelmed him and he repeatedly brought his fist down on the desk. He had counted on her dying.

The ringing phone snapped him out of his despair. It was Dexter.

"Hello, Emile."

"Hello."

"How are you?"

"What do you want?"

"You sound angry."

"What do you want?"

"I have an assignment for you. It must be done quickly. I assume that you're available."

Silva didn't respond.

"Meet me at Number Two at noon," Dexter said, and hung up.

Silva was tempted to decline the job. The plans he'd put into effect had begun to jell in his mind — bury his mother, sell both her house and his, and leave the country, go to that warm, idyllic island where he'd hidden the money he'd accumulated. He'd had enough of Dexter and his assignments. Dexter had been right: everyone's usefulness came to an end at some point. That time had come, and he wanted to leave on his own terms.

But the side of him that took pleasure in ridding society of its scum butted heads with his other intentions. He would do this final job.

Meeting place Number Two on the list was a Wendy's on Twenty-first Street, not far from the campus of George Washington University and the Foggy Bottom Metro stop. There would be many college students there, which annoyed him. He detested their immature chatter, their bravado, their smell.

Silva had already secured a table as far from the others as possible before Dexter arrived. His prediction was correct — most customers were from the university — and he sat with gritted teeth as their inane conversations and odors drifted his way. He took solace in the thought that they had no idea that the man seated among them could snuff out their useless lives at any moment. He was deep into this pleasant reverie when the little bald man entered, took the second seat at the table, and apologized for being late — something to do with a last-minute loose end to resolve — and slid an envelope to Silva. "You'll find everything in there that you need," Dexter said. "He's staying at the Hotel Rouge. Go get something to eat. I'll wait until you have."

"I'm not hungry," Silva retorted.

Dexter glared at him, left the table, and returned minutes later with his meal. "I don't appreciate your attitude," he said as he removed the wrapper from his sandwich.

"How do you want it done?" Silva asked, ignoring the comment.

"A mugging, a robbery," Dexter said, leaning close to Silva and lowering his voice. "Take his wallet, empty it of cash and credit cards, and drop it a block away."

"When?"

"As soon as possible. When you report success, the fee will be deposited as usual."

"All right."

Silva started to get up but Dexter stopped him with, "Perhaps we should talk when this assignment is over."

Silva straightened and looked down at him. "Yeah, maybe we should."

He sat in his car and opened the envelope. Inside was the dossier on Robert Brixton, two photos of him, and some additional notes. Dexter said that it was to look like a mugging gone bad, and Silva decided to use a knife. He had a collection of them in various sizes. His favorite was a nine-inch black tactical stiletto switchblade with a black Teflon-coated blade and dark horn handle. But he took note that Brixton was a private detective, which meant that he might possibly be armed. That posed a dilemma. Never bring a knife to a gunfight, as Sean Connery sagely counseled in *The Untouch-*

ables. Still, the use of a knife would more appropriately point to a street assault. He'd take a knife *and* a handgun.

He drove home and sat in his office, studying the materials and photos until he'd committed them to memory. Satisfied that he had, he followed the rules by taking the materials and photos to the garage and burning them over a metal trash can.

His anger at Dexter, and at his mother's bounce back from death, had now dissipated. Having a definite assignment caused a rush of adrenaline, a sense of purpose. Brixton's face was displayed before him as though on a screen and would remain there until it was over.

When Brixton left his breakfast with Will Sayers he went back to his hotel, where he reviewed what he would say should he actually reach Mitzi Cardell. Calling her was a long shot, but the message from Joe Cleland had regenerated his optimistic side. He reached for the phone a few times but didn't pick it up. *This is silly,* he told himself as he finally grabbed it and dialed the number he'd been given. It rang a number of times until a woman answered.

"Ms. Cardell, please," Brixton said.

"Who shall I say is calling?"

"Robert Brixton."

"What is it in reference to?"

"She'll know. Just tell her that it's important that we speak."

There were muffled female voices in the background. Finally, the same woman came on the line. "Ms. Cardell is occupied at the moment."

"Look," Brixton said, "you tell Ms. Cardell that if she doesn't talk to me she can read about what I have to say in tomorrow's paper."

He heard the phone being put down on a hard surface and chewed his cheek as he waited, drumming his fingertips on the desktop.

"Mr. Brixton?" It was a different female voice.

"Ms. Cardell?"

"Yes. I want you to know how much I resent this intrusion."

"Yeah, well, I don't mean to intrude but I have some questions I need answered."

"I'm sure I don't have the answers to any questions you might have."

"You're wrong, Ms. Cardell. Look, I'm here in D.C. to get the answers I need and I'm not leaving until I do. I'm not out to hurt anybody, including you. I just need to find out what happened twenty years ago in

Savannah when a guy was stabbed to death in a parking lot and a young black girl was paid to take the rap. That ring any bells?"

Her silence was thick.

"I also want to find out why a guy who worked for your father, Jack Felker, paid a hit man to kill that young black girl when she got out of prison."

Her silence morphed into an audible gasp.

"Am I getting through to you, Ms. Cardell?"

Her voice quavered as she said, "I know nothing about any of this. How dare you — ?"

"Have it your way, Ms. Cardell. But you'd be doing yourself a big favor by talking to me. Maybe you'd rather have the press camp at your door."

"Please," she said weakly, "it's shocking that you would think that I had anything to do with these — these — these horrible things you're talking about." He detected a sniffle on her end. "Please don't involve the press. I have a reputation to uphold and —"

"I know that, Ms. Cardell, and like I said I'm not out to hurt you or your reputation. But I have a client back in Savannah, a very nice lady who needs to know that her daughter didn't stab anybody. That's all she wants, to clear up that lousy memory she has of her kid. Her name was Louise Watkins. You knew her when you spent time together at a weekend retreat at the Christian Vision Academy. Your girlfriend back then, Jeanine Montgomery, was questioned about the stabbing and cleared. The way I figure it, she was at the club the night the guy was stabbed to death — why else question her? — and so were you. Who paid off Louise Watkins to confess to the killing? You? Your father? Ms. Montgomery's father? Jack Felker using your father's money? *Somebody did!*"

He realized that he was sounding increasingly strident and took a breath to bring his voice down a few notches. "Ms. Cardell, this whole thing went down more than twenty years ago. Why don't we get together so that I can leave the city, go home, put my client's mind at rest, and get on with our lives?"

"This all comes to me as a terrible shock, Mr. Brixton." It was obvious to him that she'd forced herself to calm down and to respond more reasonably. "I'm sure you can understand that."

"Sure. When can we get together and talk?"

"I don't know. My schedule is so busy and —"

"So's mine, Ms. Cardell. I don't enjoy laying out my client's money for the hotel while I'm here. Why don't we meet there?"

"No, no, the Rouge is too public a place." She paused. "Mackensie Smith knows about this. He called me."

"That's right. He did me a favor."

"How many other people have you told?"

"Not many. Well?"

"I need to think," she said. "I'll call you back."

"No, I'll call *you* back, Ms. Cardell. In an hour."

Jeanine Jamison's private line rang a minute after Mitzi had concluded her conversation with Brixton.

"It's Mitzi," she said to Lance Millius. "I need to speak with the first lady."

"She's not here, Ms. Cardell."

"Where is she?" Mitzi snapped.

"On her way to Savannah."

"Oh, right. I forgot. Thank you."

The second call Mitzi made was to her father in Savannah.

"He's in a business meeting," his long-suffering and loyal secretary told Mitzi when she took the call at Ward Cardell's office.

"Please tell him it's urgent," Mitzi said.

"Mitzi, darling," he said a minute later, "what's so important that I had to leave my meeting?"

She told him, including Brixton's charge that Jack Felker had paid to have Louise Watkins murdered.

"Is it true, Daddy?" she asked as she fought against tears.

"Dumbest damn thing I ever heard," he said. "Now look, Mitzi honey, you just put this out of your mind, you hear me?"

The tears won.

"Stop cryin', Mitzi. This'll all blow itself out, amount to nothing but a hill a' beans. I've got to get back to my meeting now. You take care."

Cardell returned to his meeting with his firm's comptroller. They'd been discussing how to transfer funds in order to make an off-the-books payment to the organization to which Cardell had belonged for many years, established in Oklahoma in the 1960s by a small group of wealthy oilmen, and now funded by other men of means around the country. Cardell's yearly tithe was two hundred thousand dollars, which he happily and proudly paid.

Mackensie Smith's phone sounded in his

apartment.

"Mac, it's Mitzi Cardell."

"Good morning, Mitzi. How are you?"

"Dreadful. I just got off the phone with that private detective, Mr. Brixton."

"You spoke with him."

"Yes. Mac, I'm frantic. You can't believe the things he's accusing me of."

"I didn't get the impression from him that he was interested in accusing anyone of anything. He's just looking for answers to provide a client back in Savannah. Can I be of help in any way?"

"I don't know. I'm afraid that I'll end up needing a lawyer and —"

Smith gave forth with a reassuring laugh. "Let's not jump to conclusions, Mitzi. Tell you what. We can find some time tonight after Annabel's exhibit." He was referring to a cocktail party at her gallery to introduce four drawings from the esteemed Colombian painter and sculptor Fernando Botero Angulo. They'd been given to Annabel on consignment and she was thrilled to have them in her gallery. Mitzi Cardell was on the limited invitation list and had accepted.

"You'll be at Annabel's gallery this evening?" he asked.

"Oh, God, Mac, I don't know whether I'm up for any socializing."

"That doesn't sound like the Mitzi Cardell I know."

"It's just that —"

"Let me make a suggestion. I can invite Bob Brixton to the showing, too. After everyone else has left we can sit down together in Annabel's office and put this thing to rest."

"Face him?"

"You'll have to at some point, Mitzi. This is a good opportunity. I'll be there to buffer things for you."

He waited for her response.

"I trust you, Mac," she said.

His daughter's call unsettled Ward Cardell. So did a subsequent call from his friend Warren Montgomery, father of the nation's first lady. Montgomery sounded upset, said it was important that they meet. Cardell had intended to have lunch at home that day and spend the afternoon on the golf course, but Montgomery's call changed his plans. He left the office at noon and went to the First City Club, one of three private clubs to which he belonged and where he and Montgomery had agreed to meet.

Montgomery, sporting his usual deep tan, carefully arranged silver hair, and wearing one of the dozens of power suits in his closet, got right to the point once they'd chosen a table out of earshot of others. "What's going on, Ward?" he asked.

"With what?" Cardell said.

"With this private detective, Brixton, trying to open up a can of worms."

"How did you hear about it?"

"That doesn't matter. I have my sources. The point is that he's in Washington snooping around about what happened."

"I know all about him, Warren."

"*You* know about him! Why didn't you tell me?"

Cardell glanced around the members-only dining room, leaned closer to Montgomery, and said, "In the first place, Warren, I suggest that you keep your voice down. Second, I saw no reason to bother you with it. I've taken care of everything."

"Meaning what?"

"Meaning that Mr. Brixton will no longer be a problem. I've already sent him some warnings, which unfortunately he hasn't heeded. But I'm assured by —" He now spoke in a barely audible whisper: "I'm assured by the president that steps are being taken to put an end to his troublemaking."

"You've talked to *him?*"

Cardell nodded.

"What does he intend to do to — ?"

Cardell shook his head and waved his hand to end that thread of conversation.

Montgomery looked around before saying, "Then he knows what happened. Jeanine must have told him."

Cardell exhaled in frustration. "Enough," he said.

Montgomery said, "I have a bad feeling about this."

"I suggest we have lunch and continue the conversation outside."

Montgomery accepted that idea and the two men ate in relative silence. They left the exclusive club on Bull Street in downtown Savannah and walked to the nearest of the city's twenty-four famous squares, Johnson Square, the first one created by the city's founding father, English soldier and politician James Edward Oglethorpe. Downtown bank employees who'd enjoyed their lunch beneath the square's trees had returned to work, leaving the square to them.

These two titans of Savannah business sat on a bench. Montgomery, a man seldom at a loss for words, seemed to strain for what to say next. "Ward," he said, "the ramifications for my daughter are immense."

Cardell reacted to an itch on his face as though to scratch away the comment.

Montgomery continued. "If word of what

happened in that parking lot and the cover-up ever becomes public, it could destroy Jeanine."

"And Fletcher Jamison's presidency."

Montgomery started to elaborate on his thought but Ward stopped him. "I suggest you remember, Warren, that it was Jeanine who stabbed that young punk, not Mitzi."

"An accident."

"It doesn't matter. Jeanine was responsible for his death and I came to her rescue, and to yours."

"I haven't forgotten that," said Montgomery. "But maybe it would have been better if —"

Cardell turned and faced his friend, his face red, his eyes flaring. "Better if *what,* Warren, that I do nothing? No matter what the legal outcome, their lives would have been ruined. You strut around town crowing about how your daughter is the first lady of the land. You go to the White House and sleep in the Lincoln Bedroom. And do you know what, Warren? If I hadn't acted the way I did, your precious daughter would be married to some jerk and living in a trailer park outside of town."

"That's a hell of a thing to say."

"But it's true. I told you at lunch that

Brixton is being taken care of. Leave it at that."

Cardell got up to leave but Montgomery grabbed his arm and pulled him back. "Is it true that you arranged for the Watkins girl to be killed when she got out of prison?"

"Whatever gave you *that* idea?"

"Is it true?"

"It doesn't matter whether it is or not. You know, Warren, you're spineless for a man who's achieved the success that you have. There are times when a man has to act to preserve what's precious to him, his family, his wealth, and his nation. The money you contribute each year to our group says to me that you understand what's at stake. I sure as hell don't intend to see my daughter injured by what's happened, and I also don't intend to see Fletcher Jamison's presidency torpedoed. We now have a man in the White House who shares our beliefs, who recognizes that this is a white Christian nation built upon the backs of European immigrants, who stands for what we stand for, small government, adherence to time-honored traditions of marriage and honor, fiscai responsibility, and an end to social welfare programs. I'll do whatever I can to protect your daughter from scandal because she is part of that administration, but I won't stand for being second-guessed by the man who benefits from my having taken action."

Montgomery sat silently.

Cardell resumed his seat on the bench, smiled, and put his arm over Montgomery's shoulder. "This too shall pass, my friend," he said. "Relax. The president will handle it on his end and I've set steps into motion here in Savannah. Everything will be just fine. Trust me, Warren. You must trust me."

Chapter 39

Flo Combes took Brixton's call at her shop in the historic district.

"I was getting worried," she said. "You haven't called."

"I got tied up."

"Sounds kinky."

"My kinky days are over. I think I might have hit a home run." He filled her in on his conversation with Mitzi Cardell and the call he'd just received from Mackensie Smith. "Smith has arranged for me to meet with Ms. Cardell tonight at the gallery his wife owns."

"That's terrific."

"Yeah, it is. He's a great guy. What's new back there?"

"Cooler today, and rainy. Sounds like you'll be coming back soon."

"If things work out tonight the way I hope they will."

"Have you spent any more time with the

ex and your daughters?"

"No. Marylee's got herself a boyfriend, a lawyer named Miles whose tan puts George Hamilton to shame."

"And you instantly bonded."

"I counted my fingers after we shook hands. I'd better get off, sweetheart. I'll call after I see how tonight goes. Love you."

His next call was to his office. Cynthia answered.

"Clients beating down the door for my services?" he asked, lightness in his voice.

"Have to use a baseball bat to keep them away. Oh, you'll love the story in today's paper. That guy who was running for mayor, Shepard Justin? He's announced that he's changed his mind and won't be a candidate."

"He give a reason why?"

"Why else? He wants to spend more time with his family."

"And in motel rooms with somebody *else's* wife."

"I feel like such an insider, knowing the real reason he quit the race."

"Well, keep it to yourself. I'm hoping to wrap things up here in D.C. in a day or two and head back."

"Good. Your clients are asking when you'll be available to work on their cases."

"Great to be wanted. Tell 'em I'll be back soon."

Brixton breathed a sigh of relief at knowing that Justin had dropped out of the race. Chances were that whoever ended up with the photos from the motel had provided them to Justin's opponents, who had put them to good use. Brixton was now off the hook. If the pictures were still floating around, Justin and his attorney would continue to put pressure on him under the assumption that he had copies. *Dropped out to spend more time with his family.* Brixton laughed. Another political hypocrite. Brixton decided that if Justin had admitted that he was dropping out because he'd been caught with his pants down with the wrong woman, he would have encouraged him to stay in the race and voted for him.

He puttered around his hotel room while deciding how to kill the rest of the day. He felt good.

Eunice Watkins didn't enjoy that feeling of well-being.

Her son, the Reverend Lucas Watkins, came to her house that morning. She was pleased that he'd stopped by; his visits had become less frequent lately. She warmly welcomed him, poured glasses of sweet tea, and carefully cut a fresh lemon pound cake into identical slices, which she served on her fanciest plates.

"How are things at the church?" she asked. "All the bad news on TV and in the paper these days makes me wonder what the good Lord has in store for us."

"Times are tough," he replied. "We're having trouble making ends meet."

"Like so many people."

"People don't go to church as much these days," he said. "Even those that do don't have the money to contribute like they used to. Momma, I have to talk to you about something important."

"Of course, dear."

He got up off the couch and went to the window, where he stood gathering his thoughts. Turning, he said in his deep baritone voice, "I think we should stop trying to find out what happened to Louise."

"I don't understand," she said. "You encouraged me to do it. You said that —"

"I know all that," he said, "and I meant it — at the time. But I've been praying a lot for wisdom lately and I now believe that it's wrong to do what we're doing."

"*Wrong?* What could be wrong to want to clear her name?"

He resumed his seat next to her on the couch. "I know, I know," he said. "We'd agreed that hiring the detective was the right thing to do. But if the detective is successful the only thing that will be accomplished is to drag Louise's name through the mud again. She's gone to her maker, Momma. She's in the benevolent hands of God, who's forgiven her sins. We should let her rest in peace. It all happened so long ago. She led herself onto her sinful path and paid the consequences. There's nothing to be gained by opening her life to public scrutiny and scorn."

His mother started to say something but he pressed forward, facing her and taking her hands into his. "I know that you believed Louise when she said she hadn't stabbed that man, and that she'd been paid ten thousand dollars to say that she had. But what if she wasn't telling the truth?"

"You think that your sister would lie about something like that?"

"I don't know, Momma, and you don't know it for sure, either. But what if she was telling the truth? You've said so often that she went to prison to atone for her sins and to seek a better life. She gave you ten thousand dollars and —"

"She *must* have been telling the truth, son. Where else would she have gotten such a large amount of money?"

"I don't know, and I don't think it's important. The point is that what she did led her into prison for four years, a convicted felon, and when she came out she went right back to her former life on the streets."

Eunice got to her feet, banging her leg into the small coffee table and causing some of the tea to spill. "She did nothing of the kind, Lucas. She worked hard in prison and was no longer a drug addict. She earned her GED and learned accounting. She was murdered on the street because she was in the wrong place at the wrong time. She came out of prison a good, God-loving girl, and to hear you say such things about her is —" She burst into tears and went to the bathroom.

"I don't mean to upset you, Momma," he said when she returned a few minutes later and sat next to him, "but —"

"Well, you have."

He grabbed her hands even tighter. "Momma," he said, "you must listen to what I have to say. A man came to the church last night to speak with me. . . ."

The man to whom Lucas referred had called ahead the day before and asked to meet. When Lucas asked what it was about, the man had said, "It's about the financial trouble your church is in. I can help."

He arrived driving a nondescript blue sedan. He wore a brown suit and matching tie. Lucas took note of his face, which was narrow and chiseled; he thought of a rodent.

They met in Lucas's study in the rectory. The man, who gave his name as Gerald Cosgrove, made small talk at first. He said how much he admired the work that area churches did in helping the poor and in making Savannah a better place in which to live and work. Lucas accepted the compliments, wondering all the while when his visitor would get around to explaining what he'd meant on the phone. He was about to bring up the subject when Cosgrove beat him to it. "I'm here on behalf of a wealthy businessman who wants to help you, and your church, get through the financial crisis you're facing."

Lucas's first thought was to wonder how this stranger knew of the church's financial business. Yes, its records were open to the public through tax returns and other government sources. But there were additional aspects known only to Lucas, his finance committee, and the bank that held the church's mortgage.

"I'm aware, Reverend Watkins, that your

church is in serious danger of foreclosure."

It was true. Watkins had fallen seriously behind in the mortgage payments. He had met with the bank's chief lending officer on a number of occasions in an attempt to forge some sort of accommodation, but his efforts hadn't been fruitful. At the most recent meeting, which had taken place two weeks earlier — and after assuring Lucas that the last thing the bank wanted to do was to foreclose on a church — the bank officer informed Lucas that the situation had become dire enough for that to happen unless payment was made within thirty days. The bank would have no choice but to take back the property.

"Might I ask a question?" Lucas said to Cosgrove.

"Of course."

"How do you know about our mortgage situation?"

Cosgrove smiled. "Oh, let's just say that there are ways to know *everything,* Reverend Watkins. As I mentioned earlier, I represent a wealthy individual who wishes to help you and your congregation."

"Is he involved with the church?" Watkins asked.

"Not directly. This individual is willing to bring your mortgage up-to-date with the bank. In addition, he stands ready to donate, anonymously of course, a large sum of money to help pay for your future operating expenses." He waited, head cocked. When a response didn't come, he added, "One hundred thousand dollars."

Watkins's reply wasn't verbal, but his expression spoke volumes.

Cosgrove smiled again. "I thought you'd be pleased," he said.

" 'Pleased' doesn't quite convey my feelings, Mr. Cosgrove. Are there strings attached? There usually are when such generosity is involved."

"Oh, let's not call it 'strings,' Reverend Watkins. There is, of course, something this benefactor would like in return."

"Yes?"

"There was an incident many years ago involving your sister, Ms. Louise Watkins."

Watkins flinched.

"As you know, she met a tragic death at the hands of someone after having spent four years in prison."

"I am well aware of what happened to Louise," Watkins said sternly.

"It's come to the attention of the person I represent that certain individuals are attempting to drag up her name. They claim that she was innocent of the charge that sent her away. I believe that it is your mother, Mrs. Eunice Watkins, who has instigated this. Be that as it may, using your deceased sister in this way is to me, as well as to the generous person I represent, a grave mistake with serious ramifications for certain people."

"I'm not following you, Mr. Cosgrove."

"It's really quite simple, Reverend Watkins. In return for this largesse being offered you and your congregation, all that is being asked is that your mother, and you, put a stop to this travesty involving your deceased sister. Think of it this way, sir. You are a man of God. Your benefactor is also a man of God. Rather than sully your good sister's name again by probing something that occurred more than twenty years ago, her unfortunate young life and tragic death can truly benefit the very people you so ably serve, your congregation and the community. You and your mother need only to stand by the truth of what happened in that parking lot — that your sister accidentally stabbed the young man who'd tried to take advantage of her, and truthfully admitted to the act. That's all that's being asked of you and your lovely mother."

"Louise told us that —"

Cosgrove held up a hand. "Please, Reverend, don't complicate this. I've laid it out for you as simply as possible. Your sister was guilty of the stabbing and admitted to it. That's all there is to it. I'm afraid I can't offer you the luxury of time in considering this magnanimous offer. You have until tomorrow at five. I'll call for your decision." He stood, went to the window, and looked out at the church grounds where a group of young black children were engaged in a spirited game of kickball. "It's a lovely thing you do, Reverend, instilling in children a love of God. It would be a terrible shame to see this church and the ground it stands on taken away from them by the bank, to be turned into another condominium complex, or —" He turned to face the minister. "Or to find itself burned down some night." He went to the door. "Thank you for your time, sir. It's been a pleasure. I look forward to hearing from you tomorrow."

Lucas finished relating to his mother the details of Cosgrove's visit. "Don't you see?" he said. "Louise's death can mean something, stand for something worthwhile."

"The man is blackmailing us," she responded quietly.

"Call it what you will," Lucas snapped in a voice too harsh, he knew, to be used on his mother. "I'm sorry," he said, "but this means so much to me. Without this help, the church will go into foreclosure, be shut down, taken away from those who need it most."

Mrs. Watkins took the tray of sweet tea and cake into the kitchen and methodically put things away. When she'd finished, she returned to the living room, where her son paced.

"Lucas," she said, "will you be able to sleep at night knowing that you've succumbed to this threat by a man you don't know, who represents another unknown person, people wanting to buy our silence?"

He withheld his anger. "Yes, Momma, I'll sleep very well. Will you do it?"

"And what is it that I'm supposed to do?"

"Forget about Louise being paid to admit to a crime she didn't commit. That's all that's being asked of you and of me. Louise is gone, Momma. Learning the truth about her won't bring her back."

"I don't know, son," she said wearily. "What about Mr. Brixton?"

"Call and tell him to stop his investigation. Pay him whatever he's owed but put a stop to what he's doing. I beg it of you, Momma."

"I'll think about it," she said.

Lucas exploded, "He wants my answer by five o'clock this afternoon. I'm going to accept his offer. He'll want to know *your* answer. What is it, Momma?"

"Tell him what you must, son. Please go now. I'm not feeling well."

She watched him storm from the house, get in his car, and drive away. Then, she fell to her knees, clasped her hands, and prayed for an answer.

CHAPTER 40

Brixton's days of enjoying long walks had ended with his duty-related knee injury, which eventually affected every other joint in his body. Walking any distance was painful, although that hadn't kept him from remaining mobile. Athletes were encouraged to "play hurt"; he'd adopted that approach and "lived hurt" the best he could.

The lure of getting in some exercise was appealing. He had the rest of the day to kill before going to Annabel's Georgetown gallery, where he was to meet Mitzi Cardell. He looked out the window and saw that the fair weather of the past few days had held, good weather for a stroll, as abbreviated as it might be.

He'd brought with him to Washington one of two small handguns he owned and was licensed to carry, a Smith & Wesson 638 Airweight revolver that held five rounds of .38 special ammunition. He loved its small size and light weight, and how snugly it fit into his Fobus ankle holster. Actually, he disliked being armed since retiring from the police force. He'd seen enough death and mayhem caused by people carrying weapons to last him a lifetime. But he was also pragmatic enough to realize that his work occasionally took him into situations that made carrying a prudent move.

With the Smith & Wesson secured on his ankle, and dressed in gray slacks, a red-and-white-striped shirt, and a blue blazer, he went through the trendy hotel's small, tastefully appointed lobby and stood outside among six large, alabaster nude female statues, replicas of the famous *Shy Venus* from the second or third century. He looked up into the face of one of the statues and whimsically wondered whether *she* would mind if he smoked. "You should wear something," he told her. "You'll catch a cold."

He lit up, and after a few minutes of watching the passing parade he extinguished the butt in a sidewalk ashtray and headed off in the direction of Dupont Circle, four blocks away. The streets were familiar to him from having been a D.C. cop, and he enjoyed touching base with what had once been his home. Maybe his more sanguine view of the city he'd once hated had to do with knowing that he wouldn't be staying long.

He didn't have a destination in mind. He was content to walk at his own pace, stopping now and then to peruse shop windows when his knee or back protested, and moving on when the pain had subsided.

He bought a take-out cup of coffee and sipped it on a bench while enjoying another cigarette. He was anxious for the meeting that night. At the same time, he wanted to leave D.C. and go home. Funny, he thought, how he now considered Savannah, Georgia, his home. He was thinking of Flo and what she might be doing at that moment when a man joined him on the bench. Brixton nodded.

"Hi," Emile Silva said. He wore a lightweight tan safari jacket, jeans, and sneakers. "Nice day, huh?"

"Yeah, it is," said Brixton.

"You from around here?" Silva asked.

"No. Savannah, Georgia. You?"

"Not from here. Just visiting."

Brixton turned from the stranger and finished what was left of his coffee. The street was chockablock with pedestrians, men and women in a hurry to get someplace, although when compared to New

York they moved in slow motion.

Silva shifted on the bench, his eyes darting left and right, his right hand clutching the switchblade in the cargo pocket of his jacket. *Too many people,* he thought.

Brixton stood. "You have a nice day," he said.

"Yeah, you, too. Say, I've got a question."

"Yeah?"

"I'm only going to be here in D.C. until tomorrow and was wondering what other sights to take in."

Brixton laughed. "I'm the last person to ask about that, but you can't go wrong with the museums over on The Mall, or the Kennedy Center. I'm heading there now."

"A museum?"

"The Kennedy Center. I used to go there years ago when I lived here. Have a good day."

Brixton skirted a knot of people waiting to cross the street, hailed a passing taxi, and told the driver to take him to the Kennedy Center for the Performing Arts. As the cab navigated traffic, Brixton smiled. He found it amusing that a stranger had asked him to suggest a tourist attraction to visit. As for himself, he'd decided while enjoying his coffee that as long as he was in D.C. he should take in a tourist attraction or two. He hadn't done much sightseeing during his four years there on the force, aside from a few forays with Marylee and their small children. But he did remember enjoying the Kennedy Center and looked forward to revisiting it.

When his marriage was breaking up and he was recuperating from the gunshot wound to his knee, he found the center the most welcoming and comforting of all the monuments to fallen heroes scattered throughout Washington. He would have a drink (or two or three) in the Roof Terrace Restaurant and Bar, eat dinner there, catch a free show in the Millenium Theater at the far end of the 630-foot-long Grand Foyer, and enjoy a cigarette (or two or three) on the expansive open-air rooftop terrace accessible from the foyer and offering panoramic views of the Potomac River below; the Roslyn, Virginia, skyline to the west; Washington Harbour and the infamous Watergate complex to the north; and the Lincoln Memorial and George Washington University to the east. The flight path into Reagan National Airport ran along the river and was a source of complaints from many, but Brixton liked seeing the jets scream past, wondering who was on the planes and what their lives were like.

He got out of the taxi and looked up. The

pristine blue sky was now pewter, and the wind had picked up. You didn't have to be a meteorologist to forecast that rain was on its way.

He walked the length of the Hall of States, in which flags from every state in the union were colorfully displayed, reached the Grand Foyer, and went back down the Hall of Nations, which featured flags from every country recognized by the United States. The five-hundred-foot journey wreaked havoc with his knee and he found a seat in the foyer, close to the eight-foot-tall Robert Berks bronze bust of President John Kennedy. Sitting there flooded him with memories, not all of them pleasant. He was debating leaving and going back to the hotel when he saw the man with whom he'd had the brief encounter in Dupont Circle. He seemed to be admiring artwork in the Grand Foyer, standing close to a piece, then stepping back to gain a wider perspective. Brixton considered going over to him but decided against it. Instead, he went through doors leading to the huge rooftop terrace, pulled out a cigarette, lit it, and leaned on the railing. The Potomac flowed by below; a crew from one of the universities practiced its sport on the brown water while other small craft headed upstream and down. The wind had picked up in intensity, and he felt a wayward raindrop hit his cheek. No wonder the terrace was virtually empty. It wasn't the sort of weather that enticed people outdoors.

"Well, hello there."

Brixton turned to see the man from Dupont Circle.

"Hi. I see you decided to come here, too."

"Thanks to your suggestion. Beautiful views, huh?" he said, joining Brixton at the railing.

"Yeah."

A commercial jet heading for National Airport roared down the river and disappeared to their left.

"Those things are noisy," Emile Silva said.

"That they are. I read that when they designed the Kennedy Center they made it a box within a box to soundproof the performances from the planes."

"That so?"

"It's what I read."

Silva's hand went to the switchblade in his pocket. He ran through a mental checklist. The jets were coming with regularity, their screaming engines providing the perfect cover for the sound of flicking open the blade and any sounds that might come from his victim. He glanced over at Brixton, whose exposed neck provided a vulnerable target for the blade. He'd ram it into the neck and twist, severing arteries. He looked at the jacket Brixton was wearing. It came down over the rear pockets in his slacks. Chances were that he kept his wallet in one of those pockets. He'd have to move fast to find the wallet and extract it from the pocket, pull out the cash and credit cards, run back inside, drop the wallet in the Grand Foyer, and make his escape.

The sound of an approaching aircraft using the river as its guide to the airport named after Ronald Reagan caught his attention, the deafening whine of its engines growing louder. He looked left and right. They were virtually alone. He slowly removed the knife from his jacket and fingered the button. The blade snapped into place. The plane was directly in front of them now. Perfect! He turned toward Brixton and was prepared to thrust the knife into his neck when a chorus of squeaky children's voices erupted. Silva and Brixton turned to see a visiting class of youngsters pour through the doors to the terrace. Simultaneously, the skies opened and rain came down hard.

Brixton said, "See ya." He sprinted painfully to the doors and joined the kids and their teachers as they scrambled inside. He looked back to see Silva still standing at the railing. *Must enjoy the rain,* he thought as he headed back down the Hall of Nations, through the doors at the opposite end of the center, and climbed into the backseat of a waiting cab. "The Hotel Rouge," he told the driver.

Chapter 41

Silva cursed his soggy clothing as he walked down the Hall of States and went to where he'd parked his car. His sneakers squished as he proceeded down the long promenade, and water dripped from his hair onto his nose and mustache. He didn't need this on his final assignment, didn't appreciate the mob of squealing, smelly kids and their teachers dashing this perfect opportunity.

He assumed that Brixton had returned to his hotel and further assumed that he would stay there for a while. He drove home, took a hot shower, and changed clothes. The aborted attempt at the Kennedy Center had soured him on the assignment. What had happened there could be considered an omen, he mused as he sat by the window in his study, watching the rain come down. Maybe he should scrap the hit, tell Dexter that he was quitting. The extra fee for this assassination would be nice but he didn't need it. He had enough stashed away in the Caribbean to support a nice lifestyle there for the rest of his days.

But now that he'd seen his prey up close, had actually spoken with him twice, Brixton's face continued to run before Silva's mind's eye on an endless loop, taunting him, creating a challenge. He was deep into this thinking when the phone rang.

"Hello, Emile," his mother said in her weak, singsong voice.

"Ma-ma?"

"You haven't come to see me."

"I — where are you?"

"I'm home, Emile. They brought me home."

"That's good."

She now whispered. "I don't like the woman who's here, Emile. She's not trustworthy."

"Who — ?"

"Please come as soon as you can, Emile."

She hung up.

He waited for his anger to subside before slipping into a fresh safari jacket, securing the switchblade in one pocket, his Bersa Thunder .380 handgun in the other, and going to the garage. He'd driven the third of his three cars that morning, a nondescript white Toyota Camry, preferring its relative automotive anonymity. But now as he prepared to go to the Hotel Rouge for another crack at Robert Brixton he chose the black Porsche Cayman. Driving it, he knew, would calm him down. It always did.

He was deep in thought as he drove down the sloping driveway and turned left in the direction of The District, so immersed in it that he failed to notice a blue SUV and its driver parked across the street. Nor did he see James Brockman pull away from the curb and fall in behind him.

Like Emile Silva, James C. Brockman had been in the military, the marines. He'd served in Iraq and Kuwait during the first Gulf War and had been injured there when he lost control of a truck he was driving and plowed into a command post, injuring two fellow marines. He was brought up on charges of negligence and dereliction of duty and given a choice: face a court-martial or accept a plea deal that would lower his rank from corporal to private and sever him from the corps with a general discharge.

At first, Brockman accepted the deal under the assumption that a general discharge was as good as an honorable one. He discovered that he was wrong when he returned to civilian life and found that he was denied certain rights and benefits.

Like Silva, his anger at the military and its members festered, fostering visions of lining up the sergeant who'd instigated the charges against him, alongside others who'd reviewed his case, and blowing them away, one after the other, no blindfolds or last wishes. That dream stayed with him every day he was on a civilian firing range, practicing with a variety of weapons he now possessed.

And also like Silva, he'd been recruited in a bar by someone from Dexter's organization, where after too many drinks he'd verbalized his fantasies to an interested, sympathetic stranger. At the time he was working as a truck driver for a contractor with a sizable government contract with whom he'd had numerous verbal run-ins, someone else to be gunned down by his imagined one-man firing squad.

Brockman had been a troubled teenager. His father, an alcoholic, frequently beat him and his sisters; his mother was a timid soul who also endured beatings at the hand of her drunken husband. Brockman's enlistment in the marines was his means of escape. His mother died while he was in Iraq; he hadn't had contact with his father in years. His relationships with women were characterized by sporadic bursts of violent anger toward them; none lasted more than a few months.

Dexter's kind of guy.

Brockman hadn't expected to hear from Dexter that quickly. He had received a call on his cell phone the afternoon before to meet with the little man at an I-Hop on the Jefferson Davis Highway in Alexandria. It was there, over plates of chocolate chip pancakes and bacon, that Brockman received his first assignment.

"I think you should know, James, that the person who is your target works with us. I mention that because I do not want you to think that we're disloyal to our employees. Far from it. This individual has recently behaved in a way that runs counter to our mission. In fact, James, he has done things that not only threaten to undermine us, his actions could potentially put at risk certain important aspects of the security of the United States."

"What'd he do?" Brockman asked.

"I'm not at liberty to reveal that, James. Do you have any problem with this?"

Brockman shrugged and took a forkful of pancake. "No, I don't have any problem with it. If this guy's been causing trouble, he should be taken out. Where will I find him?"

Dexter slid an envelope across the table, saying, "Everything you need to know is in here. He's currently on his final assignment for us and I want him to successfully conclude that before you undertake your obligation. I want you to stay close to him and be ready to strike when I give the word. I'll call you on your cell phone when that time comes. I will simply say, 'The sale is on.' When you hear that, you'll know it is time."

"Okay. How do you want it done?"

"I leave that up to your expertise. Of course, it is vitally important that you not be linked in any way to it. If you should be, we disavow all knowledge of you. We made that clear, as you'll recall, when we first became acquainted."

"I understand. Anything else?"

"Not unless you have further questions."

Brockman shook his head, wiped syrup from his mouth, and grinned. "This is just like in the movies," he said.

Dexter frowned. "I assure you, James, that this is not a motion picture. This is real life."

"Okay, forget I said it. Thanks for breakfast."

"I'll leave first. Follow in five minutes."

Brockman watched Dexter walk from the

restaurant. "What a fruitcake," he muttered to himself as he did the same.

CHAPTER 42

Mac and Annabel Smith spent the late afternoon at her gallery, preparing for that evening's cocktail reception. The guest list was small, only fourteen people — fifteen with the addition of Robert Brixton. Two women from Federal City Caterers arrived and helped set up a small bar. An assortment of finger foods would be passed by the women once guests arrived; the bar would be manned by a professional mixologist, the Smiths were told, prompting Mac to quip to his wife, "I wish they'd just say he's a bartender. Mixologist indeed!"

Annabel smiled and continued what she was doing. Her husband liked to call things what they were, and refused to order a Grande Latte at Starbucks, preferring to ask for a *medium* latte.

They took a break at five and sat in Annabel's office at the rear of the gallery. Mac had prepared a checklist, which they went over. That chore completed, Annabel said, "So, tell me again how it's supposed to go with Mitzi and Brixton."

"I have no idea how it will go, Annie," he replied. "What I wanted was for the two of them to get together and have Brixton tell her about the case he's working on."

"I'm surprised that she agreed to sit down with him," Annabel said.

"I was, too. He must have been pretty persuasive when he spoke with her on the phone. She sounded stressed when she called me about it."

"Do you really think that what he says is true, that she stabbed that man twenty years ago and paid off a young black girl to take the rap?"

"You know, Annie, I *do* believe him. I hope he's wrong, for Mitzi's sake, but his story rings true. He doesn't strike me as the sort of man who buys into fanciful conspiracy theories, or chases juicy gossip. Will Sayers doesn't see him that way either. But we'll see how it goes tonight. I promised Mitzi that I'd be the buffer between them. If I think he's going down the wrong path, I'll end the conversation."

"Well," Annabel said, standing, "if it *is* true, it's going to raise a lot of eyebrows in this town. Want to grab a bite before our guests arrive? I never get to eat the things we serve at our own parties."

Silva sat in his Porsche a half block from the Hotel Rouge and waited for his prey to emerge again. Brockman was at the curb three car lengths behind. It was five o'clock. The rain had stopped but the sky continued to threaten. Silva considered calling Brixton's room to be sure that he was still inside but thought better of it. Had he left the hotel during the time that Silva was at home? Possible.

He got out of the Porsche and walked in front of the hotel, glancing into the lobby for a sign of Brixton. Nothing. He reached a corner and retraced his steps. This time he saw Brixton, who stood at the reception desk talking with the clerk. Silva returned to the car. It wouldn't do for Brixton to see him for the third time that day. He'd consider that more than a coincidence. He was a private detective who'd been a cop for more than twenty years. His antenna would be up. Better to stay out of his sight until it was time to follow through. He touched the knife through the fabric of the jacket, did the same with the gun on the other side. He was getting antsy. He wanted it over with. It was dragging on too long. The rain started again and he closed the window. The windshield fogged up, interfering with his view of the hotel's entrance. He swore and wiped condensation off the windshield, turned on the engine and the AC. "Come on," he said aloud, "go someplace."

Brockman wasn't antsy. He was plain bored. He thought of a movie he'd seen three times, *The French Connection,* in which the character Popeye Doyle, played by Gene Hackman, had to stand outside in the cold while staking out a suspect. It was only minutes on the screen but it was obvious that cops spent hours doing that sort of thing. A waste of time as far as Brockman was concerned. If it hadn't been for Dexter's orders — and he would follow those orders because he'd never had such a lucrative job before — he would just walk up to that silly sports car and shoot this guy Silva in the head. But he was told to get close to him and wait for the go-ahead from Dexter. "The sale is on," he said a few times to make sure he'd remember it.

Brixton exited the hotel, causing Silva to sit up straight and to lean closer to the windshield. The rain shower had been brief. Brixton stood among the statues, a tan raincoat over his arm. He lit a cigarette and seemed in no rush to go anywhere. Silva glanced in his rearview mirror and saw a taxi turn onto Sixteenth Street. It pulled up in front of the hotel. Brixton carried his cigarette to the curb and ground it out in the gutter, opened the cab door, and climbed in. He must have called for the taxi, Silva decided. The cab pulled away. Silva slipped the Porsche into gear and followed. The blue SUV driven by James Brockman was next in line.

Silva almost lost the taxi a few times but managed to stay behind it when the driver drove into Georgetown and came to a stop in front of Annabel's gallery. He watched Brixton get out, pay the driver, and enter the gallery. *Interesting,* Silva thought. It was where he'd first encountered the beautiful woman with the auburn hair, and her husband. What was the connection? He was tempted to find a parking space and go inside, too, but knew that would be foolhardy. Georgetown was busy, lots of pedestrians and cars. He decided to circle a few times in the hope that a space would open up close to the gallery entrance. It took three passes before he backed into a vacant slot. He turned off the ignition and trained his eyes on the door and the sign above: PRE-COLUMBIAN GALLERY — A. LEE SMITH PROPRIETOR.

Brockman double-parked while waiting for a space of his own, flipping the bird at other drivers who beeped their horns at him. A car parked directly behind Silva's Porsche eventually pulled away from the curb and Brockman moved his SUV into the vacant spot. Silva glanced in his rear-view window and saw the SUV's driver, a man with sandy hair. Brockman saw Silva's eyes in the mirror and decided he'd better get out and observe from a distance.

He crossed the street and stood beneath the overhang of a store that sold movie memorabilia, where he had an unobstructed view of the Porsche and the gallery. He thought again of Popeye Doyle and wondered how long he'd have to wait. Brockman was a gun fanatic and had a large stash of weapons from which to choose. This day he carried a "Baby" Glock 9 mm subcompact handgun in a shoulder holster beneath his kelly-green windbreaker; he'd left a Heckler & Koch PSG1 sniper's rifle with a telescopic sight in the SUV.

And so the waiting game began.

Guests began to arrive a little before seven. Mac and Annabel greeted them as they came through the door. The gallery's stereo system shuffled six jazz CDs that emphasized piano and guitar cuts. Mac kept his eye out for Mitzi Cardell and began to wonder whether she'd had second thoughts and would be a no-show. That concern vanished when a gray Lincoln Town Car pulled up and Mitzi got out. She paused at the door as though uncertain whether to enter. As the Town Car pulled away, she pulled on the door and stepped through. Mac was the first to extend a hand. "Great seeing you, Mitzi," he said.

"I wasn't sure whether —"

"Come on in, have a drink and something to eat," he said, leading her to the bar.

Brixton watched her entrance from a far corner of the gallery and wondered when Smith would bring her to him for an introduction. When it appeared that it would not happen soon, he moved to where Annabel was chatting with a husband and wife. She introduced Brixton to them. The wife asked whether he was a connoisseur of pre-Columbian art.

"Afraid not," he said through a grin. "I'm here because I'm friends with Mac and Annabel." He glanced at Annabel to see whether by claiming friendship he'd stepped over the line. Her wide smile and hand on his arm said that he hadn't.

It was a lively party; the bouncy jazz music, top-shelf liquor, myriad tasty finger foods, and spirited conversation ensured that it would be. There were lots of oohs and ahs about Fernando Botero Angulo's works that were the reason for the gathering. One of the guests, a wealthy D.C. real estate man, offered to buy them on the spot. Annabel suggested that they talk in the morning, to which he agreed, with the caveat, "Don't you dare sell them out from under me, Annabel."

She assured him that she wouldn't.

As the party wound down and some guests left, Mac brought Brixton over to meet Mitzi.

"Hello, Ms. Cardell," Brixton said.

"Hello," she said, frost on her words.

"I really appreciate having a chance to speak with you," he said.

"I wouldn't have agreed to do it if it weren't for Mac Smith," she said.

Brixton nodded his thanks in Smith's direction as Mitzi walked away.

A half hour later, after the caterers had performed the cleanup in what seemed a matter of minutes, only Mac, Annabel, Mitzi, and Brixton remained. Mac led them into Annabel's office, where four chairs arranged in a tight semicircle awaited. Mitzi's nervousness was apparent. She crossed one leg over the other and it was in constant motion. Her fingers kept going to her face when they weren't tapping out a rhythm only she could hear on the arms of the chair.

"I suggest that Bob start," Smith said to Mitzi, "by telling you what his investigation has led him to conclude. Let's hear him out before asking questions or challenging what he has to say."

Mitzi's sigh was contemptuous, but she agreed.

Brixton had many times gone over how he intended to put it to Mitzi. He wanted to make it as easy as possible, to say it in a way that would acknowledge that he knew that his conclusions would be painful for her. On the other hand, he didn't want to come off as being unsure of his findings, and hoped that he could find a comfortable middle ground.

He spoke for ten minutes. Mitzi tried to protest a few times but Mac kept things on track. When Brixton was done — he made it clear that he believed that it was Mitzi who'd stabbed the young man in Augie's parking lot and that she (or her father) had arranged to pay off Louise Watkins to take responsibility — he sat back and waited for her reaction.

It was slow in coming. She squirmed in her chair as though to find a more comfortable position, and made a series of false starts. From her posture he assumed that she would issue a flat denial of everything he'd said. But to his surprise she suddenly smiled at him. He returned it.

"I assume you've already gone to the press with your suppositions," she said, struggling to inject calm into her voice. "A reporter called me about it."

"Yes, I've spoken with someone from the press," Brixton acknowledged. "But it's not my intention to turn this into a media story. I just want to be able to tell my client, Ms. Watkins' mother, that her daughter didn't stab the man at Augie's. That's important to her, which I'm sure you can understand."

"Because I'm a mother?" Mitzi said. "I don't have children."

"As a human being," Brixton said.

His comment caused her to draw a deep breath. She looked as though she might break down and cry. After a few more steadying breaths, she said, "I did not stab anyone, Mr. Brixton."

Brixton looked at Mac and Annabel before saying, "Then did your friend, Jeanine Montgomery, now Jeanine Jamison, actually stab the man?" He started to explain how he'd come to that possible conclusion but she waved him off. "It was all an accident,

Mr. Brixton. Good God, do you think Jeanine would do such a thing deliberately?"

"No," Brixton said.

"We were foolish teenage girls, unsure of who we were. We came from good families. We were raised to respect life and to try to make this a better world. Jeanine's parents had high hopes for her. So did mine. Is it so difficult to understand why our parents would do everything under heaven and earth to protect their daughters? Do you have daughters, Mr. Brixton?"

"Two."

"Well?"

"Sure," Brixton said, "I'd go to great lengths to protect them, but it wouldn't include seeing an innocent young girl spend four years in prison for something she didn't do. She was paid off to, as you say, 'protect' you and Jeanine. But nobody protected *her.* She was vulnerable. Ten thousand bucks was like hitting a mega-lottery for her. She was a hooker and a drug dealer, a disposable human being in the scheme of things." He felt his anger level rise and fought to keep it under control.

"Is there anything else you wish to say?" Mitzi asked.

"Then you *are* confirming that Louise Watkins was paid to take the rap for you,"

Brixton said.

Mitzi said nothing.

"Or take the rap for the first lady."

Mitzi straightened in her chair and smiled at him again. "I've agreed to meet with you, Mr. Brixton, and have kept my promise. What I've said to you in this room will not be what I will say to any reporter who questions me about what happened in Savannah years ago. From what you've told me, you don't have any proof to back up your allegations, just an assortment of theories. I have no obligation to be truthful with the press. This is not a matter of national security. The fate of the nation doesn't hang in the balance. No one has died because of —"

"Whoa," Brixton said. "Louise Watkins died right after she came out of prison, gunned down on a street corner. You — your father — wouldn't know anything about *that* I suppose. This guy who was stabbed in the parking lot *died.* Don't tell me that nobody died because of what happened in Savannah."

Mitzi turned to Smith. "I've had quite enough, Mac," she said. "I've been gracious enough to meet with your friend and to listen to his theories. This is all so —" She muttered something that the others in the room couldn't hear. She leaned forward in Brixton's direction. "I'm going to ask you, Mr. Brixton, to apply some common sense. I respect the fact that you're working for this girl's mother, who wants to know the truth. But is the truth so important that you would bring down good, decent people who've lived exemplary lives since that one, unfortunate night twenty years ago? I've worked hard to establish my reputation here in Washington. I bring together important people who make life-and-death decisions for a nation, *your* nation. The first lady of this land and her husband, the president of the United States, have an agenda that could determine the fate of the free world. Is it money you're after? I can see to it that whatever you lose by shelving this witch hunt will be more than compensated for. Don't you see? Can't you put things in perspective? Please, try to be reasonable."

Brixton slammed his fist onto the arm of his chair and almost came to his feet. "Buy me off the way you and your father bought off Louise Watkins? You know, Ms. Cardell, I came here tonight without any intention of hurting you or your family. I didn't vote for Fletcher Jamison but I'm not out to derail whatever the hell he intends to do with the country. I don't know the first lady and I don't want to know her. But I'll tell you this." He pointed a finger at Mitzi. "You and your kind make me sick. Keep your money. I've heard enough here to convince me that Louise Watkins' mother was right. If the press wants to probe deeper, that's their business." He turned to Smith. "I hope I haven't crossed the line, Mac, but frankly, this woman disgusts me."

Brixton got up and stood with his back to the others.

"I need to call my driver," Mitzi told Smith. She picked up a phone — "I'm ready to leave," she said — and a minute later the Town Car appeared in front of the gallery.

Smith walked her to the door. "I know this has been upsetting, Mitzi, but I'm glad you had a chance to confront him."

"Well, Mac, I am *not* pleased to have had to confront this . . . this, this vile man. I never should have listened to you."

Smith held open the door and she disappeared into the chauffeured car, which drove away. He returned to the office, where Annabel was preparing to close up for the night.

"I'm sorry that it turned out this way," Brixton said to them. "I lost my cool and —"

"It's okay, Robert," Smith said. "It's obvious that what you've said is true. She didn't admit to it in so many words, but there's no doubt that she and her friend Jeanine were involved in the stabbing, and that her father paid off the girl."

"There's something else you should know," Brixton said.

"What's that?" Annabel asked.

"Her father's right-hand man, a guy named Jack Felker, hired the gunman who killed Louise Watkins after she got out of prison."

Mac and Annabel looked at him. "You're certain of that?" Mac asked.

Brixton explained about the dying inmate who had confessed to having killed Louise Watkins and who had further claimed that he'd been paid by Felker.

"What are you going to do next?" Smith asked as they snapped off the office lights and passed through the gallery.

"I suppose I'll go back, tell my client that her daughter didn't stab anybody, and hope that's sufficient for her."

"But what will *she* do with that information?" Annabel asked.

Brixton shrugged as Annabel set the alarm and they exited to the street. "That's up to her," he said.

"How did you get here tonight?" Smith asked.

"Taxi."

"We'll drop you at the hotel," Smith said. "Our car is in the lot across the street."

Silva had been afraid that he'd doze off while waiting for something to happen. He saw them, snapped to attention, and turned on the engine.

Brockman saw the Porsche's headlights come to life and exhaust coming from its rear. He hopscotched through traffic, reached his SUV, climbed in, and started the engine.

Smith pulled out of the small parking lot with Annabel in the front passenger seat and Brixton in the back. They turned right, the opposite direction from which Silva and Brockman were facing. Silva gunned the Porsche, made a U-turn that caused a driver to slam on his brakes, and followed Smith's car. Brockman cursed the traffic. He knew he'd lose them but assumed they were going to Brixton's hotel. He turned at the corner and headed for Sixteenth Street, hoping he was right.

Chapter 43

Smith pulled up in front of the Hotel Rouge.

"I really appreciate what you did for me tonight," Brixton said.

"I'm not sure it accomplished anything," Smith replied. "Knowing what you now know is one thing. Making use of it is another."

"I'll leave that up to my client, Mrs. Watkins," Brixton said.

"What about Will Sayers?" Mac asked. "He'll want to learn what *you* learned."

"I know," Brixton said wearily. "I meant it when I said that I didn't want to turn this into a media event."

"Hard to keep things like this under wraps," Annabel commented, "especially in this town."

Brixton's laugh was sardonic. "You know what?" he said. "I think I won't worry about what goes down after I report back to my client. Will has been helpful — I wouldn't have benefited from meeting you if it weren't for him. I'll fill him in on what transpired tonight and let him make his own decision about pursuing it. Thanks again for everything." He reached over the back of the seat and patted them on their shoulders. "If you're ever in Savannah give me a call. I'll show you the sights."

"That's a deal," Annabel said. "We'll stay in touch."

Brixton got out of the car, waved, and watched them drive away. He debated going inside to the hotel bar but decided he first needed a cigarette. He lit up, inhaled, then exhaled and watched the smoke as it slowly drifted up into the night. Emile Silva watched it, too. He'd parked his Porche around the corner and was slowly walking to the hotel.

It was quiet on Sixteenth Street. Brixton stood among the nude female statues and smiled at one of them. He thought of Flo and that he'd soon be back with her in Savannah. He was engaged in that pleasant contemplation when his cell phone rang.

"Robert," said the familiar voice of Wayne St. Pierre.

"Hello, Wayne."

"Hope I'm not disturbing anything important."

"Just enjoying a cigarette. What's up?"

"You ought to give them up, Robert. Thought you'd want to know that the ME's report on Mr. Jack Felker came back late this afternoon. Poor fella died of natural causes. He was one sick puppy, Robert. ME says his body was riddled with the cancer."

Brixton's first thought was that the ME was either an idiot or had come up with his finding to suit someone else's agenda. But he was in no mood to argue it while standing on the street. "Is that so?" he said.

"Just thought you'd want to know," said St. Pierre.

"Yeah, well, thanks for the news, Wayne."

"Things goin' well there in D.C.?"

"Very well."

"Come on now, my friend, don't be coy with Uncle Wayne. What's happening with your case? What did Ms. Cardell have to say?"

"How did you know I spoke with her?"

The patrician detective laughed. "I know everything, my friend."

"I'll fill you in when I get back. You do know that the man who killed Louise Watkins has fessed up to it and fingered Jack Felker as the one who paid for the hit."

"Of course I've heard it, Robert. No credence to it, however. The man's lyin' through his teeth."

"Why would he do that? From what I hear he's terminal. What's he got to gain?"

"Oh, you know how these jailhouse types think, Robert. He figures he'll cleanse his soul for when he gets to the Pearly Gates. No basis at all for what he claims. When are you coming home?"

"In a day or two."

Brixton lit another cigarette, wedging the cell phone between his ear and shoulder.

Silva was now only a dozen feet from him. He pulled the switchblade from his jacket pocket and came closer.

"You there, Robert?" St. Pierre asked.

"Yes, I'm here. I'm going to cut this short, Wayne. I'll call you when I get back."

As Brixton pushed the Off button, Silva came up from behind. "Hey," he said.

Brixton turned.

"It's me," Silva said through a crooked grin as he lunged with the knife at Brixton's chest. Brixton's reflexive move turned him sideways to his attacker. The blade tore through his jacket sleeve and plunged deep into his biceps. Silva pulled the knife out and cursed. As he did so, Brixton squared and brought his knee up into Silva's groin, causing him to double over and fall to his knees. Brixton took steps back, bumping into one of the statues. As he reached down and fumbled to draw his gun from his ankle holster, Mac and Annabel pulled up, their car's headlights casting harsh light on the scene.

Silva got to his feet and was caught in the headlights. Brixton hadn't felt the knife's penetration but was now blinded by searing pain. He felt warm blood running down his arm and saw it spread onto his hand.

Mac Smith jumped out of his car. He hesitated; Brixton was on his knees, his left hand grasping at his right arm. The man holding the knife looked panicked. Smith braced for an attack, but Silva took off, sprinting up the street and around the corner. Annabel exited the car and went to Brixton, who now had his weapon in his good hand. "Oh my God," she said as she helped him to his feet. "You left your raincoat in the car and we were returning it," she said.

"Call 911," Mac said to his wife. To Brixton: "What happened?"

"The guy came up behind me and —"

"A stranger?"

"I've seen him before, maybe twice."

Smith looked down at a puddle of blood that had formed at Brixton's feet. Brixton sagged against Smith.

"Take it easy," Mac said. "Annie's called for an ambulance."

By this time a few hotel staff members had come to see what had happened and were joined by a couple returning to the hotel from dinner. An ambulance arrived within minutes, accompanied by a patrol car driven by a uniformed officer. Brixton, whose loss of blood had rendered him too weak to stand and almost speechless, was placed in the rear of the ambulance, where a medical tech managed to stem the bleeding.

"Get him to the hospital," the cop said. 'We'll get a statement there." He turned to Smith. "You saw it?" he asked.

"We arrived while it was happening," Smith offered, and explained why they'd returned to the hotel after having dropped Brixton off. "He said he'd seen his attacker a few times before."

The officer took Smith's name and contact information. As he did so, an older woman walking a large dog joined them. "Someone died?" she said.

"No, ma'am," the officer said.

She saw the blood on the pavement. "I knew it," she said, "I just knew it."

"Knew what, ma'am?"

"I knew that that man who almost

knocked me over was running away from something bad."

"You saw him?" Smith asked.

"He ran right into me. Billy here — Billy's my dog — snapped at him."

"Did you see where he went?"

"Yes, I did. He got into his car and sped off like a madman."

"What sort of car?" the officer asked.

"One of those little sports cars, like James Bond drives in the movies."

"What color was it?"

"Black. All black. I saw the license plate."

The cop and Smith looked at each other.

"He's from Virginia. I didn't get every number but I got most of them."

CHAPTER 44

Silva had all he could do not to drive the Porsche flat out and possibly attract law enforcement attention. He kept close to the speed limit, his eyes constantly looking in the rearview mirror for signs of the police, an endless stream of invective flowing from his mouth, shouted at times. Every hit he'd accomplished for Dexter and his people had gone without a hitch. *Now this.* His target was alive and could identify him. So could the couple who'd arrived in their car, the woman with the auburn hair and her smug husband. "Damn you all!" he yelled above the engine noise.

When he wasn't swearing at his bad luck, he was formulating his next step. Time to get away, out of the country, go where his money was stashed, sever all ties in D.C., make a clean escape and put it all behind him.

He pulled into the driveway of his mother's home, where a strange car was parked. He got out and looked back at the street. A blue SUV slowly drove by but kept going. He entered the house and found his mother in her wheelchair in the living room. A black woman in a crisp white nurse's uniform sat in a corner, reading the day's paper.

"Who are you?" Silva demanded.

She stood and said she was one of the home-health-care aides assigned to care for Mrs. Silva.

"Get out!" Silva exploded.

"Who are *you?*" the woman asked.

"It's my son, Emile," his mother said in her little-girl voice.

"That's right. I'm her son," Silva said. "You can go home now. I'm here to take care of her."

The nurse looked at Mrs. Silva, who smiled sweetly and nodded. "My son is home now," she said. "You can go."

It was obvious that the nurse wasn't sure what to do.

"It's okay," Emile said in a more modulated voice. "You'll get paid for your full shift. Go on now, please leave."

She gathered her things and left. Silva looked out the window and saw her get into her car and pull away.

James Brockman, too, saw the aide leave.

He'd turned around at the end of the street, parked, turned off the engine and lights, and waited. He'd spotted Silva's black Porsche where he'd parked around the corner from the Hotel Rouge and had pulled in behind him. He'd seen Silva's mad dash to the car, his screeching getaway from the curb, and had managed to follow him to this house.

"I'm so happy that you're here, Emile. We can have dinner and you can play me some music."

"Yeah, yeah," he said. "I'll be right back."

He ran up the stairs and went to the bedroom that had been his while growing up. He closed the door, sat on his bed, and attempted to force clarity into his thinking. As hard as he tried, every thought was fleeting, jumbled, nothing sticking long enough to make sense. He knew only that he had to do something and do it quickly.

He pulled his cell phone from his jacket and dialed a special, private number. Dexter answered. The little man was at home watching a TV cooking show.

"It's Emile."

Dexter immediately knew that something was wrong. "What is it?" he asked.

"The assignment went bad."

"How so?"

"He's alive. He saw me."

"He can identify you?"

"Yeah, I think so. Two other people he was with saw me, too. I'm leaving."

"Where are you going, Emile?" Dexter asked in a calm voice as he turned down the TV volume.

"I have a place. Look, I tried my best. Things just got fouled up, that's all. I want my money for tonight."

"I think that can be arranged, Emile. I'll have it deposited in —"

"No, no. I want it in cash. Meet me someplace with it."

"Emile, really, you don't think I can put my hands on that much cash tonight, do you?"

Silva's anger level rose. He was being talked to as though he were a child. He looked at his surroundings. A dozen unblinking, nonjudgmental stuffed animals peered up at him.

"Emile," his mother called from downstairs. "Where are you?"

"I suggest, Emile, that we meet tomorrow after you've calmed down," Dexter said soothingly. "We can have lunch at, say —"

"Listen, you miserable bastard," Silva sputtered, "you listen to me. I know enough to put you and your friends away for life."

"I will not be spoken to this way," Dexter said, and hung up.

Silva punched in the number twice more. The calls weren't answered.

Panic had been replaced by anger. Now, panic had returned. While fleeing the scene at the Hotel Rouge he'd tried to decide what to do with his house and his other cars should he flee the country. But that no longer mattered. The only thing that was important was to escape, to avoid being hunted down and put away. He could never survive being locked up, not for even one day.

"Emile!" she called in a stronger voice.

"Shut up," he said, not loud enough for her to hear. "Shut the hell up." He shook, and wrapped his arms about himself.

"Emile!"

"Coming, Ma-ma."

He slowly descended the stairs and stood before her.

"I'm hungry," she said. "I'd like some soup, and some crackers, too."

"Yes, Ma-ma."

"That woman wanted to steal things," she said after him as he went to the kitchen. "I could tell the way she was looking around. I'm so glad you came. You will stay, won't you?"

"Yes, Ma-ma," he called from the kitchen.

"Make the soup nice and hot."

"I will."

Instead, he quietly opened the door that led to the garage, went in, and picked up a five-gallon red plastic container of gasoline. He opened the overhead door, stepped outside, and poured some of the fuel around the foundation of the house. Then he returned to the kitchen, where he stood silently, the half-filled container in his hand.

"Emile! Is the soup ready yet? I'm hungry."

He sprinkled some of the gas along one wall and went through a second door to the dining room, where he did the same.

"Emile!"

"Goodbye, Ma-ma," he said as he tossed down a match. Flames shot up in the dining room, igniting the drapes and turning the white wall black. He ran into the living room and looked at her for a brief, horrified second before racing outside through the front door.

He reached the Porsche and turned to watch the frame house go up. He saw his mother through the front bay window. She tried to stand but fell back into her wheelchair as flames engulfed her, her agonizing cry the last thing he would ever hear from her.

Across the street, Brockman couldn't believe what he was seeing. He'd received a terse call from Dexter — "The sale is on" — and had moved the SUV closer to the driveway and the Porsche. He'd taken the Heckler & Koch sniper's rifle from the floor and leaned on the vehicle, the rifle propped on the hood, ready to be fired. He'd decided that if he could get off a clean shot he'd grab the opportunity and call it a day. That opportunity had arrived.

As Silva turned from observing the inferno and reached for the door handle of his car, Brockman centered the crosshairs of the telescopic sight on his chest and squeezed the trigger. His aim was dead-on. Silva screamed. His hands went to his chest as the force of the bullet knocked him backward to the ground. He was dead before he reached it.

The echo of the rifle's powerful discharge mingled with the sudden wail of sirens. Brockman got back into the SUV, tossed the rifle on the backseat, and started the engine. But before he could slip the transmission into Drive, he was pinned in by three patrol cars, two carrying Virginia state policemen, the third a District of Columbia vehicle with two uniformed cops. Brockman pulled his handgun from its holster and waved it. The officers saw that he was armed and shouted a warning to drop the weapon, raise his hands, and slowly approach. He was tempted to try to ram them but knew it was futile. He followed their orders and stepped from the car, hands up, his face bathed in the hideous glow of orange-yellow flames that by now engulfed the house.

Chapter 45

The torching of Rose Silva's house and her gruesome death in the inferno, and her son's murder by James Brockman, set off a series of events in both Washington, D.C., and Savannah.

Brixton was kept overnight at the hospital, where he was given a transfusion to replace the blood he'd lost, and Mac and Annabel spent time with him there. A windswept rain had started again and pelted the window of his room.

"I'd seen the guy twice before," Brixton told them after he'd called Flo, and after the police had taken a formal statement and left. "He sat down on a bench with me in Dupont Circle, and ended up at the Kennedy Center when I went there. I never thought anything of it."

"He'd obviously targeted you," Annabel said.

"Looks that way," Brixton agreed. "The

question is, why?"

"Has to be the case you've been working," Mac said flatly.

"But who would have sicced him on me?" Brixton mused. "The only person in D.C. with a stake in this is Ms. Cardell, and I somehow can't picture her hiring a hit man." After a silence, he added, "And the first lady."

"You mentioned that a convict back in Savannah claimed that someone who worked for Mitzi's father had ordered the hit on your client's daughter," Annabel said.

"Ward Cardell is a tough, hard-nosed businessman, and there are plenty of stories about people he's screwed," Brixton said. "I'm sure she kept her father in the loop about me and what I was after." He shrugged, causing his bandaged biceps to ache.

"It hurts," Annabel said.

"Not as much as letting the creep get away with stabbing me. I'm getting old. I'm not as cautious as I used to be. The reflexes aren't what they were."

"You had no reason to anticipate that someone was out to kill you, Robert," Mac said. "I'm just glad you forgot your raincoat."

Brixton laughed, which also caused him

pain. "Flo's coming tomorrow to drive me home. She's my lady friend."

"Like to meet her," Mac said. "I have a suggestion. We'll pick you up tomorrow when they discharge you and take you to our apartment. Your lady, Flo, can meet up with you there and the two of you can swing by the hotel later to collect your things."

"I don't want to intrude," Brixton said.

"Robert," Mac said, laying a hand on Brixton's shoulder, "you've already intruded, and it's been one of the more interesting intrusions I can ever remember. No arguments. We'll call you tomorrow."

The Smiths picked Brixton up the following morning and brought him to their Watergate apartment. Brixton had given Flo directions and she planned to meet him there at two. There was much to talk about before her arrival.

The *Washington Post* carried a lengthy story about the fire in Virginia and the man who'd been killed, Emile Silva. According to the reporters covering it, the authorities suspected that the man who had shot Silva, James Brockman, had also set the fire, for reasons unknown. A woman identified as Rose Silva, the dead man's mother, had died in the blaze. The investigation was ongoing.

But it wasn't the article's words that commanded the attention of Brixton and the Smiths. It was the photo of Emile Silva.

"That's the guy," Brixton said.

"Looks like him, although we didn't get much of a look," Annabel said.

"But I did," Brixton said. "That's him! No question about it."

"What's the link between this gunman, Brockman, and Silva's attack on you?" Smith mused aloud.

No one had an answer.

Smith had invited Willis Sayers to join them and he arrived in time for lunch.

"You sure you're really hurt, Robert," Sayers said pleasantly, "or are you just looking for attention?"

"Want to see my wound?" Brixton replied as he threatened to remove his shirt and the bandage.

"No, please no," Sayers said, "I don't need you to pull an LBJ on me. So, fill me in, buddy. Tell me what happened."

Brixton ran through the events of the preceding evening, including his conversation with Mitzi Cardell.

"She admitted it?" Sayers said.

"She admitted that her teenage girlfriend, Jeanine Montgomery, did the stabbing, and that her father, Ward Cardell, arranged to pay off Louise Watkins to go to prison for it."

"Whew!" Sayers said. "The first lady of the land a murderer."

"Whoa," said Smith. "I think we should back up a little. Robert is right. Mitzi's comments and answers to his questions leave little doubt that what he's been saying is true. But as an attorney I should warn you that none of it would stand up in court."

"Even with someone like you corroborating Robert's claim?" Sayers asked.

"I'm not corroborating anything," said Smith. "I wasn't there as Mitzi's attorney, but I am a lawyer who's advised her on legal matters. I may not practice law anymore but I'm still a member of the bar. It would be inappropriate for me to testify to what was said last night."

"So that leaves only Robert's word."

"Exactly," Smith confirmed. "Also bear in mind that before she left she said that she'd deny all of it if asked by anyone who wasn't in the room."

Sayers turned to Brixton. "But there's the word of your client, Louise Watkins' mother."

Brixton nodded. "Look, Will," he said, "I told Ms. Cardell that I wasn't out to turn this into a media event. I meant that. But you're free to do whatever you wish, and I'll help in any way I can."

"I'm going to give Ms. Cardell a call again," Sayers said.

"Good luck," Brixton said. "If you want to talk with my client back in Savannah, give a yell."

"Shall do," replied Sayers. "I'd hate to see this story die."

Brixton handed Sayers that morning's *Post*. "See that picture?" he said. "That's the guy who attacked me last night."

"The story keeps getting better," Sayers said.

"A story I could do without," Brixton said as he rubbed his aching arm.

Flo arrived early and joined them at the table. She, too, wanted a play-by-play, but Brixton declined. "We've been through it already," he said. "I'll rerun it for you on the drive home."

"I know one thing," Smith said as Brixton and Flo prepared to leave.

"What's that?" Brixton asked.

"I doubt if we're still on Mitzi Cardell's A-list."

Brixton and Flo gathered his belongings from the hotel and were on their way back to Savannah by four that afternoon.

■ ■ ■ ■

A few days later, Brockman was arraigned on the charge of first-degree murder, as well as with the torching of the house. He denied the latter, of course, and his court-appointed attorney expressed confidence that evidence was lacking to link him to the arson. Brockman told the arresting authorities that he'd killed Silva on orders from a paramilitary group headed by a man named Dexter — a patriotic group, he claimed — which was met with skepticism and scorn. He directed them to the office building used as a front where he'd received part of his indoctrination, but before anyone visited there in search of the mysterious man called Dexter, word came down from the highest echelons of government that any investigation of the firm Z-Stat was off-limits for national security reasons. Brockman's attorney was informed that there was no person at Z-Stat named Dexter and that his client was delusional: "Maybe you can get him off with an insanity plea," the prosecutor joked with the defense attorney, an old buddy, and they shared a good laugh over it.

As it turned out, there was no need to enter a plea for Brockman. He was found hanging in his cell by a sheet. A few questions were asked about why corrections officers hadn't taken steps to prevent his suicide, but these queries soon evaporated.

Brixton got up the morning after returning to Savannah and went to the window. It promised to be a scorcher in Georgia's first city and his adopted home. Everything ached, thanks in part to the long car ride from D.C. He turned and looked at Flo, who slept peacefully, a tiny smile on her pretty face. Brixton smiled, too. He hadn't realized how much he'd missed her, and made a silent pledge to treat her to a special dinner for sticking by him.

Showering was a slow, painful process; he had to be careful not to get his bandage wet and accomplished that by wrapping Saran Wrap around it. He dressed in a beige linen shirt, which he didn't tuck into his blue slacks, and wore a pair of tan desert boots he'd forgotten that he'd left in the back of one of Flo's closets.

"I'm going to the office," he said, kissing her brow.

She stirred, looked up, and grinned. "I am so glad you're home," she said.

"Me, too."

She sat up. “You’re feeling up to going to work?”

“Yeah, I’m fine. I’ll call later. How about dinner out tonight?”

“Sounds yummy.” They kissed, and she snuggled her head back into the pillow.

Cynthia was at the office when he walked in.

“You look like hell,” she said.

“Thank you, madam. Come on in and I’ll tell you about my adventures.”

She hung on every word as he recounted what had happened in Washington.

“So this Cardell character admitted that the first lady stabbed the guy, and that Cardell’s father paid off Louise Watkins?”

“Maybe not in so many words but it was obvious that that’s how it went down. Anything new here while I was getting sliced up?”

She handed him a sheaf of telephone messages. On top was a call from the Reverend Lucas Watkins.

“He say what he wants?”

“No, just said that it’s important that he speak with you.”

The second message slip concerned Will Sayers. “He called as I walked in this morning,” she said. “He’ll be here in Savannah by one and wants to see you.”

Brixton had intended to call Sayers and suggest that he come to Savannah to speak with Eunice Watkins and her son, Lucas. Whether the word of the mother and son would be sufficient for Sayers to pursue the story was conjecture — and not Brixton's problem. He'd meant it when he said he was not out to create a media circus. But there was another side of him that cried out for some form of justice to be dispensed. Would it be enough for Louise's mother simply to know that her daughter hadn't committed the act to which she had confessed, and not have the need to share it with the wider world? If so, she was a better person than he was. If it had been his daughter, he'd want everyone to know that she hadn't killed anyone, and that there were people who'd cruelly used their money to thwart the truth.

"When are you and Jim leaving?" he asked.

"Next week. I'll miss you."

"I'll miss you, too."

"Thanks. This place will go to the dogs without me."

"Thanks for the vote of confidence."

He spent the rest of the morning returning phone calls and going through the pile of mail, and e-mails on his computer. He promised the restaurant owner that he'd get started on his case within a day or two, and picked up another client, a divorce lawyer who wanted him to document the movements of a husband who the wife claimed was cheating. He hesitated before accepting the assignment, but a pile of recent bills culled from the larger group of envelopes made the decision for him.

He held off returning Lucas Watkins's call until last. He'd decided to invite Sayers to join him on a visit to Eunice Watkins. Might as well have him hear what he had to report to her, and be there to gauge her reaction in person.

"Reverend Watkins," Brixton said, "it's Robert Brixton returning your call."

"Yes, Mr. Brixton. You're back from Washington."

"That's right. I'd like to get together with you and your mother sometime today."

"I'm afraid that will be impossible," he said in his deep, officious voice.

"Tomorrow then? I've learned things in Washington that I know you and your mother will want to know."

"Mr. Brixton," he said, "I'm afraid that we've misled you."

" 'Misled me?' What does that mean?"

"You see, Mother misunderstood what

Louise had told her. Let me be direct. I believe you deserve directness. We've come to learn that it *was* Louise who fended off an attempted rape that night in the parking lot, and accidentally stabbed her attacker. All I can say is that we are deeply sorry to have put you to all this trouble. Naturally, we will pay any further fees you require, as well as expenses that you've incurred."

Brixton was speechless.

"There's really nothing more to say, Mr. Brixton. If you'll send me a written breakdown of what we owe you, we'll take care of it immediately."

"Wait a minute, Reverend," Brixton said. "I want to hear this from your mother."

"I'm afraid that's not possible, Mr. Brixton. She hasn't been feeling well and has gone out of state to be with another family member. She won't be back for some time. She's not to be disturbed."

"I'll be damned," Brixton muttered.

"I look forward to receiving your final bill," Watkins said, "and thank you for understanding."

"Yeah, I understand," Brixton said. "I understand that somebody got to you and your mother and —"

He was speaking into a dead phone.

Sayers arrived at one and they went to

lunch at the Riverhouse Restaurant on West River Street, where Sayers particularly enjoyed the Savannah crab cakes made with native blue crab and served with a mango chutney and red rice. And there was fudge walnut cake for dessert. The man loved his food.

Brixton waited until their drinks were served before telling his large journalist friend about the conversation with Lucas Watkins. When he was finished, Sayers snorted and said, "Lovely folks you run with, Robert,"

"I'm still having trouble believing this," Brixton said. "They've been bought off."

"Or scared off. I tried getting to Mitzi Cardell."

"And?"

"I was told to contact her father's lawyer here in Savannah. I didn't bother. The *Morning News* has a piece tomorrow on that convict's claim that he was hired by Jack Felker to kill Louise Watkins. They got hold of Ward Cardell for a statement. He was all bluster — how dare the media besmirch the good name of a man who isn't here to defend himself — Felker was an associate and a dear friend who lived an exemplary life — how dare anyone take the word of a convicted murderer, the scum of the earth, in a pathetic attempt to destroy a decent man's reputation — yada yada yada. You say Felker was murdered. The police say that the ME pegged it as a natural death."

Brixton sat with gritted teeth.

"What are you going to do?" Sayers asked after they'd ordered lunch.

"What *can* I do? I've been tilting at windmills ever since I got involved."

"Want my advice?"

"Sure."

"Bill the good preacher for big bucks. Hell, you've earned it, and I imagine he won't balk at anything you ask for. After that, I'd forget the whole nasty mess."

"What about you?" Brixton asked. "Will you pursue it any further?"

Sayers grinned and looked with happy anticipation at his appetizer, a double order of low-country shrimp and stone-ground grits served with tasso gravy. Brixton was content with a cup of lobster bisque.

"Me?" Sayers said after tasting the grits and indicating his approval. "I'll go back and get the bureau up and running in our nation's capital, keep the folks back here apprised of all the good deeds done for the nation by Savannah's finest, our first lady and D.C.'s leading social light. Eat up, Robert. Don't let it get cold."

■ ■ ■ ■

Brixton took Sayers's advice and billed Lucas Watkins twice what he felt was fair. The check arrived in two days. It was drawn on the church bank account and indicated that it was for a "special project." It cleared.

As he was about to leave the office that evening, he received a call from Wayne St. Pierre, inviting him to his home for a drink: "Sort of a welcome-back drink, Robert."

Brixton arrived at the house at six and found his former colleague listening to the player piano pump out Johnny Mercer songs. He was dressed in a purple robe trimmed in silver and held a large snifter.

"Robert, so good to see you. I understand you've been through quite an ordeal in our nation's capital. Come in, come in, Let's celebrate your safe return and the successful completion of your case. Bourbon? Scotch? A cold, dry martini, shaken, not stirred?"

"Skip the drink, Wayne. You knew everything that was going down, didn't you?"

"Pardon?"

"You told people everything that I was doing with the Watkins case from day one."

"What in the world has gotten into you,

Bobby?"

"Knock off the 'Bobby' crap. You're wired in to the elite of this city, aren't you? You like rubbing elbows with the movers and shakers, slip them a little information now and then to keep them appreciative, relay some gossip when it keeps them close, rich cruds like Cardell and Montgomery."

St. Pierre sat in a large red chair and crossed his legs, the snifter held like a trophy. "Sure you won't have a drink, Bobby — Robert? You're in a frazzled state. Going back to Washington must have been upsetting for you. Actually, I invited you here tonight with a proposition."

Brixton said nothing.

"I have it on very good authority that a friend of mine is looking for someone like you to head up security for his various business ventures. The pay would be substantial and —"

"Who's this friend of yours, Ward Cardell? Or is it Warren Montgomery?"

"You're such a cynic, Robert. I suppose that goes with your New York upbringing. I will tell you this. Savannah is quite a different place from New York. We do things our own way and don't appreciate outsiders coming here and upsetting the applecart, as the saying goes. It seems to me that you have one of two choices: either become an adopted son of the old South and play by the rules, or go back home where the rules are different. Your call, Robert. Sure you won't have a drink? Please. Join me. We go back a long way and despite our different backgrounds we have a lot in common."

The pianist on the disk launched into Mercer's "Everything Happens to Me."

"The only thing we have in common is that we once wore the same uniform. You were the only one who knew certain things I was doing, and other people knew it because of you. You disgust me, Wayne."

St. Pierre got up and leaned on the piano, keeping it between them. "You're treading on dangerous ground, my friend," he said. "You come here shootin' off your mouth, accusing me of God knows what. Well, I will not stand for it, Bobby Brixton. I invited you here with good intentions. Now get your sorry ass out of my home. You hear me?"

"I hear you, Wayne. You know, I had visions of coming here and shooting you."

St. Pierre laughed. "That would have been one dumb thing for you to do, wouldn't it?"

"Yeah, it would have been dumb. That's why I'm not doing it. All your rich friends are more important to you than what I was trying to do for a mixed-up young black kid who deserved better. You're a whore, Wayne. You're a disgrace to all the good, honest cops here in Savannah and everywhere else."

"Good night, Robert."

"No, Wayne. Goodbye."

Brixton went through the front door, the piano strains of "Ac-Cent-Tu-Ate the Positive" following him. He pulled a pack of cigarettes from his shirt and started to pull a cigarette from it. He looked back through the open door to where St. Pierre stood posed at the piano. He crumpled the pack and tossed it ceremoniously into the neatly cultivated bed of azaleas that had lost their yearly battle with the summer heat.

One month later to the day, Robert Brixton drove away from Savannah — destination New York.

Flo Combes joined him there months later after she'd sold her shop and house.

And in Washington, D.C., and Savannah, business went on as usual.

ABOUT THE AUTHOR

Margaret Truman won faithful readers with her works of biography and fiction, particularly her Capital Crimes mysteries. Her novels let readers into the corridors of power and privilege, and poverty and pageantry, in the nation's capital. She was the author of many nonfiction books, including *The President's House*, in which she shared some of the secrets and history of the White House, where she once resided.

The employees of Thorndike Press hope you have enjoyed this Large Print book. All our Thorndike, Wheeler, and Kennebec Large Print titles are designed for easy reading, and all our books are made to last. Other Thorndike Press Large Print books are available at your library, through selected bookstores, or directly from us.

For information about titles, please call:
(800) 223-1244

or visit our Web site at:
http://gale.cengage.com/thorndike

To share your comments, please write:
Publisher
Thorndike Press
10 Water St., Suite 310
Waterville, ME 04901